THE PANSY PARADOX

THE CHRONICLES OF KING'S END
BOOK ONE

CHARITY TAHMASEB

COLLINS MARK BOOKS

For Abby. Thank you for always being there.
This one's for you.

THE PANSY PARADOX

And though she be but little, she is fierce.

— WILLIAM SHAKESPEARE

PART ONE
BOLT FROM THE BLUE

CHAPTER I

PANSY

King's End, Minnesota
Saturday, July 8

My mother always said: *Beware of the brilliant blue sky*.

But as I stand on the front porch, hand shielding my eyes, I detect nothing. The July air is heavy and sweet, full of summer and the promise of sweat, salt, and sunburn. Today is the first day I feel like myself again, or nearly so.

I step inside and consider pulling my umbrella from the stand. She is a pale pink with a scattering of polka dots in all sizes, from dollar-size to tiny pinpricks. Also? She has ruffles. Yes, she looks like a frivolous thing. Oh, but don't underestimate her.

She is formidable.

But she is also leaning against my mother's umbrella, one of a deep rose red, an American Beauty of a color. Their straps are intertwined, a mother and daughter clutching hands. To my right, the front room is empty now, but my mind's eye superimposes the hospital bed on the space. My ears anticipate the rhythmic, mechanical breath of the oxygen condenser.

I blink, cast my gaze back to the brilliant blue day outside my house. It's time I ventured downtown. I'm ready for that.

Even if my umbrella isn't.

So, I leave her behind. She shudders with both relief and guilt. I tell her to hush as I close the door behind me.

On the sidewalk, I pause, peer to the right, and let my gaze follow the asphalt until it vanishes into the gravel road that leads to the abandoned housing development. Mind you, I *have* been patrolling that part of King's End. There's no getting around that particular chore.

All of the problems in King's End begin and end in the development's skeletal remains. Weekly, I repair any holes that appear in the chain-link fence that surrounds the half-developed acres of land and mend fissures that crisscross the ground. Farther down the road, the old farmhouse and crumbling silo stand. Occasionally, I patrol there as well, but I haven't returned there since that day three months ago.

In truth, I hope never to return.

But that part of my job is solitary. No one but me ever ventures past where the sidewalk ends. The downtown, on the other hand? I'm certain to run into someone I know, will have to accept strained greetings and awkward condolences. I'm ready, I tell myself.

I'm ready.

King's End is small enough that I can walk its streets and alleys in half a day. I'd bike, but the world passes by too quickly for me to do my job. Logging thousands of steps a day is the lot of an Enclave permanent post agent.

It's Saturday, so the pedestrian mall is teeming with tables, pop-up stalls, and a few people selling their wares with traveling trays, like cigarette girls of old. The smells of brewing coffee and freshly baked bread compete with the tangy scent of tomatoes and smoke from roasting bratwurst.

I halt, the cobblestones solid beneath my feet. With a hand on my stomach, I gauge the growl. Flickers of actual hunger—the first in three months. After my patrol, I plan to load up a plate of food, starting with a vegan brat. I'm amazed at how such a small thing can feel so rebellious.

The market is alive with chatter and chirpy music. I do a circuit, lifting my chin, not so much tasting the air as sensing what lingers beneath it. Yes, a couple of pockets of discontent, but they're small, puny things. Hard to find, but I should root them out before they have the chance to bloom into something harder to contain.

Before I can, someone calls my name.

"Pansy!" A tall woman with a cascade of braids waves from her stall of eggs and honey and preserves. Beneath the table rests a Great Dane with its head on its paws. When I approach, Tiny—she was the runt of her litter—perks up, from ears to tail, so quickly that it almost topples the table.

"Tiny!" The woman, Matilda, grabs the collar as Tiny's claws scrabble against the cobblestone. "She misses you," she says. "We all do."

"I'm sorry—" My throat clutches, my cheeks flame, and a hot flush of guilt washes through me. It really has been too long.

She hushes me, much like I shushed my umbrella, and pulls me into a hug. "We understand, honey. It doesn't matter your age. It's hard to lose your mother."

I repress a sigh. If she only knew.

Matilda cups my shoulders and gives me a once-over. "You're looking good."

No, I'm not. I'm *really* not, but only the alarmingly honest will mention how awful you do look.

"I have plenty of eggs here," she says, as if the cure is food and lots of it. "And preserves, and, lucky you, you haven't missed raspberry season."

But I'm catching the tail end of it because it's been three months. All of spring and into summer. I feel as if I've missed more than a mere season.

"Everything," I say. "Eggs, raspberries, and preserves. I'll pick them up on Tuesday."

On Saturdays, the locals cater to the out-of-town visitors, mainly from the Twin Cities and the suburbs, especially the chichi suburbs. It's so lucrative that the town council put in a row of chargers for all the fancy electric vehicles. And, of course, everyone raises their prices accordingly. I don't want Matilda to lose sales on my account.

"How are you on herbs?" she asks, jotting down the items on a notepad. "Your mother always stocked up this time of year. The usual?"

I nod. We always supplemented with herbs from the farmers market. This year, my own garden has wilted from neglect. I didn't mean to ignore it, but then I didn't expect the events of this past spring to hit me so hard.

"Tuesday as well? I don't want to keep you in case you need to —" She waves a hand at the pedestrian mall. "Do your thing."

Yes, my thing. It *is* what I do. Those pockets of discontent nag at the back of my mind, a bit more insistent, a bit craftier. That's never good.

Matilda drops her hand, a frown full of curiosity and appreciation crinkling her brow.

"Who is *that*?" she asks. "Do you know him?"

I turn to follow her gaze.

A man strolls through the market, resplendent in an actual three-piece suit. The material has the barest hint of a pinstripe, and his shirt is blizzard-white against his dusky skin. On his head sits a hat that's a cross between a fedora and a bowler but is somehow neither. Even though he's dressed like some 1950s movie icon, those cheekbones could go viral on social media. His paisley tie is loose at his neck, his only concession to the July heat. On his arm, he carries a large, black umbrella.

An umbrella? No. It can't be. It's Saturday, I reason. And while King's End is a good hour's drive southwest of the Twin Cities, we get all sorts here on the weekend, not just for the farmers market. The old-fashioned bridge across the Minnesota River, the parks, and the quaint downtown lure plenty of people. On a day like today, there are bound to be several proposals along the Rose Walk that borders the river.

"He has an umbrella," Matilda observes, voice sly.

Well, yes, I noticed that.

"People carry umbrellas." I give a little shrug. Yes, people carry umbrellas. But not on these beautifully blue summer days. Not like I normally do.

"He almost looks like an actor in a play," Matilda adds. "Doesn't he?"

Something inside my chest loosens. That must be it. He's too well-dressed, too, too much for King's End. "He probably *is* an actor, or a model. I bet he's here for a photo shoot." Even from across the pedestrian mall, those razor-sharp cheekbones are still on full display.

Matilda returns her attention to her stall and an approaching customer. "If you get the chance, stop by before you leave," she says, then whispers, "Are you sure *you* don't need your umbrella? You don't want to get sunburnt."

"I'm fine." Really? Sunburn isn't one of my problems.

But I'm wondering if this well-dressed man is.

BETWEEN THE CROWDS and an extended goodbye with Tiny, I lose sight of the man. I wipe dog kisses from my cheek and consider my next move. Find him? Or find those pockets of discontent before they can find me, or worse, an unsuspecting citizen of King's End.

I trek across the wide expanse of cobblestones, keeping my gaze on the milling crowd. A fluttering teases the corner of my eye. I glance up but don't focus. Instead, I let my gaze drift. I raise my chin and gauge the shift in the air. The back of my throat burns with bile and bitterness. My heart gives a single warning thud. I sniff and wipe a trickle of blood from beneath my nose. This is a portent, and I have bigger problems than pockets of discontent and a well-dressed man.

Near the bridge, a couple enters the Rose Walk. The town's master gardener coaxes the flowers to bloom late into the season. It's a fairytale space, perfect for romantic wanderings, wedding photos, and, of course, proposals.

I get a glimpse—two, actually—of what might happen in the next five minutes.

Squeals. Kisses. A resounding YES!

Or?

A sudden squall. A lost engagement ring. A breakup.

I *knew* it. My mother is—or was—always right. And?

I should've brought my umbrella.

Not far from the bridge, those pockets of discontent have coalesced into something far more dangerous. I'm the only one who can see the gathering storm. It's my task to dispatch it before it can strike.

My job is both delicate and difficult, challenging, and yet not. You could say I was born to it, as all of us in the Enclave are. As my mother was, even though she gave up her globe-trotting ways and settled in King's End as a permanent post agent decades ago.

Our mission, those of us in the Enclave, is to keep the world safe from things most people can't see. This is harder than you might imagine. *You* try pulling someone away from an invisible-to-them onslaught—without getting arrested.

Really, it's even trickier than it sounds.

What's gathering near the King's End Rose Walk is a tempest. It resembles a storm—at least to me—and tastes like static against my tongue. But what is it, exactly? Frankly, no one in the Enclave truly knows, despite all the hypotheses. A force leaks into our reality, something tangible, something fierce, something that doesn't belong—and it knows it. The textbook definition is temporal disturbances. But even that isn't certain.

What is, though? In the moments before an attack, that something screams.

The sound reverberates against my skin and scorches my

eardrums, although I'm the only one who can hear it. This is no job for bare hands. With a panicked glance, I find The King's Larder. The owner, Milo, has set the umbrella stand beneath the awning. I run, fingers outstretched. The biggest, baddest umbrella of the lot is canted to one side, as if volunteering. I grab it and sprint toward the couple.

Halfway there, I stumble. My fingers tingle, and curiosity sparks in my mind. This is no store-bought umbrella. The last time I saw it? The jade handle was looped on the arm of that well-dressed man.

Oh, *no*. He really is one of my problems. But not the most immediate. And while this behemoth isn't *my* umbrella, it's far more helpful than an ordinary one.

"Nice to meet you," I say.

I get the sense of a nod in return, correct, polite, with a hint of something else, something I can't name but want to call recognition.

Together, we take up the run. Images in my mind flash: the awful ones of the breakup, the ring tumbling down the bank and into the river, someone falling and breaking an ankle. This adds fuel to my sprint across the green and toward the bridge.

I wonder if the Screamers—we're not supposed to call them that, but since they scream, it makes sense—have been saving this little encounter as a welcome back. That would be just like them.

There's no love lost between me and the Screamers of King's End.

My thigh muscles strain as I pick up speed, like I can outrun this forgone conclusion. Nothing's certain until it is, so I press on. The umbrella in my hands wants this fight as much as I do. Really, it's itching for it. Not in a disturbing manner, but more of a valiant, justice-for-all kind of way. I have no idea about its owner, but I'm starting to like his umbrella.

We find the heart of the tempest not far from the foot of the bridge, on the edge of the green. It shimmers, distorts the air, visible to only me. Pedestrian traffic is lighter here. A good thing, since I tuck, roll, and stab the center of the tempest with that sharp and deadly umbrella point.

The umbrella adds its own flourish, a shockwave that pulses through the air, thoroughly dispatching the discontent that's been brewing.

Another cry goes up, a screech, really. The Screamers disperse in a flurry of what looks like crows of many colors—obsidian and emerald, sapphire and ruby, all transparent and fleeting. Static clogs my throat. Sweat coats my brow. My T-shirt sticks to my back, and my favorite trashed jeans have acquired a new, somewhat impressive hole along with grass stains that will never fade.

But in the distance, under the hue of pink roses, someone has taken a knee and pulled a velvet-covered box from their pocket. That resounding YES echoes. I catch the smiles of passersby and a smattering of applause.

With a grateful exhale, I flop onto my back, umbrella at my side, and stare at the brilliant blue sky. I swipe my palm beneath my nose and catch the last trickle of blood.

I'm on my back, basking in a job well done, when a shadow blocks the brilliant blue sky. I squint at a pair of pinstriped trousers, the creases so crisp, I cringe. The man towers over me, a glower gathering on his brow. He removes the hat, pushes a hand through his dark hair, and heaves a sigh as if *he's* the one who just dispatched some nasty Screamers.

"I believe, Agent Little," he says, his tone resonating with disapproval, "that you have my umbrella."

Oh, *no*. He *is* from the Enclave. And he's staring down at me like I'm some odious chore he's yet to complete. The sky reappears behind him, less brilliant. Then again, maybe that's just me.

We weren't in the same class at the Academy, that much is certain. True, the Enclave is small, but other than summers at the training academy, I've never ventured farther than Minneapolis. I know names but certainly not faces. While his is familiar, I can't place the name.

"I'm Agent Darnelle," he says by way of introduction.

Wait. *The* Henry Darnelle? The man who, mere weeks ago, braved the Sahara and single-handedly tamed a Screamer-fueled sand-storm? Why would the Enclave send a field agent of his caliber to a backwater like King's End?

"It's time for your field agent examination."

Oh. That's why.

"And, incidentally." His hand shoots out. "You *still* have my umbrella."

With whispered thanks, I pass him the monstrous thing. It fairly quivers with pleasure at a job well done. Agent Darnelle tilts his head and regards the umbrella before securing the strap and hanging it back on his arm.

"I've been trying to contact your mentor," he says.

That's going to be difficult.

"She hasn't been answering her phone."

And she won't be. I let his words hang in the air, feeling both irritated and bereft. I want to savor this tiny triumph, root out any last bits of discontent, and banish the Screamers—at least, for another day—not deal with Henry Darnelle and the Enclave.

"She's gone," I say once the silence between us becomes not just awkward but oppressive.

Instead of sympathy, confusion plays across his features. He frowns in what looks like consternation. "So, she's left you to complete the examination on your own?"

Technically, that's true, so I nod.

"Really?"

I nod again.

His brow unfurls, and delight chases the confusion from his expression. "Well, that's something. I find it's so much better when mentors allow their apprentices to do that."

He doesn't know. The Enclave doesn't know. Relief blooms in my chest. They don't know. Not yet. That can only be good.

"I will have to confer with her at the end, of course, give her my full report."

I nod, yet again, without conceding anything. If I make it through my examination, I'll deal with any repercussions then.

Henry Darnelle rubs his hands together, almost in anticipation. "Here's what I suggest. We'll meet at your house tomorrow morning. In fact, I'll bring breakfast. We'll create a plan for your examination, one that lets you complete your daily duties. The intent is not to disrupt your routine."

Right. Because having someone scrutinize your every move is never disruptive, especially when that someone holds your future in his hands.

"Tomorrow's Sunday," I say.

He raises an eyebrow. In that single move, Henry Darnelle transforms from exceptional field agent into judgmental schoolmaster. Of course, there are no weekends or holidays for the Enclave. It's not like the Screamers take time off.

"Tomorrow's fine." I sigh. "What time?"

"Seven work for you?"

"In the morning?"

"I *am* bringing breakfast."

A sarcastic and ill-advised reply lingers just behind my teeth. I can taste the consequences, and they are sour and fetid, indeed.

"We'll start then," he adds as if that settles it.

But he continues to hover, and his intent rolls off him. He saw me dispatch the Screamers. Now? He wants to see if I can stand. Without my knees buckling. Without staggering across the lawn, punch-drunk from my encounter. Without, of course, any help.

My examination has already begun.

I clamber to my feet, forcing a bright expression onto my face as if all I've been doing is napping in the sun. I even smile, although it's hardly convincing. Together, we head toward the pedestrian mall.

"The farmers market here is quite impressive," he says, voice raised since there's a good eight feet between us. "Wish my room had a kitchen."

"Where are you staying?" I shove politeness into my reply, but really, I want to know what part of town to avoid.

"Riverside Bed and Breakfast."

"It's a nice place." And, thankfully, just down the block. Am I supposed to invite him to dinner? Maybe? But since he's already invited himself for breakfast, I don't see the point. The man is not my friend. He's not even an acquaintance. He's here to do a job.

I can only hope that when he's done, I'll still have mine.

AT HOME, my legs give up and start their post-encounter wobble. I manage three steps before collapsing on the staircase, very much a ragdoll. Eyes closed, I let my head rest against the wall, let my breathing return to normal, and do *not* let my mind stray into the future—or, more accurately, my future. I've already flirted with the Sight once today.

I don't need a full-on attack.

Besides, the future is unpredictable; the further away from the present, the more variables come into play. Sure, I *might* see what happens this week. But the effort isn't worth it.

The Sight never is.

Instead, I pull myself up by the handrail and cast my gaze about the place. Does it look like my mother has stepped out for my examination? Or can a stranger read the grief in all the things left behind? Do I still wear that grief? Does this house?

I suspect we're co-conspirators in sorrow, the front room in particular. At the time, it was the only practical space for the rented hospital bed. The hospice nurse kept the morphine in a lock box in the kitchen, but all the other items for my mother's comfort strayed into this room, including me, often on the couch.

The medical companies have reclaimed everything, but the after-effects linger. I still expect to see her diminished form in the hospital bed, hear the inhalation of the oxygen condenser and her own labored breath, smell the antiseptic and decay.

And I still wonder what happened the last time I saw my mother.

CHAPTER 2
OPHELIA

Seattle, Washington
Friday, July 7 (one day prior)

Ophelia knows when Henry steps through the front door. With his entrance, her brother brings a reprieve. The loop—the endless, endless loop—pauses. She can take a full breath, or as full a breath as anyone in a coma can take.

She can't see him. This Sight-induced coma won't allow for that. But she can hear his footfalls on the sweeping staircase of this Queen Anne mansion. He continues along the hallway, toward her bedroom, his presence steady and sure in a house filled with sorrow and shame. Only when he visits does this space truly feel like home.

Then he speaks, and everyone around her relaxes. Their mother's frayed nerves mend. The healthcare aide releases a sigh. The nurse on duty—there's always a nurse on duty, although there's not much for them to do—wheels the IV stand to the head of the bed so Henry may sit.

"How is she?" he asks, most likely after kissing their mother's cheek, although Ophelia can't see that, either. But she knows her brother.

"Better," their mother says, "now that you're here."

"I'm hoping to be here a lot more."

This is good news. The best news. If Henry is here, he can't be *there*. If Henry is here, maybe the loop—this endless, endless loop— will fade, not plague her so.

They confer, quietly. Of anyone, only Henry is aware that Ophelia hears everything said in this room, around her bed, about her rather than to her. Granted, both the nurse and the aide let her know when they're about to do something—a blood draw, a sponge bath, an adjustment to her position. But it's routine, a habit they can't break, with words devoid of meaning.

Only Henry speaks with meaning.

Chair legs scrape against the floor, and she hears the rustle of Henry sitting. He brings his travels with him—bad airport coffee, recycled air, stale sweat. Beneath that? A lingering hint of the desert and a trace of vanilla from his cologne.

"Hey there," he says and folds her hand in his. The skin is dry and rough, his palm calloused. The desert has left its mark. "Sorry to be gone for so long."

I understand.

"I took a peek at your vitals."

Of course he did.

"You *are* doing better." A pause. "Mostly."

Because Henry doesn't lie, at least not to her.

"But it's nothing that we can't fix."

Because Henry's an optimist, at least when it comes to her.

I'm sick of hearing about myself.

"I was in the Sahara," he says. "Did they tell you? Egypt, Libya, made a stop in Morocco on my way home—quite the tour of duty."

Henry can't read her mind, although, like now, it feels as if he can. But his patterns are predictable, and perhaps so are hers, from when they were children. They continue the conversation even if she can't truly participate.

They didn't *tell me*. On purpose, no doubt. That didn't stop them from talking about it within earshot.

"Did you know that in a level five hot spot, desert Screamers can whip up a sandstorm?"

And you, like a fool, walked right into it.

"It was incredible. Nothing like it. It felt good to fight them. Honest, in a way. I needed to leave after the funeral. I was just so ..."

Angry.

"And I..."

Missed him so much.

"And I simply couldn't deal with..."

All the assholes at headquarters.

"He loved you so very much," Henry says now, his voice splintering on the phrase. "I didn't mention this earlier because everyone thought they could contest the will."

Of course they did.

"But he left you a trust. I'm managing it for now, but it's all yours. Not huge, but it's sizable, and it's certainly enough that you could..."

Walk away from the Enclave? Break her betrothal? Assuming, of course, this loop—this endless, endless loop—doesn't break it for her. Wouldn't that be a bonus?

"It raised some eyebrows, though."

I imagine it did.

Harrison Darnelle was Henry's father but not Ophelia's. Her father has gone MIA, spending his time at Enclave headquarters, overseeing the High Council, wearing her predicament like a badge of honor. *Her* father has barely been home in months.

And Henry's is dead.

From somewhere in the depths of the house, the doorbell chimes. No one in this room moves, not that they need to. They have, as her father would intone, people for that.

Oh, how Ophelia would love to answer the door. As a child, she'd race through the house whenever the bell rang, making bets with Henry about who stood on the other side. She always won. It was how they knew she had the Sight.

"Who can that be?" their mother says, her words full of annoyance tinged with something that sounds like fear. Miranda Connolly doesn't have the Sight, but she can taste oncoming calamity. She says it sours the air.

The air must be very sour, indeed.

Then the voice. The last voice Ophelia heard before succumbing to this coma and the last one she wants to hear now. The voice is a herald of things to come, a reminder of all the futures she's seen.

Henry's fingers slip from hers. The chair legs scrape again when he stands.

"I'll handle this," he says.

The loop—that endless, endless loop—presses against her mind, drawing her back into its embrace. How many times now? Once she realized the Sight wouldn't relent, Ophelia stopped counting. Whatever power keeps her in this loop can't be broken. The future has many variations, too many to memorize. Not that Ophelia doesn't try.

She always tries. It's the one thing she can do.

Even if, in the end, nothing changes. The sun is eclipsed by a Screamer onslaught, the sky fracturing with color before everything turns a dull, ice gray—as if the world truly will end with a whimper rather than a bang.

But it starts with the ominous scrape of chair legs, with Henry standing, confronting the voice. Henry, protective son and big brother, who walks into sandstorms. Henry, who would do anything to save the world.

Only Ophelia knows that he will die trying.

CHAPTER 3
HENRY

Seattle, Washington
Friday, July 7 (one day prior)

Henry waited until he cleared the bedroom door before releasing a frustrated sigh. If the newcomer heard? So be it. Henry didn't have time for anyone other than Ophelia and their mother. He'd just returned from four months abroad, a fact everyone at Enclave headquarters knew. He needed to see his sister, who had been in a coma for ten months. Something else everyone at headquarters knew.

Then again, no one at headquarters gave a damn.

"My boy, it's good to see you home." Professor Reginald Botten was a man who wore his degrees and his position on the High Council with gravitas and gaiety, as if he were still a working field agent who'd stumbled into good fortune.

According to rumors, there was no stumbling about it.

"How are you? And your sister?" Botten strained to peer into Ophelia's bedroom, but Henry was already inching him down the hallway and toward the landing of the main staircase.

"Stable."

"Excellent news."

It wasn't news at all. Ophelia had remained stable for the duration of this coma, one that was most likely Sight induced, given the brain activity. But, of course, no one knew for certain.

"I'm sorry to interrupt this little family reunion, my boy, but I have need of you."

Yes, Botten was here for a reason, no doubt using the GPS in Henry's umbrella to track him down. He'd switched it on after his flight, clearly a mistake. Henry opened his mouth to protest. All that emerged was another frustrated sigh.

"I wouldn't ask if it weren't both a crucial and delicate situation, not something I could propose over the phone."

Oh? Not routine, then. Not grunt work. All things considered, he might be willing. He nodded once to let Botten know he was both listening and interested. In that moment, the connection he'd once had with this man rekindled.

During his first summer at the Academy, he'd been so proud to earn the professor's good opinion and make the Botten's Best List—unheard of, really, for a first-year cadet. With chagrin, Henry recalled the hand on his shoulder, the confidential way Botten had declared, "You're a special breed, my boy."

But that was long before a string of broken promises and before Henry's father—a man slow to speak and to judge—had remarked, almost casually:

"He is a man I do not admire."

Now, Henry was cautious. But he'd listen to what Botten had on offer.

"Is there somewhere we might speak more privately?" Botten asked, a hand on Henry's arm as if to lead him to that private space.

Soft light bathed the stairwell landing, electric, of course. If you squinted, you could pretend to be in a bygone era of gas lamps and candles. The runner was a rich emerald green—his mother's favorite color—and the wood gleamed. The air held the scent of cut roses and lemon furniture polish. Even in a crisis, his mother was meticulous about such things.

Henry eased from Botten's grip, tucked his hands behind his back, and simply said, "Here's good."

Here was clearly not good, but Botten didn't persist.

"Very well. You recall, of course, the class you helped evaluate at the Academy?"

Wait. *What*? Henry scoffed, exhaling a dismissive breath. He should've known. This was routine. This was grunt work. "There can't be anyone left—"

"One apprentice agent, actually."

Seriously? Who waited the full five years to take their field agent examination? Granted, there were exceptions, and it was certainly allowed. Most agents wanted to pass their exam that first year and start field work. Henry shook his head. "I've done more than my fair share of evaluations. Find someone else."

"As I mentioned, this is a delicate situation."

"And you need me in particular?"

"Indeed, I do. The apprentice agent in question is unlikely to pass the examination."

Failure was rare, although every few years it did happen. These situations were always fraught with emotion and politics.

"She also hails from an old family."

Make that highly fraught.

"I'm sorry to say it's time to retire that line," Botten continued, not sounding the least bit sorry.

"Old family?"

"The Little line."

No, that couldn't be right. In his last mission, Henry had relied heavily on Rose Little's research on desert Screamers. Decades on, her white papers were still one of the best resources in the entire Enclave.

"Rose Little is legendary," Henry said.

"Hm, yes." Now it was Botten's turn to scoff. "But she married a local. As luck, or perhaps genetics, would have it, the daughter did not inherit her mother's ability. I'm afraid even a benign permanent post is beyond her capabilities."

"And you need me to do what, exactly?"

"You'll need to meet with Rose, explain the situation. I know her reputation is fiery, but at heart, Rose is a realist. As I said, a delicate situation, but one I know you can manage. Besides, I suspect hearing the news from you will smooth the way. She and your father were *close*."

Close. Which meant what? Botten didn't elaborate, and Henry wasn't about to ask. He raised an eyebrow instead. "Shouldn't I administer the examination first?"

"What? Yes, of course, my boy. Don't expect the outcome to be anything but disappointing."

So, in this case, failure was a forgone conclusion. "Right."

"We'll need you to stay on as the acting agent until a new permanent post one can be assigned."

No. Full stop. Absolutely not. It was one thing to fail an apprentice agent and then retire the entire family line. It was quite another to step into the role of a permanent post agent, even briefly. That sort of assignment was a harbinger; the most likely outcome was *remaining* a permanent post agent.

"Someone else can handle that portion of things."

"That's not an option." Botten's voice lost its joviality. The corners of his mouth turned down, his gaze steely and uncompromising. "Let me be frank. If you wish to stay in the field, you need to take this assignment, all of it."

Screw the quiet part. Henry wanted—needed—Botten to spell this out. "Or else?"

"There are those on the High Council who believe you're close to burning out, that your father's death was too much, that you need a respite."

Henry wouldn't be the first field agent forced to recuperate. This entire situation was ridiculous. Made-up games that the High

Council liked to play. He had another decade in the field, at least. He wasn't about to give that up.

"Of course, if you prefer a reassignment to headquarters—"

"No. That's fine. I'll take the job."

"I thought as much." Botten clapped him on the shoulder. "Your flight's all arranged, gear ready for pickup, and you have access to all the records you'll need, including your original evaluation from the Academy."

Botten headed down the stairs, his steps nimble, his mood light once again. At the midpoint, where the staircase curved and flowed into the entryway, he paused.

"Expedite this with discretion, and I may see my way to expediting your current paperwork problem with the High Council."

Paperwork problem. That was an interesting euphemism for breaking a binding contract. Henry gave a terse nod.

"Good luck, my boy."

In the empty corridors of the house, Henry swore he heard the echo of: *You'll need it*.

He turned his back on the retreating footfalls and the warning in Botten's words. Before he could climb the stairs once again, his phone pinged. A reminder to check in for his flight flashed across the screen, one scheduled for tomorrow morning.

Damn. It was all he could do not to toss his phone down the stairway. Instead, he pulled up the records on Apprentice Agent Pansy Little and considered what he'd written five years ago. Almost as quickly, he shut everything down, shoved his phone into his pocket, and headed for Ophelia's room.

The air felt thicker now, close and cloying. The nurse looked dour, but then they always did. He suspected the private agency her father hired specialized in dour-faced nurses, as if that would somehow complement the seriousness of the situation. The aide had anxious eyes but smiled at him. His mother, however, had frayed half a box of tissues in his absence.

"They're sending me out again." No sense sugar-coating it. Even so, he flinched at his mother's expression.

"You just got back. When do you leave?"

"Tomorrow morning."

"Where are they sending you?"

"Somewhere in Minnesota."

His mother shook her head as if that was all it took to stop the Enclave from doing anything. "I don't like it."

"You didn't like the Sahara, either." He raised his hands. "But here I am."

"This feels different."

"You said that about North Africa. I doubt I'll encounter any sandstorms in Minnesota. Besides, I'm only performing an examination."

His mother nodded, hardly mollified, and reached for another handful of tissues. Henry headed for Ophelia.

Sometimes, he could detect her presence, like earlier. Other times, she was remote, cut off from everything, the space around her bed emptier, colder. No doubt the others felt it, too. It would explain all the dour expressions.

He tucked the blanket closer around her. Ophelia had been here earlier, and Henry hoped she could still detect his presence. He knelt by her side, took her hand once more.

"I'll be back," he whispered. "I promise."

CHAPTER 4
PANSY

King's End, Minnesota
Friday, April 28 (three months prior)

My mother was forever making lists. Fun lists on pink paper, wish lists on green. Books to read in black ink on creamy stationery. Television shows to avoid on the backs of receipts. But there was one list that eclipsed them all, this one on yellow legal pad.

This particular list remains attached to the refrigerator with a set of whimsical magnets from The King's Larder. Over the years, my mother added to it, crossed items out, and rewrote it completely. This is how it stood the last time she was able to venture into the kitchen:

1. Never go into the housing development after dark.
2. Never go to the silo alone.
3. Never go to the covered bridge, period.
4. If the Enclave makes an offer, remember they always require something in return.

5. Trust no one from the Enclave.
6. When someone tells you they're not betrothed, don't believe them.
7. The Screamers don't fight fair; you shouldn't, either.

Rules to live by, rules to be obeyed, rules that sometimes don't make sense. The list is the first thing I see each morning when I step into the kitchen and the last thing before shutting down for the night. At some point, I stopped questioning, stopped asking why.

That morning, three months ago, I headed to the kitchen first, giving the list a mock salute rather than detouring to the front room. Would that have changed anything? Could I at least have said good-bye? I don't know. I can forgive myself the one.

But not the other.

That morning, strains of something light and buoyant came from the front room. Mozart, one of the concertos. No news. No television. This signaled a good day. My mother was content to watch the sunrise, listen to her music, and otherwise ignore the medical intrusion and the pain.

Dawn flooded the kitchen with pinks and golds, painting the air with hope. While coffee brewed, I spooned loose tea into a strainer and let the tension in my chest unknot ever so slightly. If I squinted through the window over the sink, a pale green haloed the trees in the backyard. It had been a long, cold April, one filled with wintery mixes and sullen sleet. Today, the promise of spring felt real.

Except the air tasted wrong. Not foul. Not toxic. Not stale like the gray-speckled snowbanks and icy mud that remained in the yard.

Wrong as in not of this world. The sort of wrong that meant I should be on my guard.

And that morning, I wasn't. I ignored the pinpricks at the back of my mind and worked overtime to push the Sight away. After all, I knew I was losing my mother. I didn't need—or want—to know when and how.

I was pulling the half-and-half from the fridge for some coffee when the air shifted again. So strange, so wrong, I couldn't ignore it. The container slipped from my fingers and smacked against the floor, cream splattering my shins. In the front room, the volume spiked, and the violins screamed. I thought we'd wake the entire neighborhood.

I'd gotten as far as the kitchen threshold when the pocket door—on its own volition—slammed shut, nearly taking a few fingers. I yanked once, twice, before realizing that was fruitless. Then I spun and sprinted out the back door.

Icy mud soaked my socks. I stumbled, arms pinwheeling, ankle twisting and singing out in pain. I peeled off one sock and then another, hopping and running. I rounded the house and halted.

A man was on the sidewalk, his back to me. In his arms, he cradled a slight figure, as if that someone was the most precious thing of all. I only caught a glimpse. The blue fleece robe. The fuzzy slippers. The hair prematurely gray. The man glanced over his shoulder, his face obscured by a sweatshirt hood. He ran.

So did I.

We raced past the last few houses on the street. The paved asphalt melted into a slurry of gravel that led to the abandoned housing development. Fear gripped me, urged me faster. He couldn't be taking her *there*, could he?

He moved as if the burden in his arms weighed nothing. I was gaining on them, but cold made my legs ache, and my stride faltered. Every last stone and pebble stabbed the soles of my feet. I was pretty sure they were bleeding, but I didn't stop to check. The air washed the perspiration from my brow as soon as it sprouted. In front of me, a preternatural glow encased the man and my mother as if it were a cocoon. Once, twice, I reached out, could just brush its edges.

But I couldn't catch them.

They passed the entrance to the housing development, and I nearly wept with relief. But the man gained speed and, with it, uncanny power. The glow thickened. The sky turned a deep, midnight blue, filled with pinpricks of light—it was like staring into the Milky Way. A force reared up, like a wave, and crashed into me.

I flew through the air, landing hard on my tailbone. The man spirited my mother away. Before they vanished into the windbreak that separated the housing development from a stretch of fallow fields, my mother shifted in the man's arms.

She spoke, or at least mouthed words. Despite the glow, the uncanny stars, and all the rest, her message was clear, as was the gentle smile, the one she bestowed only on me.

It's okay.

Was it? I sat in the frigid mud, pondering that. I understood enough about my mother to know that this was final. But my heart disagreed, and it was my heart that had me on my feet, racing past the windbreak, the fallow fields, and toward the silo.

I ignored the farmhouse—with its peeling yellow paint and caved-in front porch—and headed straight for the crumbling silo. I'd only ventured inside it once on my own—a very long time ago, before I knew any better.

Today, I didn't care.

In the mud was a single set of footprints, obvious tracks that had trekked both to and from the silo. I yanked open the door, and it shuddered and screeched, almost angry. Inside, nothing marred the dusty floor except a couple of plastic bags and a Swiss Army knife. No stardust. No glow.

Nothing but an afterimage remained. A man. A woman. An embrace.

They were gone.

My mother was gone.

And I was truly undone.

AT HOME, the music played on. Not one of the concertos, but Mozart's Requiem. And yes, that was the sort of gallows humor my mother sometimes favored. The oxygen condenser breathed its steady, mechanical breath. A strange, primal anger washed through me. All I wanted was to shut everything down. I slammed my hand against the stereo and yanked the condenser's cord from the wall. My body recoiled.

Silence was much, much worse.

But in that silence, a piece of paper caught my attention. A page torn from a yellow legal pad, attached to my mother's pillow, deliberately, with a safety pin.

To my darling girl:

1. For as long as possible, do not report my "death" to the Enclave. I owe them nothing, and they'll find out soon enough.
2. Have a funeral anyway.
3. If Adele hasn't arrived, call her. (I suspect she'll arrive.)
4. In the back corner of the pantry is everything you need.
5. In the coming months, you'll also need to break some rules.
6. Trust that you'll know which ones.
7. Always know that you are loved.
8. Lastly, memories are precious; keep them close.

The yellow legal pad meant she was serious. These rules brooked no argument, not that she was here to argue with. They sounded just like her, both explicit and cryptic. Except for that last one. That didn't sound like her at all, minus the semicolon.

Her handwriting was painstakingly correct. The cost of this list —in time, in effort, in pain—must have been enormous. Had she composed it over hours? Days, perhaps? I unpinned it from the pillowcase, careful not to tear the paper.

This was how Adele found me. Standing in the middle of the

room, feet bleeding, surrounded by silence, with the last thing my mother had written clutched in my hand.

CHAPTER 5
PANSY

King's End, Minnesota
Saturday, July 8

My mother, as usual, was right. I did find what I needed in the pantry. The will, trust paperwork, and account information all secured in a fireproof lock box. Next to that was an urn, filled with what looked like sand. (At least, I hoped it was sand.) And yes, we held a funeral, one Adele helped me plan. As a nurse, she was able to finesse the death certificate, and deal with both the medical examiner's office and the funeral home. It was days before I realized my mother and Adele had planned everything in advance.

I haven't reported any of this to the Enclave. I haven't even told my best friends from the Academy that my mother is gone. What would I say? That a stranger carried her off and that, together, they vanished? How do you explain such a thing?

Mind you, we do lose agents, mainly field agents, but a permanent post job can be dangerous, too. Those fissures that let the Screamers invade our world? While they pop up anywhere in the world, generally at the worst times, there are those the Enclave needs to tend. King's End is rated a level one hot spot. If I don't mend the fissures, especially those in the housing development, on a regular basis, they might hop over levels two, three, and four, and become a level five hot spot.

And one of those can suck an agent—or even a task force—into its depths. Once that happens, there's no coming back. At least, that's what they told us at the Academy. It's also why we have six years of summer training there, at the Academy. It's the reason for the umbrellas; they make excellent offensive and defensive weapons. I can spear Screamers with the tip or send out a pulse to repel them. I can hunker down beneath the canopy and catch my breath.

One thing that never happens? Strangers emerging from a fissure, picking up a retired field agent, and simply vanishing into the void. For weeks, I did a deep dive into our lore, into the stories that are more like fairy tales than fact, looking for something, anything, that might explain my mother's disappearance.

There have been attempts to harness the power that comes through these fissures. Make no mistake. It is powerful. There have been strangers—travelers, they're called—who fall through to our side. Although these stories, too, read like fairy tales. But nothing about actual abductions.

Now, I stand in the kitchen and ease the lists from beneath their magnets. It might hurt less if I did it quickly, like ripping off a bandage. But I can't. Removing the lists feels like a betrayal, like sacrilege. I swallow back this sour task. No choice. I must hide them —along with my mother's umbrella—before tomorrow's breakfast meeting with Agent Darnelle.

With gentle fingertips, I hold the lists, wondering, pondering, questioning.

In the coming months, you'll need to break some rules.

Okay. Fine. I can do that.

Trust that you'll know which ones.

This, on the other hand? I'm not so sure. Not trusting Agent

Darnelle makes perfect sense. But I need to know what to expect this coming week. I think I know who I can ask, too.

I put on the tea kettle. While the water boils, I rummage in the pantry. From there, I pull out the tinctures and extracts my mother concocted every autumn. Nothing feels sore, and it's doubtful the Screamers broke any skin. Still, after an encounter, my mother and I always brewed and then drank a pot of specially enhanced tea.

I take the tea, my laptop, and my phone and head upstairs to my bedroom. Once there, I message my two best friends, Mortimer Connolly and Jack Ling, in our group chat.

> Henry Darnelle is here for my field agent examination. 😁

Jack tags my text with an exclamation point. A moment later, Mortimer sends a request for a video call. I accept, and Mort comes into view. His thick blond hair is swept back from his forehead like he's just emerged from a shower. His skin is ruddy, either from steam or sunburn. In the dim light, it's hard to tell.

"Let me add Jack," he says.

"Where *are* you?"

Head down, he doesn't answer. Mort's assignments take him all over the world. He could be in any hotel on any continent. Behind him, I catch a glimpse of a king-sized bed draped with an elegant crimson and gold quilt and piled with at least ten pillows. Velvety curtains frame a door to the balcony. Pinpricks of light sparkle, inviting you to step outside. A vase of fresh-cut flowers graces the nightstand.

Only Mortimer. The room is opulent in the extreme. This is hardly Enclave standard fare.

"So, you're where?" I try again. "Versailles?" Really, the space is giving off *let them eat cake* vibes.

Mort laughs. "Close enough. You could do laps in the hot tub. If only Jack were here."

"Well, I'm not, buddy."

The screen splits, and Jack appears, black-haired, willow-thin, and tall, serious in his dark, horn-rimmed glasses. Jack Ling was my only friend at the Academy that first year, both of us the odd ones out. We clung to each other—initially out of necessity, then because we preferred it that way. We were our own tiny alliance until Mort stepped in. You could say he brought us both into the fold. But sometimes, even now, I suspect he was only interested in Jack.

And Jack wouldn't go anywhere without me.

"Hey," Mort says, and it's a soft, seductive thing.

"Hey, yourself." There's an edge to Jack's voice, and I can taste the tension between them. Mort and Jack have been on-again and off-again since they fell in love, right here in King's End, over a long Thanksgiving weekend when we were all seventeen.

If they were in the room with me, I might be able to discern which way they were headed. Has Mort done something—yet again—to upset Jack? Mort has a way of trampling other people's feelings, but he also has the sort of charm that makes you forgive him. It's a combination for constant heartbreak.

"Why the hell haven't you had your examination?" Mort says now. "It's been five effing years since we graduated."

Instead of answering, I reach for my teacup and take a sip.

"Did you get hit today?" Jack pulls off his glasses, wipes them on his shirt, and then replaces them. He leans closer to the camera. "Are you okay?"

"Fine. Just a skirmish."

"It's never just a skirmish in King's End," Mort mutters.

Behind Jack, I notice the dull gray panels of a cubicle farm. "What are you doing at work? It's Saturday."

He gives me a look and then rolls his eyes. Yes, I know. The Enclave never takes weekends. Still. He works at headquarters, and they get more time off than field agents do.

"Speaking of Henry Darnelle," Jack says. "He's the reason I'm at work. He brought a crap-ton of data back from the Sahara. We're still shifting through it."

Another thing our umbrellas do: collect information. They're loaded with sensors and a GPS. Every time we repair a fissure or fight off some Screamers, we send data to the Enclave's headquarters for analysts like Jack to study.

"That's your problem, buddy," Mort says, his tone making me think they are headed for off-again territory. "Not Pansy's."

"*Do* I have a problem?" I ask, not only to change the subject, but I need to know. Is Henry Darnelle coming in all hard-ass? Or is it just a front, and he's actually a big softy who'll check all the boxes and be on his way. I'm hoping for the latter.

"You might. He's strictly by the book. Never met a rule he didn't want to follow." Mort makes a face, lips twisting in disgust. And yes, Mort's never met a rule he didn't want to break. "Plus, Darnelle has an umbrella shoved so far up his—"

"You're going to have to finesse this one," Jack interrupts.

I sigh and reach for more tea. "Great."

"But Rose is there, right?" Mort asks.

Teacup halfway to my lips, I freeze. I hold absolutely still. I'm not sure I even breathe for a few moments. Then I drop my gaze as if I'm letting the steam bathe my face. But the truth is, I can't look either of my friends in the eye.

"Just have her give him that disappointed-mom stare," Mort adds. "You know, with that little head shake as the chaser. Always works on me."

Granted, Mort has gathered far more of those than I ever have.

"So, what am I going to have to do?" I'm desperate, again, to change the subject, and I'm hoping they'll let me.

"Standard Academy stuff," Jack says. "Obstacle courses, fissure repair, couple of Screamer battles, only all on your home turf. Really, sweet pea, you could have passed it your first year out."

"Like you guys did."

Jack shrugs. Yes, he passed, and so did Mort, the moment the post-graduation moratorium was over. "I know Rose hates the

Enclave, but you'd think she'd want this out of the way, so it wasn't hanging over your head these past five years."

"She had her reasons."

What I don't say is this: For the last five years, since I graduated from the Academy, I've been the acting field agent in King's End. I came home that summer after graduation to find my mother broken and King's End under an all-out Screamer onslaught. Both Jack and Mortimer have been so busy traveling, building their careers within the Enclave, that neither has returned to King's End in that time.

A strange, hollow feeling shoots through me at the thought. The last time all three of us were together was a twenty-first birthday celebration in Minneapolis a few years back. A long weekend when my mother felt strong enough to patrol, and Adele promised to call if there was an emergency.

I blink, my eyes damp. For a moment, I consider disconnecting the call. Instead, I ask, "Is there a test for the Sight?" I'm hoping I left that nonsense behind when I left the Academy.

On the screen, Jack glances toward Mort, who then lifts his gaze toward the ornate ceiling.

"A few years back, Professor Botten changed the examination to weave in more tests," Mort says. He exhales as if the next words hurt him. "He said we were missing agents with that sort of potential. So, it isn't just one test, it's all of them."

I swear, softly. Both Jack and Mort know about my ability. The Enclave does not.

That first summer, before I left for the Academy, my mother sat me down over a pot of tea. She explained how the Enclave tests for the Sight and how the skill is both rare and highly prized. How agents with the Sight live short, terrible lives.

"They'll make promises," she said. "Don't believe them. Never believe the Enclave. All they will do is hone you into a weapon. When you are of no use, they will abandon you." She refilled my teacup, her expression sharpening even as her eyes grew tender. "What you must do, my sweetest of flowers, is appear unremarkable. That is your armor."

I've done everything to go unnoticed, right up to not scheduling the official field agent examination for as long as allowed. It's not ideal for career advancement. But, so what? I'm not going anywhere but King's End. However, this is the final year. Even if I could log into the system as my mother and request an extension, it wouldn't work. I would have to give up my post in King's End; I would have to turn in my umbrella. And that's something I simply can't do.

"It's how they caught Sandeep," Jack says now.

"Sandeep has the Sight?" I ask. Sandeep Patel was on our team at the Academy. If he had the Sight, he hid it well.

"Yeah," Mort adds, "earthquakes. He's pretty good at it, too, so he's heading up a geological team in Italy, lucky bastard."

Says the man currently plucking buttery escargot from shells with a tiny fork. I meet Jack's gaze and we both roll our eyes.

"You know," Jack says, and now his voice has gone all conspiratorial. "We could take a look at what Darnelle said about you five years ago."

"We can?" I ask.

"Well," Jack amends, "I can. I have access as part of my work."

"You are diabolical," Mort says. "I approve."

"Seriously?" I still can't believe this. "They let you?"

"No way around it. We have to know who's bringing in the data. Each agent is different, how they fight, their umbrella, years of experience, even how they view other agents. There are too many variables to analyze things blindly."

That makes sense. I guess? Either that, or it's a huge intrusion of privacy. Not that the Enclave has ever been big on privacy.

"What are you waiting for?" Mort prompts.

Jack turns his attention to his laptop, a light tapping of the keyboard filling the speakers. "Found it," he says a moment later.

Both Mort and I lean forward. Mort's hair flops into his eyes, and he shoves it back with an impatient hand. I clutch the teacup so hard, it might shatter between my fingers.

Jack clears his throat and takes on an imperious sort of tone. "'Cadet Pansy Little is an adequate, if unremarkable, trainee. She could become a productive permanent post agent with additional instruction from the right mentor.'"

For an instant, none of us says anything. Then? We all burst out laughing.

Mort wipes tears from his eyes, his voice full of mirth. "You've got this, Pansy-Girl. You've totally got this. I told you Darnelle was completely by the book. Play by the rules, fulfill his expectations, and you'll be fine."

That's harder than it sounds, but if both Jack and Mort think I can do it, then maybe I can. We talk for a few more minutes, and when the call ends, the silence that rushes in takes me aback. My heart pounds, and there's a tender spot in my chest that aches with both loneliness and regret. Maybe I should have confessed that I'm here alone, that my mother is gone. But when she wrote:

Trust no one from the Enclave.

She meant no one. And while it isn't there, scrawled in black ink on a yellow legal pad, I know this.

That rule includes my two best friends.

CHAPTER 6
PANSY

The coffeemaker gurgles a protest as if being pressed into service so early is not something it usually does. Lately, at least, that's been true.

But it's six thirty in the morning, and I'm certain Agent Darnelle is the sort to arrive the second it's seven o'clock. I've already done an hour's worth of yoga, but I need to be caffeinated before he shows up on my front porch.

While the coffee brews, I consider what I'll need to take with me today. My umbrella, of course, and the backpack I carry whenever I venture into the housing development. It's actually the same backpack I used all through training at the Academy. The olive-drab canvas has never quite lost its musty smell from weeks of roughing it in the damp summers of Washington state.

The scent is almost like a balm, a reminder of when things weren't quite so complicated, when I dreamed of maybe—*maybe*—

taking on the world as an actual field agent rather than a permanent post one.

I tuck a water bottle into the backpack's side pocket, add wire cutters, pliers, and a spool of wire for repairing the chain-link fence around the housing development, and a few of my mother's tinctures in case I get hit on site.

While I pack, I ponder the question rolling around in my mind. Do I really want to take Henry Darnelle to the housing development? Do I have a choice? Of all the areas around King's End, it has the most Screamer activity and contains all the major fissures. It would look strange if I didn't take him there.

It's now 6:55, and I resist the urge to flash ten minutes into my future. I touch fingertips to my forehead and let out a long, cleansing breath. I push the nattering, the whispered suggestions, the temptation to the back of my mind. I hold still until those branching lines of the future fade into mere hunches that I can ignore.

When I open my eyes, the coffeemaker's clock switches to 7:00.

The doorbell chimes.

Yes. Of course it does. No doubt Field Agent Extraordinaire Henry Darnelle is *always* on time.

On my front porch, he's there, resplendent as ever in suit, tie, and ridiculous hat. On one arm is that behemoth of an umbrella; on the other is a reusable sack. He must have stopped by The King's Larder, because the aroma of still-warm bagels joins the scent of the fresh coffee from the kitchen. The combination makes me weak-kneed with hunger and possibly gratitude.

I wasn't expecting him to make good on his offer. That he has? I don't know if I've misjudged him or if this is merely a technique to soften me up. But if so, what on earth for?

The kill.

It's the one whispered thought that pushes through all the barriers I've thrown up against the Sight. Does Henry Darnelle not expect me to pass this examination? Me, unremarkable Pansy Little?

I suppose that might be a reasonable assumption, given my performance at the Academy.

True, we've only just met, but the whispered thought doesn't sound like him. I may be an odious chore, but I'm not more than that, not to him anyway. Before I can open up that line of inquiry, probe the Sight ever-so-carefully, he nods, a bit terse.

"Agent Little."

Flustered, I step back, ushering him inside. "The kitchen's this way, and you can leave your umbrella in the stand if you like."

He does, because this is not so much a suggestion as a rule. Our umbrellas *are* weapons, after all. While they're designed for Screamers, they can work on other things as well, including other field agents.

I throw a glance over my shoulder as we head down the hall. My own umbrella has perked up considerably. She tilts ever so slightly toward the newcomer, fluttering her ruffles the way a person might bat their eyelashes. Wait. Is she flirting?

"Stop," I say under my breath. The command doesn't do any good. Besides, Agent Darnelle's umbrella is leaning closer, seemingly entranced by all that fluttering, so I give up and head into the kitchen.

At the moment, I have much bigger problems.

Bagels and cream cheese unpacked, coffee poured, Agent Darnelle tugs out his phone. He ponders the screen for what is designed to be several unnerving minutes. I use the time to inhale a couple of bagels and affect an air of un-remarkability.

At last, he glances at me. With care, he takes a precise bite of his bagel, chews thoughtfully, and then sips some coffee.

"This is quite good." He sounds genuinely surprised.

"It's the only thing I can make." Or rather, it's the only thing I can make—besides tea—that other people might want to consume.

He nods as if I haven't spoken at all. Then he clears his throat, a polite cough, more for show than anything else.

"Well, Agent Little, I'm not sure I should inform you of this, but you are the last of your class to take the field agent examination."

Of course I am.

"It's highly unusual to wait so long."

This I know.

"I've been busy," I say, because he's expecting some sort of reply. Honestly, I think he's expecting tears or, at the very least, a trembling lower lip. I don't have it in me to give him either of those things. All I want is to pass this examination and for him to be gone.

"Doing what?"

I blink, not understanding the question at first. Oh, does he really want to know what I've been doing these past five years? Like I haven't been the acting field agent here? I refuse to tell him about earning my associate's degree from King's End Community College. My mother was beside herself with pride, and the graduation ceremony was the last social function she ever attended.

"Just"—I glance around, hoping to pluck inspiration from somewhere in the kitchen—"busy."

"Indeed."

That single word seals my fate—or could if I let it.

"I'd like to show you around King's End," I say, rallying. "Show you what it is I do."

"What *you* do?"

Damn it. "My mother is retired, after all."

"So I gathered. He consults the phone's screen again. "That, too, is unusual, for an agent in charge to retire before a fully certified replacement is secured."

"We're an unusual family."

This is not going well. When Agent Darnelle stands, tucks his phone away, and says, "I think I've heard everything I need to for now," I'm certain of it.

But he turns to me, and while there is no smile on his face, there is a challenging light in his eyes.

"Let's head on out, Agent Little. I'm looking forward to seeing more of King's End."

WE ARE HALF a block from my house when I notice his shoes. He's a determined walker, managing to swing the umbrella and adjust his cuffs all without breaking stride. Those shoes, though. They are black and leather—and possibly hand-tooled. If we were strolling through Nordstrom's, they'd be perfect. For the trek out to the housing development?

"Will your feet be all right in those?" I point with the tip of my umbrella. "We're going to hit gravel here pretty soon." I direct my umbrella forward to where the asphalt ends and the unpaved road begins.

"I walked here from the bed and breakfast. I'll be fine." His voice has a clipped quality, a schoolmaster disappointed in his student. The message is clear: *Worry about yourself, Agent Little.*

Fortunately, it's early, and not many people are out. Still, one of my neighbors jogs past and nearly trips for staring. If anyone is peeking through their curtains, they're going to want details. Pansy Little and a handsome, well-dressed stranger? Off on a romantic morning stroll? Yes, this is going to be hard to explain. If we don't hurry, it'll be all over the Hey Neighbor app before noon.

We leave the concrete sidewalk and the neighborhood behind. Without hesitation, I strike out onto the dirt road that leads to the source of all my troubles here in King's End. Agent Darnelle balks at the sidewalk's edge, his eyes darting from his shoes to the dust I've already kicked up. Then, without protest or complaint, he follows me.

"They were supposed to pave this road," I say over my shoulder. "But the construction company never got around to it." Then again, they were supposed to do lots of things. Just one of the many broken promises of this place.

We arrive at the entrance of the abandoned housing development. The stone façade is half-complete, and the wrought-iron gate doesn't work. I've managed to drag it a few feet, but the metal screeches and then halts. Not that it matters. No one ever comes back this way.

Agent Darnelle pauses, shields his eyes against the morning sun, and squints at the billboard that looms over the gate. The sign casts a long shadow across the dirt road. Step into its shade, and the temperature drops by several degrees. It's uncanny. Even in the sun, the chill touches my skin, and I rub my arms.

"Camelot Lots," he says.

The name is spelled out in a typeface that was trendy for a month and now simply looks sad. Beneath that, in fancy, old-timey script, is the phrase: *Because King's End needs more castles!*

"Doesn't exactly roll off the tongue," he adds.

"That's the least of its problems."

"So I gathered."

I start up again, but he remains in place. This is not an unusual reaction, not when confronting Camelot Lots. Most everyone with a bit of sense gives in to the urge, turns around, and heads in the other direction.

Hand still shielding his eyes, he peers through the gate. "I feel as though I've seen this place before."

"You've been to King's End?"

"Never."

"Then I don't know how—"

"Neither do I." He gives me a look, a quick up and down, and then says, "Shall we?"

His tone is mild, but beneath it lies that challenge. *Prove yourself, Apprentice Agent.*

I scan the area, almost hoping for an ambush today. That would prove any number of things, maybe even get Agent Darnelle to leave early. Who needs a manufactured obstacle course after thwarting a full-fledged Screamer attack?

Near the entrance, the few completed houses bask in the sunrise. The lawns are spare, but in the morning light, the brown patches aren't quite as obvious. This is the best time of day here, and I make a point of patrolling as early as possible. Hope is strongest then, and despair a mere aftertaste. If you squint, you could almost pretend to have stumbled upon a sleepy suburb not yet up for the day.

If you don't look too closely, that is. The few birds that nest here do so in empty windowsills, all the panes devoid of glass. And except for the model homes near the entrance, most houses are skeletons of themselves, with missing doors, missing walls, missing life.

"Do you patrol here often, Agent Little?"

"Nearly every day."

All that crisscrosses the dusty path in front of us are tiny mice tracks and larger ones, perhaps of a fox chasing after dinner. Yes, Agent Darnelle excels at looking closely, I'm sure. Evidence suggests I haven't been here in years, never mind the other day.

I tap the dust in front of me with the toe of my shoe. "It just does that."

"Does what?"

"Sweeps my footprints away when I leave."

He raises a skeptical eyebrow but otherwise doesn't comment.

My first task is the chain-link fence that surrounds the development. Overnight, holes appear, as if something has clawed its way out—or in. The fact that I can't tell has always unnerved me, and my mother never said. But I follow another of her iron-clad rules:

Mending the fence is my first priority.

While I'm still on alert, something tells me this will be a routine, unchallenging sort of patrol. The air doesn't taste like an ambush, so I head for a large hole, one that's directly behind the showcase home. At one time, this particular house hosted tours, and couples and families streamed in and out. It's the nicest house in the entire development, staged with furniture and high-end interior design. And yet? Something about it feels malevolent—again, hope tinged with despair.

Perhaps that's because around back, near a basement egress window, there's a fissure. Or normally, there's one. Today, I can't even detect a seam or my handiwork in repairing it. Typical.

At the fence, I attach my umbrella to the quick-release strap and sling that over my shoulder, cross-body. Then I pull a set of pliers and some wire from my backpack and set to work.

Agent Darnelle touches the fence. His fingertips light upon the silver links and send a tremor through the metal.

"Do the repairs help?"

"They don't hurt."

My mother always said if the fence goes, we all go. That's not something you confess to the man who holds your job in his hands. Neither is this: Every April, my mother mixed up a concoction on the kitchen stove, one of herbs and oils and one specific—and most crucial—ingredient.

Her blood.

She then would paint random spots on the fence with the mixture. This April, I did the same, except with my blood instead of hers. At the rate I've been repairing holes, I doubt it did any good.

We make our way through the development. I need to repair that gap by the cemetery, but I really don't want to. The tear in the chain link is large and angry, almost like it's taunting me, the hole nothing but a row of jagged, silver teeth. Worse, Agent Darnelle's skepticism shadows me like a third presence. He's not impressed.

I stop our trek and glance around, letting my gaze soften, letting the barricades I've built in my mind ease.

Nothing.

Agent Darnelle pulls out his phone. He taps away, a schoolmaster frown gathering on his brow. "I was led to believe that this area contains the main fissures in King's End."

"It does."

"Are you certain?"

It takes all my willpower not to roll my eyes and spit out a sarcastic reply of: *Well, I live here, don't I? Wouldn't I know?* Then again, the Screamers aren't simply silent today; they're absent altogether. I wouldn't believe me.

"I see that there hasn't been an official site survey since 1991. Perhaps things have changed since then. You should put in a request for a survey team, assuming..." He trails off as if something has caught his attention, but his unspoken words make my heart pound with trepidation.

Yes, assuming I pass my examination. Assuming I'll be the permanent post agent here. Assuming I even want someone—or rather, someone else—from the Enclave poking around in King's End. Which, by the way, I don't.

"Agent Little, I think I've seen enough here for today. It's time we headed back, run you through some paces. I scouted out the green where I found you yesterday—"

"I need to finish here first."

Again with the skeptical eyebrow. "I really think you're—"

I know what he's going to say; the air is filled with his displeasure. "I'm not avoiding my examination."

"Aren't you?" He casts a look around, holds out a hand like he's searching for raindrops.

That last hole remains, the one I must repair, even at the risk of failing my examination.

"Please?" I point toward the far end of the development. "Let me fix that?"

Maybe it's my voice. Maybe it's because it's suddenly devoid of its sarcasm. Or maybe it's the hole in the fence. Because it looks like a gaping maw with jagged teeth. Agent Darnelle stares at it and, after a moment, nods.

I take the path behind the last row of houses, not caring if he follows. These particular buildings really do resemble skeletons. On windy days, the frames creak and moan, the sound pitiful, as if they mourn for the families that will never live in them. Today, in the still air and bright sun, they strike me as even sadder. Agent Darnelle cranes his neck, surveys the space, and then halts as if he feels it, too.

"It's so empty," he says.

"Yes. I know."

"There's no graffiti."

"None."

"Are you safe here on your own, Agent Little?" A hint of concern touches his voice. He readjusts his hold on his umbrella. "There aren't any—?"

"Squatters? Gangs?" I shake my head. "No. Only me."

"I see."

Whether he does or not, I can't say, but that hole isn't mending itself, so I get to work. When his hands join mine, holding the two sides in place, my heart skitters. I've forgotten how much easier this particular job is with an extra set of hands. Something presses at the back of my mind, urging me to confess this.

Before I can—foolishly—open my mouth to do so, something in the cemetery flutters in my peripheral vision. The air fills with sorrow. It's so thick that it sours the back of my throat. I grip the fence tight, and the chain link digs into the flesh of my fingers.

A funeral.

Oh, *no*. That's why the housing development is so quiet today.

CHAPTER 7
PANSY

King's End, Minnesota
Sunday, July 9

From my backpack, I grab the wire cutters. I snip away at all our previous work and then some, enlarging the hole in the fence.

"What—?" Agent Darnelle begins. Then he peers through the hole I've just made.

He swears softly, then shuts his eyes. For the barest of moments, anguish flashes across his features.

I cut until I can slip through the space. Halfway through, I realize Agent Darnelle is much larger than I am, and there's no way he can follow. I backtrack, metal claws snagging my T-shirt, and pick up the cutters again. I've barely made a snip when his hands grab two sides of the hole and yank them apart.

"Enough space?" I ask.

"It'll do."

I crawl through first and scrabble against the loose dirt along the fence's edge. Before I can fully ready my umbrella, an oomph sounds behind me, and I turn.

There, Agent Darnelle is stuck, his suit coat all tangled in the sharp, exposed edges of the hole. It's almost like the fence is trying to hold him back. He squirms out of his coat, grabs his umbrella, and runs, those ridiculously expensive shoes somehow finding purchase on the lush grass.

We race uphill, only slowing our steps near the top, where the mourners are gathered. Umbrella in hand, I scan the crowd for familiar faces, but other than a few residents of King's End, most are strangers. It's a small group, possibly a private ceremony, which might explain why it's so early in the day.

A man stands with two children, their faces downcast as the casket is lowered into the waiting grave. A wife. A mother. A family shattered. I stop the Sight there, but not before my heart seizes, and a thickness collects in the back of my throat. Still, I have enough presence of mind to glance upward into the trees.

I touch Agent Darnelle's umbrella with the tip of mine and then point skyward. His jaw goes slack before firming into a taut line. No one else can see the Screamers, but in a few minutes, we'll all feel them.

"Are there always so many?" His gaze is calculating as he scans the branches.

Normally? No. Lately? Say, in the last three months? Absolutely. I manage a non-committal shrug.

His hand comes to rest on my elbow, and he leans close, his whisper brushing my ear. "I'll take the far side."

Agent Darnelle might be here to fire me, but he moves with a stealth that's admirable. He skirts the ceremony without disturbing a single mourner. No one glances up. No one sends a frown his way. I kneel next to a headstone and ready my umbrella.

Once he's directly across from me, he holds up three fingers. I count the seconds in my head.

One ... two ... three.

At the same moment, our umbrellas unfurl. We both send out a pulse that shakes the air before slamming into the Screamers. And they do scream. The sound—which only Agent Darnelle and I can hear—is like a shockwave rolling through the cemetery, up and over the grave markers and trees. One of the mourners, a resident of King's End, peers over her shoulder. Her gaze touches mine, and she nods, her expression softening in approval.

But luck is with us. We caught the Screamers unaware. So intent were they to consume the strong emotions wafting up from the gravesite that they missed our presence entirely. They try, of course. This is something you must give them credit for. They always try.

Because an event such as this? Pure Screamer fuel. I wonder what it is that attracts them, what it is they need. How can something the Enclave calls temporal disturbances be so attuned to human emotions? How, if not for our intervention, they'd leave the residue of chaos and despair in their wake.

No, I've never walked into a desert and fought a Screamer sandstorm. I'm unlikely to save the world any time soon. But I can do this.

I can protect a marriage proposal and a funeral and, by doing so, protect the residents of King's End. If happy moments are important, then so, too, are the sad ones. A proper mourning. A heart so heavy you don't think it can hold anything else, and the quiet, chaos-free opportunity to feel. Screamers can deny people all of this. It's my job to see that they don't.

Or, at least for now, it is.

The mass of Screamers splits in two and erupts into splinters that resemble those crows. The black and red ones stream off toward Agent Darnelle. On silent feet, he chases them away from the mourners. The blue and green ones head back toward the housing development. I pursue them as far as the chain-link fence. They split their mass, shooting around Agent Darnelle's coat rather than through it. I don't bother following them into the housing development. They are chastised. For now.

After the service, I shadow the father and the two children, my umbrella unfurled, protecting their walk back to the waiting cars. I pretend to investigate historical grave markers, but I'm really sending out a subtle pulse with my umbrella, letting the Screamers know it would be a bad idea to return.

The mourners drive off, kicking up grit from the gravel parking lot. I remain there, dust settling on my skin, drying my lips, stinging my eyes. After a while, the shade of a second umbrella joins mine.

"I always check the obituaries," I say, although Agent Darnelle hasn't asked or even sent a chiding, schoolmaster eyebrow my way.

I have alerts set up, not just on the internet, but the Hey Neighbor app as well. Screamers don't always invade funerals, but in King's End, there's always a good chance they will. While Sunday funerals are rare, they do happen here. King's End is accommodating that way.

"There were a lot of people I didn't recognize," I add.

"Perhaps someone was coming home after a long absence."

His words are so quiet, so melancholy, that I lower my umbrella for a better look at his expression. But he keeps his face shrouded beneath his own. I taste sorrow again and something more, something bitter and full of bile.

This time, it's coming from Henry Darnelle.

All at once, he shuts his umbrella with more force than necessary. "I think we're done for the day, Agent Little."

Done for the day? Or simply done, period? Have I completely screwed up my examination?

"I don't think we were hit." My throat is so clogged, I sound as if I've come off a crying jag. "But would you like to come back for some tea? I can—"

"No." The word is sharp and final.

I take a step back.

"I mean, no, thank you, Agent Little." His voice softens, but the bile is still there, still thickening his words. "I have everything I need in my room at the bed and breakfast. Let's meet on the green tomorrow morning, say seven again?"

I swear I don't make a face or even twitch a muscle. Agent Darnelle doesn't smile, but the crinkles around his eyes deepen.

"Make it eight," he says. "I'll see you then."

With that, he walks through the cemetery's front gates, leaving me to stand in the midday sun, still clutching my open umbrella.

It's only when he's too far away that I think to call after him, remind him of his suit coat still caught in the jaws of the fence. Even if he could hear me, my mouth is too dry to make a sound.

I take a winding path through oaks and willows and headstones. Did the Screamers lead Agent Darnelle through this part of the cemetery? I glance around as if I could trace the path he took by telltale impressions in the grass or leaves torn from low-hanging branches. I don't detect anything, but then again, he moved with such grace and stealth that I'm not sure I could.

My feet lead me to the grave markers. I kneel, consider the headstones in front of me, and trace the names, first my mother's and then my father's.

Rose Little and Maximilian Monroe.

This is where we placed that urn. Sometimes, I'm grateful for this spot, that I have a place to visit, that there's evidence that Rose Little was here in this world. Other times, it feels like a violation, a betrayal. There's nothing beneath the marker that is truly her; it signifies nothing. I can't shake the notion that wherever she is, some day, she'll come back home. That maybe I've given up too soon,

Part of me insists I should mourn.

I stand, brush the grass from my jeans, and pick up my umbrella. Because if there's a part of me that insists I mourn, there's another part that refuses.

It's this part that leads me back through the older section of the cemetery until I find the hole in the fence. Agent Darnelle's jacket is still there, swaying in the breeze. I tug it free, careful of the edges that threaten to shred it. I consider the jacket in my hands and the hole in front of me.

I decide to repair both.

CHAPTER 8
HENRY

King's End, Minnesota
Sunday, July 9

Damn it. He'd forgotten his jacket. Henry sat down hard on the bed, one already made up with mints on the pillows, the room itself pristine. On the desk, a vase of fresh flowers wafted their scent into the air, making it impossible to churn up the anger he longed to feel.

Well, almost.

A rustling came from the doorway, the sound both insistent and self-satisfied. In it, Henry heard the refrain of *I told you so.*

His umbrella loved being right. Then again, so did Henry.

It had to be a funeral, didn't it? But that was the Screamers for you. They had an uncanny prescience. They'd knocked him right off his stride, had him abandoning a fellow agent—technically, an apprentice agent, so really, that was worse—and retreating like a rookie on a first field assignment.

Henry could've handled *anything* other than a funeral.

Damn it. Again.

He turned his attention toward the door and his umbrella leaning against the wall. "Well? What should we do now?"

This rustling brought a smile to his lips, although not a particularly happy one. "No, I doubt Agent Little or her umbrella would appreciate a social call."

His own umbrella begged to differ.

"A bit distracted, are we? By what? Some fetching polka dots and pretty pink ruffles?"

A disgruntled thump, and then all was quiet.

But leaving the room was an option. As was collecting his jacket and perhaps a few readings in the housing development while he was there? Henry looked once more toward his umbrella.

"Shall we?"

HENRY ENDED up in the Riverside B&B's dining area. The establishment was more a bed and breakfast, lunch, and possibly snack sort of establishment. They set him up in a cozy—and private—alcove, kept the coffee coming, and served him a late lunch while his umbrella stewed in the seat across from him, impatient and still disgruntled.

"I need to review my notes," he said, mostly under his breath.

"Sir?"

One of the waitstaff stood next to his table, coffee carafe in hand, the aroma of a rich, dark roast clearing his head. Carrie, her name tag read.

"I'm talking to myself." Henry managed a short laugh. "About work."

Carrie gave him a grin. "Do that a lot myself." She hefted the carafe. "More?"

"Thank you."

"So, work. Does that mean you're in town on business?"

Did many people venture to King's End on business? Unlikely, but he considered the question, considered what it might yield. "I'm visiting someone."

Carrie raised an interested eyebrow.

"Perhaps you know her? Pansy Little?"

"Oh, Pansy." That earlier grin bloomed into a full-fledged smile. "Yes, of course." Her gaze went from him to the umbrella seated opposite, the latter exuding the bearing of a curmudgeon waiting on a fresh cup of coffee. "Oh, wait, you must be one of her camp friends."

Camp friends? Did she mean the Academy? Well, of course. How else would a permanent post family explain summer-long absences except with a stay at a sleep-away camp?

"You could say that."

"That first year she went?" Carrie huffed. "I was *so* jealous. But then I had nothing but summer camps from all those teen movies in my head. You know, bonfires and marshmallows and sneaking out after dark."

"I assure you, it was nothing like that."

"I *know*. Pansy came home absolutely wrecked. I think she slept for all of Labor Day weekend. It's some sort of survival thing, right?"

"Yes. No marshmallows and certainly no"—Henry cleared his throat—"shenanigans."

Carrie raised an eyebrow, her voice sly. "That's not how I heard it."

A rush of blood touched his cheeks, but the heat only made him laugh. "I assure you things never got too out of hand."

Carrie glanced away, and he had the distinct impression she rolled her eyes.

"Well, I'll let you get back to it. It's sweet of you to visit. I'm sure Pansy appreciates it."

That, Henry doubted. He was going to push, dig a little deeper, test a hypothesis that had emerged at the cemetery. But what he wanted to ask was something a friend would already know. There was one rule you always followed, whether a field agent or permanent post one: maintaining the balance, the façade, with the locals was absolutely crucial.

So, instead, he nodded.

Carrie was at the alcove's threshold, framed by eyelet lace, when she turned and said, "It's good to see her camp friends looking out for her."

Only once she left did Henry taste the admonishment against his tongue, a soft refrain of *It's about time.*

A whisper came from his umbrella, a variation of Carrie's words.

Henry ignored both and hit a key, banishing the screensaver on his laptop, and picked up where he'd left off.

Cadet Pansy Little is an adequate, if unremarkable, trainee. She could become a productive permanent post agent with additional instruction from the right mentor.

"What a pretentious asshole."

A slight rustling came from his umbrella.

"Glad you agree."

But five years ago, Henry conceded, he *was* a pretentious asshole. The first of his class to make principal field agent, the first to make the rank before turning twenty-five. That hadn't happened since his father's generation, his father being one of those agents.

Rose Little had been the other.

And five years ago, he had dismissed her daughter with barely a glance.

Henry scanned the notes from that graduation exercise. He'd made plenty, although startlingly few on Pansy. That, in itself, was odd. He always made notes, copious annotations, observations, even though his recall was impeccable, and he almost never referred to them.

Why was Pansy Little a mostly blank—and unremarkable—slate? Why could he barely remember her from that summer? He searched her records for blips in her performance during the capstone exercise, a simulation meant to replicate a major field mission. Except there weren't any.

Her yearly mentor reports yielded nothing but expected progress. But even when a mentor was less than forthcoming in their evaluations (a common occurrence when the mentor was also a relative), data from umbrellas never lied. Henry brought up those records, or tried to. Each attempt resulted in an access-denied message.

He heaved a sigh, finished off his coffee—which Carrie once again deftly and stealthily refilled—and picked up his phone to call the Enclave's personnel department.

"Yes, hello," he said when the poor, hapless agent on weekend duty answered. "This is Agent Darnelle. I need access to some records."

A long, hushed silence followed this request. Then, quietly: "*Henry* Darnelle?"

His lips twitched, and that pinprick of heat peppered his cheeks. "Yes, Henry Darnelle. And you are?"

"Agent Terrence Rupp."

"Hello, Terrence. I'm hoping you can help me. I'm conducting a field agent examination and need access to the apprentice agent's umbrella data."

"They didn't give that to you?"

"*They* must have forgotten."

An exasperated sigh came from the other end of the line. "I'm sorry about that, Agent Darnelle. Give me the name, and I'll get your access set up."

"Pansy Little."

Silence ensued. At first, Henry assumed Terrence was merely working the necessary electronic magic. The quiet stretched, no clatter of keys reached his ears, and when Terrence finally spoke, the words were tinged with deep reluctance.

"I can't give you access to that data. It's been locked."

"Locked? What on earth for?"

"The family line has been earmarked for retirement."

Foregone conclusion, indeed. "Really. Tell me, Terrence, how is that possible when I haven't completed my examination yet?"

"I'm sorry, Agent Darnelle. It says here in the system—"

"Can you override the system?"

"Can I...?"

"Can you override the system and allow me access to the data?"

"I'm ... not supposed to."

"But *can* you?"

The line went quiet again, so quiet that Henry thought they'd been disconnected, which was one way this call could end. But then he heard something that sounded like a hiccup or someone swallowing a nervous sob.

"I'll get in trouble."

"Do you have any brothers or sisters, Terrence?"

"Yeah."

"Any still at the Academy?"

"My sister Tori."

"And if I were performing her examination without the benefit of the data from her umbrella, how fair would that be?"

The seconds ticked by, but Henry was already pulling another laptop from his messenger bag and didn't wait for Terrence's response.

"Send me the authorization. As a principal field agent, I can override whatever lock is on her files. I'll take the heat, and you won't get into trouble. I promise."

Another long sigh, this one filled with trepidation. "I can't leave them unlocked."

"Give me five minutes."

"I'll give you ten. But please hurry." With that, Terrence did hang up.

CHAPTER 9
PANSY

King's End, Minnesota
Sunday, July 9

ending Agent Darnelle's suit coat is not an unpleasant task. On the kitchen table sits a teapot, aromatic steam rising into the air. I brewed my mother's version of Constant Comment, the flavor sharper—it tastes like oranges and ambition. True, the Screamers scattered without a counterattack. Even so, I've added a few drops of post-encounter tincture. Already, the concoction is clearing my head.

With tiny scissors, I cut the loose threads on Agent Darnelle's jacket. The material is oddly smooth and light. It feels resilient between my fingers. I consider whether I'm about to ruin the thing. I hold it close, inspecting the weave, and the faintest hint of aftershave reaches me, full of warm vanilla but with a distinct bite. The scent is sexy, maybe even a little wild, and at odds with the schoolmaster persona he's been projecting.

I slump in my chair, exhausted from the morning and this line of thinking. I will not dwell on Agent Darnelle's aftershave. Or on my reaction to it. I spread the jacket on the kitchen table and pick up the needle, determined to mend a completely different type of fence.

I'm finishing up the last stitch and biting off the thread—an excuse to smell that warm vanilla—when a tap-tap-tap comes on the kitchen door.

Heat floods my cheeks, although why I should feel guilty about mending a jacket, I can't say. But I feel caught out. I'm certain Agent Darnelle will charge through the door, demand his jacket *and* my resignation.

Instead, my neighbor, Adele Monroe, pokes her head inside.

Her eyes are bright and blue, her dark hair threaded with silver. She lugs a huge canvas sack full of crochet projects, and under one arm, a curly-haired dog of undetermined breed. Poodle, definitely, but the rest is anyone's guess.

"We're back!" She sets the dog on the floor, and he comes bounding for me.

With a single leap, he lands in my lap. I have to shove the suit coat aside so his tiny claws don't rip my handiwork to pieces. In the process, I nearly spill the tea. The porcelain rocks against the table. Adele drops her bag and rushes forward, hands steadying the teapot.

"Sorry, sorry." She turns to the dog, who is currently trying to lick my face. "Prince, be good."

"He's fine." Truly, my kitchen hasn't been this lively in ages, and Prince is a bundle of chaotic comfort in my arms. "Are you home for a while?"

Adele works as a contract nurse. This time of year, she takes jobs in the Twin Cities. She stays in rentals that allow Prince to tag along and attend the meetings of the crochet guild. Since it's almost state fair time, that means the house next to mine has been dark these past few weeks.

"I start a new contract on Tuesday, but there were some things I wanted to pick up from home, some extra supplies for the state fair." She waves a hand at the bag bulging with a rainbow assortment of yarn. "I'll head back sometime tomorrow."

She gives me a once over. Her eyes aren't simply bright and blue —they're perceptive. She's far too professional to let emotions play across her face, but I don't need the Sight to tell me she's worried.

"And it's good to spend a little time at home," she adds, but her voice lacks conviction.

The guild is crocheting a horse for the state fair. No, I don't understand why. I do know that the project is huge, it's coming down to the wire, and they need every last member to complete it before the fair opens next month. Sundays are prime crocheting days.

So why is Adele here and not there?

As if in answer, her phone pings. She casts it an awkward glance like she wants to grab it and silence it, and her cheeks redden. I haven't checked the Hey Neighbor app since yesterday. Judging by Adele's expression, I'm pretty sure I don't want to.

"Have some tea," I say instead.

Prince and I continue our reunion while Adele busies herself with finding a second cup and saucer. We are distantly related on my father's side of the family, second cousins or something like that. She is—or was—my mother's best friend, her confidant.

Adele understands things about King's End other residents only glean. She can't see the Screamers, not like I do, but she has a sense for them. She knows about the Enclave and why I spend my days patrolling the streets. So, news of Pansy Little strolling toward the housing development with a well-dressed, handsome stranger?

That would bring her rushing home from the Twin Cities. To test this hypothesis, I say, "Yes, he's here from the Enclave."

Her cup rattles against its saucer. Her cheeks flush once again, but her gaze narrows on mine.

"Everyone is up in arms." She waves a hand, indicating the neighborhood. "They don't know whether to call the police or start planning an engagement party. Guy Gunderson is worried he's here to foreclose on your house."

I try not to roll my eyes. I mean, I really, really try. They could always just *ask* me. But then, that would put an end to all the gossip.

"I own this house, and the property taxes are paid." I think. Maybe. I shake my head, promising myself to check later.

"I have at least twenty direct messages," Adele adds, "telling me I need to come home, and there's a long community thread full of speculation."

The retirees in the neighborhood have taken to the Hey Neighbor app with an enthusiasm that's a little frightening.

"He's here for my field agent examination," I say. "So absolutely, they can throw me a party afterward, assuming I pass, but we're not inviting Henry Darnelle."

This time, Adele drops her teacup. It clatters but doesn't break. Tea slops into the saucer. She blinks, grasping for composure and then losing her grip on it completely.

"Harry's son?"

For the first time since my mother vanished, her voice cracks. All of her does. With the mere mention of Henry Darnelle, I've chiseled something open. It lasts as long as a breath, maybe two. The demeanor of the professional nurse slips away, and all I see is the woman whose loss runs as deep as mine.

"Harry?" I echo, and my voice, too, is rough.

"Harry, Harrison Darnelle." She nods, a little frantic, and gropes for her phone.

She scrolls, and while I can't see the screen, I suspect someone snapped a picture of me and Agent Darnelle this morning.

"From the Enclave?" I keep my words as soft as possible, as if I'm afraid to touch an exposed nerve.

"Yes." Adele pulls in a breath, one hand resting against her heart as if to calm it. She sets down the phone. "The Enclave."

That's easy enough to check. I dash from the kitchen in search of my laptop, the wave of her emotions nearly pushing me through the door.

When I return to the kitchen, Prince has snuggled on Adele's lap.

She weaves her fingers through his fur. Her smile is bright again, even if her eyes hold sorrow.

Like all agents in the Enclave, Henry Darnelle has a profile. His, of course, is loaded with accomplishments and commendations. Mine? Not so much. But each profile contains a lineage. Henry Darnelle *is* the son of Harrison (Harry) Darnelle and Miranda Connolly.

And Harry Darnelle died in February of this year.

Oh. The knowledge knocks into me, resonating like a blow to my solar plexus. The funeral. The expression on Agent Darnelle's face. Now I recognize it. It's a match for my own every time I look in the mirror.

"Yes. Harry Darnelle is Agent Darnelle's father." Softly, I add, "But he died recently. In February."

"I know. Rose told me."

"She did?" This past year has been a blur, patrolling, caring for my mom, witnessing the steady decline of her health. Was she still well enough to go online in February? I rummage through the memories of those days, but the threads are tangled, full of chaos and sorrow.

"They had a connection that went beyond..." Adele shakes her head and uses a napkin to sop up the spilled tea before pouring a fresh cup. "I'm not sure I should tell you this. It was before you were born and before your mother met your father, but for a time, I thought Harry Darnelle was the one, that he'd stay here in King's End with your mother."

And now his son is here to administer my field agent examination.

Yes, the Enclave is small. Yes, a coincidence like this could happen. Yes, I'm skeptical anyway.

"Of course, he was betrothed—"

Of *course*. Always remember rule number six: *When someone tells you they're not betrothed, don't believe them.*

"—but he was planning on having it annulled."

Again, don't believe them. I suspect this rule was born from my mother's own betrothal. She never said who in the Enclave it was or even which family line. Her excuse? "Oh, you're sure to encounter him at some point in your career. Less awkward—at least for you—if you don't know."

"So, what happened?" I ask Adele.

"They went patrolling. I remember your mother saying something about the quiet of the Memorial Day weekend being ideal. And there were three of them, although I can't say the other fellow's name right now. They were ... what's that phrase? Thick as thieves? Or Musketeers? Like you, Mort, and Jack. Always planning and plotting. But that day, only your mother and Harry returned. Rose couldn't talk about it, and Harry was injured and couldn't talk at all."

My pulse kicks up a notch. Images swirl just out of reach. The Sight doesn't often take me to the past, but it can.

"Whatever it was," Adele says, "whatever happened to Harry, it wasn't just physical. It was ... well, you know, not the normal kind of injury."

We are wounded in the line of duty: psychic wounds, Screamer toxin, all manner of things that can't be solved with a trip to urgent care. Sometimes, a trip to urgent care or the emergency room can kill us.

"I was home before my last year of nursing school, and I had a friend studying speech therapy who needed the extra cash. We worked with Harry all summer long, all three of us." Adele nods toward the pantry. "I don't know how many concoctions your mother tried. It was enough, but just barely. His speech was slow, but he could talk. I don't know if he ever made a full recovery in that regard."

Adele considers her tea. "It was Labor Day weekend when your mother told Harry to go home, back to the Enclave, back to his betrothed. Miranda, I think her name was. Rose kept insisting it was the only way, that he had to secure the Darnelle seat on the High Council, although she never said why. They fought about it." She shakes her head, so much sorrow and chagrin in the gesture. "And your mother never fought fair. So, in the end, Harry left."

"And she never told you what happened?"

"She couldn't."

"Couldn't or wouldn't?"

"Couldn't. Oh, I know she tried over the years. It was like she was searching for a loophole that would allow her to."

I turn the notion over in my mind. It's so out of the ordinary that I can't account for it, like those old Enclave fairy tales. "That sounds like a curse."

"It does." Adele tips her head and stares out the window above the sink. "Come to think of it, it really does."

CHAPTER 10
HENRY

The data transfer took seven minutes. Henry even powered down the second laptop as an extra precaution, once the data was safe and encrypted. True, an additional personal laptop was a breach of Enclave protocol, but then Henry hadn't become a principal field agent by playing by *all* the rules.

At the 10:01 minute mark, he watched Pansy Little's data vanish from his Enclave-issued computer.

At the 10:10 minute mark, as predicted, his phone rang. The unlisted number that flashed on the screen could belong to only one person.

"My boy, how are you?" Reginald Botten sounded as jovial as ever, as if this were a mere check-in call.

"Hamstrung without that data."

"Really, my boy, you shouldn't be badgering the rank and file like that. They're quite in awe of you."

"I recall you mentioning I'd have access to all the records I needed."

"Precisely why I called. This data won't do you any good, and it's not anything you need."

"I'd like to be the judge of that."

"I believe it to be compromised."

"In what way?" Henry asked. "As I understand it, Rose Little retired when Pansy returned from her last year at the Academy. Five years of field data should give me an overall sense of her progress."

"That's my point. It won't be *her* progress. I have reason to believe Rose stepped in from time to time and patrolled in Pansy's stead."

"And you believe this why?"

"There's very little data from Rose's umbrella these past five years. These situations are rare, but we do allow early retirement with an apprentice agent in place. In those cases, there's always a greater influx of data from the retiree's umbrella, especially in the first year or two. But in this particular case, the data has come almost exclusively from Pansy's umbrella."

Henry considered this, considered what his own eyes and umbrella were telling him—and considered whether Botten was bullshitting him.

"It's my personal belief that Rose has been covering for Pansy all these years," Botten continued. "Any data from the umbrella will pollute your evaluation."

"Do you have proof of this accusation?" Because it was an accusation, and a serious one at that. In theory, Rose, as Pansy's mentor, could use her daughter's umbrella. His father had, from time to time, shown Henry techniques not just with his own umbrella but with Henry's as well. It was a way to train them both. But long-term patrolling?

Henry didn't buy it.

"I've known Rose since my own Academy days," Botten said, as if that settled the matter.

That was hardly proof.

"I know how she operates," Botten added as if in answer to Henry's silent objection. "No one could blame her for wanting to continue the line. Her parents vanished on a field mission when she and her sister Marigold were still fairly young. Then Marigold herself vanished a dozen years ago. Pansy is the last, and she simply isn't strong enough to continue the line. Rose has anticipated this, and she's used every delay tactic to keep it from coming to pass."

The last of the Little line. This still wasn't proof, but behind Botten's unseemly upbeat recitation was a vast and unsettling gulf— of loneliness and heartbreak—even if the man couldn't sense it. Henry could, although Ophelia was far better at detecting unspoken stories beneath mere words.

"I want to conduct a fair evaluation," Henry said at last.

"Which is why I selected you in the first place. I know you won't be swayed by what Rose has to say. Or, for that matter"—and now Botten's voice turned sly—"what I might say."

He had to give Botten credit for that. Henry wouldn't be swayed.

"So, my boy, when do you think you'll have this wrapped up?"

"Without the umbrella data? A few more days, at least, maybe a week."

An irritated exhale told him that was the wrong answer. Like Henry cared what Botten thought.

"Very well. See that you check in from time to time." Botten disconnected the call without further instruction or goodbye.

And that was that.

Except. Henry didn't need those extra days, although he was determined to take them. He'd known the outcome of this examination from the moment Pansy had run off with his umbrella to tackle that pocket of discontent, one she'd detected before he had. Granted, she was outside, and he was absorbed in all the offerings at The King's Larder.

Still. His lips twitched with chagrin.

She'd *stolen* his umbrella, stolen it, and done the impossible.

She'd dispatched the Screamers while barely breaking a sweat. With his umbrella. His finely tuned, customized umbrella, the one only he, as a principal field agent, should be able to use.

Did she even know that? Henry spun his coffee cup and pondered the question.

Certainly, they covered umbrella handling at the Academy. Outside of mentoring, using another agent's umbrella didn't work, not the way your own did. You might as well grab a store-bought one, of which there were plenty in King's End, sprouting from storefronts like bouquets. And a principal field agent's umbrella? The last time someone had snatched his umbrella without permission, they'd regretted it. The fact that that someone had been Mortimer Connolly was a bonus.

"You didn't even bother with a shock, did you?"

Nothing but resolute silence as a reply.

His umbrella had known from the start and had intuitively established a rapport with an unfamiliar agent. That evening, when Henry had reviewed the data from the skirmish, he'd known as well. He could've written up his report, turned it in, and flown standby back to Seattle.

Not that he planned on confessing that to anyone, Reginald Botten in particular.

Instead, he'd plodded on with the charade, choosing to believe he was here to retire the line, while behaving like a cur and a cad and, frankly, a pretentious asshole.

And then the funeral. And her expression. Oh, god, her expression. The sheer agony of it. He could taste the grief rolling off her. Yes, she'd lost someone, and recently. Perhaps he was a cur and a cad and a pretentious asshole for not asking, but he couldn't bring himself to do so.

All he could do was follow her through the chain link and stop the Screamers from ruining yet another graveside service.

But now he had questions. About Rose and Pansy Little. About that strange, surreal stretch of land called Camelot Lots. Fortunately, he also had a trunk full of equipment. He closed his laptop and glanced at his umbrella.

"Ready?"

Oh, yes, they were both more than ready.

CHAPTER 11
PANSY

King's End, Minnesota
Sunday, July 9

Adele insists on feeding me, even though she's the one who's just arrived home. I don't mind, since all I'd been planning to eat were some of Henry Darnelle's leftover bagels.

After she leaves, I open my laptop again. Lineage is important to the Enclave. Some families can trace their line back to an original traveler—or so they claim. Old families, according to the legends, produce the best field agents. I've never seen any actual evidence for that. But it's why here, in the twenty-first century, the Enclave still clings to antiquated notions like betrothals between families.

These are arranged, of course, by everyone but the interested parties. The Littles, like the Darnelles, are an old family. I've never received so much as a single offer of betrothal. Or, rather, not a serious one. There was Charlie Pulchenko, at the Academy, but he was desperate to escape his own betrothal. In some way or form, rule six *always* applies. Not only did my mother take care of that situation, she somehow ended her own betrothal long before she met my father. Whenever the subject came up, whenever I asked, she always said, "I saw no reason to place that burden on you as well."

Sometimes, I wonder if this is how my mother ended up a permanent post agent in King's End. Was she banished for breaking her betrothal? I'm the very last Little. Sometimes, I wonder what will happen to King's End when I can no longer patrol.

I scan Agent Darnelle's profile as if that will help me through tomorrow's gauntlet. He's a principal field agent, which means he can create and lead his own field teams without (much) interference from the Enclave. He's proficient in five languages (because, of course he is).

Beneath that? So. Many. Awards. Some I've never even heard of. It's like the Enclave made them up special just for him. How he completed missions in Crete, Brazil, British Columbia, and the Philippines all in one year, never mind that whole trek into the Sahara? Who knows. Clearly, the man overachieves.

He's not married—or officially engaged. As for those betrothals? No one talks about such things in the twenty-first century, after all. But an agent like Henry Darnelle?

Rule six applies, absolutely. There's probably a waitlist.

He has one sister, or half-sister, I guess. Ophelia Connolly is a few years older than I am, but I don't remember her from the Academy. Still, she's a Connolly, and related—somehow—to Mort. Second cousins, maybe? I'm not sure, and Enclave family trees are beyond complicated. Currently, she is on a research sabbatical, whatever that is. Certainly nothing I'll ever experience.

Because I'm feeling perverse, I check my own profile. There I am, still listed as Apprentice Agent Little, permanent post in King's End. I have, according to my profile, successfully graduated from the Academy.

And while it's not there, on the screen, *by the skin of her teeth* is absolutely implied.

When I check my mother's profile, all it has is her last official photo, taken about ten years ago, with the words:

Rose Little, retired.

I close my laptop and hide it away before the melancholy can hit too hard. I rescue Agent Darnelle's suit coat from the kitchen chair, shake out the wrinkles, and hang it in the closet near the front door. It's far too early for bed, and while I know I should save my strength for tomorrow, I pluck my umbrella from the stand and head outside.

I'm certain to find the housing development quiet.

I head there anyway.

I WILL LEAVE BEFORE DARK.

This is what I tell myself.

After Adele's revelation, I wanted, maybe needed, to see the housing development, or rather, the land it sits on. Once, it was a stretch of meadow that belonged to the Kingston heirs.

But when my mother, Harry Darnelle, and that mysterious third agent went patrolling, this was the only place they could have gone. I soften my gaze, trying to recollect what the space looked like before the backhoes and bulldozers rumbled down the road and carved a new landscape. There are still hints, like the wild roses that climb the fence that borders the cemetery.

Part of me is tempted to invoke the Sight. Even if it were safe to do so in the housing development (which it's not—it's so not), the Sight doesn't work that way. If I could drop into the past whenever I felt like it, I could leave the Enclave and make a career in law enforcement. If I could drop into my future whenever the mood struck, I could make a killing on Wall Street.

To complicate matters, be it future or past, what I see isn't always mine.

The fence remains in good repair. That's an encouraging sign. A golden hour glow flatters the houses, making them appear more like dreams than nightmares. The air is almost sweet. If I didn't know better, I would agree with Agent Darnelle's skepticism. Maybe the housing development isn't the main source of the Screamers.

But I do know better. And that golden hour can slide into twilight far too quickly, especially here. I turn to leave, but the crunch of tires on gravel holds me in place. A blue sedan crawls its way up the road, easing over the ruts until it comes to a stop beneath the sign for Camelot Lots.

I can taste the evening on my tongue before I manage to close my mouth. My umbrella is all aquiver. I don't have to ask who is behind the wheel.

But I am asking why.

Henry Darnelle steps from the sedan and pulls several cases from its trunk. He's in canvas trousers and sturdy boots, but the white button-down is pristine. He approaches the entrance with the confidence of a man who routinely walks into sandstorms. Or rather, he does until his gaze lands on mine.

"Agent Little?"

I nod.

"I thought you would be..."

Home, resting up for my examination, like a sensible apprentice field agent? Yes, I probably should be.

"I remembered that I left my suit coat here." He lowers first one case and then the other to the ground. "I thought I'd return for it."

It's a reasonable excuse. If he weren't carrying all manner of equipment, I might even buy it. I narrow my gaze not on his face but on the larger of the two cases.

"And perhaps take a few of my own readings while I'm here."

This is a breach of protocol. My job might be hanging by a thread, but I am the acting agent in King's End. A flush darkens his cheeks, making him look boyish. With him standing there in the golden hour glow, he's distracting and captivating, so much so that I could forget he's here to fire me.

Well, almost.

"And yes, I should've stopped by your house and asked permission first."

I feel a smile tug my lips. Because here's the thing. I wasn't home. Henry Darnelle could have lied.

That he didn't? That makes me wonder.

"There's just something about this space that's nagging at me," he adds.

"Yes."

"You feel it too? Well, obviously, you do. So, will you allow me? I know I suggested a survey team, but honestly, it will take them ages to schedule an actual appointment, and then they'll move the date and move it again. I simply thought—"

"Agent Darnelle, I've already said yes."

He blinks as if I've derailed an express train of thought. "Did you?"

"I did. Please. Do your survey. It might be helpful."

Considering what Adele just told me, it might be *very* helpful.

He claps his hands together. "Excellent." He reaches for the two cases but halts mid-crouch. "You know, Agent Little, if you're up for it, I could run you through your paces as well."

"You mean my examination?"

"Yes, the main part. I have all the equipment in the trunk." He shields his eyes, his gaze taking in the whole of the development. "Things seem quiet. No sign of activity."

"They're chastised," I say. "They weren't expecting two of us."

"Of course. And this is far more private than the green." He grins with the delight of a schoolmaster devising a devastating final exam. "I can deploy all manner of obstacles."

I must make a face, because that grin turns into a full-fledged laugh. "I have every confidence in you, Agent Little."

Does he? Does he really? I consider the man before me now. He is the polar opposite of the one who left me in the cemetery this morning. He's a man embracing a mission rather than slogging through a chore.

Where that leaves me, I don't know. But I do know this:
I'm not about to turn down his challenge.

"Let me get you wired up, and then I'll power on the course."

I stand, arms outstretched. I'm wearing a vest studded with sensors and recording devices. Agent Darnelle moves around me, so close that the heat of his body touches mine. A hint of that vanilla lingers in the small pockets between us. I didn't think to ask if this is appropriate. Not that we need a chaperone. Not that I'm the least bit fearful of Agent Darnelle.

In fact, I'm more curious than annoyed. Was it the shift in his demeanor, or possibly mine? True, he still might fail me. I hold no illusions about that. But it feels more like we're in this together rather than apart.

And besides, if nothing else, job termination is easy on the eyes.

"Now for your umbrella," he says.

I hand her over, and the polka dots fairly blur with excitement. His own umbrella is slung cross-body, but the strap has come undone. It flutters in the breeze. Very conveniently, the strap on my umbrella loosens as well. They ease toward one another. It's both surreptitious and blatant. They're like two pre-teens trying to hold hands while hoping no one will notice.

Agent Darnelle glances down at this interaction and then pushes his umbrella farther behind his back.

My umbrella slumps in his grip, despondent.

"I'm surprised they didn't issue you a larger umbrella, Agent Little."

Now my umbrella bristles.

"She might be small, but don't underestimate her."

"Wouldn't dream of it." He chuckles under his breath. "'And though she be but little, she is fierce.'"

I stare at him.

"Shakespeare," he says. Unnecessarily, I might add. He coughs, clears his throat before stating, "Let's see how fierce *you* are, Agent Little."

I'm starting to get annoyed again.

He hands me a pair of goggles. The course is like the best virtual reality game you've ever played. I will need to fight off any number of Screamer attacks, anticipate ambushes, discover fissures, and repair them on the fly, all while running around until I drop.

The sensors record all this and any hits from the virtual Screamers. Although, since the stings from those hits are very, very real, it's more like the worst virtual reality game you've ever played.

Agent Darnelle crouches next to the control panel. He's already laid out the course. An expanse of land near the back of the development is now strung with transponders sitting atop slender poles.

"This should give you plenty of space." His gaze travels the field. "Do they mow back here?"

"They don't mow anywhere."

"Then how—?"

I give him a look. Just one of the many features of this space. The grass may be more brown than green, but it resembles the sort of golf course turf pictured on the Camelot Lots sign. Maybe the creature that claws its way out (or in) enjoys meticulously mown lawns.

"Anyway, it's crucial that you complete the course in one go. Don't remove your goggles. Otherwise, you'll have to start all over again."

I nod to show him I understand.

"I'll be on guard the whole time, so there's no need to worry."

What he means is, he'll watch for any actual Screamers that might decide to show up and ruin my exam, which they might. But I sense they're off somewhere, pouting.

Just in case, I tip my chin skyward and scan the evening sky. The air feels calm enough, the housing development benign enough that it's worth placing my trust in him. Since it's July, the sun won't set for a few more hours. I can do this, then hustle him out of the space before dark.

"Also." He shuts his eyes for a moment as if what he's about to say pains him. "They've rigged the course to deliver more stings than actual hits. I've adjusted the settings to as low as possible, but just know it's not a true reflection of your progress or ability."

"Thank you for leveling the playing field." I mean it sincerely. It's not like the Enclave ever would.

His nod is terse. "All set?"

I put on the goggles, tighten the straps, and then ready my umbrella. She trembles with excitement and anticipation to match my own.

A virtual landscape flickers to life in front of me, full of obvious—and not-so-obvious—obstacles. I take a knee as if I plan to spring forward from a starting block. The evening is cool, but already I'm starting to sweat: a trickle down my spine, a quick wash behind my knees, pinpricks along my forehead.

Jack was right.

I am going to have to finesse this.

CHAPTER 12
PANSY

King's End, Minnesota
Sunday, July 9

The Academy's first test for the Sight is a blunt, crude series of obstacles. No sense in being subtle with thirteen-year-olds. For some, the Sight hasn't even shown up by then.

But it will by the end of that first summer, even if all you possess are mild premonitions.

The Sight can manifest in any number of ways. Jack has a variation where he can intuitively sense connections between events, objects, and especially people. He spent two years in the field—mandatory for nearly everyone in the Enclave—but moved into the intelligence section soon after.

For others, the Sight shows them specific things. For example, Sandeep, with his (newly discovered) ability to sense earthquakes. Some can predict things like all the market crashes in a one-hundred-year span (helpful for when you're not a government agency but are run like one). However the Sight manifests, there's always one thing in common.

Self-preservation.

Beyond that, the Sight doesn't have rules. It would be easier if it did. Sometimes what I consider self-preservation and what it does are two vastly different things. That's why a series of blunt, crude obstacles is ideal.

So, the rope bridge across the mountain-fed stream? The notion that the rope will fray and then snap when you reach the midpoint? The inability to place a single foot on one of the rickety slats? That telltale trickle of blood from your nose?

That's the Sight.

Of course, that trickle can easily become a gush. The stronger the Sight, the messier it is.

My mother always said she suspected when I was two—I was prone to alarming nosebleeds—but knew for certain by the time I turned four. When I asked how she knew, she'd dismiss my question with, "Oh, it runs in the family. Your grandfather had the Sight."

Starting when I was eleven, we trained. We trained for two solid years before my first summer at the Academy. My Sight was already honed by the time I arrived. My aim was much higher than that of those who hoped to avoid all the traps and prove to the Enclave that they had extraordinary ability.

I needed to decide which traps to avoid and which ones to walk into without a thought for my safety. There's no stopping the nosebleeds, but if you lock down the Sight fast enough and hard enough, you might only end up with a trickle you can wipe away. In King's End, we always passed off my nosebleeds as an autoimmune issue. But that doesn't work with the Enclave.

Some families embrace all the Enclave has to offer and throw their children with the Sight into its maw. And, yes, I'm quoting my mother. Others, like my mother, caution their children with the Sight, teach them to control and conceal. I think of what Mort and Jack told me about Sandeep and wonder which part of the course caught him.

Because the course Agent Darnelle has laid out caters to both groups. You could overachieve your way through these obstacles. My Sight is already picking up the transmissions, alerting me to this tripwire and that pitfall. Part of me wants to grab each brass ring. I could run the course on those dopamine hits alone. I duck my head, sniff, and take a quick swipe beneath my nose.

But there's another layer beneath the obvious one, a second, hidden exam. I'm only getting flashes because I've locked down the Sight. I want to ask: *Who made this?* But that would only give me away. Whoever did, their Sight is as good as mine, or possibly even better.

This isn't merely an examination. Already, my skin is prickling in anticipation of all the stings I'm going to collect. It's also a training course. For someone like me, someone whose Sight could be honed into a weapon.

"Whenever you're ready, Agent Little." Agent Darnelle's voice is calm. I want to say it's almost soothing. It's definitely self-assured.

I wonder, again, if my examination started yesterday.

I dive in. I don't have a choice. I don't even know if I can finesse the exam. Will that hidden layer activate my Sight no matter how hard I lock it down? A flurry of virtual Screamers streams past. An obvious ambush. Please. You don't need the Sight for that.

I unfurl my umbrella and dispatch them without much effort. Even so, a series of stings erupts along my shoulders. The Screamers vanish into a crevice. While I know it truly isn't there, I pitch my umbrella at an angle, hunker down behind it, and repair the fissure.

I run my fingertips along the space as if weaving invisible threads. Slowly, that blank, endless expanse grows smaller and smaller until it vanishes. In real life, fissures never truly go away, no matter how expertly we mend them. It's why the Enclave needs permanent post agents in far-flung and out-of-the-way places.

Before I can stand and tackle the next obstacle, a tree falls and I roll out of the way. Or rather, I anticipate the virtual tree fall mere seconds before it comes crashing down. A ripple of leaves wavers in my peripheral vision, what would, in real life, be a hair's breadth away. I pause for a moment. This close to the ground, the course flickers in and out. I pull in a breath and realize my upper lip is damp.

I swipe my fingers beneath my nose in what I hope looks like I'm wiping away sweat. There's a smear of red along the back of my hand. I keep my head tilted toward the earth, hoping Agent Darnelle isn't watching too closely. As a result, a few drops land in front of me, the soil sucking them up as if it's greedy for my blood.

A moment later, the earth trembles.

True, this is advanced tech, but just because it can deliver stings doesn't mean it can make the ground shake.

At least, I don't think it can.

I stand, umbrella at the ready. The next obstacle is straight ahead. I don't know what it is about the Enclave and rickety bridges, but they turned up a lot during training. And, oh, look! Here's one now in the examination. The surface trap is so obvious that if you walked into it, you *should* fail your examination.

But there's more, layer after layer of more. I don't mean to hesitate, but the choices here are almost endless. Most paths lead onto the bridge, with varying results, although a virtual plunge is almost guaranteed.

I want to go under, root out the Screamer troll that's lurking there. This is most definitely the Sight talking. What will it mean if I take this option? I'm itching to, no doubt about it.

"What do you think?" I whisper to my umbrella.

She, too, trembles with indecision. She swings about, first one way and then the other, as if she's not sure what's real and what isn't.

"The course," I say. "We have to finish the course."

But she doesn't want to. She's tugging me away from the projection of the bridge and toward where I last saw Agent Darnelle. The course flickers, so one moment, I see the bridge, and the next, the chain link along the cemetery. Something roils in the depression beneath the bridge, something I must certainly avoid or attack. But static fills my head. My thoughts scramble. My vision blanks.

This must be the Sight. A warm gush of blood coats my upper lip. So I pitch forward and land on my hands and knees, hoping to keep my clothes stain-free. Better blood splatter on the grass than on my shirt.

It works, and I'm about to stand and continue the course when the ground rumbles again. The sensation has a menacing, fairytale quality—like a groggy giant waking after centuries of slumber.

There's no warning. No ambush. No flight of Screamers emerging from a fissure. Only a single, piercing screech and then nothing but a searing pain along the small of my back. It's exquisite and deadly and very, *very* real.

I stagger to my feet and then do the one thing Agent Darnelle told me not to do.

I remove my goggles.

CHAPTER 13

HENRY

King's End, Minnesota
Sunday, July 9

Henry expected Pansy to detect the ambush quickly, but not *that* quickly. He almost missed how she elegantly dispatched the Screamers. They were there and then gone. He flinched when the exam delivered a series of stings. In real life, she would've walked away without a scratch. As for the fissure repair? Admirable.

Barely a minute in, and Pansy Little had hit every requirement for a permanent post agent. Henry could stop the exam right now and call it done. Instead, he knelt next to his laptop—or, rather, both of them—and compared the readouts.

Data from umbrellas never lied. Even with a hasty scan, the evidence was clear. It was there in the rhythm, in the choice of targets, in her anticipation of where to move and when to do so.

Pansy Little—and not her mother—had spent the last five years patrolling King's End.

Henry adjusted the settings. There were several layers to this exam. Now that she'd aced the requirements for a permanent post agent, why not see how close she was to senior field agent? He went ahead and activated every last level, including those for superior Sight.

Because Henry was testing yet another hypothesis. Pansy Little didn't have mild premonitions or an occasional flash of insight. She was like Ophelia. Better, possibly. Because, unlike his sister, she had the ability to lock down the Sight on command. That Pansy had been able to hide her ability all these years was nothing short of astonishing.

And yes, there it was. The tree. No one sidestepped the tree. He'd been caught up in its virtual branches during his own examination. To his knowledge, only Ophelia had escaped unscathed.

Until now.

The ground rumbled beneath him. Henry pressed a palm against the earth to steady himself and gauge the tremor. Odd. King's End wasn't rated for Screamer-generated earthquakes, but then again, no one had bothered with a site survey since 1991.

He could deal with that later. He turned his attention back to both Pansy and the laptop's screen. She had reached the bridge, and he wanted to see what she'd do next.

At the Academy, they taught the adage: *When in doubt, move.* It was, after all, harder for the Screamers to hit a moving target. But not in the case of this particular bridge.

He leaned forward in anticipation. The route Pansy chose would reveal how deep her Sight ran, and his money was on it running deep, indeed. Before she could choose, or, more accurately, before he could watch her choose, his umbrella went into high alert. It shook hard against his spine, the vibrations spreading all the way to his fingertips. The back of his neck prickled, the sensation that also never lied.

Henry pulled his gaze from the laptop's screen and confronted a mass of Screamers, the likes of which he hadn't seen since the Sahara.

CHAPTER 14
PANSY

King's End, Minnesota
Sunday, July 9

The housing development is in an all-out Screamer onslaught. It hasn't been this bad since I returned after my last summer at the Academy.

And there, standing in the glow of the setting sun and the fractured light of dozens of Screamers, is Agent Darnelle. That black behemoth of an umbrella is unfurled. Together, they're fighting off the attack.

I drop the goggles and run, my umbrella urging me forward. Her whole being is focused on Agent Darnelle's umbrella, and she will not stand for the Screamers of King's End assaulting it.

For that matter, neither will I.

Divide and conquer, divide and conquer. The chant fills my mind. Whether it's the Sight or my umbrella or something I intuitively know about King's End, it's the tack I decide to take.

I collapse my umbrella to a single, deadly point and aim her at the center of the mass currently attacking Agent Darnelle. I sprint and then leap forward, the point of my umbrella skewering that mass, slicing it in half. A screech pierces the air, my eardrums. I unfurl my umbrella and hunker down in the aftermath. Colors swirl. Obsidian shatters into emerald and ruby and sapphire, an explosion that dazzles my eyes and peppers my skin.

The Screamers swirl, doubling back, but I'm ready for the counterattack. I send a pulse skyward. For a moment, the air clears. I can pull in a full breath. And in that quiet moment, an outstretched hand reaches for my own.

I take it, and Agent Darnelle lifts me to my feet as if I weigh no more than my umbrella. We slip into a defensive posture—back to back—like this is routine, like we've fought together a hundred times before. Without prompting, our umbrellas link. Together, they project a protective bubble around us. It can't keep out the Screamers forever, but it certainly helps.

I brace against Agent Darnelle, his shoulders solid and sturdy. The heat of his skin penetrates his shirt and my own. So hot, it's like the man is on fire. He passes his umbrella from hand to hand, directing each Screamer pass toward me. I whittle their numbers.

This part is a long grind, a war of attrition, if you will. The mass thins, eventually. Honestly, sometimes I think the Screamers simply get bored or feel they've made their point, whatever that may be. Tonight, though, they seem intent on Agent Darnelle.

"We're almost there," he says. "If you can find the source, I can cover you."

"Yes. Hang on."

I search for a likely source, all the while noting how the sun is sinking lower and lower in the sky. No, starting my exam this close to sunset was not the best idea, and worry gnaws at the back of my mind.

The source. The source. I cast my thoughts outward, forward, and back. Tiny forays—mere seconds. I want to catch a premonition, like with that couple on the Rose Walk yesterday, not trigger a full-on attack of the Sight.

Something suggests the showcase home near the entrance. I say *something*, but really, it must be the Sight. Never mind that the fissure wasn't there this morning; it most certainly is now. A few drops of blood splatter on my T-shirt, but since I know where the fissure is, I can lock down the Sight.

"Ready?" I ask both Agent Darnelle and my umbrella, although she's already tugging me forward.

"Go!" His voice alone could chase off Screamers. There's a fierce expertise to it, to his movements, and yes, a few Screamers break from the mass and scatter.

I race toward the showcase home. A handful of Screamers give chase, and they unerringly find the small of my back, that wound from earlier. I stumble, but my umbrella unfurls, and the action halts my momentum before I can crash to the ground.

I round the house. There, in the rear, near that egress window, is the source. I always wonder whether, during the excavation, the construction company somehow created another fissure. Or worse, built the house on top of one, making part of it inaccessible for repair.

I tuck the pole of my umbrella between my shoulder and ear so the canopy protects my back. Then, with the same movements used in the exam, I weave reality back into place. A few Screamers decide to bullet through before I can close off this route completely. Even so, that blank expanse shrinks faster than the virtual one did.

Leave it to the Enclave to make everything harder.

Fissure repaired, I brush off my hands, shake out my umbrella, and stand. By the time I find Agent Darnelle, he is dispatching the final Screamers.

I say dispatching. What he's doing is having fun—at their expense. He's closed his umbrella and is now jousting with them. He spins, lunges, thrusts, and parries. It doesn't matter what they throw at him. Their numbers diminish with every pass they take.

He meets them all with a boyish grin on his face, his movements graceful. He's like a principal dancer or an Olympic fencer, each movement precise, gorgeous, and deadly.

At last, a few of the smarter ones (assuming Screamers have that sort of intelligence; no one knows for certain) stream toward the showcase home, only to find the fissure closed. They head toward the cemetery and the woods, and from there, who knows.

In any case, they aren't coming back. Not for a while, at least.

Agent Darnelle turns to me, that grin still in place. "Well, that was invigorating."

"I took off my goggles." It's the only thing I can think to say. There isn't time—and I'm in no shape—to take the exam again.

He tips his head back and laughs, and the gesture is a match for that boyish grin. "And I'm glad you did. May I see your work?"

I gesture toward the showcase home, and he follows me. He takes a knee next to the egress window and inspects the repair.

"Nicely done, Agent Little." He runs his fingers along the seam. "Excellent work. Do you mind if I reinforce it?"

"Not at all." It's what my mother and I used to do before she became too weak to patrol. This repair will hold much longer with his reinforcement, maybe even for an entire week.

"I wonder how far it runs," he says, fingers knitting an intricate pattern on top of my own. "I can only extend my reach so far beneath the foundation."

"I know," I say. "I wonder, too."

It's not quite sunset, but the shadows stretch across the main road, and I loathe having to walk through them on my way out. We can't linger, and of course, I can't actually explain *why*. The few times I've stayed close to twilight, I've regretted it. The absence of the Screamers was odd enough. It was the air: soft, seductive, and strangling, like promises laced with poison. My mother never explained why the housing development is like this, but I have no issue following this particular rule.

"Were you hit, Agent Darnelle?"

I most certainly was. The small of my back aches. Pain is building at the base of my skull. Also? My thoughts are starting to fog, and I could sleep for days. "I have tea back at the house."

"I do have a field kit." From a cargo pocket, he pulls out a case and unzips it to reveal a series of what looks like epi-pens.

"Those are good," I concede. We used them at the Academy, after all. "But I have a recipe tailor-made for the Screamers of King's End. It works wonders."

He pauses, his gaze going to the epi-pens before traversing the housing development. My umbrella shivers with anticipation. His umbrella is knocking into his leg somewhat insistently.

"All right, Agent Little," he says at last. "I'll take you up on that offer."

I REALIZE my mistake the moment Agent Darnelle pulls the rental sedan into my driveway. Up and down the street, curtains flutter in living room windows. When we step from the car, I detect a flash, as if someone has just snapped a cell phone picture, which they most certainly have.

There is little subtlety to this neighborhood watch. I'll have to concoct a story later. Right now, I need tea. Despite his bravado, so does Agent Darnelle.

Inside, we drop our umbrellas into the stand. Instantly, they snuggle next to each other. Agent Darnelle casts them a look as if he doesn't quite approve of this arrangement. But he follows me into the kitchen without separating them.

I offer him a chair before ducking into the pantry for supplies and a first aid kit. I pull one tonic and then another from the rack, giving each a sniff. The sharp, heady aroma of herbs, of oils, of spices, clears my head. I'll have enough presence of mind to brew some tea.

My legs wobble, and I really could curl up on the floor and take a nap. In fact, there's a blanket and pillow on a lower shelf for those days when I need to do just that. Today, though, I need to make tea.

While Agent Darnelle has certainly been hit this hard before, he's never experienced the Screamers of King's End.

They're their own special variety.

When I emerge from the pantry, tonics and tinctures in hand, Agent Darnelle glances up from his contemplation of the kitchen table.

"You're back."

"I just—" Hands full, I nod toward the pantry in explanation. If he's starting to talk nonsense, then he was hit even harder than I thought, which means I need to brew that tea NOW.

"No," he says, his voice tired but amused. "I meant your back." He leans forward and touches his lower back. "First, I want to apologize. I should've been more on guard."

I give my head a quick shake. "That's just King's End." Truly, I've been hit a lot worse than today. Even chastised, the Screamers definitely would work overtime to disrupt my examination.

"Are they always so aggressive? Seems odd, considering this area's rating."

"I think it was you," I say.

He touches his shirt, which is still mostly pristine white and wrinkle-free despite what we've been through. My T-shirt, I note, is splattered with blood, something Agent Darnelle hasn't mentioned.

Yet.

"They were"—I shrug—"showing off? They'd do that every summer when I returned from the Academy or when I had friends from the Enclave visit." It's why Mort claims it's never just a skirmish in King's End. When he's around, it never is.

"I see," Agent Darnelle says, although he doesn't sound convinced. "As I was saying, I'm wondering if you'd allow me to..." He trails off.

No, he hesitates. Really? Agent Darnelle? I didn't think it was in his nature to hesitate.

"I'm wondering if you'd allow me to inspect the wound." Here, a hint of pink infuses those cheekbones. Such a schoolboy blush on someone so dignified and competent is ... well, it's downright adorable.

"Make sure they didn't break the skin," he continues. "Maybe spread a little balm on the spots you can't reach on your own?"

Blush. Blush. Blush. Like I said, *adorable.*

"Of course. Let me start the tea." I deposit the bottles and jars on the kitchen counter, glass against granite singing out. I set the kettle to boil and measure the tea leaves. I line up the jars in the order that I'll add the ingredients once the tea has brewed.

"Okay." I turn toward the kitchen table, grab the hem of my T-shirt, and start to yank.

Agent Darnelle scoots back in his chair and covers his eyes as if he's never seen a bare shoulder.

"I'm wearing a sports bra," I say.

He lowers his hands. "What?"

"A sports bra. I could wear it to the farmers market, or to the gym, or wherever. No one would mind."

Not even my stuffiest neighbors would. The top is completely sturdy and utilitarian without a single whiff of sexiness about it. He nods, so I peel the T-shirt off, hiding any doubt that might be lingering in my own eyes. For good measure, I wad up the material and toss it into the pantry. Blood stains out of sight = blood stains out of mind. Or so I hope.

When I meet his gaze again, a stealth smile plays across his lips, there and gone almost before I can register it.

"Well, that is fetching."

So, yes, sturdy, utilitarian, *and* pink with white polka dots. It's a match for my umbrella, and I pull it on every time I need a bit of luck.

I turn again, fingers reaching for the small of my back. "Did they break the skin?"

He steps behind me. He is still so hot, and I mean that literally. Heat radiates from him. He smells of soil and sweat, a hint of that spicy vanilla scent lingering in the air.

"Everything seems intact, but it's a nasty hit."

"They got me more than once, same spot." Screamers are uncanny that way. I nod toward the pantry again. "Bottom shelf, there's some Tupperware with—"

"You've made a contribution." He nods toward the tea. "Now it's my turn."

From a cargo pocket, he removes a small container and uncaps it. I brace for the aroma, but nothing comes. My mother's mixture—secured in its Tupperware—uses tea tree oil and eucalyptus as major ingredients. It doesn't just reek, it clings. For days. Even after multiple showers.

But it also works.

Agent Darnelle's balm has all the presence of fragrance-free lotion.

"Special issue," he says. "I was recently in the Sahara." His tone betrays nothing. He could've been in Cabo San Lucas, baking in the sun, for how calm his voice is. "Do you mind?"

"Go ahead."

I tense, anticipating cold goo against my skin. Instead, the balm goes on light and warm, and his touch is sure and steady against my skin. It takes all my willpower not to lean into the caress.

"You have a few scars," he says, fingers exploring beyond the wound on my back. "This will help. Again, if you don't mind."

"Not at all." And really, these words emerge with more air than voice. "It's hard to reach my own back."

"Hm. Indeed."

Immediately, the balm sinks in, burrowing through my pores, rooting out the lingering toxins. Tension drains from my shoulders. I exhale a shuddering breath.

"That's amazing."

The combination of his fingers and the balm is intoxicating. Apparently, he's not only an extraordinary field agent but a master masseur as well. If he doesn't stop soon, my bones will melt, and I'll be little more than a Pansy puddle on the kitchen floor.

"It's definitely useful." He takes a final swipe. "There you go."

I should run upstairs for a fresh T-shirt, but I'm locked in place, not quite sure what to do or say next. The simmering heat in the kitchen fades, and a hint of that schoolmaster sternness returns. I'm a little disappointed, although I probably shouldn't be, and I most definitely shouldn't be flirting with the man conducting my field agent examination.

Then again, I'm probably not the first apprentice field agent whose pulse went all fluttery around Agent Darnelle. No doubt I won't be the last, either.

"Are you sure I can't return the favor?" This is maybe not the most innuendo-free sentence I've ever uttered.

"I'm fine." He's spreading a bit of the balm along his forearms, across a series of what looks like defensive wounds. He is, resolutely, not meeting my eyes.

"Even you can't reach your own back," I add.

He plucks at the shirt he's wearing. "Also special issue. The weave protects against all but the hardest of hits. I'm more than fine."

I make one last, gallant try. "You have a cut." I touch my eyebrow with my ring finger. "Right there."

"Do I?" He probes his forehead, brow crinkled in curiosity. Then he winces. "I guess I do."

"Let me? It needs to be cleaned."

"I—" he begins, and I'm convinced he'll refuse, but he surprises me with a nod and takes a seat.

I step close, and again, the pulse in my stomach takes up that fluttery beat. His skin glows with a sheen of sweat. The dampness makes his hair—close-cropped and obsidian dark—curl ever so slightly. I am the consummate professional, inspecting and cleaning the wound. His breath hisses with a sharp inhale.

"Sorry," I whisper.

"No, they broke the skin, is all. It needs to be cleaned."

The wound is small, so this is absolutely something he could do on his own, back at the bed and breakfast. But then I wouldn't get to bring my lips close to his temple. I wouldn't get to breathe in that spicy vanilla mixed with sweat and soil and success. Yes, this is a man used to triumph.

"Should I use the balm?" I ask.

In answer, he pushes the container my way. I dab the wound with a generous amount and then secure a tiny butterfly bandage along his brow.

"There," I say, feeling a bit triumphant myself.

"Thank you, Agent Little."

And with those crisp words, I am dismissed. So I finish making the tea, marveling at how wonderful my back feels. My mother's salve works, but it's goopy and smelly and sticky and feels like ten extra pounds. This balm is so light, so invigorating, I could almost head back to the housing development and dispatch another round of Screamers.

Instead, I busy myself at the kitchen counter. I add a pinch of this and a drop of that to the tea, set it on the kitchen table, and then pull out two teacups.

"There's milk and sugar," I say, "but it works faster undiluted."

We sip in silence. The combination of my mother's concoction and caffeine works immediately, warming my stomach, rushing through my veins, clearing my head. A weight lifts from my chest.

"This is marvelous." Agent Darnelle reaches for the teapot and then draws his hand back. "May I? How does it work? Should I not drink any more?"

"Go ahead. You really can't drink too much. In fact." I give him a once-over and then jump up. Oh, yes. The spring is back in my step. I grab two of the bottles from the counter and then add a few more drops to the tea before freshening both our cups.

"You weigh more than I do." By a good hundred pounds. "I should've added extra to begin with. I wasn't thinking."

"An aftereffect of an attack," he says. "I sometimes forget about my shoes." He stretches out a leg and gives his foot a shake. "If they're on, I forget to take them off. If they're off, I forget to put them on. And sometimes, one's on, and one's off."

The confession is so sweet and charming that I can't resist matching it. "I sometimes don't bother going upstairs, and I sleep in the pantry."

He peers over my shoulder. "It seems cozy enough. I see it comes stocked with its own pillow and blanket."

Oh. So he noticed. Then again, there's probably little that Agent Darnelle doesn't notice.

He raises his teacup to mine. "To the end of a successful mission."

I work to unpack that. Is he implying there's an *us*, as in a field team? We *did* fall into step with each other. It felt natural, like we were long-time partners, and this was simply another pesky Screamer attack we needed to deal with before heading home for the day.

I can't fathom the look in his eyes, but there's a hint of that stealth smile, so I touch the rim of my cup to his.

"To the end of a successful mission," I echo.

That stealth smile again, one that touches his eyes, deepens the smattering of crow's feet there.

I'm starting to suspect that this mission won't be my last.

AGENT DARNELLE IS at the kitchen sink, washing the tea things—I tried to stop him, but he insisted—when he calls over his shoulder.

"I'll alert my host at the bed and breakfast that I'll be having guests for a morning meeting."

Once again, he's completely unfathomable. So I go with, "Morning meeting? Guests?"

"It's time for your debriefing, and I thought a breakfast meeting might be nice."

"But, the examination."

"What of it?"

"I didn't finish it."

He waves my words away as if they're merely soap bubbles. "You completed the main portion."

"I did?"

"The rest is merely endurance, and I can score you on that without any help from a computer."

He sets the tea things in the dish rack gently, as if they're family heirlooms, which they're not. I'm too clumsy after an attack to trust myself with anything other than thrift store specials.

"So, nine o'clock at the Riverside B&B? You and your mentor—"

"Wait. What?"

"You and your mentor," he continues, slowly, that stern schoolmaster making a reappearance, "and myself will sit down over some scones and coffee and discuss your results."

Oh, no. Oh, no, no, no, no. NO.

"My mentor," I say, and the words feel clumsy and foreign in my mouth.

"Of course. I can't wait to meet her."

Well, he's going to have to keep on waiting.

"I'll summarize your overall performance, lay out what I'll include in the formal report that I'll send to the Enclave, and answer any questions the two of you may have."

"You can't just give me your report now?"

"I haven't scored it yet."

This I don't believe. He knows what my score will be. And really, either way, it's going to be a sleepless night of *what ifs*. Unless this is a trick to activate the Sight. Wispy tendrils of thought suggest it is, so I immediately vow not to do so.

"Besides, I'm very much looking forward to meeting your mother," he says. "In fact, I want to thank her personally for her work on handling desert Screamers."

"Desert Screamers." I've been reduced to parroting his words, which is just as well, since I don't trust my own.

"I employed several of her methods on my last mission. No doubt they saved my life." He folds the dishtowel and hangs it on the rung next to the sink, adjusting the edges precisely. "Her tenure in the Middle East is fascinating reading."

"I've heard the stories," I manage, barely.

"I envy you. She was legendary in the field. It almost seems a shame..." His gaze takes in the kitchen in all its blue and white coziness. A subtle blush touches his cheekbones. He clears his throat. "Anyway, tomorrow, at nine. Will that work?"

Without recourse, I nod. "I'll show you out?"

It emerges as a question because my thoughts are in such a whirl that I'm not certain I can do even that. But Agent Darnelle heads down the hallway and toward the front door. I follow, a hand on the wall like it's the only solid, sure thing in my life right now.

When we reach the threshold, I have enough presence of mind to remember his suit coat and pull it from the closet.

"I mended the tear." I hold it up for his inspection.

"Oh. Well. Good." He looks at me as if I'm five and have offered up a mud pie destined to ruin his Sunday best. "Thank you."

Then it hits me. His jacket is special issue, like his shirt, and possibly that ridiculous hat, which would explain a lot. Except I'm fairly certain that nothing explains the hat. The suit coat's weave is smooth beneath my fingers, and I exhale regret along with a sigh.

"I've ruined it, haven't I?"

He gives his head a vigorous shake. "No, no. Not at all. I'm sure it can be patched."

His expression says it can't.

"I'm sorry." While I'm certain to be even sorrier tomorrow morning, I do regret this.

"Don't be. How were you to know?" He takes his jacket, turning it in his hands. "It's still in prototype. Same material as our umbrellas, only wearable."

In the closet, I have gear made from that material, only not wearable. It's one thing to stroll King's End with a pink, polka-dot umbrella, quite another to do so in something that resembles a HAZMAT suit. How the Enclave made something practical and so elegantly tailored, I have no idea.

Agent Darnelle plucks his umbrella from the stand. A bit of push-pull ensues until he mutters, "It's time to leave."

See? I knew I wasn't the only agent who talks to their umbrella.

Mine slumps to one side, despondent once again.

He's at his rental sedan when Adele emerges from her house with Prince decked out in his tiny reflective harness and leash. She comes to stand with me on the porch, a reassuring arm around my shoulder. Prince spins in circles and then prances on his hind legs until I pick him up.

From behind the wheel, Agent Darnelle gives a nod that includes not only Adele and me but Prince as well. I make Prince wave a tiny paw, and I'm rewarded with the barest of stealth smiles.

It isn't until the tail lights flicker at the stop sign two blocks away that Adele speaks.

"I hope you don't mind. I wanted to see for myself."

"All the photos on Hey Neighbor kind of blurry?"

Adele manages a small laugh. "Very. He looks so much like Harry. It's uncanny."

"We're meeting tomorrow morning," I say. "For the final report."

"That's good, right? He'll leave, and then things will..." She pauses and shakes her head. "He'll leave."

Her unspoken words linger in the air, so potent I can almost taste them. *Things will go back to normal, and everything will be okay.* Except they won't. They can't. I'm not certain they can go on being anything that resembles normal, never mind good.

"My mentor is supposed to be at the meeting."

It takes Adele a heartbeat, maybe two. Her grip tightens on my shoulder, and she turns to peer into my eyes.

"Your mother."

It's not a question, but I nod.

"Maybe it's time," I venture. "Should I tell the Enclave something?"

But what? After all, even my mother put the word *death* in quotation marks. I didn't lie to Henry Darnelle. My mother is gone. I simply don't know where.

"What did you tell Harry's son?"

"Just that she wasn't here. He took that to mean she stepped out and wouldn't be a helicopter parent during the examination."

Adele's sigh is filled with weariness and woe. The weight of it hangs heavy in the air. "Rose put a lot on your shoulders. She never meant to and certainly didn't want to. It was just how things worked out."

She falls silent. There's sorrow etched around her eyes and her mouth. But after a moment, something sparks in her expression. "Let me help."

I have no idea how she could, but before I can ask, she adds, "I have an idea."

I wait, but Adele merely eases Prince from my arms and sets him on the ground. "I'll tell you after our walk."

She leaves me on the front porch, Prince's tiny nails clicking on the concrete sidewalk, his tail working furiously.

My mind goes to that first rule on my mother's last list:

For as long as possible, do not report my "death" to the Enclave. I owe them nothing, and they'll find out soon enough.

When is soon enough? I stare out into the summer night, watch the flicker of a few fireflies, and ponder whether it's time I start breaking some rules.

CHAPTER 15
HENRY

King's End, Minnesota
Sunday, July 9

Sunday evening near the Minnesota River was far more active and enjoyable than Henry had anticipated. Along with the cool breeze from the water, music and laughter wafted through the open windows. The curtains undulated, the fluttering fluid and languorous and positively seductive.

Then again, that might simply have been his state of mind.

He was stretched out on the bed, the flavor of a surprisingly superior scotch from the mini-bar on his tongue. With his hands tucked behind his head, he sank deeper against the mattress, the tension and soreness fading from his limbs. And while he knew he should rectify the *one shoe on, one shoe off* situation, he couldn't muster the energy for it.

He wondered, idly, if Pansy Little had mustered the energy to climb the stairs to bed and then shut down that line of thought. Still, the notion she might be curled up in the pantry, all cozy, brought a smile to his lips.

Shut it down, Henry.

He should lumber over to the desk and boot up his laptop, run the analysis, and score the exam. Except. The outcome was obvious. Besides, back before computers and apps and electronics in general, agents calculated scores using nothing but their observations, and paper and pencil, if necessary.

No, everything he needed to know about Apprentice Agent Little he'd witnessed today in the housing development. He'd worry about the score and the report once he'd returned to Seattle.

The curtains rolled again, and humid July air washed through the room. Streetlamps lit the space with a yellow glow. The night was so welcoming, he didn't want to pull the shades and block the light. He didn't want to close the windows and block out King's End. He found he rather liked the town.

From its resting spot near the door, his umbrella rustled in agreement.

"Yes, but we still have to leave."

A solid thump against the floor was the reply, the sound absolutely glum, and Henry couldn't hold back a chuckle.

"Still distracted, are we?"

Silence ensued.

"She was rather fierce today for something so small."

A sigh, although where it had come from, exactly, Henry couldn't say: the breeze, his umbrella, possibly himself. He touched the bandage near his eye, sparks of pain radiating along his brow, the sensation enticing, almost delicious. After a certain point, after a certain number of encounters, after a certain number of hits, a field agent started to crave not just the fight but the resulting wounds as well. As if the toxin were the elixir of life itself.

It was a harbinger of an impending desk job. Henry told himself he wasn't there yet. He had another decade in the field. And then? Well, then, he wasn't about to get sucked into the bureaucracy and politics of Enclave headquarters.

He probed the wound again, the pain subsiding. He thought of

Pansy Little and her butterfly caress along his skin, the gentle exhale against his temple. He didn't shake the thought from his head, but with effort, he used his bare foot to pry the boot from the other. He kicked it to the carpet but didn't bother with the sock.

Another rustle came from near the door.

"Yes," Henry agreed. "A bit distracted, aren't we?"

CHAPTER 16
PANSY

King's End, Minnesota
Monday, July 10

This can't be working. This honestly can't be working. But here I am, sitting across from Agent Darnelle, his phone on the table between us.

From the phone's speakers, Adele is regaling him with tales of desert Screamers.

We're tucked in an alcove of the Riverside Bed and Breakfast's main floor, the one with the view of the Minnesota River. It's a prime piece of dining room real estate—cozy and private, bathed in sunlight. The owner, Edwin, only lets you use this space if he really, really likes you.

Considering all the smiles and nods tossed our way, it seems Agent Darnelle has charmed everyone on staff. Carrie, who's been freshening the coffee carafe, has shot me several significant looks, the general meaning of which has been:

Why on earth aren't you going for it, girl?

I'm sitting up straight, like a truant hauled to the principal's office. I have my hands folded neatly in front of me to calm any nervous tics. Still, every so often, my left eye twitches.

In front of me sits my chocolate chip scone, neglected. I haven't taken more than a tiny bite, and my stomach rebels at the thought of trying to take another.

When Adele first suggested that she might impersonate my mother, I was convinced it wouldn't work. After all, Agent Darnelle had just seen Adele leave her house and walk over to mine. Despite being related, we look nothing alike, and Adele looks nothing like my mother's last official photograph.

"Do you still have her phone?" Adele asked.

Yes. Sitting on the wireless charger, on the nightstand next to my mother's bed, like I think she's going to return, fully herself, and will need to contact the Enclave. So Adele took it, drove all the way to the Twin Cities last night, and is now at a coffee shop, purportedly at an impromptu meeting with members of the crochet guild.

Perhaps that seems extreme. But as Adele pointed out, if the Enclave traces the call, it will appear as if my mother *is* in the Twin Cities, chatting to Agent Darnelle on her still-activated, Enclave-issued cell phone.

"They never did your mother any favors," Adele said before she left.

So, rule number one from my mother's last to-do list remains unbroken.

The anger and condemnation in Adele's words resonates, even now, as she chats about people I've heard of but don't actually know, agents of my mother's generation.

"I laughed out loud when I heard he'd assumed the Pulchenko seat on the High Council," Adele is saying, her voice full of my mother's intonation. "Misha was such a nonconformist, considered himself a true iconoclast. Oh, the stories I could tell you, Agent Darnelle."

He chuckles softly. "I imagine you could."

What hasn't come up for discussion? My exam. Really, I'm superfluous to this little talk. If it weren't for the fact that my job hangs in the balance and Adele sounds so much like my mother it makes my heart ache, I'd leave.

"You worked with my father," Agent Darnelle says, although it's not a question. His voice is low, and at the last moment, he swallows back the words as if he's hoping they won't reach the microphone.

There's a beat of silence. The only reason I know Adele hasn't hung up is the industrious hum of a barista frothing milk and the chatter and clank of the café.

"Your father was a wonderful man." Adele's own voice catches. The emotion is so thick that I feel a lump in my throat as well. "I'm so sorry for your loss. He thought the world of you, and I can't express how very proud he was of you."

For a moment, I think Agent Darnelle will simply pack up his messenger bag, grab his cell phone, and depart. It's there in his posture, palms flat against the table, shoulders set to push to stand. Then, the tension melts from his face. The smile he gives the phone is full of gratitude.

"Thank you."

All is quiet except for someone's hushed request for a skein of yarn.

"I hate to rush this along, but we're heading out to the fairgrounds to start preliminary work on the exhibit," Adele-as-Rose says. "After all, it's nearly state fair time."

Agent Darnelle nods as if he understands state fairs in theory but not in practice. Like he saw one once in a movie but has never actually been.

"They're crocheting a horse," I say by way of explanation, not that it's much of one.

"Not just any horse," Adele puts in, because, really, she can't help herself, "but Dan Patch!"

I give him a little who-knows shrug, but his face lights up.

"Oh, Dan Patch!"

Now I'm the one who needs an explanation.

"He was a famous, if not *the* most famous, racehorse of his time," he says. "And yes, now I remember. He did end up in Minnesota. How fascinating. I read once that—"

Yes, leave it to Agent Darnelle to know more about my state than I do. Before he can go all schoolmaster on us, he shakes his head as if banishing all things horse-related, straightens his spine, and clears his throat.

"It's a shame," he begins in a serious tone and abrupt change of subject.

That earlier lump of emotion fills my entire mouth. I reach behind me for my umbrella and clutch her so hard she might squeal. She shakes, her worry radiating through my fingers and wrist.

"That your daughter didn't schedule her examination earlier."

Like it was my idea. But I loosen the death grip on my umbrella.

"She has an extraordinary combination of abilities. There were several recent training opportunities that I would've recommended for her. Certainly, she would've been a welcomed team member in North Africa. But no matter, she's eligible for advanced training now." He glances up at me, a frown on that noble brow. "You'll be a bit older than the other agents, but perhaps maturity will make the training more meaningful."

"I had my reasons for insisting Pansy take advantage of the full five years before her examination."

My heart kicks up a notch. At that moment, Adele has so captured my mother's entire essence that I'm nearly convinced it *is* her on the phone, and these last three months have been some sort of strange fever dream.

"Maybe we rush agents into the field," he concedes.

"Maybe we do," Adele-channeling-Rose says, and there's no *maybe* about it.

I decide to interrupt before they wander down yet another conversational digression.

"Are you saying I passed?" Because, is he? He hasn't actually said one way or another, so I think it's a reasonable question.

His expression tells me it's not. "With flying colors, *Agent* Little. You are more than accomplished, and I fear a permanent post in King's End is beneath your capabilities."

"I like King's End." My heart thumps, though whether from fear or joy, I can't say. Part of me has always fantasized about becoming a full-fledged field agent, like my mother; of traveling the world, like she did back then and Mort does now. Part of me has always known King's End is where I belong, that I can't leave, even if I want to. Sometimes, that feels like a prison.

Other times? Having a place in this world is its own kind of gift.

He tilts his head, his gaze scanning the cozy alcove and then the view of the river. "I like it, too, but there's a wide world out there, Agent Little." He turns back to the phone. "I want to take a few days to draft the final report. I'll send you a copy for any comments before submitting it to the Enclave."

"I'd expect no less, Agent Darnelle. I look forward to reading it. I must go now. Love you, Pansy-Girl."

Adele cuts the connection before either of us can respond. The sunlight dazzles my eyes. The scents of breakfast—bacon, maple syrup, hot buttered toast—filter past, reminding me that all I've eaten today is a single chocolate chip.

I'm breathless, maybe even lightheaded. Carrie intuitively senses I need another cup of coffee, switches out the carafe, and pours a fresh cup without even asking. I send her a grateful smile. She merely raises an eyebrow in Agent Darnelle's direction.

Do something about that.

Yes, I probably should do something—like getting him to leave King's End immediately.

"Well, *Agent* Little?"

Oh, he's loving that, that slight stress on the word *agent*. I wonder if he does that after every examination.

"Thank you," I say.

"You did the work. I was merely the scorekeeper."

"Will you be leaving today?"

"It's early enough. I should be able to fly standby back to Seattle."

The Enclave's main headquarters is near Seattle, and many of the old families live in the area around Puget Sound. The headquarters is also close to Joint Base Lewis-McChord, where in the summer, the Enclave leases long-forgotten stretches of land for Academy training. If you're thinking these might be the most inhospitable stretches of land, you'd be right.

And yes, the military is fine with this since, during the summer, we mend all the fissures that pop up on base and in the region. The Enclave might not be a government agency, but that doesn't mean the government is completely unaware of us.

Agent Darnelle starts to gather his things but raises a hand when I do the same.

"Stay. Finish your breakfast. My treat. Besides, you'll need the fuel for patrolling."

Then the man winks at me—an honest-to-goodness, sexier-than-it-has-a-right-to-be wink.

Without another word, he leaves me with my coffee, my scone, and any number of Carrie's disappointed looks.

THE PARTY IS Mort's idea.

Then again, most parties are.

But it's why my two best friends are displayed, larger than life, on the flat-screen TV. It's why I'm clutching a champagne flute in one hand and my umbrella in the other and dancing to a playlist Jack has pulled together. It's why I'm letting myself touch the edges of joy, something I haven't felt in ages.

On the screen, Jack is nursing a gin and tonic, a *large* gin and tonic, but still just the one. It's Monday evening, and we all have to work tomorrow. Although, by the way Mort's pouring amber liquid from a cut crystal decanter, you'd never know it.

I'm drinking sparkling pink grape juice. The Sight and alcohol don't mix. But after yesterday's exam and the battle in the housing development? The nattering is there in the back of my mind. All I have to do is reach for it, and the Sight will come rushing in. If I'm careless—and let's face it, alcohol makes everyone careless—I could trigger an all-out attack.

Which is not something I need when I'm here on my own.

Tonight, though? I'm not worried about the Sight. I passed my examination *with flying colors*. I'm not even worried about what that means. Am I no longer unremarkable Pansy Little? I don't care. For once, I want to be remarkable, consequences be damned.

Besides, Agent Darnelle never even hinted about the Sight, which most people do if they suspect you possess it. Everyone wants to know their future.

Take it from me: you don't.

So I'm celebrating. I'm in the room opposite the front parlor, the room my mother always called the office, but it's more like a den with a desk and bookshelves, a computer, and a television. All of that is shrouded in the multiple strings of glowing pink fairy lights I've strung across the ceiling. Between their twinkle and the bubbles from the sparkling grape juice, I'm completely giddy.

"We need to do this for real," Mort says. "How long has it been since we had a birthday bash? Couple of years?"

I can't remember how the tradition started. One of us—Mort, probably—decided our birthdays didn't count until we all turned that age, the milestone ones in particular: sixteen, eighteen, twenty-one. He was born in January, I'm July, and Jack is an October baby.

"Halloween?" Mort is scrolling on his phone. "There's got to be something going on in the Twin Cities then. At the very least, at First Avenue. Yes!" He glances up, triumphant. As I said, all parties are Mort's idea. "The annual Halloween party and costume contest. Start planning, Pansy-Girl. We need to win."

I freeze, flute halfway to my lips. "I'll be patrolling."

"Just because Rose never took a day off doesn't mean you can't."

"But—"

"If it makes you—and her—feel any better, Jack and I can drive out. We'll triple-seal all the fissures. That should buy you a full week of parties."

"We'll do it," Jack echoes. "I can get time off. Besides, I haven't seen Rose in years."

I swallow my second protest. I should tell them. I really, really should tell my two best friends in the whole world what's going on. But I can't. The resistance goes beyond the cryptic list my mother left behind. It's the Sight, nattering louder and louder. I swear, all the words are there in my mouth, but my lips feel like stone.

Maybe, by October, things will have worked themselves out. I'm longing to see both of them again, in real life. Besides, if they do help me triple-seal the fissures before the first serious snowfall, winter will be so much easier.

So I raise my glass and say, "To Halloween!"

CHAPTER 17
HENRY

Seattle, Washington
Monday, July 10

He had a week. A single week in which to accomplish the impossible. Henry sat in what was once his father's study and was now, ostensibly, his own, and felt both time and opportunity slip through his fingers with alarming speed.

This would be a delicate operation, like catching and holding on to a single Screamer, something ill-advised and with any number of unintentional ramifications.

He leaned back in the chair, wingback, leather, and it creaked beneath him. The mahogany desk—which had once been his father's as well—felt too large, as if he weren't quite ready to step into those shoes. The evening was mild, but the air held a chill, the sort born from a house not lived in. He almost started a fire in the hearth but opted to warm himself with a scotch instead.

It hadn't helped.

A rustling came from the umbrella stand near the study door.

"Are you suggesting we should have stayed?"

Another rustling, this one far more enthusiastic.

"Yes, your motivations are glaringly obvious."

But the nudge went deeper than his umbrella's affinity for Agent Little's. It had taken Henry years to accept that his umbrella's intuition was something not only to acknowledge but respect. Still, despite their mostly one-sided conversations, he had trouble discerning what its messages might mean.

Like now.

But he'd obeyed that prodding earlier, buying his own return ticket, powering down his phone and the umbrella's GPS before leaving King's End. Of course, the rental car might prove an issue, but he doubted anyone would check.

All those precautions might buy him a week.

A single week to draft his report. A single week to figure out all the implications of what he planned to say. A single week to prepare for the inevitable fallout. His thoughts kept revisiting those words from his phone call with Terrence.

The family line has been earmarked for retirement.

That wasn't a clerical mistake, a slip of a key of someone like Terrence updating personnel data. That took intervention. It took approval from the High Council, or at least, a quorum.

Has been earmarked.

There it was again, a foregone conclusion. By a faceless authority. No one to take responsibility for the decision. *See here, what can we do? It simply happened while no one was looking. And now, we'll wash our hands of it.*

The cowardice of that rankled him.

And when he turned in his report, one that would shine a light on this misdeed?

The fallout would be immediate, political, and utterly spectacular. He would shake the High Council—and most likely his career— to the core. Indeed, depending on *who* had authorized the retirement in the first place, his report might end the career of Principal Field Agent Henry Darnelle.

His father had made any number of enemies during his time in the Enclave. For that matter, so had Henry. Despite the veneer of civility, Enclave politics were ruthless.

He pushed his hands through his hair and then pushed away from the desk. He was getting nowhere. He paced in front of the hearth until a thump came from the umbrella stand. Despite everything, he laughed.

A hand braced on the doorframe, he crouched next to the stand. "What are you trying to tell me?"

A flurry of images filled his mind, those of the funeral. He didn't want to think about his father's funeral. But his umbrella was relentless. Inexplicably, Henry found his attention turning toward the sideboard, where the polished surface was still littered with condolence cards.

He'd dealt with the immediate requirements of the estate along with the funeral (a fiasco from the start). He'd meant to acknowledge the sympathy of far-flung family and friends. If for no other reason than to prove that his father's death hadn't sent him off the rails.

Instead, he'd opted for the Sahara mission.

So much for proof.

His umbrella was oddly silent as he gathered the cards together. He shuffled through them until he found the one with the return address of King's End. It had been one of the first to arrive, although, at the time, he hadn't thought much about it or its sender.

No, this particular card was the first. He remembered that now. With care, Henry eased the card from the envelope and read the message inside.

My dear Henry,

I offer you my heartfelt condolences upon the death of your father. Although it has been some years since I last saw him in person, I feel his absence keenly.

He was a man who only needed to hear a song once to know all the lyrics, which he'd sing—usually on key. He liked his scotch neat and his steak rare. He took great pleasure in being right but always admitted when he was wrong.

And he saved my life more than once.

But his greatest joy, the light that fueled his soul, was you. You brightened his world in a way no other living person ever did. Remember that in the days to come. You were his reason.

Rose Little

The recoil was immediate and searing. Although not as sharp as the first time he'd read those words. He'd gasped out loud then. This time, he forced the intake of breath past the clogging in his throat.

You were his reason. Jesus, that hurt—his mind, his heart, his soul. It left him breathless and bereft.

Back in February, he'd shoved the card into its envelope, as if he could escape both the immense weight of his father's death and his love. Now, it was as if his body had incorporated the grief, spreading it through his veins, his muscles. It was like pressing a bruise that wouldn't heal and relishing the resulting pain that radiated from its center.

He took a closer look and considered the words she had written in a careful, if shaky, hand. Those small details spoke to intimacy, but his father had never mentioned Rose Little, not that he could remember. What Henry did recall was Botten's barely hidden insinuation: *She and your father were close.*

He picked up the envelope. The first to arrive, the postmark the day his father had died.

Which couldn't be right. They'd been in Cannon Beach the last month of his father's life, abandoning Seattle and the Enclave for the small family cabin nestled along the Oregon coast. Just him, his father, and, of course, the private hospice service.

Henry had spent his days taking long walks along the beach, staring out at Haystack Rock, letting the ocean air wash across his skin. That way, when he tasted salt on his lips, he could tell himself it came from the sea. In the evenings, they streamed college basketball and improbable spy movies.

During which his father would turn to him and intone, "For such an elite organization, they're really quite terrible at their jobs." And then a long, measured pause followed by a sip of scotch. "And their tradecraft? Simply appalling."

One unseasonably fair afternoon, he'd even wheeled his father onto the deck for a cookout. That had been the surprising thing about hospice, the allowed indulgences. Tiny bites of steak cooked rare and a glass of scotch, neat, in the evenings. Small comforts that had somehow gained all the importance in the world.

And then there was the day the hospice nurse had placed a gentle hand on his shoulder, their words soft and steady.

"Henry, you don't have to do anything right now. There's no reason to rush."

So he hadn't notified anyone in the Enclave, not even his mother, until three days later, after he'd made all the arrangements to return his father home one last time.

Three days. And yet, somehow, Rose Little had known. Rose Little. In King's End.

King's End.

The notion had him abandoning the rest of the cards, and they went scattering across the floor. He yanked open the filing cabinet and rummaged around until he found the package with the security seal—the one his father's lawyer had hand-delivered a few days after the funeral.

Inside, Henry had found nothing remarkable. Photographs, some mere snapshots, the sort that people had developed at drugstores. Larger photos, more professionally done, of landscapes at various angles. A site survey, perhaps with a bit more artistic flourish, but still, views from every conceivable aspect. At the time, all he could think of was that his father wanted some discretion in regard to these particular photographs. So, after thumbing through them, he obliged and tucked them away.

Now, Henry wondered. He wondered why those landscapes looked oh so familiar and why the drugstore where the photographs had been developed was in King's End. Most of all, he wondered what his father was trying to tell him.

No note accompanied the package. There was nothing in the will. All the lawyer said upon delivery was: "Your father wanted you to have this."

Henry tucked the photographs back into the package. He'd study them later. It was, after all, a long flight to Minnesota. Then he walked over to the umbrella stand and crouched so he was at eye level with the jade handle.

"Seems you were right. Again."

His umbrella rattled the sides of the stand with excitement and delight and perhaps just a hint of *I told you so*.

CHAPTER 18
OPHELIA

Seattle, Washington
Monday, July 10

"I shouldn't be here. If anyone asks, you haven't seen me."

Henry always knows how to make her laugh. Were she younger—and actually conscious—Ophelia might lock her lips with an invisible key or cup her hands and pretend to shout the news through a megaphone.

"I need to go back to King's End. It's a long story."

Oh, a very long story. You might say a never-ending one. It loops, and it loops, and it loops.

"My father left me all these photographs. I don't understand what they mean."

Just wait until you take a closer look.

"They all have to do with King's End, so I think I need to go back there. I need to speak with Rose Little."

That's going to be difficult.

Henry sighs, and a hint of scotch floats in the air. Ophelia hopes he only drank the one. There are many ways this conversation ends, if you could even call it that. The outcome often depends on his earlier consumption of scotch.

The chair scrapes lightly against the floor, the sound filled with impatience and barely restrained fervor. Henry is a man who walks a tightrope between thought and action. Certainly, he is more centered, less impulsive than she is. It's thanks to that impulsiveness that she's here now, confined to a bed, unable to escape her mind and the Sight.

"But I've been gone for so long. I don't want to leave you."

But you must.

This is the one thing Ophelia knows. Henry always returns to King's End, but *how* he returns matters, if only to her. He's wavering, and the Sight is taking delight in showing her those scenarios, those *other* scenarios.

In those times through the loop, Henry is stripped of everything: his rank, his status, his job. They drag him before the High Council. He's accused of misconduct, of crimes never committed. No one speaks on his behalf.

No one dares.

The public shaming is thorough and ruthless. It's far easier to blame the messenger, the one who exposes the corrupt underbelly, than it is to take responsibility. And, of course, no one does. Ophelia won't touch those particular images unless the Sight insists. It wavers because Henry still wavers.

They try to take all of Henry's assets, including the house, but Harry Darnelle ensured that this would be impossible, as if he knew that the Enclave would come for his son. But even he isn't—wasn't—strong enough to keep them from revoking Henry's umbrella.

In any other excommunication, they'd turn him out at this point, cut him loose to survive on his own. But Henry is still useful in the same way Pansy Little is useful. And so, he returns to King's End, this time under guard.

In those scenarios, the end is always quick and brutal. Ophelia wonders why blood delights the Enclave so.

But if Henry leaves now, if he returns to King's End of his own volition? The end doesn't change. At least, the Sight has never shown her a scenario where there isn't blood. But Henry is glorious. And if the world must end, let it be with Henry fighting to the last.

A rustling reaches her, the soft hush of an umbrella. Not her own. She has no idea where they've stashed her umbrella. But Henry's is here, in the room. In her mind's eye, she senses the jade handle resting lightly against his thigh, a faithful dog come to heel.

He brought it with him instead of leaving it in the stand near the front door. She's positive the Sight has never shown her this before. It's such a small thing, but she grasps on to it. Ophelia knows outcomes often rely more on the small gestures than the grand ones.

All for the want of a nail—or an umbrella.

And then she tries something else. She lets her concentration slip from Henry. No use in pretending he can hear her. But his umbrella?

So, she thinks. Not about impending doom. Not about how Henry needs to leave. Not about anything other than how sad her umbrella must be because it can't see Henry's.

Henry clears his throat, a half cough, half chuckle. "What?" he says, and Ophelia knows he isn't speaking to her. It's his umbrella voice, a bit indulgent, like he's speaking to a favorite pet. The Enclave claims these communications with umbrellas are pure anthropomorphism.

Ophelia knows that, as with other things, the Enclave is full of pure shit.

"Well, where has she gone?"

Henry's quiet footfalls fill the room. He does a circuit before kneeling next to the bed.

"Why have they taken your umbrella?"

Why, indeed.

"I'm going to go look for her," he adds. "She can't be far."

The moments tick past, her mind clocking each one. Henry's gone for a very long time. She knows he hasn't forgotten her or become sidetracked. Only a catastrophe would keep him from returning. But the Sight, in its perverseness, won't show her a thing.

At last, his footfalls sound in the hallway, barely there, without a creak to any of the floorboards. He enters the room, and the rush of joy sends her heart fluttering. She tries to calm her pulse immediately so the abnormal readings won't alert the night nurse.

But she's here! Her umbrella! Her lovely, lovely sage green and glitter umbrella. Henry tucks it next to her, and its presence soothes the ragged edges of her mind. With it here, next to her, she's a more complete version of herself. And if she isn't actually more capable, Ophelia will bask in the feeling that she is.

She can hear Henry do another circuit around her room, footsteps light and considered. He won't be the one to wake the night nurse. No doubt he is in his thinking pose, hands behind his back, a frown crinkling his brow.

"We'll have to find a place for you. Not the bed."

No, unfortunately not. It's a hospital bed with all the latest technology. There's no place to hide her umbrella where it wouldn't be discovered or, worse, mangled.

"But not too far away."

Ophelia struggles to picture her room. They've rolled up the thick Turkish carpets and removed the canopy bed, swapping it out for the contraption with all its whirring and elevations, the monitors, the IV stand, and what must be a mountain of ready supplies. Even with the Egyptian cotton sheets, down pillows, and velvet quilt, the bed is still, at heart, a mechanical thing. She doesn't despise it; that would do her no good. But she certainly doesn't love it.

"The doll house?"

Some children might have little more than a box with dividers. Others might own a Barbie dream house. Ophelia has a custom-made, four-story monstrosity that accommodates her American Girl dolls. All of them.

Never mind that she's an adult, a certified field agent, or was. Ophelia supposes now she's simply a burden. Despite everything, the doll house remains in her room, and she doesn't need the Sight to taste her mother's yearning for grandchildren. Whether from her or Henry, it hardly matters. So here the doll house will remain, a beacon of hope.

"Yes. The doll house. I'll tuck it in back, where no one will see it."

In his voice, there's the staunch belief that she hears him, that she might wake, stumble from bed, and unearth her umbrella from its hiding spot. Reverently, Henry eases the umbrella from her side. He tucks it away with whispered reassurances. Then he returns to her.

"I feel better now that she's here to look after you."

So do I.

His sigh is long, but it doesn't waver. "I think I need to go to King's End."

I think so, too.

"I think ... hope you understand."

More than you know.

"I'll be home as soon as I can."

He bestows a gentle kiss on her forehead. She tracks his footfalls along the hallway, down the stairs. He leaves by the front door, his own man, of his own volition. That should be enough. Instead, he's left her with a sliver of hope.

And hope makes everything hurt that much more.

CHAPTER 19
PANSY

King's End, Minnesota
Monday, July 10

It's later—much later, really—when I notice the tender looks between Mort and Jack. The playlist has gone from sweat-sprouting to soft and seductive. Maybe it's the celebration or the promise of a birthday bash, but I'm pretty sure *off again* is about to get switched back on.

"I'm calling it a night," I say.

Of course, they try to talk me out of it. Mort could drink for hours, nap for twenty minutes, and charge out the door to fight an onslaught of Screamers. Since he's somewhere in Europe, he might have to do just that. Granted, I've also seen him crash in the after-math of all that. Jack, on the other hand, is a bit bleary-eyed.

A look of gratitude washes across his face when I add: "Maybe you two don't have to walk miles tomorrow, but I do."

I shut everything down, place my glass in the kitchen sink, and then unearth my mother's umbrella from its hiding spot in the pantry. For a long moment, I cradle it against my chest. I always hope I'll sense a connection, somehow reach my mother through her umbrella. But the beautiful rose red is a shade darker, more subdued, now that she's gone. And her umbrella is as bereft as I am.

Still, I want to feel my mother's embrace. I want to hear her words of praise. Would she chastise me for showing off? Or would she understand?

Would she, I wonder, be proud of me?

My mother's umbrella trembles with reassurances. If it could hug me, I think it would. For now, I'm simply glad I don't have to hide her.

Gently, I slip both umbrellas into the stand next to the front door. Their handles touch. Hints of conversation filter through the air. They are a mother and daughter engaged in a heartfelt chat—about me and how I cruelly separated my umbrella from Agent Darnelle's.

Really, it's all I can do not to roll my eyes.

"'For never was a story of more woe than this of Juliet and her Romeo,'" I say to them before heading up the stairs.

Henry Darnelle isn't the only one who can quote Shakespeare.

PART TWO

WHAT'S PAST IS PROLOGUE

CHAPTER 20
PANSY

King's End, Minnesota
Tuesday, July 11

The last thing you want to see after a prolonged patrol in the housing development is someone from the Enclave on your front porch.

Especially when that someone is Principal Field Agent Henry Darnelle.

He's sitting on the porch swing, his back to me. He's in full regalia today: charcoal gray suit, a hint of white dress shirt at the collar and cuffs. Although that ridiculous hat rests not on his head but on the seat next to him. A black SUV, rather than a sedan, is parked in the driveway.

With a foot, he sets the swing in motion. From where I stand, I can hear the gentle creak, the sound relaxed and soothing. It's a patient sort of move, as if he's been waiting here for a while and has the fortitude to keep on waiting.

This is Henry Darnelle, after all. He absolutely does have the fortitude.

And I do not. I don't need this. Not today. The Screamers were extra gleeful this morning. I'm starting to wonder if the sudden reappearance of Agent Darnelle is the reason why. His being here can't be anything but bad. I'm not sure I want to know just how bad.

A voice in the back of my mind whispers that—*actually*—I do want to know.

Already my thoughts are racing as if they can outrun the Sight, which, in turn, is knock-knock-knocking against my consciousness. It's too close and far too insistent. I've been flirting with it more than I should have these past few days. My upper lip feels damp, but my fingers come away with only the barest hint of blood.

Good. I can do this. Because what I plan to do is crawl through my neighbor's overgrown lilac bushes and sneak into the house through the kitchen door. Then I will hole up in the pantry and wait him out. He can't sit on my front porch forever.

At least, I hope he can't.

Granted, the neighborhood watch might notice. Still, I can deal with anything that pops up on Hey Neighbor later. But before I can step off the sidewalk and cut across my neighbor's lawn, my umbrella slips through my fingers.

I say slipped. Really? She flings herself forward, escaping my grasp. For a mere second, she balances on her tip. Then, she succumbs to an all-out swoon. She plummets to the ground like a damsel in distress.

My umbrella? She is shameless.

Henry Darnelle doesn't notice this bit of theatrics, but his umbrella certainly does. That's all it takes. Agent Darnelle swivels around in the porch swing just as I'm scooping my umbrella from the ground. I give her a shake for all the good that will do me. She is so self-satisfied and smug that no amount of scolding will penetrate.

He stands, umbrella barely restrained on his arm. At least this reunion will be joyful for them, if not for us. I consider strolling past my house as if I haven't seen him. But really, what's the point? So I steel myself and head up the walkway.

"Agent Darnelle?" I say, deciding to play offense. "Can I help you? Couldn't you get a flight back to Seattle?"

That's a reasonable assumption, but his expression tells me it isn't, that the reason he's here has to do with me, and I'm not going to like what he has to say.

Possibilities fill my head. Perhaps he was wrong and couldn't score my exam, and now I have to do the whole thing over again. Or perhaps it's worse. As in, I failed my exam, and he's here to revoke my umbrella.

In that case, I should've gone on defense, kept my status as a full-fledged field agent for a few more hours at least. I tighten my grip on my umbrella and pull her close. I will run. He will have to track me down and forcibly take her from me.

Instead, he stands there on the porch, waiting on me. A cold sweat has sprouted along my spine, and there's little the late morning sun can do to warm me.

When he doesn't speak, I'm compelled to ask, "Did I fail?"

"Fail what, Agent Little?"

"My exam?" I hate how small my voice sounds. I hate how much passing my exam *with flying colors* means to me. I hate having to wait for his answer.

"What?" Comprehension chases the sober expression from his features. His smile comes with a hint of a dimple. "No, no, nothing like that. I meant what I said yesterday. You are an accomplished field agent and have been for some time, if I'm not mistaken."

He's not, of course.

"I was hoping we could speak, perhaps inside?" He shoulders his messenger bag and secures his hat. His gaze scans the neighborhood as if spies lurk behind the ornamentals and the oaks. Considering that curtains flutter in the living room across the street, that's not an entirely wrong assumption.

"Yes, of course." Inside is better. Honestly, inside is always better. We do not need to star in yet another thread on Hey Neighbor.

Unfailingly polite, he holds the screen door while I open the main one. My umbrella—the shameless thing—is all a-tremble, no doubt anticipating some canoodling with Agent Darnelle's. I'm about to grant her wish, tell him to drop his umbrella in the stand, when the sight there freezes me in place.

My mother's umbrella. In the stand. Where I left it last night. Her essence is nothing but full-on disapproval.

I'd shoo Agent Darnelle back outside, but he has already crossed the threshold. His hand hovers above the stand, and then he lets his umbrella fall. It lands with a clunk. I ease my own umbrella in after, but three is clearly a crowd. No one is happy with this new arrangement.

"So, your mother is home?" he asks, hanging up his hat on the coat tree.

"Not exactly."

"But her umbrella is here."

"Yes, I know." And I know all the implications of that. My mother must be home because no one from the Enclave, active or retired, travels without their umbrella.

"Then can I speak to her?"

"That's going to be difficult."

"We just spoke yesterday." Concern clouds his brow. "Is she ill? Does she need a doctor?"

I open my mouth to answer, but no words come out. Not that it matters. He's barreled his way into the house and down the front hallway.

"Agent Little? Agent Rose Little? I'm sorry to intrude." Determination replaces the concern. He will speak to my mother even though she isn't here to speak to. "It's urgent that we talk."

His voice echoes throughout the space. It's a wonder he can't hear the emptiness in reply, that I'm the only one who lives here, and this house hasn't truly been a home for three long months.

"Agent Darnelle, please. Maybe I can help you instead." I gesture toward the front parlor.

He halts, turns, and then purses his lips as if the front parlor isn't ideal but will have to do.

He paces the length of the room before easing the messenger bag from his shoulder. From its depths, he pulls out a large, brown paper package.

"Do you remember when I said I thought I'd seen the housing development before?"

I nod.

"My father left me some photographs, photographs of King's End, of the land where the development now sits." He tugs a few photos from the package in illustration. And yes, that's the space, as I remember it, with its meadow and trees and wild roses before the construction company broke ground.

"I believe he was trying to tell me something, but I can't fathom what that might be. He neglected to leave me any notes." He rubs his temples as if the next words pain him. "Your mother figures prominently in the photographs, and they're all of King's End. I thought she might be able to help me."

My mother and Harry Darnelle. I feel the tug, the temptation. I don't dare close my eyes, and I manage the barest of sniffs. I want to swipe beneath my nose, but that's such an obvious tell that I can't bring myself to do it.

"And then there's this." From his suit coat pocket, he pulls a card. "Your mother sent this. It's postmarked the day my father died."

I remember what Adele told me, that my mother somehow knew Harry Darnelle had died, that they had some sort of connection. "She would send a card," I manage, my voice shaky.

Agent Darnelle's lips twist, his nostrils flare, and it's like my response has made him angry. "I told no one about my father's death for three days."

I hold absolutely still, sensing that if I speak again or even blink, I'll make everything worse.

"Do you understand what I'm saying? I told no one." He's

emphatic in this, the envelope rattling in his grip. "No one knew. I didn't contact the Enclave, or family, or friends. So, can you explain to me, Agent Little, how your mother knew my father had died?"

No, actually, I can't. I'd call Adele if it would help, but I doubt she knows how either.

"So, thirty years ago, my father was here in King's End," he says, glancing around the room as if he's seen it before. "And I think ... I think—"

"Something happened." Oh, blame the Sight. The words fly from my mouth unbidden. I have no hope of reeling them back or explaining myself.

"Then you know? You can tell me?"

So much relief blooms in his expression that I hate to disappoint him. I shake my head.

"Then your mother—"

"Isn't here. She's gone." For a moment, I consider lying—or at least telling a variation of the truth, taking Agent Darnelle to the cemetery and showing him the grave marker. But then, what about my exam debriefing? How do I explain that? Besides, I can't say the words: *She's dead.* I simply can't. It's like my lips refuse to tell this particular lie.

"Did you send this card?" He shakes it in front of my face. That's my mother's handwriting, but all I can think is maybe Adele or the hospice nurse sent it for her.

"No," I say. "I didn't send it."

"Where is your mother, Agent Little?"

Maybe it's the card he's still brandishing, and my mother's handwriting—that careful, painful script of her last days. Maybe it's the fact that no matter how hard I try, I can't answer that particular question. Or maybe it has simply been a long seventy-two hours, and I've been battling the Sight for most of them. But a hurricane is brewing in my mind, and it's about to make landfall.

I catch the first gush of blood, hot and sticky, against my fingers but can do nothing more. I'm going down, and I'm going down hard, right into the edge of the coffee table. My world goes bright red—like a sunrise before a storm—and then black.

Before I can hit the floor, a strong arm catches me around the waist. A hint of spicy vanilla mixes with the coppery tang of blood. The last thing I hear—or think I hear—is someone whispering, "I'm sorry."

CHAPTER 21
HENRY

King's End, Minnesota
Tuesday, July 11

He was a cad, a cur, and most definitely a pretentious asshole. He also had several things to do. There'd be time for self-recrimination later.

With a hand cradling the back of her head, Henry eased Pansy Little to the carpet, a dark red Persian-style rug. For a fleeting moment, he wondered if the interior design choice was intentional. Considering the amount of blood, it probably was.

From the sofa, he grabbed a throw pillow and fleece blanket and tucked her in as cozy as possible. He pulled out his phone, rummaged around in his messenger bag for its tripod stand, and set them up on the coffee table. Then, he pressed record.

He checked his watch and addressed the camera.

"It's been about forty-five seconds since the Sight incapacitated Field Agent Pansy Little. She is resting comfortably." With an index finger, he touched the underside of her wrist, gaze on his watch. "Pulse a little high, ninety beats per minute. Respiration." He counted her intake of breath. "About sixteen." Gently, he let the back of his hand rest on her forehead. "No obvious fever, skin cool, but not clammy. Also, the blood flow has stemmed."

Not alarming, then. That was something.

"I am going to step away to find something to clean up the blood, then I will return to monitor her condition."

Henry left the video running. That was protocol, after all. Hopefully, his phone had a full enough charge. Or perhaps this episode would be a short one. There was, of course, nothing in Pansy's records about her Sight. He could only guess what might help and only pray he didn't choose something that might hinder.

In the kitchen, he headed for the pantry. There, in the back, tucked away so a casual observer might not notice, were the standard-issue supplies for the Sight. The package of smelling salts was unopened and dusty. Pansy's Sight was like Ophelia's; it would simply laugh at that attempt.

And yes, Henry regarded the Sight as an entity, a thing not to be trifled with, a thing that had a will of its own, a thing that didn't run on logic, which was why he found it so confounding.

The essential oils might help. Those, at least in his experience, never hurt. He examined the bottles in their rack, selecting the sweet basil and lavender mixture. It was the most used, which suggested it was the most effective.

He returned to the parlor with the oil, paper towels, and a soft, damp washcloth, and set to work. Blood first. It was already an angry rust color on her skin. He'd deal with the carpet later. He was an expert at getting blood out of carpets.

He looked up at the camera. "I'm now going to clean up some of this blood."

Lightly, and with patience, he dabbed, coaxing the blood from her skin rather than scraping the cloth across her cheeks and neck like some first-year cadet at the Academy. The blood had to go, one way or the other. The pulse points needed to be clean and dry before he applied the essential oil.

At last, the blood was mostly sopped up. Henry uncapped the bottle, and a rush of lavender filled the space. Immediately, his shoulders relaxed, some of the tension draining away. The sweet basil was the chaser, bringing with it an earthy aroma that cleared his head.

The concoction was almost addicting. After another long inhale, he used his ring finger to place a drop behind each of Pansy's ears. He waited, gauged her response, took her pulse again. No change, but no distress, either. He moved on to her wrists, then neck, and then the inner elbows, stopping to check her vitals after each application.

The rest? Well, the rest could take a while. Henry sat cross-legged on the floor next to her and waited.

If nothing else, he was an expert at that.

He'd been waiting a very long time. Granted, Henry was also an expert at keeping this vigil. He'd sat at Ophelia's side for countless hours. Most people with the Sight recovered on their own, even without the smelling salts and essential oils.

But then, most people weren't like his sister or Pansy Little.

There was one more thing he could try, and he was positive it would work. Well, almost. It had always worked with Ophelia. If he hadn't been halfway around the world when she'd succumbed that last time, she might not be in a coma now. There was just one problem in using it with Pansy Little.

He didn't have her consent.

Henry sighed, stretched his legs. The wait had given him a chance to think, to conduct a thorough, if somewhat limited, inspection of her home. Everything was slightly off-kilter. Small oddities, like a discarded length of oxygen tubing beneath the sofa, the lone coffee cup in the sink, the single jacket on the coat tree next to the front door. The house itself felt both lived in and abandoned in a way he couldn't discern. Or rather, he could. It felt exactly like his father's home in Seattle.

Then there was that speckling of scars across her skin. Henry could judge a scar, and those were fairly recent.

It's hard to reach my own back.

The sign of an agent on their own.

That strange insistence of her mother being gone. Gone. Not merely away. Not dead. Just gone.

"And let's not forget the umbrella," he murmured.

His own was cowering in its presence, thwarted in its pursuit of the daughter. If things hadn't been so strange and dire, Henry might have laughed at that. Rose Little had been a formidable agent, and her umbrella was no different.

Had been? Past tense? There were two reasons for an agent to be without their umbrella: excommunication and death. Protocol demanded that when an agent died, the family turned in their umbrella. For Henry, that particular act had been nearly as devastating as his father's death.

He considered the umbrella stand. There was not much to gain from Rose's umbrella. He didn't blame his own for cowering. But Pansy's? Henry glanced at the camera, held up a finger, and stood.

Upon reaching the stand, he crouched, arms braced on his thighs. His own umbrella was pouting near the back under the shrewd scrutiny of the rose-red one. But Pansy's fluttered a greeting. It was such a resourceful, effusive little thing, not unlike its owner, he supposed.

"Will you help me?" he asked.

The ruffles fluttered again with what could only be a yes.

"All right, then. Let's go."

Back in front of the phone, Henry turned the umbrella's handle toward the camera's lens. "I'm setting Agent Little's umbrella to deliver a shock if at any point I"—he paused, pursed his lips in thought—"inadvertently harm her in any way."

He tucked the umbrella next to Pansy. A sigh reached him,

whether from Pansy, her umbrella, or both, he couldn't tell. Next came the delicate part of this operation. He sat on the floor and eased the pillow from beneath Pansy's head and then her head to his thigh.

Technically, he could perform the maneuvers without this contact. In his experience, this posture was more efficient, certainly more effective, if perhaps more intimate. He had always sat this way with Ophelia. The contact produced a feedback loop that let him adjust his technique.

With care, he eased the ponytail holder from her hair, and the chestnut strands fanned out. She looked smaller like this but not doll-like. Even in this state, she had far too much expression in her features. But she appeared vulnerable, perhaps because she was.

The worry hit him like a spike to the chest. The last thing he wanted to do was hurt her. Still, no second guessing. He'd committed to this course of action, so he might as well see it through.

Then, lightly, carefully, he placed his fingers on her skull, traced the bones along her face, from temple to ear, along her jaw, and then traveled across her brow. Eyes closed, he searched for a connection. He'd just met her, and that was the danger.

This *was* an intimate technique, one requiring trust. His presence might chase her farther into the Sight, might cause more damage. He might be the reason she never woke up. Henry thought of Ophelia and what might have alarmed her to the point where she couldn't return.

Pansy's umbrella rustled slightly, not in warning but in reassurance. So Henry kept his eyes closed, he kept the vigil, and he kept his fingers moving in hopes he could draw Pansy out of the Sight.

CHAPTER 22
PANSY

Seattle, Washington
Friday, March 3 (four months prior)

I'm at a funeral. And I'm at a funeral because the Sight trades in that sort of irony. It's a wet, cold day in what smells like the Pacific Northwest: damp pine with a hint of salt. We're graveside, and the mourners all have umbrellas, which, given the rain, wouldn't be unusual.

Except the rows are dotted with multicolored canopies, some far too frivolous for a funeral. Several agents stand around the perimeter of the gravesite, strategically positioned. They're on guard, their gazes canvassing the thick clouds above. They look impossibly young, all of them. Their umbrellas twitch with nervous energy.

This is an Enclave funeral, possibly for someone from the High Council. Granted, I've never attended an Enclave graveside service, but the mood is heavy with the sort of gravitas you'd expect from a state funeral. No one particularly wants to be here, but the air is clogged with obligation.

For a moment, I wonder if I've flashed forward, that I'm witnessing the end result—or one possible end result—of informing the Enclave of my mother's "death." But I can't fathom a scenario where I disinter my mother's fake ashes and bring them to Seattle for this sort of pomp and circumstance.

Although I suppose there might be a reality where I do, and the Sight is taking perverse pleasure in showing me that.

Then movement catches my eye. Screamers are coming in with alarming speed and unerring precision. I wave my arms, trying to alert the agents stationed around the perimeter. Occasionally, these sorts of antics—the arm waving, jumping up and down, shouting— appear to work. I don't know if I can make contact like that or if it's merely coincidences that make me believe I can.

I dash around, first to one agent and then the next. None of them have detected the Screamers. Oddly, no one has. Certainly, there are several high-caliber agents here. They should be shooting to their feet, arming their umbrellas, getting ready to fight so the family can mourn in peace. But no one moves.

Except for one person in the front row.

He stands, shoulders broad, umbrella at the ready. When he turns my way, I find myself staring into the eyes of Henry Darnelle. He looks stricken, beyond bereft, as if his whole world has cratered.

The knowledge slices into me: sharp and hot and full of that perverse glee. This is just like the Sight to show me Harrison Darnelle's funeral.

The Screamers go zipping past me, intent on Henry now that he's acknowledged them. A few break off to harass me, but since I'm technically not here, their strikes don't penetrate. Although I can certainly feel the sting. Again, the Sight is perverse this way.

With his umbrella, he sends a single pulse and snaps the canopy closed. Then? He runs. Eager and rapt, the Screamers follow. He's like the Pied Piper, leading them away not only from his father's funeral but the cemetery in general.

In the quiet aftermath, I prowl the rows of folding chairs. A few people shiver, someone frowns, someone else rubs their arms.

"It's like a goose just walked over my grave," someone whispers as I scoot past. Her companion shushes her immediately.

Absolutely the wrong occasion for that comparison. But, from what I know, accurate. The caress of an icy finger against the back of your neck. I've felt it from time to time, and I wonder who from the future, or the past, is spying on me.

There's some rustling of canopies, some throat clearing. A sonorous voice from near the front announces that the service will continue once Henry Darnelle returns. In the meantime, everyone will apparently sit here and not do a damn thing to help.

I continue to weave my way through the mourners. Strands of gossip curl through the air, tendrils reaching my ears.

... this is why you don't mentor your own child ... you heard about Ophelia, didn't you ... hundred bucks says he burns out in the next six months ...

The voices grate inside my mind, and I want to tune them out. My mother always said that everything at Enclave headquarters was steeped in ambition, avarice, and malice. This funeral is no different. Hardly anyone is here to mourn. The thought makes my heart clench.

I'm moving toward the front when I spy Mortimer, in an aisle seat, parked in a cluster of Connollys. His cobalt-blue umbrella shelters him from rain that's starting to pick up. He is surreptitiously checking his phone. I think he's texting.

For the love of—I get right up into his face, inches away. I lean close, hands braced on my knees.

"Why are you sitting on your ass? You're one of the best agents here. Get up and help him."

So, fine, Mortimer doesn't like Henry Darnelle. I'm certain the feeling is mutual. But it's a *funeral*. The cemetery is infested with

Screamers. All he has to do is stand at the perimeter and send out a pulse.

"Get. Off. Your. Ass."

Nothing. I glance around, but Jack isn't here. His family lives in Portland, and while they've been in the Enclave for decades, they're not considered an old family. They maybe sent a representative, but that's it.

I try a different approach. I let my fingers hover over Mort's umbrella. I'm ghost-like here, so this is a delicate maneuver. Near enough that my skin tingles in anticipation of feeling the umbrella's fabric, but not so close that my fingers shoot straight through it.

Get him to do the right thing.

Maybe it's me. Maybe it's the fact that Mort's umbrella is far more sensitive and sympathetic than he is. But that cobalt-blue canopy shudders in response. Mort glances up, annoyed. But he puts his phone away and lumbers to his feet. With impatient stabs of his umbrella, he directs the hapless agents on the perimeter into better positions.

By the time Agent Darnelle returns, the site is secured. He gives Mortimer a single, terse nod. Yes, these two do not like each other, but there's gratitude in the gesture.

Henry himself delivers the eulogy, his voice raw from exertion and emotion. I can't hear what he says. Everything swirls like watercolor. The trees, the umbrellas, the patter of rain, and his voice blend together until I settle back into my own reality.

I know it's my reality because I can feel my umbrella in my grip. Her whole being trembles with relief. I'm not ready to open my eyes and confront this world. Everything right now is so serene. I'm warm inside a fleece throw. My umbrella is by my side. Someone strokes my brow and my face with bone-melting caresses, someone who knows what they're doing.

I brace for the post-attack nausea, the headache that will send spikes of agony through my skull.

Nothing. Or rather, nothing but bliss. I want to know who's granted me this reprieve, so I bat my eyelashes open.

Above me, his expression filled with concern, is Henry Darnelle. This close, I notice tiny flecks of gold in his irises. A smile blooms across his face, popping two dimples and deepening the crinkles around his eyes.

"Well, Agent Little, it's very good to see you."

CHAPTER 23
PANSY

King's End, Minnesota
Tuesday, July 11

His fingers still, and then Agent Darnelle lifts his hands from my face. The sudden absence makes me cry out. I want nothing more than to lounge here and let him caress the last of the Sight from my mind.

"Are you all right, Agent Little?" His voice is filled with alarm. "Did I hurt you?"

"No. It's just ... I mean, you can keep—"

"Do I have your consent to continue?"

"Yes. Please." The fingers return, and I shut my eyes, overcome by that pure bliss. "If you're not tired, that is."

"I'm not." The alarm drains from his voice. His tone is nothing but tender, a match for those fingers traveling across my skin and skull. "But I suspect you might be."

"Sort of."

"Been a while since a major attack?"

"Couple of years," I admit. At this point, there's no reason to lie about my Sight.

"Really!" The exclamation comes with a huff of admiration. "Your ability to lock down the Sight is extraordinary."

"I sometimes pay the price."

That last time, though, I'd merely been foolish, during the birthday bash in Minneapolis. I hadn't been drinking, per se, but I'd been taking sips, sampling the truly outrageous cocktails Mort and Jack were ordering. Yes, the Sight and alcohol don't mix. Mort slung me over his shoulder and carried me back to our shared hotel room. Not that I remember any of that.

"Yes," Henry says. "I can sense the build-up."

Oh, he must know someone with the Sight. His technique is just too good, and he has the intimate knowledge to match. True, they train everyone in this technique at the Academy, but it's right up there with CPR. You could go your whole career without ever using the skill.

"That bad?" Locking down the Sight is a handy, practical trick. But there's a cost; with the Sight, there always is. The build-up is like a sticky, mental residue.

"There was a lot. I'm surprised you went so long between attacks."

The only other person who could read the build-up was—is—my mother. "What's it like?" I ask, because she would never say. "Does it hurt you?" I always suspected her silence meant that it does.

"It's more informative than painful."

I have no idea what that means, and my non-response must tell him so, because he breathes out a soft laugh.

"It's hard to explain," he adds. "I can't see what you saw, obviously. I can't tell how many times you've locked down the Sight, but I can sense the toll it takes, if that makes sense. It's thick and heavy. There's no other way to describe it."

Oh. No wonder my mother never spoke of it. He must absolutely be related to someone with the Sight. I want to ask. And yet? I don't want to intrude. Before I can make up my mind, his posture shifts. He reaches for something on the coffee table.

"Now that you're awake, I can stop the recording."

Wait. Recording. Oh, no. I grope the floor, but my hands are tangled in the fleece blanket. Besides, I'm still in the newborn kitten phase of recovery. I'm not sitting up quite yet. I try, though.

"Agent Little, please—"

"Recording?" My voice cracks.

"Yes. Protocol. Also, I'd like you to review it. I hope none of my actions make you uncomfortable."

I nod, although the last thing I want to see is myself supine on the floor.

"You mean now?" he asks.

The sooner, the better. I nod again.

"I can send it to your phone."

"No!" I've made it up to my elbows under my own power. His eyes widen as if he's shocked by both this and my outburst. "I mean, let's watch it on your phone."

He helps me sit up and then starts the video from the beginning.

It's been about forty-five seconds since the Sight incapacitated Field Agent Pansy Little...

Is there a time when this man is not precise and correct? He speeds up the playback, since three hours of watching me sprawled out on the floor would be mind-numbing. During that time, he barely left my side. He barely moved except to shuck off the suit coat jacket, loosen his tie, and roll his cuffs.

Most people don't have the stamina or patience for this sort of vigil. Jack does, but only because he's one of my best friends. Then again, Mort doesn't, so maybe it's a personality thing.

We keep watching, and even I'm getting bored. I'm tempted to speed up the video, but then Henry brings my umbrella into the frame, and I slow it down instead.

I'm setting Agent Little's umbrella to deliver a shock...

She is still at my side, so I pick her up and examine the handle.

"Agent Darnelle, you set her to tase!" I never have a reason to shock anyone in King's End, never mind tase them. I return the setting to zero, and I swear she sighs in relief. "She would never tase you."

"I"—he shuts his eyes, a pained expression on his face—"didn't have your consent. I wanted to be extra cautious. The Sight is not something to trifle with."

Okay, this I understand. "Will you do me a favor?"

"Send you the video for your records? Certainly."

"Delete it."

His hand hovers over the screen. "I believe this interaction should be maintained."

"I don't want it on my phone," I say. "My *Enclave*-issued phone. I don't want it on your Enclave-issued phone, either."

Will he do this for me? Mort's warning rings in my ears, how Henry Darnelle never met a rule he didn't want to follow. I can't help but wonder what he's planning to say in my final report. Will he out me to the Enclave? He sprang into action so quickly that he must have known about the Sight, even before today.

His expression is shrouded, and I have no idea what's going on behind those dark eyes. He's turning something over in his mind, that much I can tell.

"I'll delete this, but if we ever find ourselves in this situation again, I'd like your consent to help you through it."

My consent for the most blissful head massage known the world over? Hell, yes, sign me up for more of that. I don't say this, of course. Instead, I give him the answer he needs.

"Yes, Agent Darnelle, you have my consent."

His lips purse, and a frown clouds his brow, but I don't think he's upset with me. A strange mix of concern and regret flits across his face. But he keeps his promise, and, with the tap of a finger, deletes the video.

"Feel ready for the couch?"

"I think so."

He leverages his shoulder beneath mine and helps me to stand. My legs wobble, and my knees threaten to buckle, but his arm is secure around my waist. Still, I'm like a colt taking its first steps.

We're halfway to the couch when I do ask that question churning in the back of my mind.

"Who do you know with the Sight?"

His footing falters, the muscles tensing beneath my arm, the grip on my waist tightening. If I hadn't been glued to his side, snuggled up right next to him—and the heat radiating off his body—I would've missed all these telltale signs.

"I'm sorry." I rush my words, because this really isn't any of my business. "It's not my place to ask. You don't—"

"Let's get you settled." He maneuvers me onto the couch. "Are you hungry? I can make us some lunch. Sandwiches, perhaps?"

My stomach is suddenly hollow and rumbles in response to the suggestion. *Loudly*, I might add.

"Sandwiches it is," he says, and the spark returns to his eyes. I—or at least my stomach—have provided a mission he can't wait to tackle.

"I think the bread is stale." I hate to admit it, but it's true.

"French toast, then. We'll have brunch."

"I don't have any syrup."

He waves away the objection on his way to the kitchen. "I'll improvise." At the threshold, he pauses, a hand on the doorframe. He gives me another look, this one full of challenge. "And then, perhaps, we'll talk."

CHAPTER 24
OPHELIA

King's End, Minnesota
Tuesday, July 11

If the Sight has an upside—and attributing anything positive to the Sight is a stretch, as Ophelia knows too well—then it's here, in the post-episode pampering.

And Henry knows how to pamper.

Even if he's a bit perplexed by Pansy's kitchen. As expected, he's inspecting the bread for any hint of mold. Satisfied, he moves on, locating the ingredients he'll need along with conducting a thorough inspection of the kitchen and the pantry.

He opens the refrigerator, extracting both the eggs and information.

"She's definitely here alone," he murmurs.

Not anymore.

He crouches to examine the bins and lower shelves. "Nothing." He sighs. "How does she even cook?"

Pansy Little doesn't cook. She forages.

Henry turns as if he can hear the sound of her voice. A shockwave rumbles through her. Sometimes, during these loops, when they're this close, Ophelia believes he can sense her. Other times, she's convinced it's a cruel trick of the Sight. Even so, she's greedy for these moments, no matter how false they might be.

He gestures to the mostly empty shelves. "It's appalling. Does she spread ketchup on bread and call it dinner?"

With a shake of his head, he shuts the fridge and turns toward the pantry. This space is in better shape. Jars and bottles line the shelves. What isn't store-bought is clearly labeled, complete with dates and ingredients. He selects raspberry preserves, some confectioners' sugar, but his hand hesitates when it reaches the rack with the various tinctures.

That one. She uses that one after an attack like this.

He'll ask anyway. Henry always does. Ophelia doesn't bother to follow him down the hall. It's a quick, efficient question and answer. Yes, true to form, he's back and busy brewing tea and beating eggs.

The brunch spread grows in both substance and sophistication. Enough fresh fruit for a decorative platter. A mix of spices and vanilla for the French toast. He tilts his head, considers the confectioners' sugar.

"You know what?" he says, and it's almost like he's consulting her. "I think I'll make a glaze."

Careful, brother mine. One of the ways to Pansy Little's heart is definitely through her stomach.

Still, Henry loves to cook, always has, as far back as she can remember. It's a true passion, if a bit performative. But he'll have an appreciative audience in Pansy Little.

And Ophelia can't wait.

He returns to the front room triumphant, first with the tea, then with the spread. Pansy's eyes widen, her lips part, and Ophelia can tell the moment the aroma from the French toast hits her. Wariness wars with gratitude. She dips a finger in the glaze, brings it to her lips, and gratitude wins.

"I didn't think I had syrup."

"You didn't. I merely whipped up a glaze."

Pansy stares at him, expression bemused.

Yes. I know. He's my brother, and I love him, but the man absolutely overachieves.

"It's delicious. You really shouldn't have." She takes a bite, and the look of bliss belies her words. "But thank you, Agent Darnelle."

Henry has pulled up a chair next to the coffee table. He pauses in slicing a piece of French toast. "Henry," he says.

Pansy blinks in surprise.

"I think we can dispense with the formalities," he continues. "I'm not here on official business."

And you did spend half the morning in his lap.

"And you did spend half the morning in my lap."

Yes! Ophelia raises her hands in the air and dances about the space. Henry never disappoints. There it is, the patented Darnelle deadpan delivery. Is he flirting, ladies? Or merely stating fact?

Pansy halts, fork halfway to her mouth, her eyes lit with curiosity. She's waifish, sitting cross-legged on the sofa, hair still loose and spilling around her shoulders. Those thick, dark lashes flutter. Not a single hint of mascara, *dammit*. But then, Pansy is more than practical, and who on earth would bother with smoky eyes while defending King's End from a horde of Screamers?

"All right, Henry." His name emerges with a lilt. An invitation? No, not yet. Because Pansy is her mother's daughter, and there are *rules* about men from the Enclave.

"You haven't asked me about what I saw," she says.

"It isn't any of my business."

Henry believes that with all his heart, with all his righteousness. He never once forced Ophelia to repeat what she saw—only if she wanted to, only if the confession would help lessen the Sight's hold. As incapacitating as these episodes can be, they are, in their own perverse way, an extension of the Sight's self-preservation instinct. This is something Ophelia knows far too well. After all, what could be worse than a Sight-induced coma?

The monster who put her into one.

"I think it might be your business," Pansy says. "It took me to the past. I saw the funeral."

"The funeral?" Henry's fork lands hard on his plate. The sound clatters too loudly in the quiet space.

"Your father's."

Henry exhales, and Ophelia feels as if the wind's been knocked from her. Her heart pounds, and she must be setting off all the monitors. In fact, she can feel the drag back to that bleak, sour reality, to the hospital bed in her shadowed room in Seattle.

Her greatest regret—other than not being able to save Henry in the end—is this. She was already comatose when Harrison Darnelle started hospice care. There was no comforting and supporting Henry then, no sitting at his side during the funeral, no fiercely protecting him from every last asshole in the Enclave and their so-called sympathy.

She left him alone. If things play out as it seems they must, she won't have the chance to ask him for his forgiveness.

But Pansy seeing the funeral? Is this new, or has Ophelia simply not been paying attention like she should? It's more fun to relish the sweet moments between these two opposites, who are, nevertheless, so well suited for each other.

The Sight attacks, and Henry swoops in like a knight in shining armor. Ophelia cheers on the sidelines while frantically trying to connect with Henry. She always hoped that, as siblings, she could connect, that sometimes she does, and it isn't a cruel trick, it isn't pattern recognition from those endless, endless loops. She wants to believe that his knowledge of the Sight, and of hers in particular, is the best chance of doing so. Their best chance of changing how things end.

What if she's been wrong all this time? What if, Ophelia wonders, it's Pansy.

The Sight unclenches its fist around her mind, because there are only so many scenes she's allowed to see in The Last Days of Henry

Darnelle, a highlight reel, if you will. But as the images swirl before her, Ophelia vows to try anything, to do all she can. If this truly is the last time she'll witness these events, then there's nothing to lose.

She'll be back. And God help the man who put her here in the first place.

Ophelia will fight him every step of the way.

CHAPTER 25
PANSY

King's End, Minnesota
Tuesday, July 11

Agent Darnelle—or, rather, Henry—hasn't responded. His expression is remote, and perhaps he's back there at the cemetery, reliving those moments.

And I am so, so sorry.

"I don't know why it showed me that," I say. "The Sight can be cruel"—certainly, in this instance, it is—"but it often has a reason, too."

"Yes." His sigh is heavy. "I know."

The scene will linger now, like a memory, one I won't forget anytime soon. I hear the hiss of insidious gossip, feel the patter of rain against my cheeks, the sting from the Screamers. I want to ask why everyone there was so inept, so blindsided by the attack. Well, everyone except Henry. Before I can, he speaks.

"My sister, Ophelia."

"What?"

"You asked who I know with the Sight."

"She's on some sort of research sabbatical, right?" I'm curious about what she's doing, and if it involves the Sight. I suspect it does. When he raises an eyebrow, I add, "When you came to town, I maybe took a look at your profile."

This earns me a half-smile. "I'd expect no less." But his expression is far too grim, his French toast grows cold on his plate, and his eyes hold the look of a man who has endured far too much in too short a time.

"What happened?" I ask, and then immediately follow with, "You don't have to tell—"

"Ophelia's talent is extraordinary. She's had the entire workup done. Her Sight is one of the strongest in decades, maybe a century." He holds up a hand, although I'm not about to interrupt. "Present company excepted. Although, I don't suppose yours has been measured."

That it has not.

"She was collaborating with R&D, enhancing the tests for the Sight, creating additional, advanced training—"

"Already deployed?" I ask.

"Yes, in part. I may have also woven a few of Ophelia's personal training routines into your exam, out of curiosity. I take it you noticed."

Oh, that I did. "I probably missed a few, what with the Screamers and all."

"I want to apologize for that, for not being on my guard, and I want to apologize for provoking you this morning and triggering an attack—"

"You didn't provoke an attack—"

"I know the Sight is all about self-preservation, and I was being a bully—"

"You were upset, but I wasn't afraid of you. I told you. It's been a couple of years, and I've been fighting this off for a while. I honestly think it was my mother's condolence card that did it."

"Which would still make this all my fault."

It strikes me then. He wants this to be his fault. He wants the guilt. He wants to pay penance. I consider the man across from me. The façade of a legendary field agent. Posture impeccable. Dark eyes unfathomable. Even now, I have the sense he's still on alert, ready to catch me if the Sight strikes again. It won't, but what does hit me are those insidious, whispered words.

... you heard about Ophelia, didn't you ...

"What happened to Ophelia?"

"She was working on a special project, something that might allow a real-time relay of the Sight."

I turn that over in my mind. "Do you mean like projecting our visions so others can watch?"

"In a sense, although they've been using a conduit who can see what the Sight is showing Ophelia and relay that information. Or at least, that was what the project was investigating."

This is the most asinine thing I've ever heard. Having the Sight constantly knock against your mind and then invade is one thing. Inviting someone else inside for the show? The notion burns in my chest. I want to smash something, if not for me, then for Ophelia.

"It's not like we're Netflix. Or lab rats." I want to add that what the Sight shows us isn't always true or important, except it can be both. The Enclave, in particular, would want a front-row seat to the future. Instead, I say, "Everyone can wait until we wake up."

When Henry doesn't respond, those whispered words double back and thwack me upside the head. Oh, no. Oh, no, no, no. A moment later, my mother's warning rings in my ears: *All they will do is hone you into a weapon. When you are of no use, they will abandon you.*

"Is she in a coma?"

He presses his lips together, his mouth a thin, grim line. He gives me a single nod that has me scrambling. I stop short of placing my hand on his, but I ease from the couch and lean across the coffee table. The scent of cinnamon swirls with the sorrow, and the air is heavy with both.

"I'm so sorry. I should've guessed, and I didn't mean to—"

"I believe you did guess."

"Only because the Sight made sure I overheard something at the funeral."

Henry shakes his head. Oh, he knows, even if he didn't hear the words himself. "Enclave gossip strikes again. The situation is, as you can imagine, supposed to be private, not to mention highly classified."

That's never stopped anyone in the Enclave from gossiping. This, I suspect, would not have surprised my mother. "Steeped in ambition, avarice, and malice," I murmur.

He raises an eyebrow at that, and from the twist of his lips, I can tell he agrees.

"Something my mother always said about the Enclave," I add.

The silence in the front parlor is complete.

Yes, I used the past tense. Yes, something about Henry's confession is prompting one of my own. I don't know where to start, but I think of my mother's final to-do list.

In the coming months, you'll need to break some rules.
Trust that you'll know which ones.

But in explaining about my mother, I will need to explain about King's End. I will need both of her lists, because I'm about to break a major one:

Trust no one from the Enclave.

I'm braced to stand, ready to unearth the lists from their hiding place, when the ring of a cell phone shatters the silence.

CHAPTER 26
HENRY

King's End, Minnesota
Tuesday, July 11

Professor Reginald Botten either had impeccable timing or the absolute worst. Henry couldn't decide which, but he also couldn't let this call go through to voicemail. He answered, then stood to stretch his legs but remained in the room.

"My boy, I see you've checked out of the bed and breakfast. I hope that means you're ready to wrap up this little problem."

Of course. No doubt Botten had some flunky monitoring Henry's every move. He sent a wave of gratitude toward his umbrella for that reminder to go dark. If someone dug deep enough, they might uncover his flight to and from Seattle. He was counting on bureaucratic malaise—at least for the short term—to keep from having to explain that.

"Actually, I've accepted an invitation to stay with the Littles, and I thought I'd save the Enclave some money by doing so."

Next to the coffee table, Pansy jerked her head up, eyes wide with curiosity rather than alarm.

"Do you really think that's wise?" Botten asked.

What did Henry think? Well, for one, the woman across from him deserved to know what the Enclave had planned for her. He held a finger to his lips. When she nodded, he put the call on speaker.

"I think that's the best way to go about it. I'm enjoying Rose's company. You were right. She and my father were close, and she has any number of stories to share."

The tense silence that met this proclamation was delightful. Whatever Botten wanted in this scheme, whatever he was after, this was certainly not it.

"My boy, I must insist you wrap this up immediately."

"Do you, now? I recall you needing my expertise in all this, my discretion. I can hardly arrive in town one day, fail Pansy the next, and then retire the entire family line on the third."

But, of course, that was exactly what Botten wanted. Henry could sense the man's impatience along with his malice, to quote Rose Little. Pansy's lips formed a tiny o, both of astonishment and under-standing. Umbrella in hand, she pushed to her feet and tiptoed around the coffee table, completely ignoring the emphatic shake of his head.

He jabbed a finger at the couch. "Sit down," he mouthed.

"I'm fine," she mouthed back and headed from the room.

A quiet thunk came from the hallway. Henry's heart rate kicked up a notch, but it was only the sound of her umbrella joining the others. Yes, yes, he wasn't her keeper. Certainly, she knew her limits after an attack better than he did. Nevertheless, he shadowed her into the kitchen, his phone balanced on his palm, his free hand ready to catch her.

"Perhaps you're not the agent for this task." Botten's words were mild, but a threat lingered beneath the surface.

Pansy glanced over her shoulder at this before slipping into the pantry.

"Perhaps you're right." Henry craned his neck, peered into the space, but she was merely kneeling and rummaging through some items. She was close to the ground and safe for the moment.

"Please, find a replacement," he continued, his focus back on Botten. "I'll take that offer of a desk job at headquarters. In fact, I will pack my things and fly back tonight." Henry paused for a beat and then added, "After I explain the situation to Rose, that is."

Henry knew this much: Rose Little may have opted for a permanent post in King's End, but she wasn't without influence. Even assuming she didn't have any allies on the High Council—extremely doubtful—she knew where all the bodies were buried, including those Botten himself had put into the ground. The photographs his father had left him indicated as much.

"You asked for my discretion and my finesse in this situation," Henry continued when Botten didn't respond. "I'm giving you that. If you expect me to stay on temporarily, good relations with both Pansy and her mother are crucial. Besides, I think Pansy has some latent skill. Perhaps all she needs is a bit of additional mentoring."

Pansy emerged from the pantry, something clutched in her grip. Her expression, both incredulous and amused, nearly had him laughing out loud. As it was, he threw her a wink. A hint of pink touched her cheeks, and she peered up at him through her lashes.

And he nearly forgot about Botten on the other end of the call.

Shut it down, Henry.

Botten snorted. "Your optimism astounds me. By all means, if you think it will smooth the way with Rose—"

"I believe it will."

"Very well. Do check in more often, my boy." Botten ended the call, as he did all his calls, without a goodbye.

In the quiet that followed, the air fairly crackled with expectation. It was static against his tongue and a buzzing in his ears. He'd put it all out there. For this woman, this stranger, really. He'd chosen her over the Enclave because it'd been the right thing to do.

At least, he hoped like hell it was. Pansy stood across from him, her gaze taking in his full measure. Henry wondered what she saw, what she sensed about him. At last, she let out a sigh and pushed her hand through her hair, securing the strands with a ponytail holder.

"Remind me never to play poker with you."

Then he did laugh, throwing his head back, loud and long until finally Pansy joined in as well. From down the hall came the rattle of all three umbrellas in the stand.

"More tea?" he asked once he could pull a full breath. He felt lighter, as if a stone had been lifted from his chest.

"Let me—"

He pointed to a kitchen chair. "Sit."

Instead, she lifted her chin and crossed her arms over her chest. "So, you really did come here to fire me."

"The Sight—?"

"I didn't invoke it or anything." She shook her head, then raised her gaze toward the charming tin ceiling.

Ophelia would do that, as if the Sight were something constantly looming in the air above them. In his sister's case, at least, perhaps it was.

"It was more of a nattering in the back of my mind," Pansy added.

Henry could almost see it, another—perhaps more callous—version of himself, someone motivated by promises Botten had no intention of keeping, his "paperwork problem" chief among them.

"That was the gist of the assignment, yes."

"And then you would stay on as a permanent post agent?"

"Not *permanently*, no."

Pansy glanced away, and he had the distinct impression she rolled her eyes. Then she turned back to him, her expression filled with incomprehension.

"Why?"

"I can't tell you because I don't know why. All I do know is, the Little line has already been earmarked for retirement. I had hope that your mother could shed light on this situation, that it had something to do with the photographs my father left me."

There was something devastating now in her posture. Again, the impression hit him. Pansy was here, all alone, and had been for a while.

"Can you tell me where your mother is?" He kept his voice low, coaxing, but already she was shaking her head.

"I can't tell you where she is." From her pocket, she removed a couple pieces of paper, torn from what looked like a yellow legal pad. "All I can tell you is what happened."

CHAPTER 27
PANSY

King's End, Minnesota
Tuesday, July 11

Before I can tell Henry Darnelle anything, he insists I sit. Perhaps he's right, about that and the tea. The cup warms my fingers, the liquid my stomach, which has been churning in an icy ball ever since he put Professor Botten on speaker.

With care, I spread both lists on the kitchen table, turned so he can read them.

1. Never go into the housing development after dark.
2. Never go to the silo alone.
3. Never go to the covered bridge, period.
4. If the Enclave makes an offer, remember they always require something in return.
5. Trust no one from the Enclave.
6. When someone tells you they're not betrothed, don't believe them.
7. The Screamers don't fight fair; you shouldn't either.

To my darling girl:

1. For as long as possible, do not report my "death" to the Enclave. I owe them nothing, and they'll find out soon enough.
2. Have a funeral anyway.
3. If Adele hasn't arrived, call her. (I suspect she'll arrive.)
4. In the back corner of the pantry, you'll find the necessary supplies.
5. In the coming months, you'll need to break some rules.
6. Trust that you'll know which ones.
7. Always know that you are loved.
8. Lastly, memories are precious; keep them close.

I tell him briefly about my mother's last months, about hospice. In his eyes, I see the lingering sadness.

He nods, purses his lips, and says, "Yes. My father, too."

Again, I want to reach for his hand, but I hold back.

Then I tell him about the morning my mother vanished: the strange light, the screech of music, the man who came to take my mother away. She must have known him; after all, she didn't fight, didn't beat her fists against his chest, not that she had the strength. In fact, she looked content in his embrace. If not for me chasing after them, I think she would've been completely happy to leave.

"I thought he was taking her to the housing development, but they vanished into the silo instead."

"Is the silo like the housing development, then? Do you tend to it?"

I shake my head. "There's nothing to repair. It just sits there and is wrong."

Henry nods thoughtfully.

"Have you ever heard of such a thing, Agent Darnelle?"

He raises an eyebrow at me.

"I mean, Henry." His name feels soft and forbidden against my lips. And? If I'm being honest? Absolutely wonderful. So I ask again, "Have you ever heard of such a thing, Henry? Of people vanishing like that."

"It's not unknown."

"So strangers from other..."

"Dimensions," he supplies.

"Strangers from other dimensions pop in and abduct random people."

"I'm only guessing here, but I don't think this was random or that the man was a stranger, to your mother, at least."

He's right. "How come I've never heard of this before?" This is important information. You'd think they'd cover this sort of scenario at the Academy.

"It's classified."

Oh. That's why.

"The eyewitness accounts we have are suspect, at best," he adds. "The official stance is that, in theory, it could happen, but it's doubtful it does. I suppose the line of thought is that the knowledge might be more harmful than helpful."

Unless you're the one being kidnapped. "Puts a whole new spin on alien abductions."

He snorts a laugh. "I suppose it does."

While we've been talking, Henry has been smoothing the wrinkles from the lists. He has fine, strong hands, the sort that could land a punch or perform a piano concerto. On his left ring finger, there's a pale swath, the color a hint lighter than the surrounding skin. I wonder if, in addition to losing his father, he's suffered other losses as well.

"And Adele is?" He taps number three on my mother's final list.

"My neighbor, my mother's best friend."

"The woman with the little dog?"

I nod.

"And possibly the same woman I debriefed yesterday?"

Regret leaves me with a huge sigh. "Yes, that too."

"She knows a great deal about the Enclave."

After yesterday, I'm starting to suspect Adele knows more than I do. "She's lived here all her life. Really, things are different in King's End. Everyone understands." I wave a hand in the general direction of the neighborhood. "Even if they can't tell you, exactly, what it is they understand."

"I imagine life is different for a permanent post agent. Perhaps, in some ways, more difficult."

Henry pushes back from the kitchen table, contemplating the space in front of him. He doesn't stand. It's as if he simply needs the extra space to think.

"I'll be honest," he says. "I'm not certain what to make of all this. I'd hoped your mother could shed some light on the situation. Something was obviously important enough for my father to leave me those photographs. I had it in my head that he wanted me to come here."

I pull in a breath and tell Henry what Adele told me: all about that fateful patrol, his father's injury, the strange, curse-like inability of either of them to talk about it, the mysterious third agent who never returned. My words are slow, hushed, and I'm careful not to embellish anything Adele said.

"We both thought it sounded like a curse from a fairy tale," I add when I reach the end.

"Hm. That it does." His eyes hold a knowing look, and I think I've stumbled into more classified information. But he doesn't elaborate.

Instead, he asks, "Adele doesn't know who that third agent was?"

I shake my head. "She didn't remember ... no, I'm sure that's not right." I stare at the ceiling, Adele's words just out of reach. She said something else, something that, at the time, didn't register. But now I realize it sounded odd. My eyelids flutter shut.

"Pansy." Henry's voice is a low growl. "If you're invoking the Sight—"

Damn. My eyes fly open. I catch a single drop of blood on the back of my hand, my pulse thrumming in my ears.

"Grab my wrists."

Without question, he does. His grip is strong and sure and not the least bit overbearing. He is an anchor in a storm, and I navigate my way back to the present, the Sight tucked away, locked down. I can't afford to deliberately invoke it so soon after an attack. That might put me into a coma.

I pull in a breath and gently ease my hands from Henry's. "I'm okay. It's locked down."

He's shaking his head, not in disagreement but in what looks like admiration. "Your ability to lock down the Sight is truly extraordinary."

"But what Adele said feels important."

He raises an eyebrow. Yes, that's a trick of the Sight, no doubt. It might be important, but chances are, it would only serve to incapacitate me. The Sight doesn't give without taking, and I've truly had enough of it today.

"Perhaps, but it's something we could check," Henry says. "If an agent died or vanished here in King's End, that information will be in the archives. I'll run a search. We can take this one step at a time, and we can do it without interference from the Enclave or your Sight."

That doesn't sound easy. Neither are the next words I'm going to say.

"What were you going to do? Back in Seattle? With my report?"

He refills his teacup and then mine as if we're two old acquaintances having a chat. "I was going to draft it first, send it to you"—he clears his throat—"and your mother, and then file it with the Academy to close out your record there."

"And what were you going to do when whoever earmarked the Little line for retirement saw that report?"

"I would deal with those repercussions when and if they occurred." His statement is so mild, so benign.

I'm not naïve when it comes to the Enclave and the High Council. My mother made sure of that. While the Academy is, officially, for training, it's also for networking, building relationships, currying favor with those destined to sit on the High Council, generally the old families, but not always. I'm currently staring at a man who will assume his father's seat on that High Council, providing he plays the right sort of games.

My examination report is not the right sort of game. Or rather, it is, as long as he abides by the predetermined outcome.

"You could lose your job."

He gives a cavalier shrug. "Doubtful, but Enclave politics being what they are, possible."

"I can't let you do that. They might revoke your umbrella."

From down the hall comes another rattle from the stand. I suspect it's my umbrella, rather than Henry's, and she's ready to take on the entire Enclave.

"And I can't file a false report. I cannot and *will not* lie for someone else's agenda. I simply won't do it."

He won't. I don't need the Sight to tell me that. Here's where Mort is wrong about Principal Field Agent Henry Darnelle. Does he follow rules? Oh, absolutely, but not when they contradict his true north.

"When do you need to file the report?"

"You heard Botten. The sooner, the better. But I figured I could give myself a week to finesse it, call in some favors, speak with a few of my father's colleagues on the High Council."

Translation: Henry Darnelle is not completely without friends and influence. But it might not be enough.

"Let me put it plainly, Pansy. I dislike being manipulated. I dislike the abdication of responsibility. And I will not be a party to it."

There's a low, growing warning in his voice, one that goes beyond mere anger. I would not want to be on the receiving end of that, and I almost pity the person who will be.

"A week," I say, although now I'm simply musing out loud. "Do you think that would give us enough time?"

"Time for what?"

"To figure out what happened all those years ago? Maybe see if it has something to do with this so-called retirement. I mean, you already told Botten you're staying." I wave a hand around, indicating my kitchen and the entire house. "Can't you draft your report here as well as Seattle?"

"Yes, but—"

"So why don't you?"

His gaze drops to my mother's lists, still on the kitchen table. A sly grin lights his features. "Perhaps break some rules?"

"Why not? I've already broken a couple."

He gives me a thoughtful nod. "We might be able to dig up some additional ammunition for my report."

Honestly, I think he might mean ammunition in the literal sense. "Okay, then," I say, because even if he doesn't mean actual ammo, I like having an ally. "There's plenty of extra bedrooms upstairs. Take your pick."

"Oh, I couldn't." He shakes his head now, a full-on refusal. "I only said that to needle Botten."

Well, yes. *Obviously*.

"I couldn't impose," he continues. "I'll see if the bed and breakfast still has my—"

"It's summer. They won't."

"Well, I certainly can't stay here."

"Why not?" I glance around my kitchen, seeking out any apparent flaws. Really? What's wrong with here?

A blush flashes across those razor-edge cheekbones. Oh, does the man have cheekbones. His hand goes to the knot in his tie, but he's already loosened it. He actually squirms in his chair.

"This may sound old-fashioned," he says at last, "but won't your neighbors talk?"

My neighbors? Talk? I probably shouldn't show him that thread on Hey Neighbor. "Have you met my neighbors?"

"I can't say that I've had the pleasure."

I try not to roll my eyes at that—try and fail. "There's nothing they like better than to talk. You'll be doing them a huge favor."

He doesn't respond. Again, those dark eyes are unfathomable. If he's waging some sort of internal debate, I can't tell. But I have a confession that I hope tops any of his objections.

"Besides," I say, and I'm surprised at how tentative my voice is, "I wouldn't mind the company."

His gaze alters, and those gold flecks in his irises spark into something molten, like whiskey under flame.

"To be honest," he says, his voice soft, "I wouldn't mind either."

"Then?"

"I'll stay, but I do have one condition." He stands, pulls open the refrigerator door, and gestures—a bit wildly—at the shelves. "I simply can't live like this."

FIVE MINUTES after I told my new roommate about the Tuesday farmers market, we had our first fight.

He can't go alone; he simply can't. Everyone will charge him double as an out-of-towner. Yes, he insisted on not only cooking but completely restocking my kitchen as well. I finally won him over by asserting that I am no one's hot house flower or damsel in distress.

Also? King's End is *my* territory, and I'm the full-fledged field agent in charge.

This is why I'm upstairs, deciding what to wear. I can't go down-town in a blood-stained shirt. Well, since this is King's End, I can. Me, wandering around with blood splatter, would not alarm the locals.

But clearly, he expects me to change. Can I insist he pull on some jeans and a T-shirt as well? No, no, I cannot. He is Henry Darnelle, Principal Field Agent, and he will dress like Henry Darnelle, Principal Field Agent. Even in small-town Minnesota in the middle of July.

So I veto the T-shirt and jeans option for myself, along with the comfy yoga pants. Never mind the farmers market; the moment we emerge from the house together, everyone will start talking. I might as well give them something to really talk about.

This is why I step down the staircase in a pair of black cigarette pants, a pink sleeveless top with a Peter Pan collar, and a high ponytail with a coordinating ribbon. No, I don't quite match the full regalia that is Henry Darnelle (complete with ridiculous hat), but I won't look too out of place at his side.

When he catches sight of me, a smile blooms, one that pinches those two dimples.

"You look very fetching."

"So do you," I say, although I'm not quite sure what he means by that word.

In response, he merely laughs. But he sobers, those dark eyes filled with concern. "Are you certain you feel up to this? The Sight—"

I hold in an impatient sigh. "Actually, I haven't felt this good in ages." There's something cleansing about an attack, especially when you have an expert caregiver in its wake. "I don't even have a headache. You have some seriously magical fingers."

The silence that greets this proclamation is prolonged and deeply uncomfortable. The phrase hangs heavy and awkward in the air, and the blush hits me before I can fully register what I've said. Yes, those aren't words anyone should speak outside the bedroom or, possibly, an operating theater.

"Hm. Yes. So I've been told."

His words are so mild, and I can't bear to look him in the eye, so is he flirting? I may never know. I shove my feet into some sneakers —black, with pink laces—grab my umbrella, and hope my blush will fade by the time we reach the farmers market.

On the front porch, he offers me his arm like an old-fashioned gentleman. "Shall we?"

I take that arm, and there's something so steady and sure about him. It's not like we're holding hands or anything. This move is practical. We could, if needed, whirl into a defensive position, unfurl our umbrellas, and fight off an ambush.

As it is, it lets us talk. Because *Agent* Darnelle has a lot of questions, of a practical nature.

"I'm curious about how you've managed this particular situation. Is your mother still collecting a pension?"

"She took a lump sum when she retired and invested it. It's in a trust, under both our names. Well, just mine now."

"My father wasn't officially retired, but he did much the same with his own assets."

"She bought private health insurance as well, so she wouldn't have to use the Enclave's." That I did cancel, because talk about expensive. "The house is paid for, and in my name, and all our accounts were joint accounts. She started setting this all up after I turned eighteen and came back from my last summer at the Academy."

His gaze touches mine, that thoughtful, scholarly expression in his eyes. "She clearly had a plan."

"Right up to an urn with fake ashes."

He exhales. "Interesting."

It is, now that I look back at it, and it's making me feel foolish for not asking about the rules that ran—and still run—my life.

"I know it sounds odd, like I never questioned anything, but it was just—"

"The water you swim in," he finishes. "As it is for all of us. Most of the time, Enclave rules save our lives, or at least make our jobs easier. But then there are times when..."

"They don't?" I suggest.

"Or perhaps the rules are..." He pauses as if he can't actually say *wrong* in relation to rules. "Detrimental. It's possible another agent might not have questioned the fact that your family line was already earmarked for retirement." He peers at me now. "Because why would the Enclave make a mistake like that?"

"But *you* did question."

"And I can imagine a time when I wouldn't have."

Oh, the chagrin in his voice, the self-recrimination. I wonder how close I came to losing both my job and my umbrella. She trembles in my grip, but the sensation is filled with reassurance. That big black behemoth on Henry's arm inflates its canopy, just a bit, also in encouragement.

We've reached the downtown and the pedestrian mall that holds the farmers market. It's crowded today, mostly with locals. Off to the west, clouds promise an afternoon thunderstorm. Above us now, the sky is that brilliant blue. Everything smells ripe and earthy and warm.

But it's Henry's grin that delights me the most. It's full of boyish wonder at the bounty of King's End. He turns to me, and his expression is filled with a wistfulness that makes my heart squeeze.

"This is truly a marvelous little town." He gestures with his umbrella, and for a moment, I see King's End through his eyes. The cobblestones and stalls, the quirky little storefronts selling everything from groceries to hand-thrown pottery to vintage-inspired clothing.

"It must be quite comforting to have such a home," he adds.

I'm not sure those words are meant for me, but I reply anyway. "Most of my friends couldn't wait to leave."

"The water you swim in is perhaps not as enticing as somewhere else." He considers me now. "Where shall we start? I'm in your hands."

Several highly inappropriate responses stream across my mind. With a tremendous amount of willpower, I choose none of them.

"I have an order to pick up," I say instead and point to Matilda's stall. "We can start there."

Of course, that means introducing Henry Darnelle to Matilda and anyone else we might meet. I give him a quick once-over: umbrella, suit, ridiculous hat.

"If anyone asks," I say—and they will, oh yes, they will—"You're one of my friends from camp."

"I've already established that at the bed and breakfast."

Oh? "Really?"

"It's the conclusion Carrie jumped to." He hefts his umbrella again. "I thought it best to let her."

It's not that people in King's End don't carry umbrellas. I cast my gaze toward the sky above. They tend not to on days like today.

"She seems to be under the impression that the Academy is..." He clears his throat but doesn't continue.

"More fun than it actually is?" I may have embellished a few things. Although I didn't have to try too hard. True, summers there were brutal, but we were teenagers, all hormonal and highly inventive.

Now he laughs. "Yes. That."

Matilda greets me with a hug and raised eyebrows. I introduce Henry as a friend from camp and garner a look so skeptical that I'm certain no one will believe this. Jack and Mort, sure. They're well known in King's End. But Henry is clearly a few years older than I am. He is certainly far more pulled together than I could ever hope to be. He has no reason to be here.

But he slips into the conversation as if he does, kneeling to pet Tiny, who is losing her mind over this new admirer, complete with tail thumps and drool.

"I was in the Twin Cities for some business when I remembered Pansy lived out this way." He gives that cavalier shrug and a grin that reaches his dimples. "And since I can work remotely, I thought I'd drive out and surprise her."

"I didn't recognize him at first," I add. This is really the worst explanation, but Henry runs with it.

"Well, it has been several years." He gives Tiny's belly a final rub and stands. "And I finally grew into my nose."

Then he gives us one of those sexier-than-it-has-a-right-to-be winks.

Matilda laughs, and when Henry glances away, whispers, "Oh, I *like* him."

With Matilda's seal of approval, I decide I can allow Henry Darnelle to wander around the farmers market and everything will be just fine. So I do, telling him that if he spends more than twenty-five dollars at The King's Larder, delivery is free.

"I am definitely spending more than twenty-five dollars," he assures me.

"Denisha's delivering today, so nothing will be crushed, either," Matilda adds.

Then I simply watch Henry make his way from stall to stall, conjuring net bags from somewhere to hold all the produce he's buying. Matilda raises an eyebrow at this as well.

"He plans to cook," I tell her.

"Oh, honey, *let* him."

He knows who wants a handshake, who might like a fist bump, and who would prefer not to be touched, thank-you-very-much. He visits every stall and leaves smiles in his wake. Matilda tracks his progress into The King's Larder and then pulls out her phone.

"I'm letting Denisha know to stop by here."

"I can take my things now."

That skeptical look returns. "Honey, you already have your hands full."

She's right. I do. I get a sloppy kiss from Tiny before heading off to see just how much of his own money Henry is spending at The King's Larder. I'm halfway across the pedestrian mall when a drop of rain hits my nose.

The sky is still that brilliant blue above me. I wipe my nose, and it comes away red. Another drop hits my cheek, cool against my sun-warmed skin. Hairs on the back of my neck prickle, and my mouth fills with static.

I spin. Yes, the view directly above is still blue and cloudless. But out to the west, a storm is gathering. The sky is that sickly green everyone in the Midwest associates with tornados. I blink, getting a sense of what this is, and what it isn't.

More raindrops pelt my face and arms, nonsensically since the storm hasn't reached us yet. Tendrils extend from those clouds as if they plan to grab the earth and tear it apart. The sickly green is peppered with flashes of ruby and sapphire and emerald.

Those are Screamers, and I've never seen them do this before.

I'm not sure how they've cooked up a tornado, or even why. But the storm is something everyone can see. Already, the crowd streams toward the storefronts or their cars. Merchants rush to cover their stalls. Parents are lugging their children from the play structure and into the relative safety of the bandstand.

I remain in the middle of the farmers market and unfurl my umbrella in time to deflect the first assault. The Screamers rush past, a token effort to harass me. I turn to find Henry at the door of The King's Larder, his own umbrella in hand. He scans the sky behind me, and then his gaze meets mine.

I read concern in his eyes but certainly not panic. Everyone else is panicking, including poor Tiny, whose claws are scrabbling against the cobblestones in her attempt to bolt. But not Henry.

Instead, he merely walks to the center of the pedestrian mall as if he has all the time in the world. He unfurls his umbrella, sends a single pulse into the air, and closes it. Then? Then, he runs.

It's the same Pied Piper maneuver he used at his father's funeral. The Screamers coalesce, those smaller tendrils merging into a larger one. As a single unit, they give chase. Their aim is Henry, and they want nothing more than to destroy him.

For an instant, I'm frozen with both shock and fear. This is his signature move, I realize. This is what makes Henry Darnelle, Principal Field Agent, so damn good. A flash of Sight tears through my mind. I lock it down—fast and hard—but not before it sears a path through my thoughts.

Maybe not today or even tomorrow, but some day this signature move will end Henry Darnelle.

CHAPTER 28
OPHELIA

King's End, Minnesota
Tuesday, July 11

Blood, Ophelia thinks, somewhat sourly, only makes Pansy Little look fierce. Ophelia's own bloody noses cause her eyes to water. Between the tears and the blood, she has all the presence of a big crybaby after someone's bopped her on the nose.

Not Pansy Little. She races after Henry and the mass of Screamers intent on his destruction. Her foolish, foolish big brother who can draw the Screamers to him and away from everyone else. Only his skill as a fighter has kept him alive this long. He savors the fight with a relish that borders on addiction. Does he know how close he came to that in the Sahara?

He leads the Screamers to a remote part of the green, well away from the families huddled in the bandstand and the few couples hunkering down beneath the bridge. He'd lead them away from Pansy as well, even raising a hand as if to send her back to safety, but she's having none of that.

Instead, Pansy tucks, rolls, and then stabs the main column, fracturing the Screamers into two smaller funnel clouds. One for each of them, Ophelia thinks. How egalitarian.

This time, when Henry holds out his hand, it's to help Pansy to her feet. She whirls around so they stand back-to-back in a defensive posture, sheltered by the protective bubble their umbrellas create.

She twirls her umbrella, and the ruffles splinter a counterattack into tiny shards. These Screamers hobble away from the melee like crows with clipped wings until they shatter into mist. But those two columns merge again. And again, they're intent on Henry.

The Screamers whirl, picking up bits of leaves and grass, painting the air a livid green. Anyone watching might think an actual tornado has targeted her brother, and they wouldn't be wrong, not entirely.

He's still sending out that pulse. Above the roar of wind and the shriek of the Screamers comes Pansy's voice.

"Stop it!"

He won't. Ophelia isn't sure her brother *can* stop it, or himself. He's a born protector, and denying him this would be to deny him his very essence. Pansy pushes a palm across her cheek, smearing more blood. If this fight weren't so dire, the Screamers so insistent, her aggrieved expression might make Ophelia laugh.

I know. He's a pain in the ass sometimes.

Pansy blinks, her gaze canvassing the area, ear turned toward where Ophelia is hovering. It's at that moment the Screamers see their advantage and stream through a momentary gap between the two umbrellas. The force throws Pansy wide. She goes tumbling across the green. The wind picks up her umbrella, still unfurled, and spirits it away.

Damn, damn, damn.

Despite the tiny triumph bubbling inside Ophelia—Pansy heard her, she's certain—she's made things worse. Pansy must chase after her umbrella; she has no choice. This is not an attack to counter with bare hands. She grabs fistfuls of muddy grass and pulls herself to her feet.

She glances back at Henry, who stands in the middle of the green, legs braced, umbrella open, shielding everyone from the onslaught.

Go. You can't help him otherwise.

This time, Pansy doesn't even blink. She dashes after her umbrella, racing for the embankment near the bridge, chasing a group of Screamers as they batter the umbrella so hard the polka dots blur.

The river, of course, is their destination. Ophelia's heart seizes. Her pulse skitters, and her breathing becomes erratic. What has she done? What can she do except witness her mistake? Once the water grabs Pansy's umbrella, it's over.

And while, in theory, an agent can function without their umbrella, Pansy's heart will break. They'll need to contact the Enclave. And keeping the Enclave as far away for as long as possible is the goal in all this.

Ophelia is ethereal here, insubstantial. At least, she's always assumed she is. An observer, not a participant. And yet? Pansy heard her. And earlier, back in her bedroom, Henry's umbrella heard her as well. Ophelia is certain.

So now she focuses all her attention on that clever little pink and white umbrella.

Stop. Fight back. She needs you.

The umbrella tumbles, spilling over the edge of the river walk. With a puff, the canopy folds. The next time the Screamers crash into it, that clever and cunning little umbrella uses the momentum to shove her point into the sand on the river's bank.

And sticks the landing.

Pansy scrambles to the water's edge, feet slipping on sand, and scoops up her umbrella. She holds it to her chest. Now there are tears, just a few. And yes, they only serve to make her look even fiercer.

Together, Pansy and her umbrella climb the embankment and set their sights on Henry again. Before they rejoin the battle, Pansy raises her chin, her gaze on nothing and everything.

"Thank you."

She sprints toward Henry and the fray, the determination in her expression enough to chase the Screamers from her path.

Back in Seattle, Ophelia's cheeks are damp. Her heart rate, her breathing, both are normal. The healthcare aide is no doubt dozing, the nurse possibly reading a novel. Ophelia is alone, for once, except for the soft whisper of her umbrella, tucked away in the doll house. And since she's alone, for once?

She lets herself cry.

CHAPTER 29
HENRY

King's End, Minnesota
Tuesday, July 11

What reassured him more? Pansy back at his side? Or the palpable relief that flowed through his umbrella? He couldn't say, but at this moment, it didn't matter. In front of them, the funnel cloud wavered, colors splintering. They could fight this battle of attrition—that's all it was now—or they could have a little fun.

Henry opted for fun.

"Follow my lead," he said, close enough to her ear that a few strands of hair slipped against his lips. He caught a coppery hint in the air. While her blouse was blood-splattered, her nose, at least, wasn't actively bleeding. Henry took that as a good sign.

Casually, he collapsed his umbrella and stepped away from Pansy, as if he were tired of this fight. The Screamers, sensing an opening, streamed past. He feigned a stumble and let the hat topple from his head.

The hat tumbled over itself and landed several feet away with a solid thump. He nodded toward it in silent command.

Pansy's eyes were wide, but she didn't hesitate, and followed the hat's trajectory. When she was clear, Henry stood up straight and popped the collar of his suit coat for extra protection. Now he absolutely had the attention of every last Screamer in the vicinity.

Their screech reverberated through the air, made the ground tremble beneath them. He lumbered forward, sending out that pulse, adding a limp, allowing a few hits. After all, a predator doesn't expect impervious prey. Show some weakness. Let the Screamers drive you to your knees. You might be big, but you're weak-minded —the best kind of prey. Bring them in close. Even closer. Yes, like that. Now, hold out your hand for mercy.

Not that the Screamers ever allowed for mercy. He was on the ground now, grass against his cheek, the earth damp beneath him, hand outstretched. Waiting, waiting, waiting for the right moment, waiting for Pansy.

Then, it came. A whirring sliced through the air and cleaved the congregation of Screamers. He couldn't help but smile. Pansy's timing was uncanny. A second later, he caught his hat with that outstretched hand.

He rebounded to his feet, flinging the hat from him frisbee-style. The hat spun and sent out a pulse that acted like rotors. Pansy leaped, caught the hat, and sent it back his way. They continued the game, each pass decimating the horde until the very last Screamer vanished into the ether.

From across the green, Pansy smiled at him, her hair billowing about her, the blood on her face more triumphant than grim. Henry could taste the sweetness of the air after a storm, the flavor that meant everything was safe and secure.

So he wasn't all that concerned when the ground met his knees, even less when he rolled onto his back. He stared up at the brilliant blue sky and decided to bask in a job well done.

Henry wasn't quite certain when or how Pansy came to be at his side. Or, more accurately, resting next to him, her head on his chest, his hand in her hair, a slow caress of strands through his fingers. Perhaps she'd scooted there so they could talk more easily. Perhaps he inched closer, wove his fingers through her hair to coax the last vestiges of the Sight from her mind. For those were there, just under the surface, although certainly not as intense as they'd been earlier that morning.

But however it happened, he wasn't about to give up that delicious weight and warmth on his chest and the hair that slid like silk against his skin. This was not, admittedly, the most professional of after-action reviews. It was, however, one of the more enjoyable.

"I heard something. No, *someone*," she was saying in answer to his question. He'd been curious about what had occurred, not accusatory, and Pansy hadn't taken it that way. "It was the strangest thing, like someone was talking to me."

"The Sight?"

"Not exactly. Not my Sight, anyway."

Not *her* Sight. Interesting. "Do you remember what they said?"

"They called you a pain in the ass."

Henry coughed out a laugh. Only Ophelia ever called him that, to his face, at least.

Only Ophelia. He wanted to dismiss that as a coincidence, because certainly it was. And yet? He shut his eyes against the bright blue, tried to focus, but his thoughts scattered. King's End was too real: the grass tickling the back of his neck, the scent of earth, of sweat, and something sweet, perhaps Pansy's shampoo.

"Anything else?" he prompted, opening his eyes.

"They told me to chase after my umbrella, that it was the only way to help you."

"A reasonable thing to say and do."

"Then it was like they could speak to my umbrella as well." Pansy shifted and pulled her umbrella closer. "She almost went into the river. I thought I was going to lose her."

"But you didn't," he soothed. Even so, his heart thumped in response, and he clutched his own umbrella closer as well. It trembled in his grip as if it, too, were imagining the scenario.

"This has never happened before," she added.

"Hearing voices?"

"Hearing them like that, yes. But also, this." She waved a lazy hand in the air. "I've never seen the Screamers do this before."

Most likely because King's End was—officially, at least—a level one hot spot. Screamers only manifested extreme weather in a level five hot spot. But that was something to investigate later.

"Also?" she said now. "I take back everything I thought about your hat."

He laughed again. "Yes, it's more than a mere affectation."

"But it's absolutely that as well."

"Perhaps," he conceded. "But a fairly marvelous one."

Around them, King's End was coming back to life. Children shrieked with delight, their footfalls pounding on the play structure. Chatter rose from the farmers market. The sun was approaching that golden hour glow, and Henry could almost ignore the reason they were lounging here on the green.

Almost.

"When we arrive home, I'd like permission to download the data from your umbrella."

"Of course."

"And I'd like to make a small adjustment. I want to hold off sending anything significant to headquarters." He paused, considered how to phrase this next thought. "For the short term. Until we have a better sense of what happened in the past and what's happening now here in King's End."

"Something's happening now?"

Abductions? A possible level five hot spot? Henry doubted the list ended there. "Your mother, for one," he said. "And today. Not normal for King's End, correct?"

"Not normal." She exhaled. "But at the same time? Not all that surprising. King's End is different."

"I'd like to figure out why, and I'd like to do it with minimal interference." True, he'd have to placate Botten with a few check-in calls, invent some sort of faux mentoring curriculum, as if the woman at his side needed remedial training.

"All right." Another exhale, this one filled with relief. "I agree."

"There's an override in case anything catastrophic happens. Automatically notifies HQ and triggers a response team."

"Good to know."

"I rather hope it won't come to that."

Pansy rolled, hair slipping from his fingers. She peered at him now, eyes bright with mischief. She pinned him in place with that gaze. He couldn't move even if he wanted to.

And Henry didn't want to.

She gave him a conspiratorial smile. "We'll just have to make sure it doesn't."

CHAPTER 30
OPHELIA

King's End, Minnesota
Tuesday, July 11

They should hurry. Ophelia knows they should hurry—ticking clock and all. They need to sober up after this latest encounter, analyze data, examine those photos, contact Adele.

Instead, they're acting punch-drunk. Like newly minted agents after their first face-off with Screamers in the field. Henry staggers and ends up taking a knee, planting a hand on the soggy grass. There, beneath his palm, is a sodden pink ribbon with white polka dots. He threads the ribbon through his fingers. Then, in a gesture that's both deliberate and absent-minded, he slips the ribbon into his coat pocket.

Henry stands and stumbles again. This time, intentionally, Ophelia is certain. Because a moment later, Pansy clutches him around the waist to keep him from falling. As if Principal Field Agent Henry Darnelle didn't walk out of the desert under his own power.

You're so transparent, brother mine.

They stagger from the green and then home only to discover that the kind citizens of King's End have delivered not only the groceries but also all of Henry's produce in those reusable net bags.

Then there's tonight's dinner: Guy Gunderson's famous quiche, salad from the farmers market, and strawberry shortcake from Emma's Bakeshop. Not to mention the flowers, a large bouquet of stunning summer blooms to set the mood.

No wine, because they know Pansy doesn't drink. But the last name Darnelle is familiar enough—as is the set of the jaw, the noble brow—that they've tucked in a bottle of Harry's favorite scotch.

The citizens of King's End may not understand, exactly, what it is Pansy does and what her mother before her did. But they know she is key to their prosperity, this little oasis of a town. They want her to be happy. And for the last several years, happiness has been well out of her reach.

In this loop—this endless, endless loop—Ophelia has gotten to know the denizens of King's End. Those of Rose's generation—the Gen-Xers, if you will—remember the bad old days. They don't view the past with nostalgia or through glasses tinted any color.

They remember the slow and inexorable slide into misery: storefronts boarded up, the dwindling school attendance, lack of healthcare and jobs, the drinking, the meth, the flight of anyone who could leave King's End. For those who couldn't? See above: the drinking and the meth.

They remember the old farmhouse at the edge of town, the one rented to a parade of disgruntled, uncaring, and downright surly types. One would arrive in town only to speed away twelve to eighteen months later, their penance paid.

As Enclave lore went, you had to have done something truly scandalous (or, let's be real: legendary) to land your ass in King's End. It's where the Enclave sent you to dry out, shape up, repent sins.

You did your time, and, if you'd cultivated enough contacts on the High Council, garnered your next field assignment. For the unlucky and unconnected, the other option was riding a desk at headquarters. What you didn't do, at least not in King's End, was care.

Rose Little cared. Rose Little cared so much that she bought that dilapidated farmhouse on the edge of town. She refurbished it and the yard and threw parties the likes of which weren't seen outside of Minneapolis.

She tamed the Screamers, not that the residents of King's End called them that. These were ethereal beings, after all. They went by other names: bad vibes, bad luck, bad air. All of which infected King's End and, without constant vigilance, would overrun it.

But Rose was vigilant. So the boards came down along Main Street. Small businesses flourished. A community college sprang up, and with it, an influx of students and cash. The weekend tourists came next. King's End attracted the quirky, the artistic, the outside the mainstream. Their small, diverse community blossomed like no other town in the state.

Then, five years ago, they nearly ruined all that. No one listened to Rose when she told them not to break ground for a new housing development: not her neighbors, not the town council, not the Kingston heirs who owned the land (and reaped a tidy profit).

When Rose fell ill, everyone in King's End held their breath, afraid that this rose-tinted prosperity might vanish along with the woman who'd somehow granted it.

But then Pansy returned from her last summer at camp, pink and white umbrella in hand, an expression of utmost determination on her face.

Now, there's an uneasy truce. Everyone knows something lurks down the road from that formerly dilapidated farmhouse. Everyone knows one small woman is all that stands between them and another downward spiral. Everyone knows the center can't hold, but no one knows when it will break.

Except Ophelia.

Ophelia knows this as well: Rose unearthed the secrets of King's End, those buried in strange places and deep within its ground, and she paid a terrible price for doing so. If Ophelia could name those secrets, she would. She would focus all her willpower into whispering them to Henry or Pansy, because those secrets matter.

But she can't. And tonight, she can't penetrate the bubble that surrounds the two of them, bathed in pink fairy lights. Pansy dozes on the sofa while Henry sits in a wingback chair, feet resting on a low stool, a glass of scotch, neat, at his side, ostensibly crunching data on his laptop.

Ophelia might even buy the act if it weren't for the one-sock-on, one-sock-off situation. Besides, he's spending more time glancing up, taking in Pansy's form on the couch, and smiling to himself than doing any actual work.

Do you really think now is the time to play house?

Normally, he wouldn't let himself dream of such a thing. A house. No, a *home*. With someone who can call him on his bullshit. And if ever a man needed someone to call him on his bullshit, it's Henry.

Ophelia's heart is sore from battering against her ribs. She can't help but want this for Henry, too. He deserves this. But this right here, this gauzy, wistful tableau? Its seduction is just as dangerous as the Screamers that emerge from the housing development.

And when Henry scoops Pansy from the sofa and carries her, bridal-style, to her bedroom? That tender expression as he tucks her in, then pauses at the doorway? That quick scan not of Pansy but of her surroundings, as if he needs to reassure himself that she is safe? And when he nods to himself, steps from the room, and shuts the door gently behind him?

That's when Ophelia knows he's a goner.

CHAPTER 31
PANSY

King's End, Minnesota
Wednesday, July 12

I'm not entirely sure how I ended up in bed last night. Fuzzy notions fill my head, ones of floating up the stairs. Since that isn't possible, I'm pretty sure Henry was involved. I'd ask him, except the thought makes my cheeks flame.

I'd ask him, except his umbrella is missing from the stand. Mine is slumped to one side, utterly despondent, ruffles sad and deflated.

"Want to do some yoga?" I ask her.

She does not.

On the other hand, that red-rose umbrella is all puffed up, looking unduly proud of herself. She's been taking her chaperoning duties far too seriously. I pluck her from the stand—under protest—and carry her upstairs to my room.

On the way, I tell her, "Sometimes you have to let children make their own mistakes." Which is something I overheard my mother saying to Adele when I was sixteen.

Was it a mistake? It involved a boy. So, at least in part, it no doubt was. I haven't thought of Daniel in ages. The last I heard, he was at Oxford as a Rhodes Scholar, one more achievement in a long list of them. The only thing he hasn't done is return to King's End after leaving seven years ago. His family moved not long after he graduated early from high school. Really, he doesn't have a reason to return. Even so, the Sight insists he will someday, with a leggy Italian model in tow.

But then, the Sight is just perverse that way.

In the kitchen, I find the space transformed. The contrasting gold and blue from sunflowers and delphiniums fill the space with joy. On the table sits a strategically placed and overflowing fruit bowl.

Someone—me, perhaps, although I don't remember—tacked the note from The King's Larder on the fridge.

Dinner is on us! Enjoy!
Guy and Milo

Guy and Milo own The King's Larder, although Guy is officially retired. Except for all the extra time he spends on Hey Neighbor, you wouldn't actually know it. He's as busy as ever at The King's Larder, as the quiche from last night proves.

Coffee is in a carafe on the counter, with a clean cup next to it. The French roast mingles with the scent of flowers and the hint of sweetness from the fruit. The kitchen smells like someone lives here rather than that same someone simply existing.

How Henry managed that in less than twenty-four hours, I'm not sure.

I'm on the back porch, in the midst of a downward-facing dog, when a pair of running shoes enters my field of vision. Next, I spy some high-end track pants and one of those fancy, sweat-wicking shirts.

What do you know? Henry Darnelle *can* dress for King's End.

There's a healthy flush to those cheekbones and a sheen of perspiration along his brow. I'm certain Henry Darnelle never actually sweats, not even in the Sahara. He has his umbrella strapped cross-body. From inside, a rattling comes from the umbrella stand, the noise loud and insistent. I send my umbrella a quick *told you so* and then ignore her.

"Good morning, Agent Little," he says. "I hope you're ready for your training today."

My training? I land with a thump in table top, the wooden slats beneath my yoga mat creaking.

He's holding his phone in the palm of his hand and continues to speak as if I'm not actually in front of him.

"I've completed the daily patrol of King's End. Screamer activity is negligible. The fissures Agent Little and I repaired on Sunday continue to hold. However, there are pockets of discontent that will make for some excellent remedial training opportunities."

Remedial training?

"There are a few hairline fractures in the old part of the cemetery as well. We'll be able to refine her mending technique with those. I've attached a lesson plan, and I have every confidence Agent Little will complete these tasks satisfactorily."

Oh, will I, now? I'm not exactly sure what to make of this. His tone is officious. He's channeling that schoolmaster persona but hard. I'm about to show him how I feel about remedial training—with a well-aimed downward dog—when Henry adds:

"I'll send another update on Friday." He taps the phone's screen and tucks it away before giving me a full-on grin, one with dimples and a mischievous glint in his eyes. "That should keep Botten off my back."

"Are there really pockets of discontent and fissures in the cemetery?"

"None that I detected. However, it lets us roam King's End and stream some innocuous data to headquarters. I'd like to break a few of your mother's rules. I have a good sense of the housing development, so I'd like to explore other areas."

"How did the fence look this morning?"

"Intact."

"Huh." I consider that. After yesterday, I was planning an all-day field trip, certain I'd find the fence shredded.

"Out of the ordinary, then?"

"I repair the fence nearly every day."

"Even in the winter?"

I nod. Yes, there's nothing like working with metal in sub-zero windchills.

"That sounds miserable," he says as if reading my thoughts. "And something to look into, but for today, I thought you could show me the silo or perhaps the covered bridge."

"Silo, yes, but I'm not sure where the bridge is."

He raises an eyebrow.

"Apparently, I wandered there when I was four and almost fell into the river. I don't remember that part, but I have it in my head that I was looking for my father." That's the extent of my memories, and the Sight has declined to show me anything about that day. "I sometimes think my mother left that one on the list because it was so ... so..."

"Terrifying," Henry supplies.

I exhale and nod. Even after all these years, I hate having scared my mother like that.

"Perhaps we'll start at the silo, then," he says, "and figure out where the bridge might be later. Someone in King's End must know, right?"

I give him a blank look; I know I do, because a slight frown creases his brow.

"Don't they?" he prompts. Again, he's curious, not accusatory. He genuinely wants to know what's going on in King's End. For that matter, so do I.

"I don't know." I feel so stupid when it comes to my own back-yard. How can I not know these things? "I'm sorry. It's just that King's End is—"

"Different. Yes, I'm starting to understand that. In any case, we can make a plan over breakfast. Blueberry pancakes?"

"You don't—"

"Blueberry pancakes it is."

I'm about to protest, again, when Matilda's refrain of *Honey, let him* whispers through my mind.

Instead, I say, "Thank you."

He rubs his hands together as if he simply can't wait to tackle this next chore. "Excellent."

He takes the stairs two at a time. He's full of boundless energy, and it strikes me that this is a much different man than the one I met on the green a mere few days ago.

It strikes me that I'm different, too. That, in some way, he's helping me stitch my life back together. I send out a wave of gratitude and get one in return—from my umbrella. She's been reunited with Henry's. Now that they're alone? She's about to commence with some serious canoodling.

Shameless thing.

WE'RE NEARLY DONE with the pancakes when Henry's cell phone rings. Annoyance flashes across his face, and I'm certain it must be Professor Botten, no doubt calling to encourage Henry to fire me.

But then Henry's eyes go wide. "Excuse me," he says, stands, and heads for the back porch.

I catch a murmur of, "Is everything all right?" before the screen door clatters behind him.

The dishes beckon. Actually? Eavesdropping beckons, but I do not let my ears or the Sight stray toward the back porch. By the time I have everything rinsed and stacked in the dishwasher, Henry returns. He appears sober, and perhaps a bit puzzled, but not bereft.

"Is everything ok—" I begin.

"Someone broke into my house last night," he states as if he can't believe it himself.

"Broke in?" I echo, and the air is filled with static. I give my head a good shake to chase it away.

"Nothing was stolen, at least, not that Cameron can tell." Henry starts to pace now, from pantry to sink. He even opens the dishwasher as if to check my work. I suspect he simply needs to think.

"Cameron?" I ask.

"The butler."

Wait. Henry Darnelle has a butler?

"Or rather, my father's butler and housekeeper," he amends and then pauses. "And his companion these last few years. Cam's really more of a family friend. He keeps an eye on the place when I'm away. He's a comfort, and I saw no reason to turn him out after my father died."

Because Henry Darnelle is a decent person.

"Anyway," he continues, "whoever it was, they tore apart the study and even broke open the wall safe. Although that's the extent of the damage."

Okay. Butler *and* a wall safe? Who is this man?

"Wall safe?" My words come out with a squeak.

He must catch my bemused expression, because his own softens, and he manages a chuckle. "Yes, a wall safe."

"Is it behind a painting?" I ask, because I can't help myself. My head fills with images of a well-appointed study, book-lined shelves, imposing chairs near a hearth, and lots of gleaming dark wood. I can absolutely picture the man across from me sitting in a space like that.

"It is, actually, and at least they didn't damage that. Or steal it. Although its only value is sentimental. According to Cam, there may have been a note inside the safe."

"How does he know?"

Henry halts in his pacing and pulls out his phone. He brings up the photo app. The first picture shows a crumpled piece of stationery and envelope. Both are tossed on a floor strewn with so much paper that only hints of the carpet peek through. The next picture shows the note up close. On rich, creamy stationery are a few lines in precise, black script.

Really, my friend,
Do you suppose I'm as foolish as all that?
H.

"Your father?"

"Yes, that's his handwriting."

"Are you going to call the police?"

"No forced entry," Henry says, and the words come slowly and with some reluctance. "Whoever broke in had access to the alarm system or the security codes. So that's either myself or Cam, or..." He trails off, comprehension lighting his features. "Or possibly someone from the Enclave, because the codes would be on file there, as an emergency backup measure. Wellness checks and that sort of thing."

"So, no police, then."

"No. Besides, there was nothing of value in the study."

"Identity theft?" I suggest.

"Not even that. The cabinets were filled with references, resources, and all the notes my father made about his hobbies and nothing more."

I consider the papers, books, and magazines scattered across the floor. "He must have had a lot of hobbies."

"Gardening, bonsai, several different historical eras. He kept commonplace notebooks as well, not to mention the years of March Madness brackets, model railroad, coin and stamp collecting—"

"Did they take those?"

"Locked up. Anything of value is either in a safe deposit box or with the…" Henry trails off, his mouth slightly agape. I can almost see the thoughts swirling behind his eyes. "Lawyers," he finishes, at last. "Like the photographs my father left me."

"You don't think—" I begin, but we're both heading for the front room where he—oh so casually—left the package of photographs yesterday morning.

My heart thumps, and I'm certain the photos will have vanished. But they're still on the coffee table, tucked neatly away.

"I thought they might be a message." Henry sits down hard on the couch. "Or perhaps a nudge, my father's way of telling me to contact your mother. He was a man of few words, so this sort of thing wouldn't be out of character." He grips the package in his hands but doesn't open it. "My parents divorced when I was young. I spent every other weekend with him. All those hobbies? I think they started out as a way for us to connect."

Henry glances up at me. I've knelt opposite him, the coffee table between us. His eyes are dark with anguish. "Every other weekend, he'd show me how to do something. He taught me how to cook, how to make a three-point shot, even how to darn socks."

He eases the photographs from the package. "He was a solitary man. Unlike my mother, he never remarried. He was always so stoic, so dignified."

Much like his son? Henry's expression is a combination of bewilderment and embarrassment.

"I'm telling you all this so you can understand my confusion about these photographs."

He spills them across the coffee table, in an orderly fashion, mind you. Landscapes to one side, snapshots of people to the other. What strikes me, physically, is how young my mother looks. My chest constricts, and my eyes water just a bit.

The house, *this* house, is a disaster, as is the yard. The man at her side, who looks so much like his son, is helping her reclaim both. Yes, there's my mother, clad in a barely-there halter top and some short-shorts that are even more revealing than a pair of Daisy Dukes.

My mother. She is shameless. Not that Harry Darnelle seems to mind.

In a montage of photos, they're pulling up hideous shag carpeting, coating walls with fresh paint, and clearing the way for the garden. I wonder if it's Henry's father who's chronicling this transformation. It seems like a family trait.

Then, post-transformation, come the parties.

"Oh." I work to sort through these and put them in order, but honestly, I suspect it's one nonstop celebration.

"Yes. I *know*."

He sounds so chagrined, so pained by all this. Not that I blame him. I keep my gaze on the photographs in case he's too embarrassed to meet my eyes, or possibly vice versa. Okay, so there's nothing truly obscene in these photos. But there's the irrefutable evidence that our parents weren't always our parents. They were young. They had lives wholly separate from our own.

They were in love.

It's there in the way Harry Darnelle is looking at my mother in every single photograph and how her gaze reflects his. The look goes beyond infatuation. If someone stared at me like that, I'm not sure what I'd do. Run away? Or possibly throw myself into their arms.

"You have to understand." Henry pushes the photos around on the table as if he's trying to bring order to the chaos. "I never knew this side of my father. I never saw him this..."

Happy. The word clogs the air between us.

He pushes a picture my way. "Do you know what he's doing here?"

In the photo, colored lights brighten a dark corner, and Harrison Darnelle is master of his domain with two turntables and a microphone.

"It's called scratching."

Henry gives me a blank look.

"He's DJ-ing."

"My father."

"Apparently. And here." I tug another photograph from the stack. We've yet to examine even half. "He's proficient at air guitar, too."

"I simply can't reconcile this." Henry drops his head into his hands. "I don't know the man in these photos, and it's..."

Killing him. My chest constricts again. I, at least, witnessed my mother's parties, sneaking out of bed, peering through the stairwell railings, working to make sense of the gossip below. Grownup talk of sex and politics, the secret ingredient in Guy Gunderson's tater-tot hotdish, and the *extra* secret ingredient in his brownies.

I glance around at the walls Harry Darnelle helped to paint, the floors he sanded and refinished. This house is what it is due to him: his sweat, his care, his love. How much of him still lingers here? How much of Harry Darnelle did King's End steal?

"I'm sorry." The words escape me with a rush of guilt.

Henry raises his gaze to mine. "This is in no way your fault."

"I'm sorry for what King's End did to your father."

Something happened on that fateful patrol, something so catastrophic that it fundamentally changed Harry Darnelle. Something unspeakable, figuratively and literally.

"We don't know King's End is to blame." Henry's voice is both soft and mild. "I'm inclined to think it's not. More often, it's human interference, and even Enclave interference, that makes these situations worse."

"Like in the Sahara?"

He heaves a sigh. "Yes, exactly like that."

The notion has me returning my attention to the photographs. "These people." I push several pictures across the table toward Henry. "They're from the Enclave, right?" I've been so isolated here in King's End that I can't tell.

Henry slips from the sofa to kneel on the floor opposite me. "Not just the Enclave." His voice is contemplative. "It's a who's who of the up-and-coming agents of their day. Several now sit on the High Council, and the rest certainly hold sway."

"And they all came here to party with my mom?"

"It appears your mother turned a slap on the wrist into the place to be." His lips twist, and he gives his head a little shake. "It's what the Enclave does to their field agents for a variety of reasons. Burn out, transgressions, perceived insubordination, that sort of thing."

"So, working as a permanent post agent is a punishment." Oh, of course it is. I lift my chin and study him. "And are you being punished, Agent Darnelle?"

He laughs at that. "Probably. But I prefer to embrace the challenges the Enclave throws my way."

I point to a man I recognize, mainly because he spoke at my Academy graduation. "Isn't that—"

"The current chair of the High Council doing body shots with someone who is no doubt grateful to be anonymous? Why, yes. Yes, it is." He resumes sorting the photos, lining them up in a way that doesn't make sense to me but must have meaning for him. "I suppose if worst came to worst, there's always extortion."

"Really?"

He laughs as if this is just a joke but then sobers, considers, and adds, "Yes, really."

I cast the arrangement a skeptical look, but then I start pawing at photos, because other familiar faces appear in the crowded rooms, around the kegs, and on the back porch. "Look. Here's Milo."

"From The King's Larder?"

"Yes, and Guy, too." I shove more photos his way. "And Adele."

They all look so young. They look like us. Guy is a big bear of a man, but in these pictures, his face is still plump, his cheeks round and ruddy like a little boy's. The deep grooves around Milo's mouth have yet to make an appearance. Adele's hair is glossy without a hint of silver, fanning in an ebony arc as someone twirls her.

"Do you think they could tell us anything?" I wonder about that. Could we ask? *Should* we?

"Didn't Adele already try?"

"She did, but maybe she'll recognize a face?" I push to stand, to go grab my phone, but Henry holds up a hand.

He leaves the room, and his footfalls sound on the stairs. Moments later, he returns with something in his palm.

"Use this." He hands me a burner phone.

"Why, Agent Darnelle, you're full of surprises."

"Sometimes you have to break a few rules," he says, and gives me that sexy wink.

CHAPTER 32
HENRY

King's End, Minnesota
Wednesday, July 12

Pansy's description of the silo was apt. It did feel wrong. The sort of wrong that had Henry turning the dials on his equipment every few minutes, changing the sensitivity, gauging the quality of the air and soil.

Once or twice, he adjusted his umbrella, slung cross-body with the quick-release strap. Other than a soft tremble at the small of his back, his umbrella remained quiet.

He held up one of the photographs from that long-ago site survey. Decay was the first word that popped into his head. The structures were the same: the silo, the house, and, farther back, a stable with a corral. But unlike in the photos, everything was weathered and gray. The peeling yellow paint on the farmhouse looked diseased. The air in this space was dry and tasteless, without a whisper of a breeze.

"When was the last time someone lived here?" he asked.

Pansy shielded her eyes against the sun's glare, momentarily lost in thought. The dreamy look reminded him of Ophelia. Henry wondered, not for the first time, if those with the Sight simply had better access to memories.

"Five years ago or so, about the time they broke ground on the housing development. The family that was renting said they didn't like the noise, but"—she waved a hand toward the road and the development—"it wasn't just the noise."

He nodded. "Who owns this land?"

"Technically?" She cast her gaze toward him, and her eyes held a glint of amusement. "I do."

Henry lowered the photograph and stared at Pansy straight on. "Excuse me?"

"My mother bought it at the same time she bought the house. At least, I think she did. When she signed that over to me, this parcel of land came with it." She scanned the area again. "I keep thinking I should do something with it, but at this point, I'm not sure I could even sell it."

"Who owns the housing development?"

"The Kingston heirs owned the land, but who, exactly, they sold it to, I don't know. Some big development company, I think. Every once in a while, the town council talks about doing something, then they table the motion."

Yes, he could understand that. Both these spots were festering wounds. Henry pulled out another photo for comparison. And yet, these particular pictures didn't have that feel. But this was not his forte. He eyed Pansy. Asking her, a mere day after an attack? He shook his head and pulled out yet another photograph as if sheer numbers could make up for lack of expertise.

"You can ask me," she said a few moments later, her voice soft and inviting.

"Pardon?"

"You want me to do something, and I said you can ask me."

Oh, well, damn the Sight anyway.

"And it's not the Sight." She waved a hand at him. "You're all frustrated and twitchy."

"Am I, now? I beg to differ." He was about to launch into a lecture about seniority and protocol in the field and any number of things that would make him sound like a pretentious asshole. Meanwhile, Pansy merely stood there, her expression mild.

Henry heaved a sigh, not so much in defeat but in relief. To be fair, he was frustrated and twitchy, although he blamed the latter on the silo's looming presence. "I don't want you to invoke the Sight," he said, because yes, he wanted, *needed*, her opinion. "However, I would like your take on the disparity between the photographs and—"

"The here and now?"

"Exactly."

He handed her a photograph, and they stood side by side, arms extended, taking in the same view, comparing it to the same past. They remained like that until Henry could feel the tremble in his arms, the muscles protesting.

At last, she lowered the photograph. Then Pansy turned and met his gaze. That dreamy look had returned, and Henry swore he could almost see the past play out behind those dark eyes with their thick lashes.

"We know something happened," she said, her words cautious, as if she were afraid to chase away the wispy strands of the past. "But there's more to it. There was a before and after, and five years ago was just part of the after. This." She raised the photo. "Is the before."

He held out a hand. "Do you need an anchor to keep you connected to the present?"

Without a word, she took his outstretched hand. The connection zinged through him. Her Sight had the same force as Ophelia's, but its texture and essence were different. He could read King's End in her touch, but beneath that was something vast and unfathomable. It was like touching starlight, and the expanse nearly had him drawing his hand away.

How did she live with that?

"My mother," she said, her voice echoing that starlight. "And your father. And the other agent. They did something. It wasn't simply a patrol. It was intentional."

Those words, the ones he had spoken so casually over Pansy's coffee table, came back to haunt him.

More often, it's human interference, and even Enclave interference, that makes these situations worse.

"Can you tell what it was?"

"No. The Sight won't show me that."

Henry cursed himself. She was, perhaps unintentionally, invoking the Sight. He should've known better. Her Sight, like Ophelia's, was too strong to be flirted with like this.

"Yet," she added.

That single word felt like a death knell against his heart. He'd have to remain vigilant so the Sight wouldn't ambush her—and him—once again.

"And the third agent? Anything?" he prompted. They were already deep into this, might as well go all the way.

"I can see my mother and your father. You look like him." Pansy gave her head a little shake, her words so airy that Henry had to lean closer to hear her. "And someone else, a man, I think. It's funny, but I can't say his name, I can't describe him. It's like there's a veil shrouding him. He and your father, they both want something from my mother. It's a rivalry between them. Your father thinks it's friendly." Her voice turned cold. "But it's not."

Without letting go of Pansy, Henry knelt and rummaged in the messenger bag he'd dropped by his feet. He pulled one and then another photo from the envelope. At last, he held up a group shot. Nearly everyone who was anyone of his father's generation, all there, gathered around the backyard fire pit, Rose in the center, their undisputed queen.

"Was it someone in this photograph?"

Without hesitation, without a breath, without opening her eyes, she said, "Yes."

That was when Henry reeled her in, back to the present, the here and now, tugging her closer, willing her to look at him.

"Pansy, Pansy. Come back to me." He dropped the photograph and cupped her face in his hands, hoping the contact would help. "Let go of the past. You can't change it, so it has no right to hang on to you."

Her lashes fluttered. She gripped his wrists as if she needed something to tether her to this time and place.

"Are you okay?" he whispered.

"I think so."

"I apologize. I didn't think your Sight—"

"Don't. It wasn't your fault." She gazed up at him, her expression full of wonder. "That was amazing, having your help. I wasn't the least bit scared, and I could focus without having to worry about losing myself."

Her exhale was soft and sweet against his lips. For a long moment, they stood there, his hands still cradling her face, hers still gripping his wrists. Their breath mingled in the way it did moments before a kiss. And Henry wanted to kiss her, felt his mouth inch closer to hers, her chin tilting slightly. The promise of it was thick and rich, and he longed to indulge. But now wasn't the time, and here was hardly the place.

And yet, he couldn't admonish himself. No *shut it down, Henry* played in his mind. No guilt, although, really, that was warranted. But sometime between his father's death and now, he'd let go of so many things, Enclave rules and the prescribed track for his life in particular.

Even so, he took the first step back, gently, as if merely giving Pansy some space to breathe.

"Are you with me?" he asked.

She nodded. "I'm here."

Something stirred the photos he'd scattered across the ground.

The caved-in porch creaked, although the breeze wasn't strong enough for that. The wind barely chased the wisps of hair from Pansy's face. But it, or something, was strong enough to snatch those photos and whirl them around.

He swore, loudly. Pansy jumped, her eyes wide. A moment later, she dived for several flying toward the house. Henry chased down the others that were heading toward the silo, of their own volition, or so it seemed.

He grabbed for one, the group photo, and it felt shaky in his grip, as if invisible fingers were intent on plucking it away. He shoved it deep into a cargo pocket and secured the zipper. He pursued the other photos as far as the silo, catching a few before the rest slid beneath the door.

Pansy approached, a handful of photographs crushed against her chest. "Some went into the house, but I didn't think I should go in alone."

"Or at all," he added.

"Or that."

"What was your mother's rule?" he asked, working to catch his breath. "Never go to the silo alone? I'm beginning to understand why." He gestured toward the door. "Does this open?"

"It did three months ago."

Henry placed a hand on the door and shoved. The screech tore through the air, the sound inhuman. No, the sound *was* human. Somehow, that was worse.

Inside, no torn photographs littered the floor. No tiny rodent tracks. No cobwebs. Dust motes floated in the air, bathed in a light source he couldn't quite detect. Henry took one step back, then another, and slammed the door shut.

He surveyed the countryside. The hair on the back of his neck and along his arms prickled. The sensation of being watched flooded him, although he knew if he spun, he'd find nothing. Then his umbrella shuddered again, this time in warning.

"I think," he said, voice low and cautious, "that it's time we left."

THE HOUSING DEVELOPMENT didn't beckon. At least, that wasn't the word Henry would use. It did, however, tempt him in a way that was disturbing, much like that sandstorm in the Sahara. Still, no reason to venture past the gate. He already had readings from the day of Pansy's exam. The fence was intact. Besides, what he wanted was here, at the entrance, in this liminal space.

In the shadow of the Camelot Lots sign, Pansy helped him set up the equipment. With a little luck, he might be able to triangulate the location of the covered bridge. Some quick readings, and then they'd head home—or rather, back to Pansy's house.

Head down, he tweaked the settings and sent a few innocuous bursts of data to Enclave headquarters. Even here, at the entrance, it was too quiet. No birdsong, no hum of insects, but what felt like a breeze washed over them, full of dry static and stale air.

Then Pansy yelped.

Henry leaped to his feet. By the time he had his umbrella unslung, Pansy stood with hers at the ready. She used the tip to point toward the far end of the development, toward the fence that bordered the cemetery.

A hole had emerged there, distorting the chain-link. The gap was at least four feet tall and just as wide. Its jagged edge was like a circular row of silver teeth.

All the better to eat you with, my dear.

Through the hole, on the other side, was nothing. No headstones or ancient oaks, no lush green of the cemetery, nothing but an endless, gray expanse. The urge to investigate tugged at him. Because this phenomenon was worth noting, inspecting, studying.

Henry stepped forward only to have Pansy's hand come to rest on his shoulder.

"No," she whispered. "Don't."

He turned to look at her, but she was staring straight ahead, her gaze locked on that mass of nothing.

What had gone wrong in King's End, and why hadn't anyone reported these findings? Certainly, Rose Little understood. Those rules of hers were exact, if somewhat inexplicable. If what happened all those years ago cursed those involved, someone could have filed a report, no matter how vague. His father, for one. His father would never neglect duty in such a way.

Unless, of course, there was no other option.

The wind picked up, like a hand at the smalls of their backs, pushing them forward. Henry felt the rightness of it. They—no, *he*—needed to investigate. All he had to do was break contact with Pansy, get a running start, then he'd be there at the chain link.

Yes. Of course. It made perfect sense. The images swirled. He could almost taste the discovery. This would be a breakthrough. This would save the lives of agents all over the world. And he'd be the one to do it.

The buzz, buzz, buzz of a cell phone shattered these thoughts and pulled him into the present. Henry inhaled, his breath ragged, and yanked the burner phone from his messenger bag. His heart pounded, only now recognizing the precipice.

When he glanced up, the hole was gone.

Pansy, at least, had the presence of mind to answer the phone.

"Adele?"

The connection was scratchy. Pansy walked backward, away from the entrance and that menacing shadow cast by the signage. Henry followed, and once the sun was warming his head, touching his cheeks, he could finally pull in a full breath.

What the hell had just happened? He shook his head to clear the cobwebs and dreams of saving the world. He'd interrogate himself later. But now?

Now, he had a few questions for the woman on the other end of the phone.

"I'm working the swing shift," Adele was saying, the reception through the speaker still dodgy. "I just now got your message, but I can't—"

"You don't have to," Henry said and inched them even farther into the midday sun. The static faded from the line as both he and Pansy stepped across some invisible border. "I know there's an issue with speaking about that day, but what if we tried a process of elimination?" From his cargo pocket, he pulled the photograph of everyone gathered around the fire pit.

"I'll say a name," he added, "and you can tell me yes or no."

On the other end, Adele pulled in a shaky breath. "I'll try."

"Arthur Connolly?"

"No."

The word was firm, nonnegotiable. Henry felt himself sag with relief. Bad enough that the image of Ophelia's father doing body shots was burned into his retina. There was a small but definite comfort in the fact that the chair of the High Council was not that third agent.

"Misha Pulchenko?"

"No."

"Patrice Farmington?" he asked, although, from what they'd gleaned, the agent was most likely a man.

"No."

"Portia Worthington-Wells?

"No."

"Mortimer Connolly, Sr.?"

"No."

"Reginald Botten."

The silence on the other end stretched and stretched. At last, Adele whispered, "I can't say." Her voice was tight as if the words hurt.

Interesting. "All right. How about Rajeev Patel?"

"No."

Multiple times, he ran through the list, repeated names, mixed them up. He named every agent in that photo, even those he doubted were involved, like Anya Pulchenko, Ashwin Patel, and George Ling.

Then, when Adele's tone had calmed and her replies were automatic, he'd say:

"Reginald Botten."

Each pause was filled with the dread that surrounded the silo. It had the feel of that gaping maw in the fence. Adele's breathing would pick up, distinct through the phone's speaker. At last, as if the words cost her dearly, she'd utter:

"I can't say."

Henry glanced at Pansy, who stood stock-still and wide-eyed. If this was true? If Reginald Botten were the third agent? Henry supposed it would be one thing to go against the chair of the High Council, but Botten?

Reginald Botten headed up the Academy. He was the nominal director of R&D. He was also the undisputed—if unacknowledged—power behind the throne, the Enclave's kingmaker.

"It's okay." Henry kept his voice soft and gentle. He had enough to go on, and it was time to stop this. "You don't have to say."

"I can help, though," Adele added. "Pansy, you remember the code for my house?"

"I do."

"The room in the basement, the one with the keypad? Here's the code for that."

Pansy dug around in his messenger bag, pulled out a pen, and scrawled the number on the back of her hand.

"There's a notepad in there," Henry muttered under his breath. While Pansy didn't glance up, he was nearly certain she rolled her eyes.

"Inside, you'll find all your mother's files, notes from when she was in the field, notes about King's End, drafts of all her white papers—"

"Including the desert?" he asked, unable to help himself.

"Yes, all of it. Rose kept everything. And I kept it legible, organized, and safe. Also, Agent Darnelle?"

"Call me Henry, please."

"Henry." There was a tenderness in her voice that soothed the ragged edges of his soul. "I am sorry for your loss and for the deception the other day."

"I'm starting to understand why it was necessary."

"But I meant what I said about your father. He was truly one of the best men I have ever known. When we first met, I was so unsophisticated." Adele's laugh was warm with nostalgia. "But he was always so kind, never looked down on me. He encouraged me to apply to nursing school and then helped me find a way to pay for it. He taught me about wine, and I showed him how to crochet."

Henry shut his eyes. Never mind the photos. That, right there? *That* was his father. "He tried to teach me, but I never made it past the chain stitch."

"Also?" Adele's tone was light now, almost happy. "You'll find many of your father's field notes in the basement as well."

His eyes flew open. "My father left field notes?"

"There's a whole file cabinet drawer full of them. I know he'd want you to have them."

His father's field notes. Henry had seen precious few. Normally, the Enclave required agents to turn in all notes and drafts along with the final report or white paper. From a security standpoint, this made sense. But Henry often wondered how much was sanitized in those final drafts.

"And?" Adele pulled in another breath. "I'm afraid I need to get ready for work."

"Of course. We don't want to keep you." Henry considered the phone in his palm, the menacing view of the housing development, and the revelation about that third agent. "If you need to contact us, use this number."

Even after the goodbyes, he remained rooted in place. He needed to think, needed to figure out what this all meant. That third agent was the same man who had been at Ophelia's side when she slipped into the coma. He was the same man who had sent Henry here to conduct Pansy's field agent examination. He was no stranger to

King's End. Somehow, Botten sat in the middle of this web, weaving a pattern only he could see. One misstep might irrevocably entangle both him and Pansy in the strands.

Pansy's fingers lighted on his sleeve, the touch a mere whisper. "We should leave."

Yes, she was right. "We should." He wanted to wink, show her he was on an even keel, but couldn't muster one. Then again? He *didn't* need to, not with this woman, this wonderful and capable agent at his side.

So, when she offered her hand, he took it. Together, they walked back to the equipment and loaded it into the SUV.

And then they went home.

CHAPTER 33

OPHELIA

King's End, Minnesota/Seattle, Washington
Wednesday, July 12

Henry shouldn't be this happy, not under these circumstances. While it's true Ophelia can see him gnaw at the puzzle of King's End, a dog with one of those indestructible bones, her brother is content. Never mind the furrowed brow, the impatient hand through his hair. Henry loves to problem-solve. He truly believes there isn't a puzzle that can't be cracked with a little research.

The basement room is finished and cozy, lined with cabinets and bookshelves. On a low table, a makeshift tea service throws aromatic steam into the air. Add in the two overstuffed chairs and a desk, and it's the perfect place to excavate the past. Add in the woman at his side? Let's just say Henry's romantic daydreams run toward the academic.

Their umbrellas have already abandoned the pretext and nuzzle close together against the wall next to the door.

Henry is sitting on the floor, surrounded by piles of papers and notebooks meticulously annotated. Harry Darnelle was nothing if not thorough. Ophelia knows this: the desire to read his father's field notes must have made Henry's heart lurch with both joy and anguish.

"Oh," Pansy says. "What's this doing here?"

Henry glances up and places a finger to mark his place in the notebook he's reading. As always, he's on high alert, even though Pansy's tone is more curious than alarmed.

She tugs a cedar box from the bottom of one bookshelf. The lid is adorned with decoupage roses and pansies, with reds, pinks, and purples, a celebration of mother and daughter. The box is sizable, with enough room to store elementary school artwork and small photo albums, which, Ophelia knows, it does.

"It's my mother's memory box," Pansy tells Henry.

They stare at each other from across the room, and Ophelia can see the wheels turn in Henry's mind.

"Memories are precious—" he begins.

"Keep them close." Pansy finishes. "It couldn't be that simple." She places her palm on the lid. "Could it?"

Henry raises an eyebrow. "Maybe we should take a look."

Pansy lugs the box to the low table, but then there's the lock and no key. This isn't an issue for long. Henry has his messenger bag. From one of its pockets, he pulls out a set of lock picks.

He starts to work, and Pansy leans forward, clearly fascinated.

"More surprises?" she says. "I think I've misjudged you, Agent Darnelle."

"No." He meets her gaze, that deadpan delivery in place. "You haven't."

Pansy blinks, her cheeks flushing a delicate pink. Their faces are close, so close that they must share a breath. Henry forgets all about the lock pick clutched between finger and thumb. They've approached this precipice before, possibly more than Ophelia has witnessed. She is thankful the Sight has spared her most of these near misses.

Shut it down, Henry. Get back to work.

He does, although she's certain it's his internal compass that's guiding him rather than anything she's thought in his direction.

"I don't want to scratch the plate," he says and bends forward, intent on this task.

The lock is brass and not all that challenging. Someone with less finesse and patience will scratch that little brass plate and not care. But that isn't Henry. And that, Ophelia knows, comes later.

"Any idea what might be in here?" he asks.

Pansy shakes her head. "None. This was a mother-daughter sort of project. Maybe for Mother's Day? The King's End Community Center sponsors things like that. I remember, though, it wasn't long after my father died. So I must have been around four or five."

Inside is the expected artwork, and a collection of letters bound with a ribbon. The Enclave doesn't let cadets have phones during the summer. The only way to communicate with the outside world is by letter, and yes, those are routinely censored. There are several small photo albums, but Henry grabs the one on the top. He always does, as if some instinct is steering his hand.

He opens the album and is lost immediately. Pansy stays on task. Perhaps it's the Sight. Too much flirting with the past, and it might decide to take you there. Pansy only realizes Henry has stopped sorting through items when his low, amused chuckle reaches her.

"No," she says, her face stricken. "Just no. What do you have?" She holds out a hand, demanding the album. "The prom photos? Because if those are the prom photos—"

"So, who's your lucky escort?"

Pansy closes her eyes. "Can we not do this?"

Oh, but they *are* doing this. Henry is a dog with yet another bone.

"Really, it's delightful, and I'm just curious." His smile is disarming, the crinkles around his eyes deep and sincere. "I went to an all-boys boarding school. We didn't have dances, and certainly not a prom."

"No dances? Did you have any fun at all?"

"It was very academically focused."

Pansy glances away and rolls her eyes, her gaze on the spot where Ophelia stands. Although Ophelia isn't here physically, this exchange feels so intimate. It shoots through her with a force that surprises her. For a moment, Pansy hesitates, her expression full of wonder. Ophelia thinks Pansy might even stretch out a hand and test the air, but then she turns back to Henry.

"His name is Daniel, and he's a genius." Her tone clearly implies she wants to get this over with.

Henry raises both eyebrows at the proclamation. He's not through, not yet, not even close. He's always assessing the situation, and this one contains a potential rival. And not just any rival, but one who's a genius.

Be a shame if you weren't the smartest person in the room at some point.

Ophelia can't help herself. She flits over to Henry and peers over his shoulder. He's studying the photo from the prom's grand march, Pansy and Daniel at the apex of the bridge leading into the King's End Community College ballroom. Ophelia knows this story well and is mightily jealous of Pansy's dress: a strapless, 1950s cocktail dress, black, with polka dots—of course—and massive petticoat ruffles. Daniel is in a vintage tuxedo, complete with a top hat and cane.

Pansy, Ophelia suspects, has a thing for smart men in ridiculous hats.

Ophelia's about to get comfy when something tugs at her consciousness. Indeed, she was about to curl up in one of the over-stuffed chairs and listen as Pansy relates this tale of high school sweethearts—one that starts innocently enough and ends with Pansy nearly bleeding out.

That something is back in Seattle. That's a problem because Ophelia is very much here, in King's End. The plaintive cry of her umbrella reaches her. The small sliver of herself that remains in that hospital bed, the part of her mind that tracks her physical surroundings, knows something is wrong.

An exchange comes from the threshold of her bedroom. The nurse, arguing with someone, a man with a sonorous voice. Her mind seizes. Here, in this cozy basement, her form freezes. No matter that she's ethereal, and the laws of physics don't apply. She can't move.

The man overpowers the nurse, not physically, although Ophelia wouldn't put it past him. He takes a seat at her bedside and takes her hand in his. His palm is fleshy but not soft, and his grip is strong. This is a man who can still wield an umbrella, tame Screamers, and best most agents currently in the field.

If she could recoil, if she could slap, if she could spit, she would. All she can do is remain as she is, frozen in both realities. It's the worst sort of option: no fight, no flight, only freeze. From the doll house comes the involuntary shudder of her umbrella.

"Hello, my dear," the man says. "It's Professor Botten."

Yes, I know who you are. I know what *you are.*

"I'm wondering if you might be willing to share what's going on in here." With a finger, he taps her temple.

It sounds like a request and a simple one at that. It's neither. Botten has never peered inside her head. He doesn't possess the skills for it. He must rely on a third party, a conduit, who can describe the images in Ophelia's mind.

Botten turns, the sound of the chair scraping against the floor filled with impatience. "Don't just stand there. Come in."

"I'm ... I mean, Aunt Miranda isn't—"

Oh, that second voice gives away so much. Her mother must be out. While Miranda Connolly doesn't need to run errands (again, they have *people* for that), Ophelia knows the escape does her good. She hardly needs her mother constantly at her side. Until, of course, she does.

Like now.

Because that second voice belongs to Leah Connolly—her cousin, her former best friend, and the other person there the day Ophelia slipped into this coma.

Ophelia can admit now that it was the tedium that got to her, made her reckless, enticed her to play. She lacks Henry's focus, his dedication to even the most mundane tasks. Her research sabbatical was exciting at first. She was the star of the show, after all. It was all about her, and Ophelia loves when it's all about her. Besides, maybe, by sharing her visions, she could relieve some of the pressure of the Sight and keep it from spinning her into unconsciousness and despair.

Only weeks into her two-year-long commitment, she was bored. It was easy to invoke the Sight. Botten's gentle hypnosis lulled her in and out of sessions with a simplicity that was deceptive. And those first weeks he was gentle, was encouraging. Ophelia was a special breed and had every reason to be proud of her ability, or so he claimed.

It was easy to establish that Leah was the best conduit for her; they're cousins, after all, born three days apart. Twins, they called themselves, even though Ophelia is dusky, with the dark curls and birdlike bone structure of her mother. Leah is a golden goddess, blonde and blue-eyed like so many of the Connollys.

It was easy to establish that Leah could only convey what was in Ophelia's direct line of sight. The constant commands to turn one way, then the other, to walk the perimeter, look up, now down, with Botten's voice growing ever more impatient, began to wear on both her and Leah. Ophelia felt like a dog on a leash, tethered to Botten, her master in all this.

Research, Ophelia decided, was hardly her strong suit. She wanted to be back in the field, not a lab rat stuck in Seattle. She found herself wondering if the Enclave would even let her back into the field now that it'd been established that her Sight was so strong, so exceptional.

Was she condemned to this, then? If it wouldn't harm her Sight, might the Enclave crack open her skull, peer inside, and discern how it all works? Not for the first time did she wonder if that would be her ultimate fate.

So Ophelia started doing what she always does when she's bored. She played. Leah could only see what Ophelia showed her. Why not make her extraordinary Sight so utterly ordinary? Certainly, after a few months of that, they'd have no recourse but to send her back into the field. With some small adjustments, Ophelia became a master at the art of deception.

This, she realizes now, may have been her downfall. Or perhaps her salvation, such as it is. That first time she stepped into this loop, the Sight didn't show her the start—the scrape of chair legs as Henry stands—but events near the end.

The Sight is all about spoilers, after all.

Ophelia ignored the obvious signs of an Enclave task force, hastily deployed. Instead, she focused on those lovely things on the periphery. The cemetery with its ancient oaks and weathered head-stones; the fields, both cultivated and fallow. The breeze that stirred the leaves and kissed her cheeks.

She skirted the decrepit, cookie-cutter houses, the hideous sign above the gate, not to mention the gate itself. For all anyone—and by that, she means Leah—knew, Ophelia was standing in the center of a lush meadow, one filled with a startling number of wild roses.

It's taken her any number of those loops to realize it's this last detail that sealed her fate. Roses. Wild ones. And there's a connection to Rose Little that Ophelia can taste but can't discern.

It was then, with the mention of the roses, that Botten sent Leah from the room, ostensibly to fetch fresh towels, a cold compress, and some bottled water. The refrigerator in the lab was conveniently empty, those soft, Turkish-cotton towels nowhere to be found. Only the best for their star.

When Leah was gone, Botten's voice changed. He leaned in close, the coffee on his breath pungent and persistent. There was no escaping its stench. Even now, if she ever wakes, Ophelia swears never to drink coffee again.

"I know where you are, my dear," he whispered. "And I know *when* you are."

I doubt that.

"So you see why I can't let you return."

Only then did she truly see as she stood there in the center of the King's End housing development. She caught glimpses of familiar faces: Mortimer Connolly, Gwyneth Worthington-Wells, and many of her peers from the Botten's Best List. Everyone milled about the space, darted in and out of tents, walked the perimeter.

And then there was Henry. An angry purple bruise had bloomed beneath one eye. His cheekbones were battered, his lower lip swollen, and blood trickled from the corner of his mouth. Although he wavered, his stance was strong. Perhaps most frightening were the field agents—brutes, every last one—at his side, restraining him.

A moment later, Reginald Botten stepped from an air-conditioned communications van, his gaze on Henry, his face alive with a cruel smile. And Ophelia realized the Sight had shown her something irrevocable.

"Not that anyone will believe you if you do return," Botten, or at least, the version of him in Seattle, added. "Not even *Daddy* will. The Sight is *so* unreliable, and everyone knows that Ophelia Connolly acts out for attention. Any investigation will take months. And in the meantime?"

Botten let this question hang in the stench between them.

"In the meantime, your brother will be in the field. And you know how dangerous that is. Accidents do have a way of happening to even our most dedicated and resourceful field agents."

Even then, even with the threat to Henry's life hanging over her,

Ophelia was determined to do the right thing. She would emerge; she would tell Henry. He would believe her even if no one else did.

Except for one small thing.

She couldn't fight her way to the surface. Not without Botten's help, not without Henry's. Her brother was an ocean away. He'd never make it back in time. And Botten let her sink deeper and deeper, the Sight protecting her in its own way. Ophelia sometimes wonders what would have happened if Leah hadn't burst back into the lab with towels and water. If she hadn't flung herself over Ophelia, sobbing at this unexpected turn of events.

Would Botten have taken a pillow, covered her face? Or would that have attracted too much scrutiny? She doesn't know. This is one outcome the Sight has never shown her.

So now, Ophelia exists in this netherworld. If she emerges, Henry dies. If she remains, Henry dies. As for the world, there's no guarantee it will continue to spin no matter what she does. Except for the thing Botten doesn't know, the one thing he can't know.

He doesn't know that Ophelia has seen the future, or at least its many permutations. The future isn't nearly as threatening as the past. The past is certain. If Ophelia hasn't seen the past, then that means someone else will. That someone must be Pansy Little. Ophelia thinks: yes, Botten should be afraid of that.

But now he's sandwiching Ophelia's hand between Leah's. Ophelia's heart beats a cadence that must alert the nurse, but no one comes. Has Botten tried this before? She casts her mind through all those endless loops, certain he has. He's not a man to leave things to chance or grow complacent.

But he's never caught her here, in Adele's basement. She's never had to worry about what Leah sees and then relays to Botten. Ophelia casts about, but there's no safe place to rest her eyes, and Leah's connection worms through her thoughts, grasping and growing stronger. At the start of her sabbatical, Ophelia had the strength to kick her cousin from her head whenever it pleased her. Now?

Now, Leah's the one with the power to push past Ophelia's defenses. Her heart continues to flutter in her chest, wild and chaotic. She ignores Henry and focuses all her will on Pansy.

Can you hear me? I need your help.

Pansy raises her head, lips parted in a tiny o. She blinks as if that will help her see Ophelia and then nods ever so slightly.

Find something that I can look at, a photograph, an old one. Whatever you do, don't look at Henry.

Pansy abandons Henry mid-sentence. His mouth is open, ready to carry on the discussion. He looks taken aback, but his brow is wrinkled in concern rather than exasperation. Pansy crawls over to boxes that line the lower shelves and shuffles through their contents until her hands grasp several packets of photos.

Yes, those! Dump them all out.

By rote, Pansy does and spreads them across the floor. Ophelia scans them, hoping one will yield something she can use.

"What do you see, my dear?" Botten croons. He's always patient and charming at the start of a session.

"It's a jumble." Leah's voice has that faraway quality, half in her mind, half in Ophelia's. "It's a series of images, and I can't unscramble them. Maybe the Sight—"

"No, no. Keep going. It will resolve itself, I'm sure."

Ophelia's scrambling now, keeping Leah out and letting Pansy in, working to direct her. Then she spies something red. It's gorgeous and perfect.

That one. Pick that one up and hold it out in front of you.

Without question, Pansy does. Her arm doesn't even tremble. Must be all that yoga.

"Pansy, are you—?" Henry's there, hovering, ever protective.

And get him to shut the hell up. His life depends on it.

Pansy raises a finger to her lips. By some miracle, Henry obeys. He obeys without another word, without protest. If Ophelia ever escapes this loop, she swears she'll ask Pansy for her secret.

"Oh, a car," Leah exclaims. "Wait, no, it's a convertible, a red convertible. It's an old-fashioned one, but really sweet. I'd love a ride like that."

"What model?"

A long pause follows Botten's question. Really, he knows better and should be content that Leah can tell the difference between a sedan and a convertible. Asking her what kind of convertible is taking things a bit too far.

Leah's hands convulse around Ophelia's, an involuntary response full of fear and dread. Botten can lavish praise and condemnation in equal measure. Fail him one too many times, and you'll find yourself with the sort of shit assignment not even permanent post agents endure.

"It's all right, my dear." Botten is back to crooning. "That part doesn't matter. What else do you see?"

"A man. I think it's Henry Darnelle."

Ophelia's heart seizes and shrivels. She's certain her attention hasn't strayed from the photograph. Certainly, Pansy's hasn't. Her arm is still outstretched, still defying gravity. But it's possible that Leah caught a glimpse of Henry and has named him rather than the man in the photograph.

"God, he's *so* handsome. I always wanted to sleep over at Ophelia's and not the other way around, in case he'd be there."

Ophelia longs to roll her eyes at this but doesn't dare. A side effect of this connection is that Leah's ability to filter dwindles to nothing. Yes, she'll tell Botten what Ophelia sees. Leah will also recite every last thing she feels about that.

"Let's try to stay on task, shall we?" Ah, there's the eyeroll, right there in Botten's tone. "How about an inventory of the surroundings," he continues. "A convertible, yes?"

"Yes."

"And it's red."

"Yes."

"And there's a man. Where is he?"

Ophelia's pulse pounds in her neck, but her gaze never wavers.

"He's in the convertible, like he's going to drive somewhere."

If Ophelia could, she'd release a breath. As it is, she keeps her focus locked on the photo.

"Anything else?" Botten prompts.

"There's a woman, but I can't really see her face. She's wearing a head scarf like she thinks she's glamorous or something." Leah snorts, the sound dismissive.

"Ah, yes. A convertible has a way of tangling the hair."

Botten's soft, strange revelation sends a shockwave through Ophelia. The words contain a surprising amount of tenderness. It's almost as if Botten is there, just outside the frame of the photograph. Or perhaps behind the camera.

There's a whisper of a sound, almost like a gasp, and then a commotion reaches her. Maybe because she's tethered to Leah, the noise is amplified. Maybe it's her mother's avenging anger. Whatever the case, everyone in the bedroom gets an earful when Miranda Connolly bursts in.

"How dare you! How *dare* you! I cannot leave my child alone for even an hour without you and the Enclave assaulting her once again—"

"Miranda, please, calm down. It's nothing like that."

"Oh, really?" Her mother's tone is arched and bitter cold. "Then, what is it? What is it you think she sees that's so important?"

"I was merely assessing her situation, seeing if Leah could perhaps reach her—"

"Bullshit."

A hush falls over the room. Ophelia's certain she's never heard her mother swear, and she's also certain no one else here has either.

"You've lied to me one too many times, Reggie." Her mother's voice is low and controlled. "I forbid you from setting foot in this house ever again."

"As you wish, Miranda."

While Ophelia is still half in King's End and half in Seattle, she feels the full force of her mother's wrath when she whirls toward the other person in the bedroom.

"And you, Leah Annabelle Connolly. You should be ashamed of yourself."

Leah is full-on sobbing now. It is, as Ophelia knows all too well, her cousin's go-to response.

Her mother softens slightly. "I suppose you weren't given much of a choice." Her fury returns, but now her words are calculated, all the more frightening for their brittle precision. "I don't care who you are or what sort of sway you hold with the High Council, or my husband, for that matter. You come near my daughter again, and I will personally end you."

"Miranda—"

"I may not have the Sight, but you forget that I know things, Reggie. Things you might not like out in the open."

"I see." Botten's voice is clipped. "We understand each other, then."

Ophelia's breathing rate increases to the point where the monitor starts to beep.

"I suggest you keep a careful eye on your daughter," he adds. "Her health appears *fragile*."

"Get out."

"Come, Leah."

"Leah, stay. Please. I didn't mean to shout. I know Ophelia appreciates your company."

"Now." Botten's command comes from far away, as if he's already stepped into the hallway. "We're leaving now, *Agent* Connolly."

Her cousin dithers; Ophelia can sense it. But it doesn't last. There's no contest in this seemingly impossible choice. Leah sniffs, the sound thick, full of tears. After shuffling footsteps, the front door closes, a gentle click full of regret. In its wake, the house feels colder.

PANSY IS STILL HOLDING the photograph outstretched in front of her. Her arm doesn't tremble. She is like a statue. She is like nothing Ophelia has ever encountered in all these loops. She flutters about, working to get Pansy's attention.

Thank you, thank you! You can let go now. It's safe. Henry's safe. I can't thank you enough, but you can let go now.

But Pansy doesn't. Ophelia flits over to Henry and swirls about. He remains quiet, still obeying Pansy's silent command. In forestalling Botten, has she made matters worse? Ophelia has trod this path to the end so many times. And yet, how is it that things continue to change? How can she help when everything she does makes things worse?

Help her, Henry. It's safe now. Get her to sit, pour her some tea. It must be related to the Sight, but I don't know how—

He moves then, easing the photograph from Pansy's grasp. Her arm is pliant beneath his, and a shuddering sigh fills the space as if only now she feels the toll. Henry touches her brow, her temples, with slow, almost sensuous strokes, all the while murmuring.

"Come back to me, come back to me. It's safe. We're safe."

"I heard her again," Pansy says, her voice soft and dreamy, as if the Sight is reluctant to let go. "She was worried about you."

Both of you, really. Ophelia huffs.

"Who was worried?" Henry takes her hands and rubs them gently between his own, a concentrated frown on his brow as if this task takes all his attention.

"I'm not sure."

"Was it the same voice, the one from the green?"

"Yes. I'm certain it was."

Get her to sit, give her some tea. Come on, Henry.

"I'd like some tea," Pansy says, and Ophelia nearly laughs.

"And maybe to sit down?" Henry adds.

Now you're getting somewhere.

Ophelia leaves them to it, lets go of the cozy basement, and fully returns to her bedroom in Seattle. Her mother is at her side, fussing with the comforter, placing items in Ophelia's hands: a silk scarf she'll never wear, the buttery leather of a purse she'll never carry. Her mother smooths a rich balm across Ophelia's skin, the sweet scent of gardenias banishing the sharp medicinal smell and the hint of decay that normally fills her room.

It's only when something hot and wet lands on her cheek—and is hastily swept away—that Ophelia realizes her mother is crying.

CHAPTER 34
PANSY

Henry is sitting on the low table across from me, as if the proximity will help him examine each sip of tea I take. My shoulders ache, but the cup warms my fingers, and the caffeine clears the fog from my head. Still, I could really do without the scrutiny.

Well, almost. His knees brush against mine. This close, I can detect a hint of five o'clock shadow along his jaw. Those dark eyes with the gold flecks don't miss a thing, though. I can't even sigh without him mentally recording the response.

"Are you sure you're okay," he says, maybe for the fifth or sixth time. I've lost count.

"Yes, *Agent Darnelle*, I'm fine."

That earns me a smile with a dimple. "Forgive me. I'm simply worried. This is uncharted territory. It's most curious."

That it is. "She cares about you," I say. "This person on the other side."

"She?"

I nod. "And she knows you, in the way a family member would."

I realize that I shouldn't implicitly trust random voices that pop into my head. But I can't help wondering if this particular voice is Ophelia Connolly. She sounds young—young and trapped. Or rather, young and trapped and desperate. It's Henry she's trying to save. But from what? That isn't clear.

"Have you ever heard of such a thing?" I ask. Who knows, maybe it's in all the classified information the Enclave doesn't let permanent post agents see.

Henry shakes his head. "No, but then, agents with Sight such as yours or Ophelia's are rare, a once-in-a-century occurrence."

"Or so the Enclave thinks."

Henry gives a mirthless laugh. "Exactly."

"Do you think it might be Ophelia?" I hate to ask. It feels like a crass sort of question. The last thing I want to do is hurt him.

He doesn't recoil, doesn't stand and walk away. Instead, he eases the cup from my grip and then takes my hands in his.

"I'm afraid I'm pinning all my hopes on the fact that it is. Part of me wants you to continue to forge this connection with her because it might be the one thing to..."

He falters, and I hear the words he can't say: *Bring her back.*

"But these trances." His grimace is full of self-reproach. "They scare me. I can't ask you to risk yourself like this."

"I'm not sure I have a choice. Besides, it doesn't feel risky."

He raises an eyebrow at that. Yes, he's correct. This is the Sight we're dealing with, and it absolutely could be risky. He's still assessing me, chin tilted, lips compressed, a million thoughts swirling behind his gaze.

"I'm wondering what it is about your Sight that's different, that's allowing this," he says at last.

"You think it's me and not Ophelia?"

"We can trace Ophelia's Sight back to our maternal great-grandmother. It manifested very much the way Ophelia's does, although to be honest, our great-grandmother had far more discipline when it came to the Sight."

"My mother always said my grandfather had the Sight," I offer.

"No, he didn't."

Oh, really? And Henry knows this how? My expression must turn stormy and sour, because he quickly adds, "At least, it's not in his records."

"You checked?"

"The second I realized *you* had the Sight."

Of course he did. This is Henry Darnelle. He probably constructed a complete Little family tree.

"Just because it's not in the Enclave's database doesn't mean he didn't have the Sight," I counter.

"Yes, I thought of that," he concedes. "I went back as far as we have records. The Little line has any number of fine agents, your mother in particular."

See? He did create a family tree.

"But there's no hint that any of them had the Sight. So, your father—"

"Was a local," I finish.

"Are you certain?"

Am I? I sigh. "Not anymore."

Henry leans back and reaches behind him. He plucks a photograph from the floor, the one that Ophelia—yes, I'm certain it's Ophelia—had me hold. He lets it rest in his palms so we both can study it.

"Why this photo?" he asks. "Any idea?"

"She said she needed something to look at. No matter what I did, I wasn't supposed to look at you. And I had to get you to shut the hell up."

This earns me yet another arched schoolmaster eyebrow.

"Her words, not mine. She said your life depended on it."

Henry falls silent and remains so for several long moments. Then he holds up a finger, although I'm not about to say anything or go anywhere. The only thing I'm going to do is pour us both another cup of tea. So I do, and that's when Henry pulls out the burner phone and makes a call.

"Mother, it's Henry. I'm calling to ask how—" he begins.

Words stream from the phone, drowning out his question. I can't discern what Miranda Connolly is saying, but the panic, the sorrow, and the anger in her voice vibrate in the air around me. That telltale temptation to activate the Sight presses against my skull. *Just for a moment. Dip into the past.* The voice almost croons.

That's when I lock it down, because that particular invitation sounds wrong. It scrapes against my ears, and I want nothing to do with it.

At last, Henry hangs up with a promise to return home soon. He holds a hand over his mouth, in contemplation again, weighing something. His sigh, before he speaks, is heavy.

"My mother stepped out for a bit, and when she returned, she found Professor Botten with Ophelia."

All of me turns cold. I grip Henry's hand. "Is she okay?"

He nods. "My mother threw him out, along with Leah, our cousin. She's the one who can, apparently, relay what Ophelia sees."

I pick up the discarded photograph, the one where Harry Darnelle and my mother look like movie stars from a bygone era.

"And she wanted them to see this." I consider that. "Do you think Ophelia witnessed what happened all those years ago?"

"It's a distinct possibility," he says, but then shakes his head. "But we can't know for certain. Ophelia wasn't allowed to talk much about the research in its early stages. Unfortunately, I was constantly in the field, so I don't know what, exactly, they were able to do."

I point to the convertible. "For what it's worth, the car's still in the garage."

Henry's expression brightens a bit. "What?"

"Under a tarp. Hasn't been driven for years, though."

"It's quite a specimen," he says, his tone appreciative. "An Alfa Romeo Spider in good condition could probably net you a tidy sum."

"Really?"

"My father knew a little bit about cars." He shrugs, supremely cavalier. "It rubbed off."

I'm beginning to suspect that for Henry, "a little bit" is everybody else's definition of encyclopedic knowledge.

"So, what do we do now?" I mean, we're hardly going to jump into that convertible and drive off into the sunset, although there's a part of me that insists this would be an excellent idea.

Henry graces me with a warm smile that deepens the crinkles around his eyes and makes those flecks of gold positively glow. "First, we get you something to eat."

"I'm really not—" I begin, but then my stomach growls.

"Like I said, we get something to eat. Besides, cooking helps me think. We'll have to plan our next steps cautiously." He glances around, gaze landing on the files and photos we've scattered around the basement. "Do you mind if I bring back some of these files?"

"No, not at all, and you can keep your father's notes."

"Technically, they belong to your mother—"

"*Technically*, they belong to your father, which makes them yours, and I know my mother would want you to have them."

"All right." Henry nods, but instead of reaching for those file folders, his hand lands on the album with the prom photos. "You never did tell me what happened."

Are you kidding me? "You really want to know?"

"Oh, I do." And there's an enthusiasm in his voice I can't quite place.

So I give in and tell Henry about the ill-fated high school romance between Pansy Little and Daniel Lombardi.

I DIDN'T LIE when I said Daniel's a genius. He, and as far as I know, still is. At the start of our sophomore year, he was so smart—and by smart, I also mean bored—that the school and his parents agreed he should skip to his senior year. (And he was still bored, so he started knocking out his generals at King's End Community College.)

His parents wanted him to have a "real" senior year of high school, but his friend group, including me, were all sophomores and a few freshies we adopted. So he brought us along. Since he was the golden boy of King's End—perfect test scores, robotics team state championship, academic awards, and a slew of scholarships—everyone let him.

"I imagine that can be quite isolating," Henry observes. "That level of intelligence."

Daniel would get frustrated when the rest of us couldn't keep up, but he was never cruel about it. He just wanted us all to understand. We just wanted him to have fun. We made it our mission. For most of the year, it worked. We *all* had the best senior year.

Then came the day after graduation. And the picnic, just me and Daniel. Strawberries, sparkling grape juice, and a red-and-white checked blanket. We liked to hike deep into the old part of the cemetery. At the crest of a hill sits a welcoming willow tree. It's calm and comforting there, one of the few spots where I'm not constantly on alert for Screamers. That day, Daniel had tied back the sweeping branches with red ribbons. He created something that felt like a sanctuary.

And a trap.

"He wanted me to skip my 'summer camp,'" I tell Henry, drawing quotation marks in the air. "He said *I* didn't care that he was going away at the end of August, and how could *I* be so selfish? And this was our only chance to make things work." I knew what he meant; when it came to high school romances, the statistics weren't on our side. And Daniel was all about statistics.

Then he turned things around—as if reverse psychology might

help—and started talking about staying in King's End forever. No college, nothing.

"I told him he was going to do great things, but he had to leave King's End to do them."

"The Sight?"

"In part. It would show me things, just glimpses, now and then. And then he said, 'Not without you. If you're staying, I'm staying.' He got down on one knee and pulled out an engagement ring—his grandmother's."

Henry's eyes widen. "And you were both—?"

"Sixteen."

Now he cringes, and I suspect he's about to launch into a lecture about age-appropriate relationship milestones.

I raise my hands and shake my head. "I know. I know." Even though I was only sixteen, I didn't need hindsight, or even the Sight, to tell me this could only end badly.

"It's so painful, that first time." Henry covers his mouth again, as if he's holding in the agony of a first heartbreak. "I'm guessing you turned him down."

"The Sight did it for me. My nose started bleeding. I mean, *really* started bleeding. Blood soaked my shirt within moments. I ruined the blanket, trying to get it to stop. I got blood all over Daniel." I shake my head as if I can banish the memory of all that red. "We looked like something from a slasher movie."

Henry stares at me, astonishment and sorrow and deep concern playing across his features.

"Even at home, it wouldn't stop." I pause in my retelling, because I've been longing to ask this question for years. Nosebleeds are common, yes. But not this sudden and aggressive bloodletting. "Have you heard of such a thing? Of this happening to anyone with the Sight? Ophelia, maybe?"

"No, I'm afraid not." He gives me a sidelong glance. "I'm not going to lie. It is rather alarming."

"It was only that one time. It's never happened again with that kind of force."

Yet. It's never happened again *yet.* Every once in a while, that fear assails me. What if it happens when I'm alone? With no one here to help? I don't want to imagine that. I was a wreck, and it was my mother who took over once I stumbled into the house.

She called Daniel's parents, because he was shell-shocked and in no condition to walk home alone. What she told them? About me? What was happening? I don't know. I was in the downstairs bathroom painting the sink, mirror, and walls red. I couldn't help but swallow some blood—there was just so much—and then I started vomiting as well.

Henry turns a page in the album as if he can discern what happened from the photographs alone. "What did your mother do?"

"There wasn't much she could do. She called Adele, and they debated taking me to the hospital. My mother said that would make things worse and asked if there was some way to do a transfusion at home."

Depending on their lineage, some agents can't go to a local hospital. It might kill them, and blood incompatibility is the reason why. The Enclave even has its own blood bank for such emergencies.

"You know," Henry says, "assuming your father was a local, that might not have been an issue."

I open my mouth, close it, then try again. If he's right, then my mother should have absolutely rushed me to the hospital or dialed 911. "The bleeding did stop, though, and then it was just the cleanup."

The details are fuzzy. I was lightheaded, vomiting, and in no condition to remember much. But the more I let go of Daniel—and the idea that we could be together—the more the blood flow stemmed. I remember my mother crouched next to me on the bathroom floor, her hands gently cradling me, her words soothing the Sight. *I know, darling girl. I know how much this hurts. It's so hard to let him go.*

"That's the last time I saw Daniel," I add. "I spent the next two weeks trying to recover in time for the Academy."

That year, I was so anemic from blood loss that I didn't need to pretend. I was utterly unremarkable. My Sight had depleted itself. It only perked up in August, in time for our last field exercise, much to Mort's relief if not mine.

It was a brutal summer, made worse by Daniel's utter silence. Not a single letter, and he had written daily the year before. Our friend group didn't survive, either. I wasn't friendless, but King's End is a small town. Word got around. Nobody said anything mean, of course. But no one here has asked me out since. Which, considering the Screamers and the patrols and vanishing mothers, is probably just as well.

Henry turns another page in the photo album. "I want to apologize for making you relive this."

"You didn't know. Besides, it was years ago."

Of course, when I arrived at the Academy that summer, Jack immediately sensed something was wrong. He folded me into a hug the moment I stepped from the airport shuttle. I told him and Mortimer an abbreviated version, redacting the part with all the blood. Jack thought I was suffering from a broken heart; Mort thought I was just moping.

Now I place a palm on my chest, not because my heart hurts but because it feels lighter, the shredded strands mending themselves back together. "It felt good to tell someone who'd understand."

"Still. It was unfair of me, when you clearly didn't want to talk about it." Another page turn. Despite his words, the man can't get enough of my prom. Does he find it quaint? Charming? Was that the word he used?

Then he freezes. Shock plays across his face, although he schools his expression immediately. He turns the album so I can see the photo. It's a couples dance. Daniel is trying to maneuver me and all my ruffles around the floor. No easy task; there were ruffles for days.

In the background, the chaperones have congregated, my mother included. Next to her is a man. They're in animated conversation. My mother's head is tipped back as if he's just said something enormously funny. He's leaning in close, a hand on her shoulder. And while I've never met him, I know who he is.

I lift my gaze to Henry's. He looks as befuddled as I feel.

"Can you explain why my father is at your prom?"

CHAPTER 35
PANSY

Hours pass. Or maybe it's simply several excruciating minutes with neither of us speaking. I don't have an answer or even words. It's clear that Henry doesn't either.

On the surface, there's nothing untoward about Harry Darnelle (divorced) visiting Rose Little (widowed). Considering Henry's obsession with my prom? There may be something crucial we should consider.

"Did you ever meet my father?" he asks.

I give my head a shake. "I never made it home that night, so—"

Oh, and there it is. The schoolmaster eyebrow. Despite everything, I burst out laughing.

"Not like that. Every year, King's End throws an after-prom party. Guy and Milo host it in the community center. The reasoning goes that if everyone is snacking and playing games, they can't be sneaking off to drink or do whatever."

"*Especially* the whatever," Henry says, but he's laughing now, too.

I scan the room, taking in all the photographs and files. The memory box has been a bit of a disappointment, unless, somehow, we were supposed to find this particular picture. I think of Henry's obsessive page-turning. The man has a knack for finding things. The Sight does run in his family, and I wonder if this might be a variation.

"Do you think they left clues for us?" I wave a hand, indicating the mess. "Is that why your father was here?"

"Possibly." He picks up the other photograph, the one of his father and my mother in the convertible. "Although I'm not sure it was the only reason for his visit."

The note of sadness in his voice makes my heart clench. Henry's earlier words come back to me: *He was a solitary man.* That gulf opens. I can almost taste the undercurrent of abject loneliness.

But then Henry rallies. This, I suspect, is something Henry Darnelle always does.

"Let's take a couple of boxes back with us," he says. "We can sort through them after dinner and then come back for more in the morning."

We both start gathering up papers and files and photographs. I secure the memory box. After all, memories are precious. I might as well keep them close, or closer, as the case may be. I pause when I find an automobile title.

I hold it out to Henry. "Something else that belonged to your father."

His brow is furrowed in thought, and he doesn't even glance at what's in my hand. "I've seen this name before," he mutters.

I raise up on tiptoes to peer at the paper he's scrutinizing. My birth certificate. I have a copy in the file cabinet at home. Is it odd that Adele should have one, too? She was always my mother's backup, so perhaps not.

"That's because it's me," I say.

His gaze meets mine over the certificate, amusement lighting his eyes. "Well, yes. And happy early birthday, by the way. But I meant your father, Maximilian Monroe."

"My Enclave records?"

"Your father isn't listed."

"Why?"

"Because he wasn't a member of the Enclave."

That sounds elitist. "What does it say in my records? That my father was just some local guy?"

"Not in so many words, but yes, essentially."

"That's ridiculous."

"It is, for a variety of reasons, but locals aren't included in the records or agent lineage."

"But why?" I ask again. "Couldn't they have descended from a traveler, but no one knows it?"

"Absolutely." He considers me from over the top of the certificate. "But it doesn't explain where I've seen your father's name before."

Oh, he looks so exasperated. He fairly radiates frustration. "This is going to keep you up all night, isn't it?"

He opens his mouth to protest. I know it's a protest; those have their own flavor. Then he simply sighs. "Most likely."

"Well, here's something to keep you busy." I hand him the title.

It takes a moment for it to sink in. Because yes, the title is for the car in my garage. The red 1986 Alfa Romeo Spider Veloce does not belong to Rose Little. Instead, the name on the title reads Harrison Darnelle.

"Surprise!" I say when Henry doesn't speak.

"You don't mean ... I couldn't possibly—"

"It was your father's. That makes it yours."

"I really don't think—"

"Dinner," I counter. "You promised me dinner."

He pauses, and his lips twitch. He's repressing a smile, but there's a hint of dimple anyway. "I did, didn't I?"

"We can talk about who owns the car over—"

"Enchiladas and some lime and coriander rice?"

That. Sounds. Amazing. "Yes. We'll talk about who owns the car over enchiladas." And when I say *who owns*, I absolutely mean him.

Henry returns to packing boxes, and I can't help but bask in a bit of triumph.

I'm pretty sure I've won this round.

PART THREE

THE EDGE OF NOWHERE

CHAPTER 36
PANSY

King's End, Minnesota
Thursday, July 13

It's early Thursday morning, the sun just cresting the horizon, and I'm following Henry's circuitous trail through the cemetery. He stops every few minutes, consults his phone, and then picks up the walk again. He's certain we're on the right path to the covered bridge.

I'm certain we're going in circles.

The grass is soft beneath my sneakers, the air heavy and sweet. Pink and gold streak the sky. My pulse thrums with anticipation when I press my hand against my belly. I strain my ears, cast my gaze over the benign oaks and graying headstones. We've reached the older part of the cemetery, where rain and snow and wind have worn away the names, the dates, and the history of those buried here.

Henry holds up a hand, halts, then turns around. His grin is full-on mischievous as he readies the camera on his phone.

"Well, Agent Little?"

Well, what? The earth beneath my feet shudders, the slightest tingling reaching my toes. My umbrella, too, picks up the disturbance and trembles against my back. I'm standing on top of the world's smallest fissure.

"Oh!" I say, and kneel down.

Henry aims the camera's lens at me. "Without assistance, Agent Little detected the presence of a hairline fissure in this part of the cemetery."

I'm about to protest that I did no such thing until I was standing right on top of it, but he's off and running, intoning like a narrator for a nature documentary.

"I believe this makes her uniquely suited to be the permanent post agent for King's End. I was unable to locate the fissure myself without aid. Furthermore, her skills at repair—"

I take this as my cue to start mending the fissure. Honestly, it's such a tiny thing. Hardly worth noting, right up until it starts spewing Screamers, that is. Now that I'm here, I might as well mend it.

"—are second to none. She has a deft hand that, again, is suited to King's End. I'm enormously pleased with her progress. In a few years, I can envision Agent Little mentoring other permanent post agents."

That sounds like a backhanded compliment. I keep my gaze on the ground, my fingers in the soil, and use every ounce of willpower not to roll my eyes. Henry is schoolmastering but hard. Really, could the man be any more pretentious?

"I've taken the liberty of copying the High Council on my findings in King's End as well. I know several members have a vested interest in how Rose Little and her daughter are faring."

I nearly lose the thread of that fissure, but I keep the connection, keep mending, the grass scratchy and cool against my fingers. Dampness from the earth is working its way through the knees of my jeans. Despite the morning sun against my neck, I shiver.

"I'll send another update tomorrow." Henry stops the camera, uploads the video, and then shuts off his phone. He's still grinning like a little boy in the midst of an enormously clever prank.

"Are you sure you're not overselling it?" I ask.

"Not in the least."

"And those other members of the High Council?"

"Insurance. I have a good sense of who my father's allies were. I suspect they may have also been your mother's."

Enclave politics. I make a face; I know I must, because Henry bursts out laughing.

"A necessary evil, I agree." He crouches next to the fissure and places his hands on the earth. "Well done. You know, your skills really are suited for King's End. But elsewhere is available, if you so choose."

There's that offer again, of becoming a full-fledged field agent. Assuming, of course, the Enclave doesn't override Henry and retire the Little line. "You know," I say, because I can't help myself, "I didn't actually detect the fissure until I was standing right on top of it."

"And I didn't detect it without the app."

"Wait. There's an app?"

"Which you don't need." He gives me one of those sexy winks. This, combined with the boyish grin, nearly unravels me. Again, who is this man? There are so many layers to him: stern schoolmaster, field agent extraordinaire, stealth flirt in an impeccably tailored suit. Then there's this man across from me now, giving me his full attention.

And then, suddenly, not. It's caught by something beyond my shoulder, his gaze curious but cautious.

"No, it couldn't be," he mutters. But he stands and weaves among the headstones.

I have no choice.

I follow him.

"The funeral," he says over his shoulder.

I glance around, but we're in the wrong part of the cemetery for one. These are the legacy graves, names and memories washed away by time and rain and neglect.

"On Sunday," he clarifies. "The Screamers led me back this way. I think I know why."

"All the way back here?"

He nods and picks up the pace. Again, I follow. His excitement is contagious. I have no idea what we're looking for, but I keep pace as he jogs through the headstones, footfalls silent against the grass.

At last, he halts at a row that hasn't seen as much weather or neglect. Henry crouches at the side of one headstone and, with careful fingers, wipes away dirt.

Maximilian Monroe
August 3, 1960 – September 15, 1960
Little boy
Little angel

My knees give out, all at once and somewhat violently. I stare at the headstone, understanding the words and yet not understanding at all. Could there be two men named Maximilian Monroe, even in a town as small as King's End? Maybe. Two with the same birthday?

Doubtful.

"The Screamers showed you this?"

"They led me past this spot half a dozen times."

Of course they did.

"What do you remember about your father?" Henry asks.

"Not a lot. My mother always said he was local, that he grew up in Mankato, a town south of King's End, and that I was distantly related to Adele."

"And the date of birth?"

He doesn't need me to answer, but I do. "The same."

"Hm." Henry stares into the middle distance, and I can practically see the thoughts churning. "A birth certificate, especially without a corresponding death certificate, is a first step in establishing an identity."

"You mean a fake identity?"

"Yes, I do."

"Isn't that a crime?"

"It's that, too, a federal crime. That doesn't mean it's unheard of in Enclave circles."

"Fake identities for—?"

"Travelers."

"How many travelers fall through in a given year?"

"Generally, a couple per decade, although there haven't been any in the last twenty years or so. Still, it happens, and there's a protocol." He nods toward the headstone. "Which your mother, as a principal field agent, would have known."

"Are you saying my father was from another dimension?" I'm trying to parse this, but really, my mind simply spins.

"I'm saying it's a possibility." He gestures toward the grave. "Perhaps this was the source of the birth certificate that established his identity."

"So my mother knew he was a traveler, she broke the law, and then kept everything from the Enclave?" Now that I'm saying it out loud, I absolutely believe she was capable of such a thing. With Adele's help, once again, no doubt. But to keep it from me? Then again, I was four when my father died. He is someone I peer at through a mist—a face I can't quite discern, a feeling I can't quite name.

"Again, it's a possibility." He raises an eyebrow. "After all, I believe your mother's kept a great many things from the Enclave."

Yes, my Sight first and foremost. "Did you find anything in her files?"

"It's what I didn't find. No tax returns in your father's name, W2s, or automobile titles. Although there is a Social Security card and a marriage certificate. It's sometimes too difficult to integrate first-generation travelers. That may have been the case with your father."

"Assuming he was a traveler, from another dimension."

"Yes, assuming."

"Why would the Screamers lead you here, though?" What I really mean is, why on earth would they help? Both in general and me in particular. Screamers don't help at all. At least, that's never been my experience.

"Do you want the party line or my personal theory?"

"Your personal theory."

"I don't believe the Screamers are evil, which doesn't make them good. I believe they—or something that's larger than them—are trying to correct an imbalance. They shouldn't be in this dimension, which is why we mend fissures to begin with."

"Is that why they feel so..." I pause and consider. I want to say *emotional*, but I'm not sure that's quite right. "Insistent? Like with that couple on the Rose Walk? The Sight was convinced they should break up."

Henry's nodding like he agrees. "I don't sense the emotions or motivations the way you do, with your Sight. But I believe that the Screamers are simply trying to course-correct, if you will, match our reality to theirs."

"Might explain why funerals are so awful."

"Hm. Indeed."

When Henry falls silent, I add, "My mother always said the first travelers were trying to fix what they broke by falling through, and now it's our job to try to repair what they couldn't."

"I tend to think they didn't so much as fall as punched their way through and only realized after the fact that they'd done something irrevocable."

"Something irrevocable." The phrase catches in my mind, something about it familiar, although I can't say what, exactly. Except. "Like the housing development?"

"It's a possibility."

"You're just full of possibilities today, Agent Darnelle."

He laughs at that and offers me his hand. "Shall we see if we can uncover yet another possibility?"

"Do you know where it is?"

"I believe I do."

I take that outstretched hand and nearly fly to my feet. "Then let's go," I say, and my umbrella beats against my spine in her excitement. "Let's go."

CHAPTER 37
HENRY

King's End, Minnesota
Thursday, July 13

Henry did have a good idea of where the covered bridge was. He'd manipulated the data, ran the calculations, and mapped the most likely location. He'd plotted several avenues of approach, accounting for the density of the surrounding woods. He was hardly surprised to find the most direct route skirted the cemetery.

It was Pansy, though, who actually found the bridge.

"I remember now!" She pointed toward a narrow path leading into a dense thicket and then pushed past him. "The fairy lights! Do you see them?"

Fairy lights? The morning sun was still gentle, but nothing glimmered or sparkled. Nothing resembled fairy lights in the least. Henry lunged forward, his hand catching Pansy's for a moment. Her fingers slipped through his, but she spun around and stopped.

"Hold up," he said.

"But—"

"Fairy lights?"

Her expression cleared, the dazzled look leaving her eyes. She drew in a breath and pressed a hand against her chest. "That makes no sense."

"I know. Do you see them now?"

She turned, gaze canvassing the trees and sky and undergrowth. "Maybe. They're not as bright."

He exhaled, heart rate settling into something less panicked. "Good. Can you follow them while staying with me?"

"I think so." She turned again, this time her focus on him. "What's going on?"

"I'm not sure. Tell me again what you remember."

"I remember thinking that the lights would lead me to my father. All I had to do was follow them." She closed her eyes. "My mother was so angry when she found me, although I think she was mostly terrified. She was shouting." Pansy gazed at him now, her expression clearing. "But not at me. Honestly, it feels like a dream. If it weren't for the rule on her list, I'd doubt that it happened at all."

"I think I know what's at the covered bridge."

"We shouldn't keep going, should we?"

"Absolutely not."

"But—?"

He managed a curt laugh. "I also think this is one of those rules we need to break." He swung his umbrella around and adjusted the settings. "I'm not going to upload anything to the Enclave, but I'd like to collect what data we can. If you're willing, that is. We'll go only if you want to."

She nodded and held out a hand. "I'd go anywhere with you, Agent Darnelle."

Those words. That smile. They sent his heart racing once again. Henry tried not to read more into the statement than a mere surface flirtation, tried and frankly failed. But he took her hand, and the contact melted the tension gathering at the base of his skull. They were stronger like this, both more grounded. This felt right in a way nothing had in ages.

They pushed forward into the woods, easing their way around and beneath branches. Evergreen needles stroked his cheeks. The scent of pine filled his nose and mouth. The rush of water on rocks grew louder.

The clearing was small and sudden. One moment, they were in the woods, the next at the edge of a steep ravine. At its bottom, a stream tumbled over rocks and pebbles and meandered toward what must be a tributary of the Minnesota River at the heart of town.

Directly across from them was an old-fashioned covered bridge. Or there was until it vanished. Then it reappeared. The bridge flickered in and out of existence. As it did, it went from new construction to decrepitude in a matter of seconds, and not in any particular order.

"Is there a bridge, or isn't there?" Pansy whispered.

"Yes."

She gave him a sidelong glance. "I wish I'd paid more attention during physics."

"I wish I had too."

The Enclave provided instruction in this sort of thing, although the standard operating procedure was to back away slowly, cordon off the area, and then call for reinforcements. The bridge continued to flicker. That made sense. Then, much to his alarm, Pansy too began to flicker.

That did not.

Light came at them in what he could only describe as waves. It fractured and bent, bathing the small clearing in rainbow colors. The force barreled into him like Screamers, but all was silent. Then, at the center of the covered bridge, an expanse opened, gray and endless.

Except for the man who stood there.

The man was perhaps a decade older than Henry. Dark-haired, lanky, with a lean, hungry look to him. As he stepped closer, the man solidified and stared straight at Pansy.

"I never thought I'd get to see you again." His eyes were wide with a tenderness that belied the rest of his appearance.

"So it *was* real." Her words were so soft that Henry barely heard them.

"Yes." Henry adjusted his grip on her hand, clutching it tighter. "I believe this man is your father."

Moments passed that felt like an eternity. Or perhaps it was an eternity that felt like mere moments. Both were true, and somehow not. Now Henry understood why Pansy's Sight was vast and unfathomable. This was why it was like touching starlight, because it literally was.

"Your father's a traveler," Henry said, mostly to see if he could prompt the man across from them to talk.

The man inclined his head. "I am."

"So you fell through to this side," Pansy said, her words still soft, still tentative, as if she couldn't quite believe what she was seeing. "And then you left?"

"I did," the man, who was no doubt Max Monroe, said. "I had to. It was what your mother—"

"Mom!" Pansy surged forward, her hand slipping from Henry's. "Is she there? Do you have her?"

Henry lunged, managed to catch Pansy around the waist, and held on, his arms straining with the effort.

"Hang on to her!" Max shouted. "Don't let her slip through!"

The pull from that unseen force was slow, steady, but inexorable. Henry braced his legs against its power, his feet sliding on loose dirt and pebbles, millimeter by millimeter, edging them closer to the bridge that was both there and wasn't. If they went through, what then?

"Your mother is here," Max said. "And yes, I collected her that day."

"Can I see her?" This time, Pansy's voice cracked. With her back against his chest, Henry could sense the anguish in her question.

"I'm afraid not, sweetheart." Max held up his hands as if that could stop their forward momentum. "She misses you, but she's safe."

"I don't understand." She glanced back at Henry as if he might explain, then looked to her father again.

"I ... your mother and I ... we're between dimensions," Max said. "Not fully in either, although there are opportunities to slip from the stream and into one dimension or the other."

"Like three months ago, when you came for her."

"Yes," Max acknowledged.

"So that's why you left. To save her."

Max shook his head. "No, sweetheart, I left to save you."

The earth rumbled beneath their feet. Henry wondered if the vortex was putting too much pressure on their dimension, if they'd fall through no matter how hard he fought against it. He knew from experience that these portals didn't last long. He'd watched one in the Sahara swallow up that sandstorm of Screamers while nearly taking him with them.

Sweat soaked his spine. His muscles trembled. He wanted to pull them both back to safety. At the same time, he wanted, *needed*, to keep listening.

"In all the threads, all the possible futures, one thing was clear," Max was saying. "If I left and then returned later for your mother, it gave you a fighting chance."

"A fighting chance?" Pansy shook her head. "To do what?"

"With your mother here, with me, with her still technically alive, her stopgap measure remains in place. A piece of her remains in your world, and you're stronger because of it. You're the key to everything."

Pansy craned her neck to peer at Henry again. She looked as confused and skeptical as he felt. "What does that mean?"

Max ignored her question. Instead, his attention shifted, and he pinned Henry with a glare. "Wait. Don't tell me. You're a Darnelle, aren't you?"

"Henry Darnelle."

"Harry's son?"

Henry nodded.

Max swore, the exact words lost somewhere between dimensions, and he rubbed his eyes. "It's always the son. Listen to me, Darnelle. If she slips through, you'd better come with her."

That went without saying.

"You protect her with your life," Max added. "That's your role in all this. Understand?"

Again, Henry nodded, but a shudder washed over Pansy. For one brief instant, it was like touching starlight again.

"What? No. No one's dying." Her gaze went to Henry, then to her father, and back again, and he had to wonder what it was the Sight had shown her—for certainly it had shown her something—or, at least, had tried to.

"Someone dies, or everyone does," Max said. "That's the way this works. Understand that your mother was betrayed, a bargain was made without her knowledge, and that price has yet to be paid."

Pansy went dangerously still in his arms. Henry prayed that the Sight hadn't attacked. But then she pulled in a deep breath.

When she didn't speak, he asked, "How was Rose betrayed?" He already had a good idea of who had done the betraying.

"I think you know, Darnelle," Max said, "or are at least smart enough to figure it out."

Pansy was shaking her head, but there was resolve in the gesture, a fierceness. "So, what now? How do we fix this?"

"Oh, sweetheart, I wish I knew. There are still too many threads, too many players. Each time I catch hold of one path, it splits and then splits again. But you're here now. And that gives me more hope than I've had in a very long time."

Max's attention was fully on Pansy now, a deep, abiding love in his gaze. "I last saw you when you were four. Do you remember that?"

She nodded. Henry still had her around the waist, and when her breathing hitched, he felt her exhale against his chest. "I wanted to see you, and the lights told me where I could find you."

"Yes. They would." Max shut his eyes briefly, as if the memory itself was a wound. "Your mother was furious."

"She put the bridge off limits."

"For good reason. You're half in your world and half in mine. At any moment, mine might assert itself, draw you to this side. That's the danger."

"What happens then?"

"Oh, sweetheart. I don't know. You might fall all the way through to the other side, become a traveler there. Or you may simply end up here, somewhere in the stream."

"Are you there forever?"

Max shrugged, although Henry wondered if Pansy's father did know his fate, and it was this: an eternal guardian between worlds.

Slowly, the force that was tugging them toward the bridge was dissipating. Light fractured again, the colors receding, the expanse shrinking. The vortex was closing, folding in on itself, and taking Max with it.

"Will I see you again?" Pansy called.

"I hope so, sweetheart." Max went gray, then faded from view until only the echo of his words remained. "I hope so."

For a long time, Henry continued to hold Pansy as if that vortex might suddenly open and swallow her whole. She turned in his arms, her eyes wide with wonder.

"You knew?"

"I guessed," he said. "Your Sight is simply too strong, too different from Ophelia's."

It occurred to Henry that no one else in the Enclave would have a basis for comparison. And Rose Little had made very certain that no one would. The Enclave's renewed interest—no, Botten's interest—in the Sight took on a more sinister implication. Had Botten been searching for Pansy all this time, and Ophelia had simply been caught up in that net? Or was there more, something about both of them?

"And this?" Pansy nodded toward the bridge, her question pulling him from his thoughts.

"Another guess."

"An educated one."

He managed a short laugh. "Perhaps. I suspected that your mother uncovered something significant here in King's End."

"And she trusted your father enough to tell him?"

"Along with Botten, which clearly was the wrong thing to do."

"Do you know how she was betrayed?"

Henry loosened his grip on her, shoulders to elbows, elbows to hands. He cast a glance toward the bridge, mundane and dilapidated. "Apparently, I'm smart enough to figure it out."

"You are that." She exhaled again, a long breath that deflated her. "I wish I knew what was going on."

So did Henry. But here wasn't the place to figure that out. He doubted the vortex would open again anytime soon. Mosquitoes nattered around his ears, one finding a spot on the nape of his neck before he could slap it. Birdsong filled the morning once again. The light, though, was the giveaway. The sun filtered through the leaves, painting the forest floor in a wash of benign gold.

"Shall we go home?" he asked, his voice low and gentle.

Pansy looked at the covered bridge, the sorrow in her gaze tangible. "I suppose we should."

"On second thought, I have another idea." For the briefest moment, he cupped her cheek. "Trust me?"

"I do."

He tried—oh, how he tried—but Henry couldn't discern a second's hesitation in her reply.

CHAPTER 38
OPHELIA

King's End, Minnesota
Thursday, July 13

They don't often come this way, and Ophelia wants to warn them that nothing good can come from this visit. Henry means well; she knows he does. Under ordinary circumstances, his suggestion would help Pansy immeasurably.

But these are no ordinary circumstances.

Ophelia doesn't know if she can sense the storm or if it's merely a matter of this loop, endless as it is, that she knows it's coming. Is the anticipation in her mind, her memory, rather than the air? But pausing in the cemetery is the last thing these two should be doing.

Ever the gentleman, Henry unfurls his umbrella with a snap. The canopy flutters, his umbrella fairly bursting with pride at protecting that pink and white polka-dot one. The pulse it sends out is meant to repel Screamers rather than attract them. Henry has created an Enclave gravesite service in miniature.

Pansy kneels between graves, Rose's light with fresh sod, Max's a darker green of nearly two decades.

"They're not really gone," she says.

"They're no longer here, either." Henry cants the umbrella, blocking the sunlight, shielding Pansy from the growing heat of the day. "Your mother was wise when she told you to have a funeral. She knew you'd need to mourn."

Not that Pansy has. Ophelia's not certain she will. But Pansy shuts her eyes. When a single tear slips down her cheek, she doesn't wipe it away.

The breeze picks up and batters Ophelia. She hovers near Henry because he's so solid, so sure. In some ways, she is like Rose and Max. Not gone, but not here either. She is somewhere in between, and how do you mourn someone like that?

If you're Henry Darnelle, you don't. The sorrow is there, in the grooves around his mouth, in the way it flavors his words, cast shadows in his eyes. He doesn't mourn, not like her mother does. Deep down, he believes that he can find a way to bring her back.

Even if Ophelia could tell him there is no way, she's not sure she would. She sometimes thinks it's his belief that keeps her—well, not grounded; there is no grounded—an active participant in these loops. Before all this, Ophelia would have said there were only so many times you could watch the world burn without tuning out, especially when you couldn't do a damn thing to douse the fire.

But with this loop, this *last* loop, she wonders if she is actually helping, not hindering. She flits about Henry, projecting as much of herself into the air as she can.

I know you don't want to rush her, but the sooner you leave, the better.

The urgency of her request evaporates like so much morning mist. Henry is implacable in his task. Beyond that, he's adept at ignoring his little sister when his mood dictates. She casts her gaze toward Pansy.

Forgive me, she says to Henry, *but you simply don't listen.*

Pansy's eyes are open, and she's running blades of grass through her fingers. Ophelia can almost taste the soil against her tongue, feel the damp earth against her skin, sense the dull ache in her chest. For one instant, it is almost like being fully herself again. She spins in abject wonder. Are these even her sensations? Or is she channeling Pansy?

She eases in front of Pansy and stares into her sorrow-tinged eyes.

If you're ready, you should leave. Actually, even if you're not ready, you should leave. They're coming for you, and they won't be kind.

Pansy's eyes light with recognition, and she stares into the space Ophelia occupies. "Ophelia?"

Her name is little more than a whisper. Ophelia nods, which is ridiculous. Or perhaps not. She feels seen, the sensation foreign, disconcerting, after having been invisible for so long.

"When?" Pansy asks, the word more air than question.

Any minute now.

Pansy glances over her shoulder at Henry, still dedicated to the task at hand. "What should we do?"

Ophelia isn't entirely certain. Always, the Screamers arrive en masse, coating the cemetery so thickly that day turns to night. Both Henry and Pansy are beaten ragged. The Screamers manage to soften them up nicely for the Enclave.

Get out in front of them.

Whether this is good advice or not, Ophelia can't say. If that scenario exists, the Sight hasn't deigned to show it to her. But getting caught unaware in the cemetery has never ended well.

Pansy peers over her shoulder again, not at Henry but beyond him. She springs to her feet, frees her umbrella from the quick-release strap, and braces for the onslaught—all before the Screamers can converge. Even Ophelia hasn't sensed them yet, and she knows to search for them, knows each one of their trajectories.

Today's trajectory happens to be right where Pansy is aiming her umbrella. She sends out a tree-rattling pulse before tugging Henry to the ground. It's a near miss, the Screamers shrieking past, skimming their umbrellas, shaking the canopies in their wake.

Ophelia has witnessed this attack before, of course. She's seen that mass of Screamers clip Henry, watch them gouge that noble brow and strong jaw, carving a permanent scar across the left side of his face.

Now, though, he escapes without a scratch. Now, he's on his feet, bringing Pansy with him; now, he's ready and more than willing to fight.

But not here. And not now. Ophelia channels every last bit of her strength. She focuses all her intention, every last drop of willpower, on both Pansy and Henry. She concentrates on one crucial message.

Run!

To her immense relief, they do.

CHAPTER 39
PANSY

King's End, Minnesota
Thursday, July 13

I've never seen this many Screamers in King's End. Not even when I returned home from my last summer at the Academy were they this bad. They were insidious, yes. If there's one thing you can count on, it's Screamers being insidious. And yes, my mother was broken. But she was still fighting them, still mending the fence, often with Adele as lookout, shielding her while my mother did the slow work of weaving the chain link together again.

Back then, the Screamers were that odd blend of angry and gleeful. It took me a full weekend to beat them, although we both knew I eventually would.

This is nothing like that. This isn't a game; this is war. And we're outnumbered.

They push us farther into the cemetery. On purpose? After all, I know this space. I wouldn't say it's an unfair advantage, but it's one of the few we have.

I slip beneath Henry's arm to take the lead, to steer us around half-hidden markers jutting from the earth. We don't have much of a choice. We're going wherever they're herding us. But we don't need to add a broken ankle to that.

The sensation of needles erupts along my back. I think I've been hit, and then the same slap strikes my face. Rain. Too cold, too sharp for July. It's a late October sort of rain, full of wet, rotting leaves and decay.

I dart a glance skyward but only catch that brilliant blue above us.

Wind and rain lash the leaves and drench the grass. I slip, and then Henry does. But together, we counter-balance each other. The Screamers are pushing us ever deeper into the cemetery, toward the fence that borders the housing development. Their intent is so strong I can taste it, full of salt and bile and terror.

My terror? Or theirs? For the first time in my life, I can't say.

But I'm not going to the housing development. At least, not yet. I have a different idea, one that might buy us some time and space to think. So, instead of breaking right and taking the path that the Screamers are insisting we should, I veer left. It's a trudge up a hill made slick with rain. But at its crest sits a lovely old willow.

Yes, that same willow where Daniel proposed. I haven't been back since. First, for obvious reasons. It was our spot, after all, and it would only hurt to visit. Then, because patrolling and caring for my mother left little time for afternoons spent in the willow's embrace.

Part of me regrets that I haven't been back sooner. Mostly, though, I'm relieved that her embrace is still welcoming and that there is peace behind the curtain of her sweeping branches. The Screamers don't follow. In fact, it appears as though they've vanished. No telltale hint that they're lurking in the cemetery beyond, waiting to ambush us.

Although I'm willing to bet they are.

Henry opens his umbrella, shakes water from the canvas, then collapses it again. I do the same. She doesn't mind getting wet but hates staying that way.

"This is"—Henry surveys the canopy of willow branches, the leaves fairly glowing—"quite remarkable."

"I used to come here all the time." I stop myself before adding *with Daniel*. "It's the one place in King's End where the Screamers never bothered me."

"Probably because it's not technically King's End."

I freeze at that, a chill running across my damp skin. "Like the covered bridge?"

He crouches and plants a palm on the earth. "No, this is different. This is, for lack of a better word, safe."

"So, no portal or anything like that?"

"No, but I'm detecting the latent indications of some fissures. It's almost like scar tissue." He surveys the branches above us, investigates the soil beneath his fingertips. "Odd. I missed that during my initial assessment, but it fits the data."

I have no idea what he's talking about, but I don't think it's our most pressing problem at the moment. "So, the Screamers?"

"In a sense, they're here with us."

Oh, this can't be good.

"And when we leave?"

"They'll still be with us."

See? I knew it wasn't good. "They're not bothering us, because—?"

Henry exhales, a concerted frown forming on his brow. "I'm not entirely certain. Tell me, you came here often with your young friend?"

Despite everything, my cheeks sprout with heat. "Before then, too. This was ... is one of the spots in King's End that I could relax completely."

"Your mother didn't mind?"

I shake my head. "She always said a girl should have a spot of her own, and this one was mine."

I run my hand along the willow's branches. When my fingers stray too close to that invisible border, the Screamers kick up a fuss.

A screech reverberates in the air but dies completely the second I pull my hand away.

What now? How on earth are we getting out of here? Obviously, we'll need to leave at some point. We can't stay here indefinitely.

"I don't suppose we could reason with them?" I ask.

"Ever the optimist. That would be ideal, wouldn't it?" He pokes the point of his umbrella through the branches. A cacophony resounds, full of venom and spite. He shakes his head. "But I suspect we'll have to make a break for it."

So do I. The question is, which is the best route? "They want us back at the housing development."

"Yes." He gestures in that direction with the point of his umbrella. "I can tell."

"Any idea why?"

"No, except for the fact that it always seems to come back to that stretch of land."

If only we knew why, knew what happened all those years ago. Honestly, I'm *this close* to invoking the Sight. Yes, it's risky. Yes, this is the exact spot where I once nearly bled out. But this is like trying to solve a jigsaw puzzle with several pieces missing. We need more information, and there's one way to get it and get it quickly.

"Pansy, don't."

"What?" I ask, feigning innocence.

"This is the last place where you should invoke the Sight."

He's right. I know it. "We need more to go on. What did my father say? I'm some sort of key? If I could just—"

Henry raises a hand, a placating gesture. "I know, I know. But not here."

"Then you think I should invoke the Sight at some point?"

"Let's say I'm not against the idea of exploring the possibility of you trying to invoke it."

What? I blink at that, trying to work out what he really means. "You could just say no."

He manages a laugh. "Perhaps, in a controlled environment, with support—"

"Meaning you and your magic fingers."

That earns me a real laugh *and* a quick blush. "With my full support." Henry clears his throat. "Then, yes. We could explore whether the Sight might yield something." He looks at me straight on, his eyes hollow with sorrow. "Because all it might do is incapacitate you."

Yes, that's a real possibility.

"The Enclave is too damn cavalier with the Sight," he continues. "I don't think it's occurred to them that perhaps we're not meant to see the future."

This isn't about me; I know that. So I remain silent, prepared to let Henry vent as much as he needs. But he doesn't. Instead, he gives me a smile full of apology.

"Forgive me."

"There's nothing to forgive. I understand."

"Yes." He shuts his eyes and exhales. "I know you do."

He rallies then. Honestly, the man is a first-class rallier, no doubt one of the reasons he's a principal field agent.

"I think we should try to get back home. The question is, which way should we go?"

"They want us in the housing development. That's the path of least resistance. But—"

"They want us in the housing development." Henry peers through the branches, and I follow his gaze as he considers one path and then the other. "You know what?" he says. "I'd like to know why they're so keen to get us there."

"*Keen?*"

"It means eager, desirous."

The schoolmaster is back, and I have no willpower left. I cross my arms over my chest and give him a look. To his credit, he has the good grace to appear contrite.

"Well, then, Agent Darnelle." I ready my umbrella. We'll need to repulse the initial attack before making a run for it. "Let's go find out why they're so *keen*."

Henry sweeps back the willow branches. "After you, Agent Little."

THE SCREAMERS DID WANT us in the housing development. No, they didn't make the trek easy, but when we reached the fence that borders the cemetery, that gaping maw of a hole greeted us.

Henry's lips twitched at the display. "They do love their symbolism."

That they do.

Now, though, I'm wondering if we've made a horrible mistake. The weather comes at us in waves: from monsoon-like rains to blistering heat, to devastating frost, to hailstones that leave tiny bruises along my arms. In flashes, the development around us changes, from how it might have looked fully completed, filled with happy families, to cultivated farmland, to nature reclaiming this space.

My hand is secure in Henry's, but the Screamers are intent on driving us apart. So he reels me in until I'm flush against his chest. And while our umbrellas are collapsed—this gale is too much, even for them—they have enough power to create a protective bubble around us.

Granted, we can't maneuver like this, but we can catch our breath.

It's warm here in his embrace, even though sleet lashes my back. My hair is plastered to my scalp, and my T-shirt and jeans are drenched. Rivulets of rain cascade down the side of Henry's face. We take tiny, stuttering steps, but at this rate, we won't reach the main gate by next week, never mind before dark.

Something tells me we really need to leave before dark.

"I think we should split up," he says, his breath so hot against my cold ear, it nearly scorches. "Force them to divide their strength. They can't manifest weather if they're stretched too thin."

All this sounds reasonable, but I don't like it. I don't want to split up. I don't want to stretch *ourselves* too thin. Most of all, I don't want to let go of Henry.

"I want you to run as fast as you can for the gate." His words are nonnegotiable.

I protest anyway. "I won't leave you."

"Listen to me." All at once, his voice turns deadly serious. "This isn't normal Screamer behavior. This isn't something the two of us can fight."

Yes, something's changed. I sense that. But what that is, I can't say. These Screamers don't even feel like King's End Screamers. My mind reaches out, curious as to why that might be, and the rush of blood is hot and thick against my upper lip.

I swipe my nose with the back of my hand, and the flow stems almost immediately. But not before one, two, three drops of blood spatter on the damp soil.

The ground rumbles beneath our feet. I watch in horror as the earth swallows up those drops of blood. Henry looks ashen. It's this, more than anything else, that makes my throat constrict with panic.

He takes me by the shoulders. "Run as fast as you can for the gate. Don't look back. Just run. I'll be right behind you."

That last sentence is a full-on lie.

"Promise me, Pansy. Run and don't look back."

I make no such promise.

But I do run.

CHAPTER 40
HENRY

King's End, Minnesota
Thursday, July 13

So, this was how it was going to be, then? Here was where it would end, in King's End and not the Sahara. Polite of the Screamers to make the trip halfway around the world just for him.

He could only hope Pansy had run when he told her to. He didn't have the margin to check. Yes, he was most likely going to die today. But no, he wasn't going to make it easy for the Screamers. Henry stood, the rain battering him, umbrella humming with anticipation. He would miss this. Whatever was on the other side, he felt certain he'd have to leave both this fight and his umbrella behind.

Well, yes, you can't take it with you.

What first, then? Which of this mass was the nastiest of the bunch, the ones destined to give Pansy the most trouble? Start there. What had Max Monroe said?

You protect her with your life. That's your role in all this.

Henry could see that now, although if he were honest with himself, he'd known his role from the moment he'd arrived in King's

End. It was there, flavoring the air, swirling just out of reach. Ophelia, no doubt, could've told him.

Ophelia. He shook thoughts of his sister from his head. Pansy could reach her; Pansy might be the one to save her. With that idea, that hope, he raised his umbrella and sent out a pulse. Then he smiled.

"Let's do this."

CHAPTER 41
PANSY

King's End, Minnesota
Thursday, July 13

Of course I look back. Why Henry thought I wouldn't, I can't say. But he's standing in the middle of the housing development, busy playing hero, so he hasn't checked.

Which is just as well. Because I have other plans.

The pulse his umbrella sends out resounds. The saplings, the framed-in houses, the chain-link, all of it shakes and rattles. The force clears the area of Screamers. The rain stops. The wind dies. Sunlight touches my cheeks, and above, that blue, blue sky appears surreal.

This, I know, is my cue to run, to escape the development. Instead, I skirt the showcase home. If Henry does spare a glance, he'll think I've gone. I can't leave him alone. He's just executed his signature move. And I know what comes next.

The mass gathers on the far side of the development, near that hole in the fence. From the fissure near the basement egress window, more Screamers emerge. They all but ignore me. A few dive-bomb my head, more harassment than a precision move meant to incapacitate. Then they take off as well. Henry is still sending out that pulse.

And it's irresistible.

The Screamers gather, coalescing into a tornado again. The sky above him is that sickly green, a bruise that simply won't heal. The air is full of static. It raises the hairs on the back of my neck and along my arms.

I inch closer, planning my next move, gauging which tactic might work best. Hit them straight on? Flank Henry and the entire mass and strike from the side or even from behind? As I consider my options, the tableau freezes me in place.

Henry, standing alone against a gathering so large, I can no longer detect individual Screamers. They are a cyclone, or a sandstorm, or possibly a mushroom cloud. They obliterate the landscape. They are destruction itself. This is what the Sight showed me at the farmers market. Seldom, if ever, is it so precise, so exact. Something always changes; there are too many variables for it not to. Except now.

I'm witnessing the end of Henry Darnelle.

And I can't let that happen.

CHAPTER 42
OPHELIA

King's End, Minnesota
Thursday, July 13

Ophelia is holding her breath. Or, at least, it feels that way. She has seen Henry die so many times, too many to count. The Enclave always comes for him, and the Enclave always wins.

But she's never seen him die like this, facing down what must be the largest gathering of Screamers outside a level five hot spot, maybe larger. Certainly, larger than the Sahara.

Now Ophelia wonders if urging Henry and Pansy to get out in front of the Screamers simply condemned them both. Because Pansy isn't leaving, and Henry certainly isn't. Pansy will have to drag him from the development, assuming he agrees to come at all.

But the alternative wasn't any better. Ophelia knows this. The confrontation in the cemetery left them both incapacitated. It was so fierce that Henry's umbrella sent out that automatic override and alerted Enclave HQ that something catastrophic had occurred, which, to be fair, it had.

Henry and Pansy never make it back home in that scenario. The

Enclave—or rather, the portion that Botten controls—swoops in, finds them broken among the headstones, and then gets on with the business of ending the world.

That last looks an awful lot like what's happening now.

If a full complement of top-notch Enclave field agents can't fight the coming storm, Ophelia can't imagine how Pansy and Henry might. She supposes now, at least, the Enclave—and Botten in particular—are denied any part in this. It's a pyrrhic sort of victory.

From behind the showcase home, Pansy is weighing her options. Does she see things Ophelia can't? Pansy swipes at her nose, that blood again, making her appear as fierce as she is.

She runs, then, not toward Henry or the Screamers, and not even toward the gate and freedom, but toward the center of the housing development. Because something is happening on the far side of the development, something Ophelia just now has noticed. A mighty force strikes Henry, strikes his heart, and sends him flying backward. He is airborne, umbrella still clutched in one hand.

He lands hard, right where Pansy is standing. With the help of that clever little umbrella, she breaks the impact. But Henry is sizable, tall, broad shoulders, all muscle. Pansy, while no slouch, most likely weighs half of what he does. Henry should crush her.

He doesn't. True, he crashes into her, and they go tumbling. Pansy cries out in pain but swallows it back immediately. Then they come to utter stillness. Both are coated in mud and debris.

Ophelia flits around them, urging one or the other to move. She tries to pat a cheek, shake a shoulder, to no avail. Henry is on his back, eyes closed, and his skin has a sickly gray cast to it. Pansy is slumped against his chest. They would look like lovers, like sweethearts, if not for the mud and the blood and the stillness that feels so wrong.

Henry is oblivious to the world, so she kneels next to Pansy, her words urgent.

Can you hear me? You need to move. You need to get out of here.

Ophelia scans the sky. It roils above them. The Screamers aren't through, not by half, but they've stopped their attack. Not out of politeness, certainly, but wariness. Something about Pansy and Henry *together* is giving the Screamers pause.

Pansy's eyes flutter open. She winces, then pushes to her knees. She brings her cheek to Henry's mouth and her fingers to his neck. Her exhale of relief tells Ophelia everything she needs to know, and she releases a sob.

"He's alive," Pansy says to the space where Ophelia hovers.

Pansy gets to work, deploying and then anchoring both umbrellas. Their affinity for each other creates a protective bubble. She uncurls Henry's fingers and extracts the epi-pen there. She tugs off the cap with her teeth and plunges the needle into his thigh, none too gently.

Yes. I know. He's too much of a hero.

The Screamers have gathered their wits and their strength. They circle, circle, circle above the shield created by the umbrellas. This space is a refuge, a respite, but it's unsustainable. At some point, they will need to leave the development. Moving will shatter that protective bubble. Henry's in no shape to walk, never mind fight. Pansy can't lug him home and keep up an active defense.

But Pansy's full focus is on Henry. From her pocket, she pulls out a small bottle. With a hand behind his head, she eases the contents between his lips. Henry coughs, sputters, but his eyes flutter open. A moment later, color returns to his cheeks. He scans their arrangement and then peers up into the sky.

"Yeah," Pansy says. "I know."

But even as she speaks, Pansy herself is scanning the area, a frown creasing her brow. She touches Henry's hand, and the Screamers recede. With her hand still in his, she touches her umbrella, and they recede farther.

Henry catches on. Immediately, of course. He reaches behind him and latches on to his umbrella. He grips Pansy's hand, and she holds tight to her own umbrella. Another trickle of blood coats Pansy's upper lip. Then, again, one, two, three drops of blood splatter against the earth.

The sonic boom is like nothing Ophelia has ever heard. The shock wave rolls through the development. Somehow, the umbrellas remain anchored. Somehow, they maintain that protective bubble. The world quakes. The Screamers shriek, one piercing blast of anguish and anger.

That thunderclap of sound is so strong that it hurls Ophelia from King's End and all the way back to Seattle.

CHAPTER 43
HENRY

Yes, the sky was clear. And, yes, his heart was broken. Tendrils of agony snaked through his chest, tightening, squeezing. Was this an actual heart attack or merely a metaphorical one? Did it matter?

No, it didn't.

The universe had made known what it thought of Henry Darnelle.

It wasn't much.

With caution, he unclenched his umbrella. Whatever Pansy had done, whatever they had done together, Henry didn't trust it would last. They needed to move.

If only he could.

"We don't have much time," Pansy said.

She was right in more ways than one. The Screamers would return. This ache in his heart would redouble, make it impossible for him to walk or run, never mind fight.

"You should leave me behind," he said.

Pansy simply stared at him as if he'd babbled nonsense. Then she turned to the task at hand. She collapsed both umbrellas and slung them cross-body over her shoulder. She crouched and, with unexpected strength, levered Henry to his feet.

"You are ... full of surprises ... Agent Little."

"Can you walk?"

Could he? Perhaps. If he focused on his feet, on how his muscles should move. "I think so."

He tried not to collapse against her, like an umbrella himself. His legs were unsteady, and his head swam with their first steps. They weren't that far from the main entrance, and he marked each footfall. Main gate. The shadow of the Camelot Lots sign. The gravel road that led to the sidewalk.

Henry wasn't the least bit surprised when a bear appeared on that sidewalk. The creature loomed. Pansy flinched, her sharp intake of breath a warning. Then she relaxed. After that, the bear, the creature, the man slipped his shoulder under Henry's.

"There we go," the bear-man said. "I got you."

Henry's world receded until all he saw was a single pinpoint of light, and then that, too, blinked out.

CHAPTER 44
PANSY

King's End, Minnesota
Thursday, July 13

"My car's faster than 911." My neighbor, Guy Gunderson, steers us in the direction of his house and the EV that's charging in the garage.

He's so substantial that I can't fight against him. I'm caught in the current, and since he's shouldering most of Henry's weight, I don't have an option but to follow.

"No hospital." I trip over my feet, then Henry's, and stumble a few steps. "No urgent care. Help me get him home. Please, Guy."

"He's barely conscious." Guy considers me, his gaze calculating and critical. "And you're not much better."

Physically, both Henry and I are battered. My hip aches from when he crashed into me, or rather, the landing after he crashed into me. But our main issues are Screamer related: the toxins, the build-up, the wounds no ER doctor could detect, never mind treat. I need to brew a huge pot of tea. I need to swallow back some of my mother's emergency tinctures and force Henry to do the same.

What I don't need to do is talk my way out of the ER under the scrutiny of some sharp-eyed nurse.

I've never spoken with Guy about the Enclave, not like Adele. But he's in all those old photos; he attended all those parties. I think of that grocery delivery with Henry's favorite scotch. Maybe Guy knows something, and maybe he doesn't, but he does know *someone*.

"He can't go to the hospital," I manage between panting breaths. "Because he really is Harry Darnelle's son."

Guy freezes in our trek up the sidewalk. I use his hesitation to pull a full inhale. The morning sun touches my forehead, but my clothes are soaked, and the warmth can't chase away the chill. Guy's expression is incredulous, then understanding lights in his eyes.

"Really? Harry's son?" He breathes the words, his voice full of awe. His gaze scans Henry, no doubt evaluating that noble brow and firm jaw, those cheekbones. "I mean, we thought, or maybe guessed. Milo was sure, but I wasn't totally convinced. Seemed like a—"

"Coincidence," I finish.

Guy nods. "But yes, I can see it now. He's Harry's son, absolutely."

"And I need to take care of him."

With a mighty huff, Guy switches directions, and we head for my house.

I shed most of my muddy layers on the porch and rush inside. Tinctures first, tea second. The next half an hour is chaotic. I knock back one of the nastier of my mother's concoctions, and between Guy and myself, we force Henry to do the same. He shudders and coughs the way I wish I had time to.

"Find him something dry," Guy says to me.

I take the stairs by twos, barge into the room where Henry is staying, and glance around.

The space is so tidy, it hurts. Items are lined up carefully on the dresser. A thick book on the nightstand with a ribbon bookmark. On the bed, tucked beneath the pillow, are a pair of pajama bottoms and a matching T-shirt. The material is silky soft between my fingers, and a hint of that spicy vanilla reaches me. I'm relieved, actually. Part of me suspected Henry Darnelle slept in a three-piece suit along with tie and ridiculous hat.

Guy cleans up Henry while I brew tea. I bring out my mother's entire arsenal, consult her notes, running my finger down the check-list of items and adding ingredients as I go. A few years into my Academy training, I asked her why we needed so many emergency supplies. The Screamers are nasty and certainly have their tricks, but back then, even on their worst days, they were nothing like this.

"King's End may surprise you one day," is all she said.

It certainly has.

By the time the tea is ready, Guy has Henry settled on the couch in the office, clean and dry, tucked into a fleece blanket.

"I tried to take him up the stairs," Guy says, shaking his head with chagrin. "I'm afraid I'm not as young as I used to be."

"That's okay. It's easier if he's downstairs." I assess Henry. He's still far too pale, but his skin is not nearly as gray. I set the tea service on the coffee table and pour a cup.

Guy scoops up the muddy clothes, and as he leaves the room, I call over my shoulder, "Just toss them in the laundry room."

Then I turn my attention back to Henry, but not before a wave of exhaustion hits me. It's a good thing Guy didn't carry Henry upstairs.

"Henry? Can you hear me?"

His breathing is steady and sure. That's a good sign. With finger-tips against the underside of his wrist, I take his pulse and check the feel of his skin. He's running hot, but when I check for a fever, there is none. So maybe Henry Darnelle always runs hot.

If I had a penlight, I'd check his pupils. He needs more tea, but not if he's unable to swallow. There's always the standard issue epi-pens. Not nearly as good as my mother's tea, but they might get him to the point where he can drink some.

I'm about to ask Guy for a penlight when a better idea occurs to me.

"Agent Darnelle, can you hear me?"

A brief stirring, and something that sounds like a disgruntled sigh.

"Agent Darnelle, this is important."

A deep intake of breath followed by an exhale. "I ... thought ... we agreed ... on ... first ... names."

There he is. I can't help but smile. "All right, *Henry*. Can you hear me?"

"Could ... the first time."

I can't tell if that's sarcasm or if he's merely stating fact. I sigh, and I swear his lips twitch in response.

"I'm a terrible patient," he adds.

"Can you behave long enough to drink some tea?"

It takes Guy to help leverage Henry to a sitting position. The first sips go down rough. The first sips always do. I know that from experience. Once Henry can sit without Guy's support, I pour myself a cup and drink it down, wincing as I do.

"Is it supposed to be this foul?" Henry stares at the remaining liquid in his cup like a five-year-old staring down a plate of Brussels sprouts.

"It's the toxins, actually. The worse the hit, the worse this tastes." I raise my cup. "Once it starts neutralizing things, it won't be so bad."

"I'm not quite sure how it could be any worse."

I want to agree. I want to tell him this is the worst I've ever tasted, and *that* has nothing to do with my inability to cook. Tea, I can make. But I don't want to mention any of this, not in front of Guy. The Sight, maybe, is keeping me from uttering those words.

"You're doing better," Guy observes. "Both of you."

I look at him, and a wave of gratitude washes over me for this big bear of a man who can't help but keep tabs on everyone in the neighborhood.

"Thank you," I say. "I don't know what—" I'm about to say that I don't know what I would've done without him, but he holds up a finger and then tugs his phone from his pocket.

For one horrible moment, I'm afraid we'll end up as a thread on Hey Neighbor.

"You would've managed, Pansy-Girl. You always do. But." He taps out a message. "I'm having Milo send over some dinner and maybe a little something for tomorrow morning as well."

"That's kind of you," Henry says.

"You both look like you need some comfort food. I'll have Milo check to see if we have any tater-tot hotdish left in the back."

Oh! Guy's pulling out the big guns. Not everyone gets the tater-tot hotdish, especially the ones Guy conjures up. Never the same dish twice. Henry looks askance at the prospect. I'm pretty sure he'll change his mind after the first bite.

Guy tucks his phone away and then studies Henry. "I knew your father." Again, that long stare, the light in his eyes, an unreadable history. Not even the Sight is willing to spare a single hint.

"He was a good man," Guy adds after a long moment. "And I'm sorry for your loss."

Henry nods, and I can taste the heartbreak.

Guy sits with Henry while I shower the mud from my skin. I'm still fighting exhaustion, but the toxin is leaving my system. My head is clear enough to know what both Henry and I need, which is some solid sleep.

A short while later, I'm at the front door with Guy, and his reluctance to leave creases his brow. He's a huge, worried Teddy bear.

"You'll be okay?" he asks. "I can stay."

Milo's delivery is tucked safely away in the fridge for later. Henry is sleeping, and that's next on the agenda for me.

"We're fine." Fine being one of those relative terms. I pause, considering what it is that's pinging the back of my mind. "Actually, could you do me a favor?"

"Anything."

"Make sure no one goes near the housing development."

"No one ever does, except for you."

"I know." I shut my eyes, because now there's an overlay to my memory. I see multiple developments, or rather, multiple versions of the land the housing development sits on. "Things are different. And someone might..."

Might what? Be tempted there? What does this mean for the citizens of King's End? Can this new reality hurt them? I don't know, but I can't let anyone near the development until we know for certain.

"And maybe the front door?" I don't expect anyone to show up, but I'd rather not be surprised.

Guy pulls me into a hug. "I'll keep watch."

I know this: he absolutely will.

I ease the door closed behind him. My umbrella and Henry's are snuggled together in the stand. Their canopies are a bit deflated, but they are definitely cozy and content.

"Thank you," I whisper. "Thank you both."

From the pantry, I pull out the pillow and blanket and lug them to the office, grabbing my phone along the way. I switch it back on in case something does happen, and Guy sends a text.

Henry appears serene, dark eyelashes brushing those cheekbones, mouth soft, like a little boy's. His chest rises and falls in a way that reassures me, makes my own chest loosen, my own breathing relax.

Yes, I could sleep, too, possibly for days. I shove the coffee table out of the way and then curl up on the floor next to the couch. The last thing I feel before sleep takes me is the reassuring brush of fingertips against my forehead.

☂

I ENTER THE OFFICE TRIUMPHANTLY, a tray with two plates of hotdish, a pot of fresh tea, and the aroma of both wafting ahead of me.

Now, even if you've never tried tater-tot hotdish, you probably know what it is: ground beef, cream of mushroom soup, and frozen tater tots, obviously. You can doctor it up. You can make it fancy with fresh ingredients and a rack full of spices. No one but Guy can do all that and still infuse it with nostalgia. It simultaneously tastes like your favorite childhood casserole and something from a Michelin-star restaurant.

Henry raises an eyebrow, his skepticism melting in the wake of the scent. He's sitting up, barely, but he's managing it. Earlier, he tried to push himself from the couch to help in the kitchen, but his legs refused to cooperate.

He needs to eat. We both do. But more than that, I suspect he's injured somewhere and trying to hide it. The Screamers landed a direct hit, and the wound is draining him. I hand him a plate, pour tea, and then sit on the coffee table directly across from him. I'm determined not to miss a single wince.

Henry sips from his cup and then raises it. "Same recipe?"

"Exactly."

"Not nearly as foul."

My tea tastes floral, like sugared petals. His should, too, assuming no injuries. But I let him eat, which he does, two huge platefuls of hotdish.

"That was quite extraordinary," he says as I clear the dishes. "I admit to being skeptical, especially since I've never had tater tots before."

"No. You must have."

He shakes his head.

"Not even at school?" Then I remember he went to a fancy boarding school and that his family had an actual butler. So no, tater tots weren't on the menu.

"I rather like them," he adds.

"I'll be sure to tell Guy."

I heft the tray with all its rattling dishes and head for the kitchen. When I return, I'm lugging the bin with all my mother's first aid supplies, or at least the ones we use for a direct hit. I set it and then myself on the coffee table. Elbows on knees, chin on fists, I stare at him.

I'm good at this. The only person I can't stare down is—or was—

my mother. But Jack? He folds immediately. Mort? He'll invent a reason to glance away. Never mind the tea, the telltale winces, or that tic near his left eye. I have the Sight. I *know* Henry's injured.

Still, I may have met my match with Henry Darnelle. He returns my gaze, seemingly content, as if a standoff is normal after-dinner behavior. He's not giving an inch. If I don't, the wound is only going to fester.

So there it is: I break first.

"I know you're hurt," I say.

"I'm fine."

"You're not. You're wounded, and it won't resolve on its own, so let me treat it." I pat the Tupperware next to me. "Unless you have something in your own field kit I should use. That balm, maybe?"

He shakes his head.

"Won't it work?"

"The issue is that it perhaps works too well. Do you remember how it made you feel?"

"It was amazing. Like I could charge out the door and take on more Screamers."

He raises that schoolmaster eyebrow.

"Oh." The problem hits me, a sharp stab of worry. "And in your condition, you shouldn't charge out the door and take on more Screamers."

"Exactly. It's not addictive, not technically. But its uses are limited. The worse the wound, the more discretion is warranted."

"So, what you're really saying is you are wounded, and we should do something about it."

He tips his head back and stares up at the ceiling. "Yes, I suppose we should, Agent Little."

"I thought we agreed to first names."

The barest hint of a stealth smile touches his lips. Then he sits up and pulls the T-shirt over his head. And I can't speak. I'm not sure I can even breathe. I've seen my share of Screamer wounds. My mother had several when I returned from the Academy. Adele was doing her best to heal them, but there are reasons the Enclave treats its own, and this is one of them.

This wound needs treatment. Honestly, I should've insisted on seeing it before we both fell asleep. It's not the jagged gash left in the wake of most direct hits. Instead, the wound is perfectly round. A swollen, angry circle sits on the spot above where his heart is. The bruising radiates outward, red and purple and nearly black.

I'm afraid to touch it.

"What happened?"

"Trousers, cargo pocket, right-hand side."

This must be where the answer is. I head for the laundry room and the muddy clothes on the tile floor. The scent of cold rain and damp soil reaches me as I search. The air is clammy, and the sensation of it crawls across my skin. My fingers brush something small and cool in that cargo pocket. I sit back on my heels and consider the object in the center of my palm: an exquisitely crafted platinum wedding band.

CHAPTER 45
HENRY

King's End, Minnesota
Thursday, July 13

Pansy returned faster than Henry had expected but slower than he'd hoped. If he were honest with himself, he'd wish the ring away, lost between here and the housing development. Although he knew it hadn't been. That wasn't how his luck was running.

Pansy was sitting across from him now, the ring in the center of her palm. While he didn't necessarily owe her an explanation, he wanted to give her one.

"A few months back, when I was in the Sahara, I walked into a sandstorm."

"You know that's legendary, right?"

"It shouldn't be." Henry shook his head as if shaking that long-ago sand from his ears. "Because I didn't do anything. I didn't tame the Screamers. It wasn't long after my father died, and all I wanted to do was fight."

Indeed, he'd walked into the desert without an exit strategy. It was enough to take the physical and psychic beating, more than enough. After losing his father to death and Ophelia to the Sight, all Henry wanted was to lose himself. The Sahara and the Screamers gave him that opportunity.

Pansy nodded. Yes, she understood exactly what he was saying. "So, you were fighting the Screamers? And?"

"I pulled off my ring—"

"This ring?" She held it up between her index finger and thumb. When she tried to give it to him, he refused.

"Yes, that ring. I pulled off my ring and threw it into the heart of the sandstorm, right into the Screamers' center of mass."

He hadn't planned it that way. He'd been driven to the ground, his umbrella valiantly sending out a defensive pulse along with an SOS, not that anyone would venture a rescue at that point. Henry figured that if he had to go, he'd go free of obligations.

"Let me get this straight. You threw the ring, this ring." She held it up again, and it glinted dully in the low light of the office. "Into a sandstorm, the one in the Sahara?"

"Yes, and a moment later, a vortex opened. The ring vanished, along with all the Screamers. *That's* how I defeated them." The stillness in the wake of that had been breathtaking and bewildering, sand settling like a gentle rain. "That's the only reason I walked out alive."

"And now, four months later?"

He nodded. "Four, or thereabouts."

"Four months later, it reappears. Here. In King's End."

Like a shot across the bow. He pressed his lips together and gave another nod. "So it would seem."

"That's—"

"Unprecedented?"

"I was going to say bizarre, but sure, let's go with unprecedented. Whatever it is, this can't be good."

"I'm assuming it's not. It's also why I was so interested in your mother's encounters in the same area."

"Do you think it's connected?"

"I'm not sure. Perhaps it's a piece of the puzzle. Or perhaps it's completely unrelated, and we're chasing ghosts. It's also not the entire story." Now, he did pluck the ring from her fingers. "This is my betrothal ring."

"I figured as much."

He tucked the ring into the pocket of his pajamas, where it could burn guiltily against his thigh. "I should've been honest with you."

"About being betrothed? Please." This time, Pansy didn't glance away. Instead, she treated him to a full eye roll, and the gesture nearly made him laugh. "Everyone I know from an old family is betrothed. I'm sure my mother is the only reason I'm not. She said it was all nonsense."

"Not that you didn't have offers."

"Wait. What?"

He waved away the question. "Several, in your mother's files, from every last old family in the Enclave. I'll show you later."

Pansy scooted back on the coffee table, her expression bemused. Then her eyes brightened with a mischievous light. "I guess rule six applies to me as well."

"It's clear your mother never entertained any of the offers, so you're free." Henry pulled in a breath. "I was hoping for the same thing. Before my father's health declined, we spoke a great deal about regrets. He wanted me to know that I could make my own choices, especially when it came to the person I'll spend the rest of my life with."

Or not, given the divorce rate in the Enclave. Never, for a moment, did Henry believe his father regretted having a son. But following one of the Enclave's rules meant following another, and yet another, until you had no choice but to follow them all.

"I grew up with my betrothed, and I do care for her, but I don't love her the way someone should love the person they hope to marry. So I submitted my paperwork for an annulment. This was a few months before Ophelia's coma, and my father's death, but the High Council used both as an excuse to table the matter."

Indeed they did, indefinitely. True, the jaunt halfway around the globe hadn't helped matters. Nor had his anger.

"Well, that explains this." She reached out and traced that pale band of skin still visible on his left ring finger. Her touch was so light, so careful, it was no wonder she could repair fissures so precisely.

"And then," Henry added, "Botten sends me here with the implicit promise that if I do what he wants, he'll push the annulment through the High Council."

"Oh." She tilted her head in thought. "You had a lot to lose in helping me, Agent Darnelle."

"If I hadn't, I would have lost something far more important."

She didn't ask, and he didn't volunteer. A piece of him had been missing, perhaps the one that had kept him, in the past, from putting up and shutting up. This piece reminded him that there were rules, and then there were *rules*. The ones he followed were entirely up to him and his moral compass.

"Can I ask you something?" she said.

"Of course." Henry braced for the question. At this point, she had the right to ask him anything from the name of his betrothed to what he planned to do next.

"There's a waitlist, right?"

It took him a moment, took seeing that mischievous glint in her eyes. Then he laughed. "Not as long as yours, Agent Little, should you care to avail yourself of it."

"No one's come knocking on my door."

"Not yet. Don't be surprised if there's renewed interest once I submit your examination report."

"No one wants to end up in a permanent post assignment."

"I'm not so sure anymore." Henry let his gaze wander. If he wasn't mistaken, this room belonged to Pansy. It was a bit more whimsical than the front parlor, what with the pink-hued fairy lights, the shelves filled with books, the scattering of polka dots: a cup and saucer, multiple pillows and their matching blankets. "I think a permanent post assignment might suit me very well."

CHAPTER 46
OPHELIA

King's End, Minnesota
Thursday, July 13

Once again, for those in the back: Is he flirting, ladies? Or merely stating fact? Whichever the case, Ophelia notices he's neatly managed to delay treatment of his wound.

Another fact about Henry Darnelle: He truly is a terrible patient.

But Pansy's having none of it. She gestures toward his chest, the aggressive wound that seems to be getting worse rather than better. That could be the physical compounding the psychic damage, but Ophelia isn't so sure.

Because she's never seen this before, not the wound, and not that tidbit of Henry chucking his betrothal ring into a sandstorm. The latter delights her more than it should. Even at his lowest, her brother never disappoints. He could start a trend. She can see it now. Enclave agents all over the world tossing their rings off cliffs and into hurricanes and posting the videos on social media. #DoneWithIt.

Pansy digs around in the container on the coffee table. "If we can't use the balm, there's always this." She pulls out an opaque tub of what looks like goo. The second she cracks the lid, the aroma strikes them all, hard.

Henry jerks back. The scent is so strong, it infiltrates the ephemeral space where Ophelia hovers.

Oh, that is foul, like Vicks VapoRub on steroids.

"I *know*," Pansy says, though it's unclear whether she's addressing Henry, Ophelia, or both of them. "Two of the main ingredients are tea tree oil and eucalyptus. It reeks, and you're going to reek for days. But trust me, it works."

"It's not that," Henry says. "It ... my father ... he would use this. He started mentoring me quite young, and I remember this from the aftermath of those sessions. He always said a good friend taught him how to make it. It smells like..."

Love.

Henry drifts off, blinks, and comes back to himself. "My childhood. It's one of those smells I'll always associate with my childhood. When things settle down, I don't suppose you'd teach me how to make it."

Does Henry see that smile, feel the full force of its weight and warmth? How Pansy practically glows?

"Sure, but I warn you, it's an afternoon in the kitchen."

"Really?" Henry raises an eyebrow. "And you claim not to cook."

She proffers the tub. "Have you smelled this?"

Henry laughs, and Pansy's smile grows even wider.

"When you're better, and when things are better, I'll show you how." She dips her fingers into the goopy mess. "But now, Agent Darnelle? Would you like to do the honors, or should I?"

Something flickers in Henry's expression, the slightest of hesitations, a bit of warring between the better and lesser angels of his nature. Pansy sits there, expression placid, unaware of the conundrum she's put Henry in. Ophelia hovers closer, watching the thoughts behind his eyes, a tally of pros and cons.

"Would you?" he says at last.

Yes! Her brother manages to surprise and yet never disappoint.

"I'm not certain I can see the full extent of the wound," he adds.

Fairly flimsy excuse, brother mine.

But Pansy doesn't seem to mind, not in the least. And, in fairness, she is better at this task and with the sticky goo in general. The first layer goes on thick, and the wound absorbs it so thoroughly that no trace of it is left. She applies layer after layer, and in due course, the thick coating forms a seal on his chest. Even so, the goo gets every-where. On Henry, obviously, straying to his biceps and neck. But on Pansy, too, including, somehow, the tip of her nose.

Henry lets out an exhale, one full of relief and recuperation. "That *is* amazing. I can feel it working. I think it's better than the balm in some ways."

"In *some* ways," Pansy echoes. "Just wait until you try to shower it off."

"Still, why isn't something like this part of our standard issue?" Henry frowns, full of contemplation. "When things *are* settled, I'm going to bring that up with R&D."

"It's just a home remedy."

"And those should never be dismissed out of hand. Our ancestors managed to do this job all without an Enclave, electronics, or an R&D department."

Oh, look, the schoolmaster is back. Henry *must* be feeling better. But he studies Pansy with a tender expression in his eyes, a smile that starts slow but eventually pops both dimples.

"I don't suppose you'd allow me to return the favor, Agent Little?"

It's not so much the words but the tone that brings Ophelia up short. Henry's voice is full of seductive promise. Before Ophelia can pull herself from this vision and flee to Seattle, Pansy offers him the tub of goo.

He scoops a bit on his fingers and then, with the utmost care, paints Pansy's throat with long, languid strokes. Ophelia averts her eyes, hoping something else will capture her attention.

Really, there are some things a sister should not see.

"Better?" Henry asks.

Pansy nods, her gaze dreamy and unfocused. Her grip loosens on the container, and it nearly pitches to the floor.

Now, *that* would've been a mess.

Pansy sits back on the coffee table and secures the lid, not that it helps with the stench. Henry reaches for his T-shirt and, after a brief tug-of-war, allows Pansy to help him pull it back on. The cotton catches on his chest, and he cringes, ever so slightly.

"I know," Pansy says.

"I believe it will be worth it." He plucks at his shirt. "My head is definitely clearer, and the wound is subdued."

"You'll feel better in the morning. Maybe not fully back to normal. That's going to take a while to heal." She shakes her head as if still seeing that wound in her mind's eye. "But now? I think you should rest. That will do you the most good."

"We both should rest." He nods to the blanket and pillow and the cozy nest they make on the floor. "And you shouldn't have to sleep there. Can you make it up the stairs?"

"It's ... I mean, I don't—"

Before Pansy can finish, Henry plucks the pillow from the floor, scoots over on the couch, and pats the space next to him in invitation.

"Merely resting," he says. "We both need to recuperate."

Anyone else, and Ophelia wouldn't believe it. Even if his lesser angels steer once in a while, Henry's moral compass is strong and sure.

"Besides, I don't like the idea of you being alone," he adds.

Not that he's in any condition to play knight in shining armor.

He casts the floor a dismissive glance. "Nor should you sleep there."

"I don't want to leave you alone, either." Pansy is wavering, weighing those pros and cons in her own way. But her expression is so soft that Ophelia suspects Henry has already won.

"See?" He gestures to the couch. "We're stuck with this."

Gingerly, oh so gingerly—as if she hasn't been held in a very long time—Pansy eases herself next to Henry. He snuggles her in close, in the crook of his shoulder. They fit together, flawlessly. Pansy's expression is a delicate blend of caution and bliss. Her hair spreads across his arm, and the look of pure contentment on her brother's face is nothing Ophelia has ever seen before. This perfect moment hurts so much that Ophelia wishes she could scoop up some of that goo and spread it across her heart.

Pansy falls asleep almost immediately. Henry remains awake, a furrow of concern on his brow. His gaze doesn't track Ophelia, but she knows he senses what she does.

The coming storm—the one triggered by the SOS his umbrella sent out this morning—rests heavily on his mind. The Enclave will arrive, and soon. That much is certain. Not even calling in an all-clear will stop that. In a matter of a few hours, King's End has gone from a permanent post assignment—and a shit one, at that—to a level five hot spot.

Her brother weighs each course of action, taking into account the machinations of sending a response team and how many players will have a hand in that. Botten, certainly. But all members of the High Council will also be notified. No one likes to let a good crisis go to waste, the High Council in particular.

What happens once the response team arrives? The scenarios play out in Henry's expression, a tic here, a twitch of his lips there. But they've never trod this path before.

And not even Ophelia knows the answer to that.

CHAPTER 47
PANSY

The insistent buzz of text messages pulls me from a sleep I don't want to leave. Checking my phone means moving, and I don't want to do that, either. I'm here, next to Henry, and this couch is somehow wide enough for the two of us.

Waking means facing whatever we need to face today. Waking means leaving his warmth, this comfort, the way my feet nestle against his, how my head fits in the crook of his shoulder, his hand resting against my waist. His fingertips have found that sliver of skin between my pajama bottoms and cami. The feel of that is so delicious and forbidden that I could hold still for hours and soak it in.

Waking means leaving all that behind. I know, without a doubt, that this is not my new normal.

My phone buzzes again, impatient. A rattling comes from the umbrella stand, full of frantic warning. That has me slipping off the couch and to the floor. I paw the coffee table for my phone. On the screen is a series of increasingly anxious text messages from Guy:

Pansy-Girl, there's someone in your
driveway.

Rental sedan would be my guess. High end.

They've been sitting there for a while.

Oh, getting out now.

Umbrella! One of yours, then?

Oh, my. She's severe.

Let me know if you need me to run
interference.

On your porch.

That's when the doorbell rings. I glance at Henry and swallow the urge to hush both the sound and the person on my porch.

"Coming," I whisper-shout, as if someone behind layers of glass and wood can hear me, but not the man sleeping on my couch. The taste of eucalyptus is thick against my tongue, and my mouth is sticky with residue from the toxins leaving my system. I'm rumpled from sleeping next to Henry, and I wonder if we should make that look less obvious.

The doorbell rings again.

With a final glance at Henry, I decide we don't have time for social niceties and tiptoe from the office.

My umbrella is agitated, ruffles beating a frenzied rhythm against the stand. Henry's umbrella appears morose. It's slumped to one side, so dull and despondent that it looks like a mere store-bought version. And here I thought my umbrella was overly dramatic.

On the front porch stands the tallest, blondest woman I have ever seen. Since King's End is in Minnesota, I've seen any number of tall, blond individuals—Guy Gunderson being a prime example. This woman? Statuesque. Her suit? Royal blue and impeccable, and her hair is pulled back into a sleek bun.

The sight of her leaves me feeling even more rumpled and unkempt.

She clutches a silver-sided briefcase. Over one arm, she carries a butter-yellow umbrella, whose canopy looks to be as soft as butter as well. It's pristine, and while my own umbrella is dry, she still bears splotches from the housing development.

She also feels rumpled and unkempt.

"Apprentice Agent Little?"

I channel everything I have not to recoil, not to dislike this woman on sight. Henry hasn't submitted my report, so technically, I am still an apprentice agent.

She doesn't have to rub it in.

"I'm Agent Worthington-Wells." She pauses for the briefest of moments. "From the Enclave?"

Well, of course, from the Enclave. With that umbrella, she couldn't be from anywhere else. The question is, why is someone from the Enclave on my doorstep?

"Yes?" I manage, glancing toward the office and keeping my voice as low as possible.

"We received an SOS from Agent Darnelle's umbrella. I'm part of the response team."

Oh. That's why. No doubt others will follow. Won't that give everyone in the neighborhood something to talk about? I swallow a sigh, knowing none of this can be good.

"I'm trying to locate Agent Darnelle. I stopped by the bed and breakfast, but they said he checked out."

"He's here, actually. He took a direct hit—"

"*What?*"

I want to shush her before she wakes Henry, or has Guy dashing from his house. Before I can, a voice comes from the office.

"*Gwyneth?*" Henry sounds as if his entire throat is lined with sandpaper.

"Henry?" She drops both her umbrella and briefcase, the latter landing with a thump, and charges past me.

She vanishes into the office, leaving me alone on the threshold. Outside, the morning is mild, but there's a promise of July heat in the air, the taste of humidity that will leave everyone limp. For now, though, the flowers wave in the breeze, and windows in the houses across the street are open.

I shut the door but stand there, gripping the handle, considering the umbrella at my feet. It looks brand new or perhaps little used. The color really does evoke butter, a cold and unblemished stick on a porcelain dish.

My hip still aches, but I lean down to pick up the newcomer. A fizzle of electricity races across my skin, from fingertips to shoulder. I jump back, dropping the thing.

It shocked me!

I'm not sure I want it in the stand with my umbrella. Still, it needs to be somewhere. I pull my jacket from the coat tree and use a sleeve as a buffer before slipping it into the stand. Henry's umbrella is still morose, and mine is inching away from Gwyneth's. This is not a happy trio. I crane my neck but catch nothing from the office.

Toothpaste, I think. And then tea. Maybe some actual clothes? I cast the office another look and my nose prickles. I wipe away the blood with a finger and lock down the Sight without a second thought. Even so?

I decide to stay in my pajamas.

CHAPTER 48
HENRY

King's End, Minnesota
Friday, July 14

Of all the things Botten could have thrown at him, Henry hadn't expected Gwyneth. In retrospect, he probably should have. The man could not have orchestrated a more unwelcome situation if he'd meticulously planned it. Henry considered that Botten actually had. After all, Henry had yet to fulfill his part of their Faustian bargain.

Gwyneth now sat in the space where Pansy had slept. The telltale hint of her warmth lingered in the couch cushions. Were last night's sleeping arrangements obvious? Pansy answering the door in her pajamas, the two pillows, one with an indent that clearly wasn't from his head. He waited for the pang of guilt, but the only emotion to wash over him was deep annoyance.

Gwyneth knew how he felt, after all. It wasn't as if they'd never discussed their betrothal and what to do when their parents started pushing. During her research sabbatical in England, she'd even confided that she'd found *the one*. Henry had given both his blessing and hearty congratulations. But Gwyneth returned to Seattle alone and refused to speak of what had happened. Still, before he petitioned for an annulment, he'd called her. They had talked for hours. No recriminations, simply a gentle letting go. They both agreed it was the right thing to do.

Or so he had thought. Because Gwyneth never submitted her own petition.

A long-standing Enclave tradition was ignoring your betrothal obligation, and often your betrothed as well. Generations of agents had paired up only to switch partners and do it again and again—a game of romantic musical chairs that long summers isolated in the Pacific Northwest only encouraged. The arranged marriages, when they inevitably happened, were often short, dismal, and brutish. Certainly, his parents' marriage had been.

But no one appointed to the High Council—with the exception of Reginald Botten—had ever reneged on that obligation, no matter how short the marriage. If the union produced an heir? That opened doors for the politically inclined. His father had stepped through that door, secured a seat on the council early, and held on to it with the grace of an elder statesman and the tenacity of an underdog.

As for Gwyneth Worthington-Wells? The woman who, right now, was holding a stethoscope against his chest?

She was many things. First and foremost, a brilliant research scientist. She was undoubtedly politically inclined. However, she was not someone who'd be sent during that first wave, as part of a response team. Her time in the field had been in a support role, arriving only after the task force had secured the area and set up a field lab.

For all his achievements, all his accolades, Henry knew he was expendable. But not even the Enclave would risk a mind like Gwyneth's.

So why had Botten sent her?

From down the hall came the clatter of cups and the whistle of a tea kettle. He wondered, again, about Botten's agenda, his fixation with King's End, Rose Little, and her daughter. Ah, yes. That fit. And that something told him this orchestrated situation was meant not only for him, but for Pansy as well.

CHAPTER 49
PANSY

King's End, Minnesota
Friday, July 14

I carry a tray with a pot of tea, three cups with matching saucers, and pastries, this last courtesy of Guy. I send a silent *thank you* his way. I'll follow up with a real one later. My culinary skills truly do not extend past brewing tea. I suspect Agent Worthington-Wells might even turn up her nose at Guy's hotdish.

Is there a rational reason for disliking her? Other than the fact that her umbrella shocked me? No, there isn't, except for the Sight nattering at the back of my mind. Honestly, I think it's trying to stir up trouble because it's bored. Or it's so tied to King's End, and we only like out-of-towners during Saturday's farmers markets.

Despite her surly umbrella, I resolve to treat her with kindness. I enter the office and discover Gwyneth Worthington-Wells perched on the couch, her hip next to Henry's. The silver-sided briefcase now rests on the coffee table. Gwyneth herself is aiming a penlight at Henry's eyes. He's enduring the onslaught stoically, his hands resting on top of the fleece blanket, the skin across the knuckles bruised and battered.

On the left ring finger sits a platinum band.

It's all I can do not to drop the tray. The items rattle. A bit of hot liquid sloshes from the teapot's spout. Something hollow and vast opens up in my belly as if the Screamers have walloped *me* with that betrothal ring. There's no gush of blood or even a telltale trickle, but a rush of emptiness sweeps through me. I feel like I did after that picnic with Daniel, like I have very suddenly and almost completely bled out.

The tray somehow lands on the coffee table. Everything jangles, including that briefcase. Gwyneth scowls, but I busy myself with the cups. The steam bathes my cheeks, and the teapot warms my fingers. I'm beyond proud when only a tiny ripple mars the surface as I pass a cup to Henry.

"This is a special blend," I tell him. "Morning-after tea."

My words fall with a thud. The icy silence that follows has me rewinding what I just said. Gwyneth looks at me as if I've uttered something vulgar, and she's expecting an explanation and an apology, ASAP.

Pillows. Pajamas. And, oh yes, *heart-shaped* pastries. I retract that earlier thank-you to Guy.

"For the morning after an attack," I clarify, not that my voice is any match for all the frost in the room. "My mother swore by it."

Henry sips his tea and gives a nod in my direction. "Excellent. Quite rejuvenating."

"You should drink as much as you can. It will help you recover."

"I really don't think—" Gwyneth begins.

Henry holds up a finger. The gesture stops her words and freezes me in place. Despite his injuries and the fact that he's reclining on the sofa, he's still Principal Field Agent Henry Darnelle, and he is most definitely in charge.

"I was just telling Agent Worthington-Wells about what happened yesterday."

His voice contains a precise cadence, perhaps a heartbeat slower than his normal speech. Gwyneth doesn't seem to notice, but my ears prick. I wonder what it is he's truly trying to convey.

"About our encounter in the housing development," he continues. "What we confronted there."

I nod but glance away because I can't stand the way he's looking at me, full of intent and remorse. Something hot tickles my nose, and I reach for a tissue, then think better of it and grab a thick handful.

"I was also detailing how your mother was lost."

I catch the stream of blood with those tissues and shut my eyes. I nod again but don't utter a sound.

"How she vanished when the three of us were there, in the development," he continues, still using that strange cadence, "possibly swallowed by a fissure."

I open first my mouth to protest and then my eyes to confront Henry. My mother was not in the housing development and did not vanish through a fissure, as he well knows. I'm about to recite how she was swept away by my father, who waited nearly two decades for that exact purpose, like some time-traveling, fairytale prince. Henry's gaze halts me. There's such pleading and desperation in his expression that I can't make sense of it.

Until I do. Because as far as anyone in the Enclave knows, my mother was, up until now, alive and well.

For as long as possible, do not report my "death" to the Enclave. I owe them nothing, and they'll find out soon enough.

Well, here we are, then. Breaking that rule, and yet, somehow not. While it feels like he's torn the bandage from my grief and taken the scab with it, and while he appears extra-cozy with the woman who is most definitely his betrothed, I know this:

Henry Darnelle has just saved me.

Gwyneth turns to me now. To my surprise, I discover that her eyes aren't an Arctic blue but a warm autumn brown. "Agent Little, I'm so sorry. I know how hard this is."

To her credit, she does sound sorry. And she does know. Everyone in the Enclave has lost someone.

"When you're up to it," she adds, "your perspective on what happened yesterday will also be helpful."

I nod, yet again, grateful for that bunch of tissues in my fist and for the Sight—of all things—that had me reaching for them in the first place. I appear bereft, which is a good match for how I feel.

From the hallway comes a racket, the exact sound of the umbrella stand thumping against the wall. Something crashes with so much force, I feel it against the soles of my feet.

"I should—" I gesture toward the hall, but under the circumstances, I don't need an excuse to leave the room.

I'm relieved to have one.

The umbrella stand lies on its side. The big black behemoth of an umbrella remains inside, as does the butter-yellow one. The pink polka-dotted one is several feet down the hallway, almost to the kitchen. I can't make sense of the altercation, only that there was one. Whether my umbrella flung herself from the stand—it's happened before—or was shoved is anyone's guess. But she looks so forlorn at the end of the hallway. Isolated, a bit rumpled, friendless.

I right the stand and then go collect my umbrella. I don't return her to the others. Instead, I climb the stairs and lock myself in the bedroom. There, in my closet, I find my mother's umbrella. We cling to each other, the three of us.

"See?" I tell the red rose one. "Sometimes it's best to let children make their own mistakes."

I AM SHOWERED, presentable, or mostly so, and wondering how long I can hide in my room when the doorbell chimes. A knock follows, loud and obnoxious, then the creak of the front door opening. A voice booms up the stairs, one that takes me back to summers at the Academy.

"Anyone home?"

I fly from my room and take the stairs two at a time until I'm three steps from the bottom. There, I leap, without thought and with the utmost trust that Mortimer Connolly will catch me.

He does, pulling me tight against his chest, one hand cupping the back of my head, the other, still clutching his umbrella, around my waist. Mort is a Norse god of a man, complete with dirty blond hair and eyes to match the brilliant blue sky.

"Pansy-Girl, Pansy-Girl. I just heard. I'm so sorry, I'm so, so sorry. You know Jack and I loved Rose as well."

His umbrella's canopy flutters against my spine as if it, too, could console me.

"Have you told him?" My question is muffled against Mort's chest, but he answers anyway.

"Yeah. He could barely—" Mort shakes his head as if *he* can barely as well.

"Is he okay?" Jack loves my mother, maybe as much as I do. His sense for connections means when one is lost, he feels it deeply. He once told me it was like watching a favorite constellation wink out of the night sky.

"You know how Jack is. He'll call later, I'm sure." Mort eases me to my feet. "More importantly, how are you?"

I nod, which is becoming my go-to response. What can I say? Untangling the events of the last few months, untangling the grief—over and over again—has me balancing on a precipice. There's my version of events, and the one Henry's invented for the Enclave, and keeping my mouth shut seems the best course of action.

"You sure?" He peers down at me, hair swooping across his forehead, and then cups my cheek with his free hand. "Because you can sit this one out. You can head upstairs, and I'll keep the tea and snacks coming. You have my full permission as response team lead to check out completely."

"I don't want to check out."

"I didn't think you would, but the offer stands."

The soft tap of high-end heels on the hallway's hardwood floor has Mortimer tensing ever so slightly. He nods at the presence next to us.

"There you are, Gwennie."

"Mortimer." His name stretches her voice taut, a fine wire of a thing that, if real, might double as a garrote.

"Thanks for waiting at the airport."

She gives a cavalier shrug. "The arrivals board said your flight was delayed. I thought it best to drive straight here."

"Things well in hand, then?"

"As best as can be expected under the circumstances."

"And Darnelle?"

"Recovering."

My gaze pings back and forth during this exchange. Something feels off, something I can almost taste, a thick and sour layer of deceit over these polite words. Mort turns to me.

"I could use something to eat, and I imagine we all could. How are you, really? Up to kitchen duty?"

"Absolutely."

"Lunch, then." He nods toward the kitchen, then gives me a once over and shakes his head. "Or rather, I'll handle the edible portion, you can brew the tea."

I sock him on the arm, but he only laughs.

"Unless you want to help?" He directs this at Gwyneth.

"I don't suppose that's under my list of additional duties." She does a neat about-face, impressive in those heels, and vanishes into the office once again.

"Ah, Gwennie," Mort says. "A real team player." He goes to drop his umbrella into the stand but halts. His umbrella is shaking, clearly distressed.

"Where is she?" Mort asks.

I point toward the ceiling and my bedroom upstairs. "There was a squabble."

A thump of protest comes from my bedroom. I raise my hands, palms skyward. "Or something more than a squabble."

Mort's umbrella continues to shudder—it is outrage itself—even after he drops it into the stand.

"I swear, it only acts up around yours." He leans down, hands planted on his thighs. "Behave, or you won't get to see Pansy's umbrella at all."

That does the trick, although a wave of petulance hits me. From upstairs comes a theatrical sigh.

Mort wraps his arm around my waist, and we head for the kitchen.

"Tell me what's going on," he says.

I shake my head. "No, tell me about Paris, or wherever you were."

"Paris. Got it in one."

"I just want to hear something..." I can't quite articulate what. Something that has nothing to do with King's End. Something that sounds like an adventure in a faraway land.

"Want to hear how I was mending fissures in the catacombs?"

Oh, yes. That will do nicely. "Got it in one," I say.

☂

LUNCH IS A TERRIBLE, trying experience. Gwyneth refuses to unmoor her hip from Henry's. It's almost like she doesn't want him eating Mort's sandwiches or drinking my tea, this last in particular.

Every time Henry utters some piece of polite small talk, Mort glances my way and rolls his eyes in a manner unbecoming a senior field agent. Every time Mort pontificates about a field assignment, Gwyneth looks as if she's swallowed shards of glass. Gone is the dark fairy tale of the Paris Catacombs that sent delicious shivers up and down my spine. True, Mort has always bragged, but now his voice holds an aggressive, competitive edge that grates against my ears.

Then Mort spills his tea, and Gwyneth rolls *her* eyes at that. I'm down on the floor, sopping up what I can, when I glance up. A hint of a stealth smile lights Henry's face, and he gives me a barely there, sexier-than-it-has-the-right-to-be wink.

He schools his expression so quickly, I'm not sure if I imagined the whole thing or not. Except for the tea. The rag is sodden in my hand. The rest has sunk into the carpet, which makes a squishy sound anytime someone walks across it.

I'm clearing the dishes and pouring more tea—grinding through these hostess duties keeps my mind and gaze from straying toward Henry—when Mort rubs his hands together.

"All right, then," he says. "The infamous Camelot Lots. Charming place. You feel certain it's transmuted into a level five hot spot?"

This last is directed at Henry rather than me.

"I do," Henry says. "I've just drafted my initial report." His laptop sits on the coffee table, although how he found the elbow room to type with Gwyneth attached to his hip is anyone's guess.

"Enough evidence to call in a task force?" Mort asks.

Henry shakes his head. "We were ambushed almost immediately. There was no time to collect data or take any readings beyond what our umbrellas recorded."

"Which was surprisingly little."

Beneath Mort's observation is an accusation that sends my heart fluttering.

"We were doing a bit of training in the cemetery beforehand and didn't have our umbrellas activated." Henry brushes this off with finesse, as if Mort couldn't possibly understand what goes into mentoring a field agent. "No sense sending headquarters erroneous data. As I said, we were ambushed almost immediately. Adjusting the data settings was the last thing on our minds."

Henry speaks as if this actually happened. In a sense, I guess it did. Sort of. We were in the cemetery. We were ambushed. We eventually made it to the housing development.

Mort regards Henry with a cagey expression. He doesn't believe any of this, that much I can tell. He doesn't have any proof, though, to contradict Henry. That nervous fluttering starts up again, this time low in my belly. One of my best friends pitted against my ... well, I'm not sure what Henry is. But it feels like a showdown.

"No other way around it, then," Mort says at last. "We'll have to go to the development and remember to turn our umbrellas on this time."

"Do you think that's wise?" Henry asks.

"To turn on our umbrellas? Well, yes, that's the only way to collect data." Then Mort slaps his forehead as if the thought has just occurred to him. "You mean going back? Don't see how we can gather evidence otherwise."

Henry ignores this sarcasm the same way a schoolmaster would ignore a student acting up in class. "You might want to review my report first."

Before Mort can respond, I stand and pluck the teapot from the coffee table. With my back to Henry and Gwyneth, I hover in front of Mortimer.

"Stop being an ass." I hiss these words, and then, louder, add, "More tea?" I pour him some before he can cover his cup with a hand. He's getting more tea whether he likes it or not.

"Might as well," he says, clearly resigned to another full serving. "Works as a prophylactic." He raises an eyebrow at Henry. "Did you know that?"

Prophylactic, indeed. Of course it does, against Screamer toxin. Still. This entire situation is disintegrating. Mort is only going to get worse. I know these moods of his. I can't bear to look at Henry, but my gaze finds Gwyneth's.

She's still wearing that shards-of-glass expression, as done with the testosterone in the room as much as I am. Her nod is so slight that it barely registers. Mort misses it entirely, and I'm not sure even Henry caught it.

"How do you propose we obtain these samples?" Her voice is as sharp as those shards and twice as deadly. "You can't go alone."

Apparently, patrolling isn't under Gwyneth's list of additional duties, because she sits back more snugly against Henry's hip, crosses one leg over the other, and waits.

"Let's see." Mort points to himself and then each of us in turn. "Eeny, meeny, miny, Pansy. Up for a stroll?"

"Absolutely not," Henry says.

Mort spares Henry a look. "I wasn't speaking to you." He swivels in his chair, shining his full attention on me. "How are you feeling, Pansy-Girl?"

"Good." This is perhaps the truest thing I've uttered all day. Physically, I *do* feel fine. Not even my hip is troubling me that much.

"I still don't think—" Henry begins.

"Gwennie." Mort nods toward the briefcase still resting on the coffee table. "Do your doctor thing."

Her lips compress into a hard, thin line. But she stands and opens her silver-sided briefcase. Because Mort is the response team lead, not even Henry can contradict his orders. The air in the room shifts, its flavor full of bitterness and resignation.

"There is one way to find out if Pansy is toxin-free," Mort adds as Gwyneth places several items on the coffee table.

"It's a relatively new development," she says. "We've rolled it out to field agents on priority assignments. It's not yet available to permanent post agents."

Yes, why give us anything that might make our job easier?

"It won't hurt, but I'll need a little of your blood to run the test." For the first time today, her eyes light with anticipation and satisfaction.

I suspect this will actually hurt. A lot.

On the coffee table, she's readied a test strip, a lancet, a monitor, and alcohol wipes.

"It looks like a blood sugar monitor," I say.

"Same principle." Gwyneth pulls on some purple nitrile gloves. "Only we test for toxin, obviously."

Well, yes. *Obviously.*

"Finger, please."

The notion flits across my mind—no doubt encouraged by the Sight—of just what finger to give her. Behind me, Mortimer lets out a quiet snort. Instead, I choose to act like an adult, hold out my left hand, and offer up my index finger.

She jabs me with the lancet. The sting radiates all the way to my wrist. And she massages my finger more aggressively than necessary to produce blood. But then I'm away, cotton swab against my sore finger, hoping for an all-clear.

The Sight hasn't shown me much; I've been actively locking it down. But I know this. Staying in this room, or even this house, with all three of them? That will bring someone to the breaking point. A queasiness suggests that someone is me.

Mort has stood, and he's leaning over the coffee table, gaze locked on the monitor's screen. It beeps rather cheerfully, and he straightens, a huge grin on his face.

"Looks like you're good to go, Pansy-Girl. Rose's tea does it every time." He downs the last of his and turns to Gwyneth. "Really, you should take some of this back to the lab. It's better than anything R&D has put out in the last five years."

That's awfully specific, and perfectly awful for Mort to phrase it that way. No, I don't know how long Gwyneth has been in her position in R&D, but I suspect it's been at least five years.

"I'll look into it," Gwyneth says, jaw stiff.

Oh, no, she will not.

A thump sounds above our heads. My umbrella, beside herself with excitement. Mort gives an indulgent smile toward the ceiling.

"Someone's ready to go. Grab your things, and we'll head out."

I'm at the door when Henry's voice stops me.

"Agent Little?"

I turn and meet his gaze as best I can. It's like that earlier sting, fleeting but still oh so real.

"You don't have to do this," he says. "If you're not feeling up to it."

"She's *fine*," Mort insists.

I wonder what it is Henry thinks I should do. His expression is unfathomable, like when we first met. His demeanor is absolutely correct, and he looks the part of a field agent recovering after a major attack. And yet. So many emotions swirl through the air. So many agendas. Really, it's a passive-aggressive free-for-all. I'm not sure what Henry wants me to do, but if nothing else, I need to get out of the house.

"I'm okay," I say to him. I try to channel meaning or subtext, or whatever it is he's so good at, into my words. "Besides, after yesterday, I should really check on the fence."

"Always practical, our Pansy-Girl," Mort says. "Go on, I'll meet you on the porch."

I leave the tea things behind, certain I'll be cleaning them up later. I find my umbrella at the threshold of my bedroom. Honestly, she'd throw herself down the stairs if it got us out of the house any faster.

"Are you ready?" I say to her.

Oh, she most definitely is.

CHAPTER 50
OPHELIA

King's End, Minnesota
Friday, July 14

"Why do you reek?" Gwyneth shoots to her feet and rounds the coffee table as if that will help her escape the stench of tea tree oil and eucalyptus.

Ah, yes, Ophelia thinks. Her presumptive sister-in-law. Always the charmer. As is the entire Worthington-Wells clan. Ophelia should know. She's betrothed to Gwyneth's twin brother, Wendell Worthington-Wells, who insists on being called Big W, which is wrong on so many levels.

These sorts of arranged marriages are what make the Enclave tick. It also makes the entire enterprise slightly incestuous. Nepotism, at least in the Enclave, is a feature, not a bug. In any event, they'll have to drag Ophelia to the altar. Henry, too, by the looks of it.

A deep furrow carves a line between his eyebrows. He wants nothing more than for Gwyneth to leave the room. It's a wish Gwyneth is studiously ignoring.

"I seriously want to know." She glances around as if both the smell and the décor are offensive. "Why do you reek? I can barely stay in this room."

Just wait.

For a moment, Henry shuts his eyes. When he opens them, the steel has returned. He points to the Tupperware container that's rolled to the floor. Gwyneth bends down to retrieve it. Yes, her presumptive sister-in-law is many things, but she certainly doesn't lack curiosity. Without hesitation, Gwyneth cracks the lid.

The odor barges into the space. Ophelia imagines that it's corporeal, a living, breathing stink bomb that doesn't plan on taking any prisoners.

Gwyneth slams the lid shut, gagging and gasping for air.

"Are you kidding me? This?" She hefts the container and then tosses it across the room. "And this?" She flicks a dismissive fingernail against the teapot, and the porcelain cries out. "Explain to me, please, why you're being subjected to nineteenth-century cures."

"Because they work."

"I have given you *everything* from R&D."

Of course. The idea, the certainty, that Principal Field Agent Henry Darnelle owes his life not to his skill but to the largesse of R&D, or rather, its head researcher.

"And if I had used everything from R&D yesterday, we wouldn't be sitting here, having this conversation. Best case scenario? Emergency airlift back to Seattle. Or the more leisurely option of a body bag."

"But the epi-pens, the balm—"

"Only work for so long. The balm is dangerous after a certain point, as I've mentioned before, and the epi-pens lose their effectiveness over time." Henry's voice softens. "I've been in the field for a decade, and it's been years since something has worked as well as Agent Little's home remedies."

"Then perhaps it's time for you to come out of the field."

"I won't argue that point."

Not that Henry doesn't want to. Dragging him out of the field will be as challenging as dragging him to the altar.

"You know I'm not anti-science," he continues, "and that I admire the work you do. But what if this—" He nods at the teapot. "And that." A chin-tilt toward the wayward Tupperware. "Could augment your research?"

"You're asking me to keep an open mind."

"I believe I am, yes."

Gwyneth heaves a sigh, the sound far happier than the situation warrants. Ophelia swirls around the coffee table, wondering what it is her presumptive sister-in-law is up to.

"Then, perhaps—" Gwyneth picks her way across the floor and takes up a seat on the coffee table. "You'll return the favor?"

"I will certainly try."

"Honor our betrothal."

Henry stares, expression blank. It isn't often someone can knock her brother speechless, but Gwyneth certainly has. Maybe it's a pretext, or maybe he simply needs the strength, but he points to his teacup and remains silent while Gwyneth—somewhat reluctantly, it's true—pours another serving. Henry sips, eyes closed, as if gathering the patience for this conversation.

"Gwyneth, we've talked about this, and I thought—"

"You don't understand. What I'm proposing is a marriage of the minds."

Oh, no, honey, you should not be proposing anything at all.

But her face glows, and Ophelia thinks of the expression *stars in her eyes.* But what, exactly, is making them glitter like that? Love? Certainly not. This is a woman who has mapped her future down to the last meticulous detail. Judging by the way she's gazing at Henry, he is key to much of it.

"Marriage of the minds," he says, lips pursing ever so slightly.

"We can't play anymore, Henry. We need to assume our intended roles in the Enclave." Gwyneth nods at the band on Henry's ring finger. "That means honoring our betrothal. Otherwise, I'll go no further than research flunky, and you'll simply burn out." She tilts her head. "*If* you're lucky, that is. Or there's the more permanent option of a body bag."

Henry finishes the tea and heaves a sigh of his own. Before he can speak, Gwyneth raises a finger. "Open mind. I will look into that"—a barely-there nod toward the Tupperware container—"and you'll hear me out."

"Go ahead."

"Your father's allies could be yours, for the asking." Gwyneth leans forward, warming to the subject. "They're waiting, in fact, hoping you'll assume his seat on the High Council. Think of it! Principal Field Agent before twenty-five, High Council member before thirty. Not even your father did that!"

Oh, so that's her agenda. Of course it is. The High Council. Within Henry's grasp? Absolutely. Within Gwyneth's?

Not at all, except by proxy.

Wendell is his mother's favorite, as Ophelia knows all too well. As the oldest (by four minutes and thirty-eight seconds), Wendell will assume the Worthington-Wells seat. He knows it. Gwyneth knows it. Everyone in the Enclave knows it—and really, no one in the Enclave is looking forward to that day.

"And what if I don't particularly *want* to be a member of the High Council?"

"Please, Henry. That was before."

"Before what?" When Gwyneth falls strangely silent, he prompts again, "Before what?"

Still nothing.

"Oh." Henry slumps back against the couch cushions. "Of course. Your mother."

"She refuses to let the annulment go through. Without your father's advocacy, it's going nowhere."

"My mother—"

"Recusing herself. Besides, she's merely the wife of the chair, and trust me, he isn't budging either."

No, Ophelia thinks glumly, her father wouldn't.

"So you see," Gwyneth says, trying to gather Henry's hands in hers. After a moment, he relents. "It's this, or nothing. Why not beat these bastards at their own game? We give them what they expect, and then we go on to rule the Enclave."

Henry looks drawn and pale, but whether that's from his injuries, the prospect of sitting on the High Council, or the fact Gwyneth is still gripping his hands, Ophelia can't say.

"I don't want to rule the Enclave, Gwyneth."

"It's rule or be ruled. You know that."

"And you know I've never wanted that."

"Things are different."

"Nothing's different."

A frown furrows Gwyneth's brow. She glances around as if the source of Henry's reluctance is here, in the room with them.

"Oh!" she says. "Do you think I mind your little flirtation?"

Apparently, the source of Henry's reluctance *was* here in the room with them, mere minutes ago.

"After all," she adds, "you've put up with enough of mine."

True enough. Henry is a saint that way.

"Goodness, *that* doesn't have to change. Besides, in this case, I understand the appeal. She's very rural pixie dream girl—"

Rural pixie dream girl?

"—and she's been through a great deal—"

"Excuse me. Are you suggesting I slept with *Agent* Little out of pity, or that I took advantage of her vulnerable state after this recent tragedy?"

There goes the marriage of the minds.

"I mean, no, of course not. All I meant was—"

"Do you think so little of me, Gwyneth?"

No one does righteous indignation like her brother. The steel in his gaze hardens into titanium, his jaw clenched so tight he's going to snap a tooth if he isn't careful.

"No. Of course not. Henry, you're twisting this all around."

The gaslighting's not going to help, honey.

"Will you get me that?" Henry frees his hands from hers and points a commanding finger toward the Tupperware.

While she does, he tugs the T-shirt far enough up his chest to expose the wound. When Gwyneth turns around, the container slips from her hands, her mouth drops open, and for a long moment, she says nothing at all.

"Henry?" She rushes toward him, only grabbing the Tupperware again when he points to remind her.

Ophelia hovers close. She worries that the source of the wound will be obvious, that it will somehow give Henry away, weaken his position.

But no, the wound now resembles a lopsided doughnut; no trace of the small, circular band remains. Bruises bloom across his skin in a riot of deep purples and reds, sickly greens, and angry, aggressive yellows. Ophelia doubts there are enough, or any, cases of agents being punched in the chest with their own betrothal ring for it to be an actual diagnosis. And all Gwyneth does is gape.

"That should have—" she begins.

"Killed me. Yes, I'm well aware of that."

"Maybe we *do* need to airlift you—"

Ophelia feels her pulse kick up a notch. Henry in Seattle can't be anything but bad. Already, the Sight is weaving a new scenario, insidious and sour, full of degradation and shame. Because Gwyneth isn't the only one who knows of this so-called little flirtation.

"No," he says. "That won't be necessary."

Gwyneth arches an icy brow. "And you're the doctor now?"

For the first time during their conversation, Henry's lips twitch in amusement. "Agent Little was precise and quick in her response. She did use the epi-pens, but she also employed an array of nineteenth-century cures that saved my life. You might consider being kinder to her."

Henry lets out an exhausted sigh, and after an awkward moment, Gwyneth manages a terse nod. Then she leans closer, the scientist in her overcoming her shame, or what passes for shame when it comes to a Worthington-Wells.

She sits on the coffee table with a thump that rattles the tea service. "Is it actually healing better than it should?"

"I believe it is." He reaches for the Tupperware container. "I would like it to continue to heal, and I would like to rest. This conversation has exhausted me."

To be fair, Gwyneth is never not exhausting.

"Do you want me to?" Gwyneth gestures at his chest.

Do the honors? Sorry, honey, someone beat you to it.

"I can manage on my own." Henry tilts his head, and his voice softens. "There's plenty of space in the kitchen. You can set up your equipment there for when Agents Little and Connolly return."

And there we go, children. Class dismissed.

"Besides," he adds. "It's going to reek in here."

Gwyneth stands and leaves the room without a backward glance. With a hand hovering over the container's lid, Henry waits, ear turned toward the door, tracking those kitten heels down the hallway and into the kitchen. Only then does he open the Tupperware.

He tips his head back, half grimace, half smile on his face. "That *is* foul."

But the Henry Darnelle finesse is back in full force. He coats the wound without the goop sticking to everything and then carefully wipes his fingers with a napkin from the tea tray. Ophelia thinks he'll sleep then. Instead, her brother tugs his laptop, or rather, his *second* laptop, from beneath the couch cushions.

She marches over, leans forward, and gets right in his face, despite the stench.

You big faker.

She can't quite see the screen. And his fingers fly so fast across the keyboard that she can't keep up. Even if she could, Henry is no doubt crunching data in a way that will leave them all behind. But then, all at once, his hands droop as if the fatigue has caught up with him.

"I know they're friends, but I wish she hadn't gone off with him."

You just don't like Mortimer Connolly.

"Feeling's mutual. Besides, I believe he started it."

How old are you again? Twelve?

The corner of Henry's mouth lifts in a half smile. Ophelia wonders if he's more receptive because of the wound, or perhaps it has something to do with the latest events at the housing development. He isn't acting like he actually hears her, but is merely imagining her responses. It's not much, but she'll take it.

"Still, I wish she hadn't gone."

Ophelia moves to the window and peeks through the gauzy curtains. It's only then that she notices that the sheer material is studded with tiny, translucent polka dots. Instead of making her smile, the sight brings a solid lump to the back of her throat. Her chest tightens in a way that will probably set off the monitors back in Seattle.

There's no sign of Pansy or Mortimer on the road leading to the housing development. How long have they been gone? When she's in this loop, time loses meaning. And the path they're now treading is so unfamiliar.

But new paths bring new dangers. This, she knows all too well. Something is off about this response team. Gwyneth Worthington-Wells and Mortimer Connolly? Henry's betrothed and one of Pansy's closest friends? The idea of it is both calculating and cruel. So Ophelia swirls back to her brother, who has now tucked his laptop away and is staring at the ceiling, hands behind his head, those thoughts of his never ceasing.

You'll need to watch your back. Pansy's too.

Ophelia whispers the words. Although, really, does she need to?

She supposes she could shout. But whispering feels right. When Henry gives her the smallest of nods, she knows it is.

"I will," he says, his voice low and careful. "I won't let them hurt her."

And that is what Ophelia is afraid of most.

CHAPTER 51

PANSY

King's End, Minnesota
Friday, July 14

Patrolling King's End, my arm linked with Mortimer's, fills me with nostalgia. True, it's been a long time since either he or Jack came for a visit, never mind an actual patrol. Still, having him here so solid and sure at my side weaves some of those tattered threads of my life back together.

"I wish Jack were here," I say.

"You may get your wish. Before I left, I put in a by-name request for him."

I can't help it. I give a little squeal. "Really?"

"I need an intel analyst, so why not send one who's actually familiar with King's End?"

"Look at you, Mr. Responsible Response Team Lead."

We've left the last of the houses and the sidewalk behind, but we're not close enough to see even a hint of the development. A few more steps and the Camelot Lots sign will greet us with its dour, looming presence, assuming it wasn't devoured by Screamers yesterday.

Mort halts suddenly and with great purpose. He waits until I'm forced to look at him.

"Tell me what's going on," he says, his voice unusually soft. "What's been happening here in King's End? What's been happening with you?"

Here's the thing about being a permanent post agent, at least in King's End. I never have to explain myself. I never have to lie, not much, anyway. The locals simply accept what I do and that a pink polka-dotted umbrella helps me do it.

Pretending to be someone I'm not, the way an agent in the field might? Like Henry in the Sahara or Mort down in the catacombs? I barely passed the classes on that sort of tradecraft at the Academy. The goal, after all, was to appear unremarkable. And I managed that.

To my detriment, it seems, because Mort is surveying me with a gaze that leaves me unnerved. I need to act like someone who just lost their mother yesterday, not three months ago. It isn't hard to channel grief, but it feels different. I'm no longer free-falling through some endless void. Despite the sorrow, my feet are back on solid ground. But I need to be unmoored, at least in front of Mort.

"I'm ... it's—" I shake my head. I can't explain anything. Not without explaining how my mother vanished three months ago, carried off by my father, who—surprise!—is actually a traveler, all the things a dutiful permanent post agent *should* have reported.

"Okay, I'll go," Mort says, something angry churning beneath his words. "Why the hell is Henry Darnelle still here?"

I shake my head again to show I don't understand what he means.

"You passed your field agent exam on Monday. I had a hangover all day Tuesday to prove it. It's Friday, and he's still here."

"He was wounded."

"Which, if he had returned to Seattle to write his report, he wouldn't be." Mort unclenches his jaw. "What's really going on,

Pansy? He hasn't submitted your report. It's not in the system. I checked. Is he holding it over you?"

"Is he holding what over me?"

"Your report."

"Why would he do that?"

"Do I have to spell it out?"

Yes, he does. "I don't know what you're talking about, so go ahead."

"Is he using your *unsubmitted* report to garner sexual favors."

"What?" I try to temper my laughter, but really, what a thing to say. "You're kidding, right?"

"Not at all. It isn't unheard of. There are rumors."

"About Agent Darnelle?"

"No," Mort admits somewhat sullenly.

"There won't be any, either. If you must know, he's been giving me some extra tutoring."

"You hardly need extra tutoring."

"From a principal field agent? Really? I've been learning a lot," I add primly. "Plus, his father knew my mother. There have been reminiscences." I resist the urge to pull in a deep breath after this rather moralistic tirade. Technically, nothing's a lie. I mean, I didn't say who's been doing all that reminiscing.

"Also? You think I'd put up with something like that?" I poke him in the chest, and my umbrella shakes with indignation against my spine. "You think my *mother* would?"

I decide that now would be a good time to disengage and end this conversation. So I march toward the housing development, leaving Mortimer behind.

He catches up moments after I've reached the Camelot Lots sign, still intact, its shade as depressing as ever. I continue to ignore Mort and scan the development. Everything appears deceptively benign. And yet, I suspect something lurks beneath that. It's the taste in the air, the slightest shiver beneath my feet.

Henry and I did something yesterday. The sonic boom that rolled through the space rattled my limbs and shook my skull. For the briefest of moments, I thought my heart would stop beating.

A few strategically placed holes mar the chain-link fence. So calculated, so obvious. It's an apparent attempt at luring us into an ambush. Reality flickers, or so it seems. I see the development as it is now and how it was years ago. Back and forth, back and forth, like one of those paintings that shift between two images.

I squint. "How are they doing this?"

Mort remains still and quiet. The last time he saw the development, they hadn't broken ground yet. My mother had been waging a one-woman campaign to stop the construction, and the work had been delayed.

Even so, the Camelot Lots sign hung over the entrance, and the survey team had staked out spaces for all the houses. Of course, the fence bordering the cemetery has been there for ages. We've always repaired holes in the fence.

I turn to Mort and wonder what the development looks like through his eyes.

"Things get interesting in a level five hot spot," he says at last.

Clearly.

"Hey." His voice softens a touch. "I'm sorry, okay? I was worried, is all. Can I be forgiven?"

"Hm? Maybe. I'll think about it." But when his arm goes around my waist, I don't resist.

Mort has always been bombastic, always so sure of himself. It serves him well as a field agent. In relationships? Not so much. He'll bully and barge his way into every situation, often not caring what he breaks. And trust is a fragile thing.

"Just a bug Botten put in my ear, is all," he adds.

My pulse jumps in my throat, and something small and fragile fractures inside my chest.

"He thought Darnelle might be taking advantage of you or leading you on, making you think you could pass your exam, but I told him you're more capable than your performance at the Academy might suggest."

My insides turn to ice. "You didn't—"

"No, I didn't, and I wouldn't. Screw the Enclave, right? They don't need to know about your Sight."

It's all I can do not to sag with relief. "Okay," I manage, the word insubstantial in the late morning air. I nod toward the housing development. "What do you make of this?"

"It looks like Thanksgiving from…? When was that? Years ago."

"Six." I scan the area, realizing that when it flickers, the development does look like that, the year both Mort and Jack spent Thanksgiving in King's End, the year when they first fell in love.

"It's almost like it's taunting me," he adds.

"How so?" Not that the Screamers wouldn't taunt Mort, or me, or anyone, for that matter.

He pulls me a bit closer. "I'm thinking of asking Jack to make things permanent."

"What!" I squeal for the second time in half an hour. This is news. This could be wonderful, assuming Mort can pull it off, if he's truly serious about their relationship. Because, let's face it, he hasn't always been. "Have you asked him yet?"

He spins me around, gripping my hands, squeezing my fingers in what feels like near panic. "No, and please don't say anything."

I shake my head. "Of course not."

"You know how he is."

I do. And Jack's trust? Exceedingly fragile, the sort that should come with a warning label.

"What about your betrothal?"

"Working on it."

Jack's family isn't caught up in the betrothals the way the Connollys are. They haven't been in the Enclave long enough for that. But Mort can't walk away from his without an annulment.

Any number of possible outcomes for Mort and Jack whisper

through my thoughts. I lock down the Sight before I even have to swipe blood from beneath my nose. I don't need it interfering at the edge of the housing development. I don't need it to suggest outcomes that have no bearing on this reality. Too many emotions are tied up in their relationship for the Sight to be anything but unreliable.

Mort doesn't answer or elaborate, and once the quiet stretches between us, I don't think he will.

"What did we do back then?" I ask, simply to break the silence. "Do we play their game this time around, or—?"

"Do we change it?" He scans the development again. "That's the question, isn't it?"

"Didn't you catch one last time?"

"I did. I thought Rose was going to ban me from King's End for it, too."

Because Mort can do the near impossible. He can capture a single Screamer with his bare hands. Not that single Screamers last that long. Not that they're actually a living thing. And yet, somehow, he manages it. And somehow, once caught, they manifest as if they are a living thing, briefly, at least.

My mother hated it, and to be fair, I don't care much for it either. It feels wrong, like a violation. Although, considering all the trouble the Screamers give me, you'd think I wouldn't mind. But I do.

"Would it help," I ask, "if we brought one back?"

"Gwennie would love it." Mort shields his eyes and scans the development. "It might actually give us some clues to what's going on, between that and whatever data we can pick up going in."

I shut my eyes. November. Six years ago. No snow yet, but the trees in the cemetery had shed their leaves, and the grass was more brown than green. The air had that winter bite to it. In my mind's eye, I see the two of us, Mort and me, all baby-faced and hopeful. Jack stayed back with my mother, helping with Thanksgiving dinner. We returned to the heady scent of sage and the promise of warm pumpkin pie.

And yes, after Mort proudly displayed the prize in his hands, my mother made him return it to the development before it could ruin someone else's Thanksgiving, never mind our own. We were halfway there when it vanished in a fracture of light. In the aftermath, my nose bled enough to soak the front of my jacket.

I unsling my umbrella and point to the holes in the fence. "I probably went there first."

"If the fence goes, we all go," Mort says in an uncanny imitation of my mother. A moment later, he cringes. "Sorry, Pansy-Girl. I didn't mean—"

No, Mort never does. "It's okay. If she were here, it would be something she'd say."

Now he unslings his umbrella and adjusts the settings. "You know what? I'm going to walk the perimeter. See if any of those fissures have extended into the cemetery, get a sense of what's happening beyond this." He jabs the point of his umbrella toward the development.

"Do you need me to come along?"

"Actually, you're the base. I'll relay the data to your umbrella. That'll give us a fuller picture of what's happening here." He graces me with a roguish smile. "But you know, if I'm swarmed, I'd appreciate a hand."

I can't help it. I manage a laugh. For a moment, he cups my cheek.

"Ah, there she is, our Pansy-Girl." He strikes out for the left side of the development, nodding over his shoulder toward the right. "See you on the flip side."

CHAPTER 52
HENRY

King's End, Minnesota
Friday, July 14

It was the rattle of his umbrella that pulled Henry from his contemplation of the ceiling. The racket was insistent rather than sullen. He wasn't quite ready to face Screamers. The dull ache in his chest told him that. But his legs had enough strength, and stealth, to move through the house.

Henry marveled at that. He hadn't healed this quickly after the Sahara, and he'd been airlifted to an Enclave trauma center in Cairo. When things were settled, he'd insist Gwyneth research the teas, the tinctures, and yes, the salve-from-hell.

He eased the office door open by degrees and put a finger to his lips the moment the umbrella stand came into view. Gwyneth's seemed supremely bored. His umbrella and hers had never established a rapport. Plucking his own from the stand wouldn't be cause for alarm.

From down the hall came the clank of lab equipment, the scrape of a chair, and the murmur of conversation, someone on speaker, someone with a resonating voice.

Someone who sounded a great deal like Reginald Botten.

"No, it's my professional opinion that he's simply not ready. You must understand. Henry was gravely injured. He'll need twenty-four hours, at least, if he's to be an active participant."

The sound of running water drowned out both Gwyneth's voice and Botten's reply. For a moment, Henry hesitated at the threshold. Eavesdropping, if he could manage it, might prove fruitful.

Then his umbrella shook again, quieter this time but just as insistent. So, instead, Henry pulled it from the stand and retreated to the office.

He was halfway to the couch when he understood what was going on. The buzz of incoming data radiated through his palm. His umbrella was shaking, trying to hold as much as possible in its buffer.

With quick, precise movements, he tugged his second laptop from beneath the couch cushions and set up the relay.

"Oh, they are clever, aren't they?"

His umbrella shuddered in agreement.

Pansy must have been watching more closely than he realized, or perhaps this was something Rose had taught her. Either way, she was streaming data not only to the Enclave but to his umbrella as well. And it was glorious. *She* was glorious. It might contain the last pieces he needed to confirm his hypothesis. If nothing else, he'd have the same information as Botten, and that was no small thing.

Because Botten wanted something here in King's End, or perhaps wanted to finish something that had started decades ago. What had Max Monroe said? Pansy was the key to everything. The key to this sudden level five hot spot? Perhaps. But perhaps there was more to it than that.

Because Henry was fairly certain King's End was more than a level five hot spot that contained a two-point juncture. Those created the sort of fissures that might swallow up an agent or spit out a traveler. But a three-point juncture? The sort the silo, the covered bridge, and the housing development created?

That was an actual gateway, a door into another dimension, one that might allow two-way travel, with the right technology. Which, as far as Henry knew, the Enclave hadn't developed. At least, not *yet*.

Had Rose Little discovered this gateway? Had she trusted both his father and Reginald Botten with the secret? The power contained in a gateway was vast, unmanageable, and, more often than not, dormant. The Enclave did not tangle with gateways. They had a tendency to swallow up task forces and towns. When one was discovered, the Enclave swooped in, evacuated the local populace, and spent years mending the fissures. A long, slow, dangerous slog that no field agent wanted on their résumé.

But as folklore went, in the past, the Enclave—or at least some of its members—had attempted to command that unmanageable power with predictably disastrous results. That didn't keep the ambitious from trying. In theory, if you could control that sort of power?

You could rule the world.

His umbrella continued the data feed. The information flowed by too quickly for Henry to absorb it. Still, bits and pieces jumped out. Not enough, not yet, to confirm his hypothesis, but he was getting a sense of the whole. Mortimer Connolly was no doubt conducting a perimeter scan. The information was taking shape, and yet, at the same time, the scans were all-encompassing. It was a scatter-shot search, and a notion lit in Henry's mind.

"Like mother, like daughter. So very clever."

Again, his umbrella shook with agreement, its demeanor entirely too smug.

"Yes, I know. I was wrong, and you were right."

Henry continued to watch the download, his attention trained so fully that the sudden spike of data sent his heart racing. That looked like an attack. Before he could review this new information, a clattering came from the kitchen, the sound of heels on the floor. He gauged whether those heels were approaching. He gauged the input flowing across his screen and held on to the hope that since Pansy's umbrella was still sending data, then Pansy herself was unharmed.

The footfalls advanced, a rapid-fire click down the hallway. With a sigh of regret, Henry closed his laptop and secured it in the couch cushions once again. He shoved his legs back beneath the throw, tucked his umbrella next to him, and managed one quick whisper.

"Hold on to as much as you can."

He had just closed his eyes when Gwyneth cleared the threshold.

CHAPTER 53
PANSY

King's End, Minnesota
Friday, July 14

I do not see Mortimer on the flip side. Instead, that gaping maw opens in the fence, the chain-link curling back, the jagged edges like fangs. There's no running forward and mending this particular hole. The air rushes through the development as if that gap is the mouth of some enormous creature, and it's inhaling for all it's worth.

Then, with another violent gust, Mort comes spewing out. It's almost as if the housing development has decided he tastes quite awful. He tumbles down the center of the development, missing saplings and structures in a way that speaks of luck rather than skill. His umbrella unfurls and is caught by both the wind and a contingent of barely-there Screamers.

My legs are already moving when Mort's shout echoes behind me. I race after his umbrella. The cobalt blue canopy flutters in the eddies and streams of the air. Light fractures, and I know with undeniable clarity where the Screamers are taking it. I don't even pause to swipe the blood coating my upper lip.

Mort's shouts grow more frantic as I swerve. He's in command mode, ordering me in the opposite direction. No time to reassure him. No time to explain. Hardly time to stop what I fear is inevitable. My thigh muscles ache with the strain. My hip renews its complaints, loudly. But I run, my aim the showcase home, that basement egress window, and the fissure I'm certain has opened up once again.

I skid across the muddy grass seconds before Mort's umbrella comes cartwheeling toward the window. I shoot my hand out and catch the strap. For a moment, the umbrella hangs over that abyss. It's narrow—the perfect size for swallowing an umbrella—but vast. The churning gray is endless, without bottom.

I'm flat against the earth, but I pull Mort's umbrella toward me, clutch it close, and it quakes with relief. Before I can move, blood drips from my nose, slips from my lip, and falls not on the ground but into that fracture in the earth.

Colors swirl in that endless gray expanse, knitting it together, healing it, in a way. I should push from the ground. I should look away. I can't do either. All I can do is witness.

By the time Mort reaches me, the fissure has mostly mended itself. He spares me a glance before planting a palm on the soil to finish the task.

"You okay, Pansy-Girl?"

"Yeah." The word is soft and absorbed by the grass, but he nods as if he's heard me loud and clear.

"The Sight?"

It's not really a question. My upper lip and chin are tacky with blood. Rivulets are snaking down my neck, making the skin itch. I've gone from nearly presentable to unkempt in a matter of five minutes.

"I should've trusted you," he adds, "and I'm grateful. Thank you." Mort sounds unusually contrite, as if this encounter has sucked all the wind from his sails or at least deflated his ego a bit. "But the good news is, I have a surprise."

It's only then that I notice he's using one hand to mend the fissure. In the other? Tucked against his chest?

A single Screamer.

All is quiet now except for the pitiful mew coming from the creature trapped in Mortimer's grip. He holds the thing gently, the way one might an injured dove. Above us, the brilliant blue sky has returned. The other Screamers have fled, leaving this one to its fate.

"Are *you* okay?" I ask. Not only is catching a Screamer ill-advised, it's also a good way to end up wounded.

"Not a scratch. And they're harmless like this." He secures the Screamer with both hands now. It strains against his grip, but the effort is halfhearted, as if it already knows there's no going back.

Mort lifts his chin, gaze scanning the development, eyes narrow, assessing. "It doesn't taste like they'll counterattack, but—"

"This is King's End." So, yes, they absolutely could.

He gestures toward his umbrella. "Mind managing both?"

"Not at all."

Mort's umbrella is a kinder version of its owner. The two of ours have always had a big brother, little sister vibe. In fact, mine is currently fluttering her ruffles in a way that speaks to an unburdening of the past week or, perhaps, months.

On the other hand, Mort and I don't talk until we've cleared the gates of Camelot Lots. I release a sigh. He chuckles at the sound but immediately sobers.

"We need to get back to that incredibly awkward situation in your house—"

I start to protest, but he cuts me off.

"*Incredibly* awkward. What the hell is going on between you and Darnelle?"

"I thought we established that *nothing* was going on."

"No, we established that he isn't being a creeper or a dick. What we haven't addressed is why everything is so effing awkward in your house."

"Because of what happened yesterday?" I suggest.

"It's more than that."

I take a few steps forward, hoping I can outrun this conversation. I have no way of explaining anything to Mortimer, not without the whole situation unraveling around me. I want to get back to Henry, see if he's managed to capture any of the data I sent. Mostly, though, I want to make sure he's okay, still drinking tea, still healing.

"There's another side to this," Mort adds. "One you're not going to like."

The warning in his tone halts me.

"First, you might want to do something about the blood."

I sag. He's right. Normally, of course, I wouldn't worry. But with Gwyneth in my house? I can't risk anyone else knowing about the Sight, and certainly not a Worthington-Wells. My mother always said ambition, avarice, and malice applied double to them.

I ease the field pack from my shoulders and pull out some towelettes. Their chemical scent always brings a wave of nausea, but I scrub my skin with more force and determination than necessary.

"Second—"

"I was hoping you were done."

"Not a chance. Second, let's assume Darnelle isn't a dick."

I frown at the blood beneath my fingernails rather than at Mort. "He's not."

"Debatable. There could be another problem with your exam results."

"And that is?"

"Favoritism. Was he biased in any way when administering or scoring your exam? Because if someone decides he was, then you'll have to retake it."

Now I do stare at Mort, aghast.

"Darnelle figured it out, right?"

I don't nod; I don't shake my head. Instead, I hold absolutely still.

"And did he tell you about Ophelia?" Mort doesn't wait for my answer, not that I plan to give him one. "Ah, I see that it's yes to both of those." He steps closer, as if his next words require privacy. "Listen, Pansy-Girl, this could get very complicated and very political very, very quickly.”

I swallow hard. “How so?”

“Gwyneth Worthington-Wells is a bullet train, and you need to step off the tracks.”

“I’m not on any tracks.”

“You spent nearly a week with her betrothed.”

“My exam—”

“Principal field agents do not routinely administer exams unless they’re being punished for something or they’re interested in the examinee. And right now, Enclave gossip says it’s the latter.”

“Wait. What? There’s gossip? About me?”

“Well, to be fair, it’s more about why Henry Darnelle would extend his stay in some backwater permanent post like King’s End. But yes, you’re involved.”

“You’d think field agents would have better things to do than gossip.”

Mort laughs. “And deny the Enclave the fuel it runs on?”

“So does Gwyneth think—?”

“Oh, she does, indeed. And if she wanted to press the issue?”

The Screamer in Mort’s grip squirms at this. It’s very crow-like in its manner, and I wonder if we simply see that because we can’t comprehend what it truly is.

“Does she?” I ask, voice smaller than I’d like. “Want to press the issue?”

“Not quite yet, but all it will take is a phone call to Botten, and then you’ll find yourself with a null and void exam on your record. She’ll probably rope Wendell into doing it.”

“Wendell?” I give my head a shake. I’m pretty sure I don’t know him.

“Worthington-Wells. Her brother. He’s an idiot, but keep in mind that Gwyneth is not. She’ll be pulling the strings, and trust me, she won’t miss a thing.”

In his grip, the Screamer squawks in agreement.

"How is *that* unbiased?"

"Oh, Pansy-Girl. That's Enclave politics at their finest, or worst, however you want to think of it. She's Botten's protégé, and Darnelle is her one-way ticket to the High Council. You're inconsequential in all this."

Along with being unremarkable, I suppose. "So, what do I do?"

"First, stop making eyes at Darnelle."

"I'm not making eyes."

Mort rolls his own at this. "And get him to stop as well. He will if he knows what's good for him."

"Anything else?"

He raises the Screamer caught between his palms. "We can start by bringing Gwennie a peace offering."

A HINGED PLEXIGLAS container sits in the center of my kitchen table. Inside that, the Screamer hunkers down. It remains the size and shape of a crow, but its feathers, for lack of a better word, catch the light and fracture it into a prism of color.

In the office, Henry is sound asleep on the sofa. This worries me. If he's been drinking tea and reapplying my mother's salve, he should be alert by now, if not fully recovered. The house certainly reeks as if he has. I want to speak to him, find out for sure, but then Mort's warning echoes in the back of my mind. And it's one the Sight insists absolutely will come true with a single misstep.

Out of some sort of strange perversity, Mortimer has left me alone with Gwyneth. He claimed there was nothing to eat in my house, at least nothing that would feed four people. He's right, of course. We've already inhaled the last of the food from The King's Larder. I suspect he only wanted to escape further confinement with Gwyneth.

Earlier, she drew a couple of vials of blood, a routine sort of thing, she said, after the encounter Henry and I had. The bandage at the crook of my elbow itches. I expected another jab, but the needle slipped in without a sting. It almost felt like an apology.

"How long do they normally last?" I ask her now. The Screamer is pacing like a zoo animal trapped behind bars.

"It depends. Some, mere minutes. Others go on for days." She adjusts a sensor that's connected to one side of the container. "Once, one survived for two whole weeks, exactly, to the second it was caught."

"Do you ever feel sorry for them?" Because I do, I want to say. I feel sorry for this one trapped and on display in my kitchen.

"I ... it's funny. I do."

I nod. "Do you ever grow attached?"

"Agent Little." Her voice is stern.

I glance up.

"They aren't real," she says.

"Aren't they?" Despite its ephemeral nature, something about this lone Screamer feels very real to me, in a way that knots something in my chest, something I can't quite name. A deep sorrow, perhaps, or a loss. I place my fingertips against the Plexiglas. The creature hobbles over and rubs its face against the spot as if it can feel me. It's a very cat-like gesture, and while the thing isn't purring, I imagine that it could.

"It seems very attracted to you," Gwyneth observes.

They always have been. I sigh. "Not enough to catch."

"Mortimer is—"

"An anomaly," I suggest.

"I was going to say oddity."

My laugh is soft, since I do not wish to disturb the Screamer. It's a strange and alien impulse, but one I can't deny. "It's dying."

"They don't really die."

"Don't they?"

She holds up her hands. "They simply vanish."

"Isn't that like death?"

She doesn't answer. A moment later, a burst of light fills the container, followed by a puff of blue smoke, and then that, too, dissipates.

"You see?" Gwyneth shrugs and then pushes a few buttons on the sensor before detaching it. "Simply gone."

I doubt anything about this is simple. She reaches over and loosens a hinge. The Plexiglas container folds in on itself, and she tucks it away in her hard-sided, silver briefcase.

"I'm going to go check on Henry," she says.

I give what I hope is both a noncommittal and uninterested nod. "I'm going to make some tea if you would like some later."

Gwyneth returns my nod and then leaves the kitchen without another word, her heels punctuating each step until the carpet in the office swallows the sound. I remain seated, contemplating the space that so recently held all my fears and all my pity.

WHEN MORTIMER RETURNS WITH GROCERIES, he finds me in the kitchen, still in self-imposed exile. I've managed to brew the tea, but that's all I've accomplished.

"Pansy-Girl, what are you doing?"

I glance from my contemplation of the empty space. If I close my eyes, the afterimage of the Screamer remains. "Sitting," I say to him.

The grocery sacks crash to the kitchen table. He is at my side, kneeling by my chair.

"Pansy-Girl, Pansy-Girl. Don't do this to yourself. Rose lived a good life." He glances around the kitchen as if he can still feel my mother's presence. "She was content here in King's End, even if you aren't."

"I like King's End."

"You need to get away from it, if only for a while." He tilts my chin toward his face, and I get Mort at his most sincere, blue eyes unbearably kind, a lock of blond hair dipping to his forehead.

"I promise you, once this mess in King's End is cleared up, we'll do an early birthday bash. All three of us will escape. I'm thinking tropical, somewhere with endless beaches. We'll find you someone, someone not from King's End, and certainly not someone with an umbrella stuck so far up his—"

"Stop." I pull back. Mortimer runs as hot as Henry, but his heat feels more aggressive. "I am perfectly capable of finding my own someone."

"Recent evidence would suggest otherwise."

"Or maybe I'm not all that interested in finding my own someone."

"Liar. There hasn't been anyone serious since Daniel, has there?"

"At the Academy, Charlie Pulchenko—"

"Like I said. Someone *serious*."

I give my head a little shake, because Mort is right. No one *serious*. Not that I need someone serious, but all my friends have drifted away. I patrol. I visit the farmers market. I chat with Matilda, with Guy and Milo, with Adele. I call that my life, and on the surface, it isn't a bad one. But I wonder. How obvious is my loneliness? I suspect it's something I wear. That it's something everyone can see, except, of course, me.

"I have a thought," Mort says.

"Just the one? I'm proud."

"You will be when you hear it. Let me make dinner and play host tonight." He sweeps a hand at the discarded groceries on the kitchen table. "I'll even clean up. And you—" He pushes a finger gently against my collarbone. "Can go upstairs. I'll bring you a tray."

"I really can't let you—"

"Yes, you can. Do you really want to play hostess? Sort out the sleeping arrangements?"

No, I do not.

"I'll tell them you needed to be alone, and this is assuming Darnelle is even awake for dinner."

That worry pings me again. Yes, Henry was hit hard, but his incapacitation has gone on far too long. I swallow the urge to rush to the office and do things like check his temperature, his pulse, the whites of his eyes, anything that might indicate the toxins haven't left his system. Normally, the Enclave would've airlifted him back to Seattle, and I wonder at the inaction. But Gwyneth *is* a doctor. She would know best, or at least better than I do. I sigh, and it's such a sad sound that Mort's expression grows tender.

"I'm guessing you'd rather mourn for Rose than make small talk with Gwyneth."

Something thick and salty gathers in the back of my throat and flirts with the corners of my eyes. Mort pulls me close, his broad chest capturing my sorrow.

"It's the coward's way out," I murmur against his shirt, the material soft against my lips.

He pulls back and cups my cheeks. With his thumbs, he chases away the tears. "Then be a coward. For once in your life, Pansy-Girl."

It doesn't take more prodding than that. I don't want a reprise of today's lunch, and I really don't want to think about tonight's sleeping arrangements. I race up the stairs, not even pausing to eavesdrop at the office door.

Once in my room, instinct has me locking the door behind me. Something feels different. The barest trace of tea tree oil and eucalyptus lingers in the air. My gaze travels the space. The comforter is neater than I left it this morning, and the pillow shams are wrinkle-free, lined up like down-filled soldiers ready for inspection.

And on my nightstand, tucked unobtrusively next to the lamp, is a burner phone.

CHAPTER 54
OPHELIA

King's End, Minnesota
Friday, July 14

Mortimer Connolly is not the chef Henry is, but he isn't half bad. The scent of pesto—of basil and pine nut—wafts in the air. A pot of water boils on the stove, waiting impatiently for the pasta. He's finished chopping the last vegetables for a colorful salad and set fresh tea to brew.

All of this, the actions of the best kind of friend. He's even made a dessert, a rich crème brûlée that only needs a dusting of sugar and a blast from a torch before it's complete.

But Ophelia sits cross-legged on the kitchen table, chin planted on her fists, and glares. She doesn't move, doesn't flinch, not even when Gwyneth enters the kitchen.

"How's our patient?" Mort asks.

"Asleep again, but otherwise, better than he has a right to be."

"Then we're lucky."

"Hm. I suppose you could see it that way."

"Botten have any idea about his wound?"

Gwyneth scowls and shakes her head. "Nothing. He assumes I'll figure it out. 'I have every faith in your capabilities, m'dear.'"

The imitation is spot on, and Mortimer snorts. "In other words, he's not too concerned."

"Apparently not."

"Are you?"

Gwyneth pauses, lips pursed in thought. "I saw him, briefly, after he walked out of the Sahara. I was at a conference in Switzerland and rerouted my flight home so I could visit during a layover." She shakes her head. "He wasn't this bad. This morning he was fine, all things considered. But since then—" She pauses, her gaze tipped toward the ceiling. "It's his awareness more than anything. He's so unresponsive. Even injured, Henry is always mentally sharp. I can't make sense of it."

"It's been barely twenty-four hours. A bit of backsliding is normal, especially with what we're dealing with."

To her credit, her presumptive sister-in-law's sigh is filled with regret. Perhaps, in her own way, she cares for Henry. Still, in every path Ophelia has traveled, that concern comes too little and always too late.

Mort dumps a box of rigatoni into the pot. Steam hisses and rises into the air. In the clatter of dishes, no one hears the slight creak of the floorboards in the hallway. No one, that is, except Ophelia. She doesn't turn, doesn't even glance in that direction. Ridiculous, really. She's not here, not corporeal, and her attention can't betray Henry.

Even so, her heart grows so tight in her chest that she can't bear to risk it.

"Blood draws?" Mort asks.

"Yes. Both of them. More than enough." Gwyneth pulls a cup toward herself and reaches for one of the teapots sitting on the counter. Mort lunges and covers the spout with his palm before she can pour.

"Nope. Not that one. Not unless you want to sleep until noon." He nods toward the ceiling.

"Really?"

Mort turns back to the pasta. "Really."

Gwyneth lifts the lid and brings her face close to the liquid inside the teapot. Then she pours the tiniest amount into a spoon, dips her ring finger into the cooling tea, and places the drop on her tongue. "I'm assuming it's safe."

Mort gives her a grin. "Don't trust me?"

Gwyneth bristles. "I didn't say that."

"It's a restorative, one of Rose's recipes, ironically."

Yes, Ophelia thinks, it's always ironic to drug your best friend.

"I've simply doubled it," Mort adds. "She'll actually wake up stronger."

"That could be a problem."

"Not with the task force in place. Besides, she can't be incapacitated. Botten was clear about that. If Henry's barely conscious and Pansy's sound asleep, all we need to do is wait. Once they're both ready, we let Botten know, and he'll give the command to move."

"Can they really deploy and be operational in eight hours?"

"Heads will roll if they can't." Mort chases the pasta around in the pot before setting the strainer in the sink. From all appearances, he seems more concerned about the noodles than the particulars of this conversation.

Gwyneth watches him, ever the scientist, evaluating these simple, domestic tasks. "Do you worry about what's going to happen?"

Ophelia leans forward. Behind her, she feels Henry do the same. In her times through this loop, she's never heard this exchange, never known what Botten has said to all the others. She imagines he has spun all manner of fairy tales, depending on the audience. Once upon a time, she believed one herself. But this is not a story with a happily ever after.

"No," Mort says, and his tone is strident. "We know this isn't their fault. This is all on Rose and Darnelle, Sr. That's why Botten sent *us* and not the usual sycophantic, ass-kissing suspects." He stirs the pasta again, water splattering. "Things could get rough. That's the nature of this job, but Henry and Pansy will be fine. Absolutely." And now Mort sounds like he needs to convince himself along with Gwyneth.

All Ophelia has now are her memories of all the outcomes the Sight has shown her. It stubbornly refuses to reveal this particular future, even for mere seconds. It's unsettling not to have those threads to grasp on to, and her heart flutters again in near panic. At any moment, Mort or Gwyneth might decide to use the powder room tucked beneath the staircase and catch Henry hovering in the dark hallway.

And then? She can't see that. But she knows all too well Botten's anger, his aim in all this, not that he's actually planning on ending the world. That's merely an unintentional consequence. She doesn't know what it is that Rose Little and Harry Darnelle supposedly did, only that Botten had a hand in it; only that of the three, he is the most culpable.

Ophelia knows when the end comes, it's always drenched in blood, and the chain reaction can't be stopped, not by the military, not by governments banding together, and certainly not by the Enclave.

"Botten is only setting things right, making them better." Mort dumps the rigatoni into the strainer, and steam mists the window above the sink. "What if we didn't have to live like this anymore? What if no one did? No hunger, no disease. Wouldn't that be something?"

"No betrothals?" Gwyneth adds, eyebrow arched.

"Oh, that too." A smile blooms across Mort's face, one filled with so much hope and so much love.

Ophelia shuts her eyes, because she can't bear the desire she sees there. She knows how this dream dies, too, and it isn't pretty or pleasant or peaceful. She can almost taste Mortimer's betrayal and subsequent remorse.

The clatter of silverware pulls her from these thoughts. On a tray,

Mort has arranged a plate with pasta, a salad, a roll and butter, the crème brûlée, and, of course, the pot of tea.

"You want to take care of our patient?" He hefts the tray. "I'll head upstairs."

Ophelia flings herself from the table. Her fear is so strong, she could almost fly. All her willpower is focused on a single word:

Run!

She beats Mortimer to the hallway by mere seconds. He's cleared the space before Ophelia realizes Henry is no longer tucked into the shadows. Only when Mort's heavy tread pounds on the staircase does the powder room door creak open.

Her brother. Her daring, dashing, foolish brother slips down the hall and into the office. Ophelia tries to run interference, but Gwyneth merely steps through her, pauses for a moment, shudders, and then marches on.

In the office, on the sofa, Henry is silent and pale. He blinks groggily at Gwyneth and gives her a sleepy smile. He looks like a little boy, home sick from school. He accepts the tray and Gwyneth's fussing with a display worthy of an Oscar.

Miffed, Ophelia settles on the coffee table and shoots scowls at the woman who would be Dr. Gwyneth Worthington-Wells-Darnelle. (Yes, that's a side shoot the Sight has shown her. Yes, it's completely disturbing. And yes, it ends exactly how one might imagine.)

Don't believe what you've heard. You won't be fine. They are going to kill you and Pansy.

Ophelia still wishes she knew why. But maybe the why doesn't matter. She watches, unsure which Henry is the real one. This sickly patient? Or the man sliding soundlessly through the house?

It's only when she's certain he isn't feigning this malaise and only when Gwyneth's back is turned that Henry's gaze zeroes in on her spot on the coffee table. And maybe she imagines it; maybe it's wishful thinking.

But really, did her brother just wink at her?

CHAPTER 55
PANSY

King's End, Minnesota
Friday, July 14

The burner phone has one contact, a contact who has sent me a series of text messages.

> Adele said Rose kept everything. We need to make certain none of it goes missing.

I search first beneath my bed and then try my walk-in closet. There, the boxes we brought over from Adele's basement are shoved near the back, along with my mother's memory box and the thick envelope of photographs. It's a hasty arrangement, and speaks to Henry not having a moment to spare. What I want to know is where he found the time, not to mention the strength, to lug them upstairs in the first place.

Or is his slow recovery simply a ruse? I consider how completely the man can shift personas and think: yes, it absolutely could be.

I rearrange the files, then stack sweaters on top of one box and shoes on top of another until it looks like I'm collecting items for donation, tucking the memory box to one side with the photos behind that. Halfway out of the closet, I realize my mother's umbrella needs a better hiding place as well.

No one, but no one, will think to search the zippered garment bag that holds my prom dress. As I'm slipping her between some ruffles, I wonder: who are we hiding all this from? I'm so used to hiding things from the Enclave that I haven't questioned Henry's text message. Of course we'll hide things. But why? Is it Mortimer that Henry doesn't trust? Is it Gwyneth?

Then I read the next text message:

> Rule #5 is in full effect.

Trust no one from the Enclave. Okay, then. I wonder if he's including himself in that.

> With perhaps an exception. 😉

We may need to have a talk about all this winking.

> Also, I think it's time we break rule #1.

The housing development after dark? Something about that scares me more than the silo or even the covered bridge. My mother's rules changed over the years, but ever since the construction company broke ground, that rule has sat at the top of every list.

The heavy sound of footfalls startles me. The floor shudders beneath my feet, and only one person can make that much of a racket. What sounds like a shoulder smacking my door comes next, and the wood quivers, and then the lock rattles.

"Pansy, what the hell?"

My feet have grown roots, and I'm standing next to the bed, clutching the burner phone, unable to move. My heart grates against my ribs. Part of me wants to fling open the door and demand the truth from Mort. The trickle of blood tells me that's the most foolish thing I could do.

"Pansy? You okay?"

I swipe my nose and then shove the burner phone between the mattresses. In my mad dash across the bed, I scramble the sheets and comforter and knock those pillows out of alignment. Before I unlock the door, I pull the ponytail holder from my hair and muss the strands.

"Sorry," I say. "Sorry. I dozed off. I must not be fully recovered."

Emotions flit across Mort's face. Anxiety, yes, but there's a hint of anger or perhaps just annoyance. But then his eyes grow tender, and he's the big brother to my little sister. The urge to confess washes over me. This is Mortimer. He's one of my best friends in the entire world. Why wouldn't I trust him?

Wavering, I step back, and he sets a dinner tray on my desk. The scent of basil fills my room, followed by warm bread and a hint of caramelized sugar. My stomach growls and insists that Mort must be a true friend, because who else but a true friend would whip up such a dinner on short notice?

"This is perfect," I say. "Thank you."

Mort steps close and cups my cheek with his hand. "How are you doing? I mean, really."

"Sad." That's not a lie. I do miss my mother completely, even if I'm no longer trapped in that sticky morass of deep grief. "Tired," I add.

"I thought you might be. I can't fix the one, Pansy-Girl. I wish I could. But the other?" He nods toward the teapot. "I made one of Rose's special teas. I'm not sure I got it right, so it might taste a little off."

"Which one did you make?"

"Her after-action one. I'm sure you've had plenty, but—"

"More doesn't hurt. You're right. It will make me feel better."

"My thoughts exactly. Drink the whole pot." Again, that tender look sears straight through me, as if Mort is searching for something he can't find. He opens his mouth like he's about to say something, then shuts it, shakes his head, and gives me a benevolent smile.

"I'll let you rest," is all he says.

The door shuts softly behind him. I pour a full cup of tea before crossing the room and engaging the lock. Out of some instinct—not to alert Mortimer, not to offend him—I do this as silently as possible and only when I'm certain he's reached the first floor.

With a sigh, I sit on the bed. I should probably dig out the burner phone and reread Henry's instructions for tonight. Tea first, I decide. I need to calm my heart and clear my head.

I know my mother's recipe will do just that.

CHAPTER 56
HENRY

Would he be fast enough?

Mortimer Connolly's footfalls shook the entire stairwell. The noise felt deliberate, a jab in Henry's direction. Yes, why let the injured man rest?

He'd stashed the burner phone deep beneath his pillows. Even as he shut his eyes and feigned exhaustion, he could sense the phone's presence beneath his skull, a guilty sort of feeling straight from an Edgar Allan Poe story.

Henry couldn't risk a message while Mortimer Connolly was in Pansy's room. Certainly, he couldn't pull out the phone and start texting in front of Gwyneth. Or perhaps he could, tossing off a cavalier, "Just one of my many flirtations."

That was unfair; Henry knew it. But his mood had soured, and playing the invalid hampered as much as it helped.

Like now, with Gwyneth in the room, fussing over him—stethoscope, penlight, and frown. After a decade in the field, Henry could adopt almost any persona. True, some were a bit beyond his grasp. Slipping into someone flippant was a stretch. But he could play possum with the best of them.

Gwyneth perched on the edge of the coffee table. "I'm worried, Henry. You're not—"

"Recovering fast enough after a near-fatal blow?"

Gwyneth exhaled, a half sigh, half laugh. "I know, I know. Seems odd, is all. You were fine earlier."

"Bit of a relapse. Same thing happened in Cairo after you left." It wasn't a complete lie. Still, he was feeling better than he had a right to, all things considered.

"Any idea what hit you?"

"None."

"Screamers generally don't attack like that."

No, not without an agenda, and clearly, they had one. "They were manifesting weather," he said. "And then?" He raised a hand, palm up, and let his fingers tremble slightly before dropping his hand again. "Then anything can happen."

"I just worry."

"I know you do."

To Gwyneth's credit, she always had. If Henry had to give the feeling a name, he'd call it sisterly love. Why they simply couldn't agree to that—and leave the betrothal behind—he couldn't say. Or rather, he could, and it was all due to Enclave politics.

"You should get some rest," he added. "It's been a long day for you as well."

"I was thinking"—she waved a hand at the office—"maybe Agent Little has a cot or something?"

"There's enough spare bedrooms upstairs for both you and Agent Connolly to each have your own."

"Perhaps you could join me?" True, the invitation was more soft than seductive, but a hint of the latter lingered in Gwyneth's voice. Open mind, indeed.

If he said the wrong thing? Refused in the wrong way? It would dash all his plans. With a task force hovering, he needed to move tonight. There was only so much he could fake. By morning, Gwyneth would, he was certain, declare him well enough. For what, he wasn't sure. But his vitals would be stable. There would be no reason to delay whatever it was Botten was planning, which narrowed this window of opportunity. Henry wasn't certain he could pull this off, even if everything did align.

And Gwyneth was one of those things that needed to align.

"I'm not certain I can make it up the stairs," he began.

"See? This is why—"

"But I can make it to the powder room down the hall. I can reach my phone." To demonstrate, he tapped his Enclave-issued phone on the coffee table next to the dinner tray. "If I need anything, I'll text. I know you have reports to submit and questions to handle. What does your inbox look like right now?"

Gwyneth sagged under the weight of all those administrative tasks that came with her position. "You're right. I have work to do."

It took a few more reassuring murmurs to get Gwyneth to leave the room. When the door whispered shut, Henry pulled out the burner phone and started pecking out a frantic text message. He was so intent that when the door swung open again, his thumb hit send before he could finish. He palmed the phone, tucked it beneath the fleece blanket, and tried to calm the pulse that hammered in his throat.

Mortimer Connolly shadowed the threshold. He was a big man, taller and broader than Henry. Five years in the field had sharpened the man's skills. His gaze was canny, and it assessed Henry with nothing but skepticism.

"Just seeing how you're doing." Mort's words were mild, although his tone implied something else entirely, something along the lines of *what you're doing* rather than *how*.

"I'm recovering. Slowly."

Mort gave a nod but remained silent. This was a fairly standard interrogation tactic, and really, it was beneath the man to even try.

Henry could go for days without uttering a word. He slipped into his invalid persona, let his eyelids droop, wincing as if even shifting his position was too strenuous. He was working up a good bit of drool when Mort let out a dismissive snort.

"Right. I'll let you sleep."

Oh, how the mighty have fallen. Yes, it was there in Mortimer's tone, pity mixed with contempt. It was there in the way he eased the door closed, nothing but solicitude and disdain. Well, let him think that. Let him tell Botten that.

Let everyone believe that Henry Darnelle was down for the count.

CHAPTER 57
PANSY

King's End, Minnesota
Friday, July 14

My lips touch the rim of the teacup, the porcelain warm and comforting. But at that moment, I'm not sure what startles me more: the aroma or the drops of blood that, thankfully, hit the saucer. A few more drops land, my hands tremble, and watery pink liquid threatens to spill over the edge.

Beneath me, the burner phone buzzes with an incoming text, but I don't have enough hands or focus to deal with that now. Instead, I return the teacup and saucer to the desk, and the dishes jangle. My nose continues to drip, so I dig out a bath towel from the hamper. The terry cloth is musty, and it's also a pale pink, which I'm currently ruining by bleeding into it.

I sit on the floor and contemplate the very obvious fact that my best friend is trying to drug me.

I made one of Rose's special teas. I'm not sure I got it right, so it might taste a little off.

It might taste a little off. No, it tastes exactly like my mother's restorative tea when you double, or possibly triple, the recipe. Pungent, yet soothing, almost seductive, with the lull of lavender. Why on earth try to pass it off as something other than what it is? Why not suggest that I need the restorative? Clearly, there are times when I do. And now, all things being equal, this might be one of them.

Except nothing is equal. Nothing is right about any of this. My stomach churns as if I did drink the tea. Mort should know better. That much restorative has a way of coming right back up. Unless he counted me on drinking so much, so quickly that it would knock me out. I consider this along with what to do next. Can I eat dinner? Or did he poison that as well? Honestly, if I can't trust my best friends from the Enclave, who can I trust?

The burner phone buzzes a reminder.

I crawl across the bedroom floor, the towel draped over my shoulders just in case. The bleeding has mostly stopped, but I don't want to leave a trail across the carpet. I paw under the mattress until I find the phone. Several more messages have arrived, and I read them one by one.

> Don't drink th

> The tea, damn it. Don't drink the tea. Mort did something to it.

Yes, indeed, he did.

> If you can, when you leave tonight, make it look as if you're still in bed. Pillows, blankets, clothes. That sort of thing.

> Leave your Enclave phone on the nightstand. Bring the burner.

> If you have one, bring a go bag.

Are we running away, then? To the housing development? Subterfuge and go bags. It's like something out of a spy thriller. Then again, so is my best friend drugging me. The housing development after dark might be the lesser of our problems right now.

My phone buzzes again.

> And eat. The food is safe.

> Memorize this number, delete these messages, and then the contact.

Henry's leaving nothing to chance.

> If you're caught, blame everything on me.

Oh, but I can't do that.

> If I'm caught, run. Maybe to Adele's. You could hide in that basement room, but I'd like you farther away. But don't tell me where.

Henry's worry coils around my heart and squeezes. Is it truly that bad? I think of how he so readily kept my Sight a secret, how cautious he was in not sending data to the Enclave. I think of what the Enclave has done in turning Mortimer against me.

The text messages stop then, so I dutifully do as he says. I eat. I open a window and splash tea into the hydrangeas below. They're hardy, mostly. I unearth a go bag because, yes, my mother always insisted.

I think about invoking the Sight, but I can't risk it. So I sit on my bed, fists clenched, and wait.

CHAPTER 58
OPHELIA

King's End, Minnesota
Saturday, July 15

At one in the morning, Pansy's farmhouse is full of secret night noises. Creaks and whispers, the scrabble of little feet. (She should look into getting a cat.) The ventilation system sighs its last burst of cool air before the morning sun will heat the space once again.

From down the hallway come rhythmic snores punctuated by the occasional elephant-sized snort. Mortimer, most likely. At least, Ophelia hopes it's him and not her presumptive sister-in-law. Okay, a small, petty part of her does hope it's Gwyneth.

Mort has left his bedroom door ajar as if he doesn't trust any of the inhabitants, to no avail. Pansy already stands at the top of the staircase, her footfalls down the hall so quiet that Ophelia could barely track her. Pansy casts a glance around the dark hallway. In one hand, she clutches her umbrella. On her back, a field pack. She has the air of someone saying goodbye.

Ophelia wants to ask her if she's used the Sight. Can Pansy see what Ophelia can't? Or is Pansy going into this ignorant as well? The hallway is too dim to see any telltale signs of a bloody nose. But Ophelia thinks not. Pansy's better with her Sight than Ophelia is, more cautious and more in control.

Pansy sits and eases down the first step. A well of laughter bubbles in Ophelia. This is obviously an old childhood trick, one Ophelia's used many times herself. Something to do with weight distribution; Henry explained it to her once. But yes, Pansy reaches the bottom without creaking the floorboards of a single stair.

The rooms where Mort and Gwyneth are sleeping face the backyard, so Pansy slips out the front, slings her umbrella over her shoulder, and hops the rail around the porch. With a running start, she plows through her neighbor's lilac bush.

Where she tumbles straight into Henry's waiting arms.

They stand like that, embracing, and yet not. Henry steadies her with a hand on one shoulder and plucks a few leaves from her hair with the other. The lilac bush shrouds them, shielding them from the yellow glow of the street lamps and line of sight of everyone's doorbell cameras. Not even Guy Gunderson, should he happen to peek through his living room window, will see them.

"How are you feeling?" Pansy whispers. "Are you okay?"

"Thanks to you, I'm more than okay."

Pansy lets out an exhale full of relief. "I was worried you really weren't recovering."

"I was doing a bit of playacting."

And spying.

His fingers go in search of another leaf, but Ophelia suspects it's more of an excuse to run his fingers through Pansy's hair.

"It's interesting how people talk around the injured and the sick," he adds, voice contemplative, "as if they were insensible."

"I was never sure how much my mother could hear or understand near the end. I just assumed she could. Or maybe I just hoped that."

"Hm. People speak around Ophelia as if she's no longer"—Henry breaks off and coughs—"conscious. In a physical coma, I suppose she wouldn't be. But there are times when I'm certain she's here."

Pansy scans the area, her gaze not quite meeting Ophelia's, even though Ophelia is mere inches away, as if this was some sort of group hug. Perhaps, at the moment, she's too insubstantial to create a connection. Her pulse is thready. In the background, a beep, beep, beep nags at her.

"It's like those phantom voices. You hear someone call your name, but no one's around. Or a parent and a baby's cry." Henry sighs. "I also suppose I could chalk that up to wishful thinking, or perhaps trauma."

Pansy shakes her head. "No. I think she's really here, at least some of the time." She places a hand on his chest, over his heart. "And I think you have a version of the Sight."

Henry scoffs at this. "We need to get moving."

Yes, they do. With the task force hovering so close, this is no time for heartfelt discussions. But Pansy is on to something. Ophelia swirls around them as they begin a zigzag approach toward the housing development. Really, how does Henry know where all the cameras are, which security lights will flicker on, and what path will keep them hidden? Yes, his skill as a field agent is on display. But there's more to it than that.

Maybe you do have the Sight, brother mine.

"Why couldn't you have a version of the Sight?" Pansy echoes, and Ophelia laughs with delight.

"I failed all those tests."

"Maybe the Enclave gives the wrong sorts of tests. How is it you're still alive, especially after the Sahara?"

The question brings Ophelia up short. How *has* Henry managed to stay alive all these years? The Enclave never places its most talented field agents in reserve. They throw them at the fissures and the Screamers over and over again until either their minds or bodies break, and they gratefully accept a position at headquarters. Or the other option: the toxins, a nasty hit, or one of those fissures that decides it needs a meal—or the agents themselves succumbing to the thrall of all that.

"I've been extremely lucky."

Pansy gives her head a vigorous shake. "It's more than that. But the Enclave doesn't care about their field agents. I wish I didn't have the Sight. Most of the time, it hurts more than it helps." She pauses to pull in a breath. "Except for maybe earthquakes. That would come in handy."

Henry's laugh is quiet. "Yes, knowing about earthquakes would be beneficial. But even then—"

"They're not a hundred percent predictable."

Pansy halts, and Ophelia recognizes the stubborn tilt of her chin. "No one, and I include my mother in this, has ever been able to connect with my Sight the way you do."

Henry spares her a look before moving forward again. "I've had lots of practice."

"Part of it is skill, but a large part is intuition."

"That simply isn't—"

"Logical?" Pansy jogs the few steps between them and reaches his side again. "Whoever said the Sight was logical?"

Henry inclines his head. "I'll give your theory its due consideration."

Now Ophelia snorts so loudly that Pansy glances her way.

Yes, children, summer's over, and school is now in session. And oh, look, here's your instructor, Principal Field Agent Henry Darnelle.

Ophelia can't help it; she snorts again. Her brother, painfully predictable, unlike those earthquakes.

Pansy and Henry leave the sidewalk behind, along with the crickets that have serenaded their trek. Henry steers them to the weedy edge of the gravel road, where their shoes will leave less of an impression. They walk silently now, single file. Neither speaks until they reach the entrance to Camelot Lots.

The development appears so benign in the dark. The houses are little more than outlines, suggesting cozy abodes and suburban splendor rather than decaying dreams. This far from the center of King's End, light pollution isn't an issue, and the stars emerge brighter in the night sky. It's enough to steal your breath. Ophelia tips her head back and marvels at the view.

"You could almost see the appeal," Henry says.

"It was supposed to turn King's End into more of a bedroom community. We're close enough to the Twin Cities. It would be a long commute, but..."

"No worse than the gridlock in Seattle. Better, perhaps."

"Not in the winter."

Henry manages another laugh, but already, the serious field agent persona is locking in place. Pansy adjusts the strap of her umbrella as if she, too, feels this resolve.

"My mother never wanted me to come here after dark," she says, and her voice cracks as if it hurts to break this most important rule.

"It's the only way to get out in front of the task force. They're waiting on Botten's command, but they can be here and operational in a mere eight hours."

"Botten's command? Does that mean—?"

"This has been in the works for a while? I believe so. Botten's been waiting for the right moment, and we seem to have triggered that." He pulls a small electronic device from the pocket of his cargo trousers. "I hope to scramble the readings they'll initially collect. Battery operated, but it should buy us a little time."

"Time for what?"

"For one, reinforcing the fissure—"

"Under the showcase home," Pansy finishes.

"Yes, that exactly. I believe King's End sits on top of a juncture, one your mother discovered when she was assigned here as a permanent post agent. I believe she confided this knowledge to both my father and Reginald Botten."

Pansy gapes, her eyes huge in the dark and with these revelations. "My mother...?"

"I also believe this is no ordinary juncture, but a gateway. A gateway needs three points, three holes in the fabric between dimensions, if you will, to be activated. This is the epicenter." Henry points toward the showcase home. "Then there's the silo." He gestures down the road toward that uncanny stretch of abandoned farmland. "And the covered bridge."

"So, all those years ago?"

"Yes. All those years ago. Something happened, perhaps with the gateway."

"Was it something our parents started?"

Henry's sigh is heavy, full of doubt. "I don't know."

"There aren't any photographs of the covered bridge."

"I suspect your mother may have kept that location a secret, even from my father." Henry pauses. "Although, perhaps not. But certainly Botten. The scans he's had Agent Connolly run indicate that no one is certain where all three points are, exactly."

"Trust no one from the Enclave," Pansy whispers.

Henry nods. "But someone on the task force will be sharp enough to figure it out, eventually. After all, your mother did with the bare minimum of equipment and support, as did I with what I brought with me for your examination." Henry pauses, a frown clouding his brow. "Your father mentioned a stopgap measure. This leads me to believe all they need to proceed is the precise location of the epicenter."

"Jack," Pansy says. "Jack Ling. Mort said he put in a by-name request because Jack knows so much about King's End."

"As does Agent Connolly himself."

Pansy's expression crumples. A moment later, the full realization hits Ophelia, a sharp stab in the solar plexus. She steps away from Pansy, not that it lessens the anguish rolling through her. The air is heavy with betrayal and the unspoken, heartrending refrain: *Were they ever my friends?*

Ophelia wishes she were solid, that she could wrap her arms around Pansy, hold her close, and let her cry. She'd be the fierce protector and announce to the world: *Who needs them, anyway?*

"Botten's been playing a long game," Henry says, his words as gentle as possible. "I don't think either one of them has consciously deceived you."

Pansy swallows hard, pushes her palms against her eyes, collecting tears and sorrow.

"Do either Jack or Mortimer know about the covered bridge?"

Pansy shakes her head. "It was one of those unspoken rules. It was bad enough that they knew about my Sight, but that couldn't be helped. I needed friends at the Academy."

"See? There's your clue. Botten has no idea about your capabilities."

"As far as we know."

"Yes, I suppose it could come to light. But trust me, Botten would pay dearly for that sort of knowledge. He used Ophelia relentlessly." Henry waves a hand toward the development. "Perhaps because of this. No one knows what Ophelia saw that last time, not even Botten."

Well, he thinks he knows.

But the recrimination in Henry's voice deflates Ophelia. She feels herself coming apart, almost like mist, and scrambles to hang on. There's nothing for her in Seattle but her mother's tears, so why the Sight insists on booting her back so often, she doesn't know.

Pansy, too, looks deflated, maybe even defeated. Her voice is low, still full of anguish. "I wish she would've told me all this."

"I believe your mother did, in the only way she could." Henry turns her toward him, a hand on her shoulder again, his expression tender. "Listen to me. For whatever reason, Botten needs both you and me to open, or perhaps reopen, the gateway. I suspect that was his purpose in sending me here in the first place. He needs us here, in King's End."

"And if we're not here?" Pansy's voice lightens, and her resolve returns.

These two, Ophelia thinks, read each other so well.

"Exactly. I'd like for us to get a head start and leave before the task force is activated. I wouldn't put it past Botten to send an advance party tonight." Henry glances around, taking in his surroundings as if he can detect Enclave agents lurking in the cemetery and the surrounding fields. "But they won't deploy unless the epicenter is located."

Of course. Ophelia's spent enough time in the field to know setting up in the wrong place has nasty consequences. Losing an entire task force is one of those career-limiting moves.

"I'm more than capable of planting the devices and mending the fissure," he adds. "But in case I'm not fast enough and I get caught, I think you should leave now."

Something that feels like hope sparks in Ophelia's chest. Maybe Henry's hit upon the answer. Eliminate one, or better still, both of them from the equation? In all her trips through the loop, Botten has never proceeded until both Henry and Pansy are secure in his grasp. He needs them here, alive, at least initially.

Then, yes, the obvious answer *is* to remove the players from the board. She flits around them, cajoling, shouting, waving her arms, aching to get their attention.

"I won't leave you," Pansy says, and that stubborn tilt to her chin is back.

Yes, yes, you can. Leaving means you'll save him.

Ophelia doesn't know if this is true, but it feels right in a way that things haven't felt right in a very long time.

Henry's chest swells in what looks like a burst of righteousness and chivalry.

"You need someone watching your back," Pansy adds. "We'll do this together, and then we'll both leave." When he doesn't answer, she says, "I mean, you did pack a go bag, right?"

His lips twitch. Indeed he did.

"All right." Henry holds out his hand. "Together."

Ophelia dances around in triumph, waving her arms in the air, head thrown back. Yes! They'll do it! They'll really do it! Henry won't die. The world won't end. Once they're far away, they can figure out how to deal with Botten, the Enclave, and everything else.

Pansy takes Henry's hand. He nods as if this, despite his earlier words, is where Pansy belongs, at his side, palm against palm, fingers laced. Together, they cross the threshold of the housing development.

Ophelia surges after them. She will stand watch, alert for the first signs of an advance party. She will force them to listen to her warnings. Except when she tries, she slams into an invisible and very solid wall. She pounds her fists, throws herself against it, but the barrier is uncompromising. It isn't smooth or cool. There's nothing tactile about it. The wall simply is. And it's more than a physical barricade, it's a psychic one as well, one with an agenda all its own, one that does not include Ophelia.

On the other side, the housing development remains, as eerie and tranquil as ever.

But Henry and Pansy are nowhere.

PART FOUR

THE KEY TO EVERYTHING

CHAPTER 59
PANSY

King's End, Minnesota
Saturday, July 15

"Is it me," Henry says, "or is it almost peaceful like this?"

We've just finished planting the last of the devices. According to Henry, they'll scramble any readings the Enclave tries to take of the area, essentially sending anyone searching for the epicenter on a wild goose chase. Although he's made certain to steer them away from the covered bridge.

I've been standing sentinel, umbrella ready, scanning the area for any hint of activity, Screamer and human. Everything has been calm, deceptively so, and I can't wait to leave. First, we need to reinforce the fissure.

As we turn to do just that, a breeze flutters against my cheeks like a butterfly kiss. The air itself is warm, sweet, almost seductive. My hand tucked into his feels right. If not for the field packs, umbrellas slung over shoulders, and the fact that we're eyeing the space around us with suspicion, we'd be the picture of a romantic couple out for a stroll. Yes, in the *housing development*. I count the seconds until this illusion will shatter and the Screamers come roaring in.

When that doesn't happen, dread fills me. Beneath the scented air lingers a current of unfulfilled promises and false dreams. It's a saccharine taste that coats my tongue.

"Something's wrong," I say, keeping my voice low, barely a whisper, but Henry doesn't respond.

I scan the area, searching for evidence of Screamers, for the source that's transforming the development into a place where people live and thrive. Everything is enveloped in the glow of streetlights that hover in my peripheral vision but clearly don't exist. Near the back, instead of empty frames and skeletal remains, a playground sits. Farther back, what looks like a community garden stretches, lush with tomatoes and peppers and green beans.

This can't be true, and yet Henry glances around as if he endorses these improvements.

"I'm finding it difficult," he murmurs, "to remember why we're here." He turns to me with a puzzled expression. "We don't live here, do we?"

Live here? His question shoots a burst of panic through me. He's not playacting. At least, I don't think he is. This is not a performance for the benefit of the Screamers. It's in the way he holds my hand, the gentle way his thumb travels over my knuckles. There's something so deeply contented about the gesture that I can't find the words to answer his nonsensical question.

"But it is rather nice," he says when I don't respond. "I wonder if any of these homes are for sale."

Homes for sale? I glance around again, and there's a For Sale sign in the yard of a house near the community garden. It's as if his belief has manifested it.

I choose my words with the utmost care. "We don't live here. We don't live ... together."

He tilts his head as if I've uttered something both adorable and ridiculous. Then he draws me close, his arms wrapping around me, cocooning me. Laughter rumbles against my cheek. It's so very warm in his embrace, so very safe. I plant my palms against his chest, but I can't find the willpower to push away.

"We'll just have to make it official, then, and buy ourselves one of these houses." He punctuates this declaration with a devastating wink that has my head spinning.

Oh, something is very wrong. My thoughts are slow and sticky. Henry's embrace might be a cocoon, but everything else is like being wrapped in a spider's web, and we're the prey.

Panic seizes my throat, so tight I can't speak. This is the time for a strike, when only I'm aware of the deception. But the night around us is calm. I see no sign of the Screamers, but that means little.

Henry gazes down at me as if I'm the answer to everything, as if he wants to give me everything. All I have to do is ask, and he'll buy that house near the garden, set up his kitchen, and cook me meal after meal.

His mouth inches toward mine with the promise of a lingering kiss, as if we have the rest of our lives for those sorts of kisses. I feel myself lean in to him further, wanting that kiss, wanting it to never end, wanting to fall under the same spell that has him bewitched. Because wouldn't that be lovely? Wouldn't that solve everything? An ache in my chest insists that yes, this does solve everything. It makes the hurt go away; it makes the world go away.

Never go into the housing development after dark.

The words swirl in my head, so easy to push aside and forget. Except I can't. At the last moment, before the dream can crash over me, I shove hard against Henry's chest.

"Agent Darnelle!"

His eyes lose that bedroom glimmer. He blinks once, twice. His posture shifts, the cocoon breaks, and I'm cast to one side. He still grips my hand, but it's the hold of a field agent on high alert. He shakes his head hard as if trying to shake off the hallucination.

"Never go into the housing development after dark," he echoes.

"Yes, I'm beginning to understand why." He looks at me, expression abashed. "I'm not actually sure what I said, but I hope—"

"It was nothing," I say, words rushed, as if, for one tiny moment, I didn't believe either.

And that's the real problem of all this: It. Was. Nothing. Gossamer strands of dreams that can never be.

"We can't stay for long." Henry continues to shake his head as if he must work to keep the spider's web at bay. "But we should reinforce the fissure."

"No." Even as I protest, a rivulet of blood heats my upper lip. I don't need the Sight to tell me there isn't time. "We can't."

"Damn." Henry pulls a handkerchief from a pocket. With a hand on my shoulder, he steadies me and presses the cloth gently against my nose. It's unbearably soft, and he's unbearably tender. He pauses in his ministrations, chin lifted. "I don't like the way the air is changing."

I feel it, too. Beneath the sudden and seductive scent of chocolate chip cookies, a dry crackle of static.

"Something's coming." Henry shoves the handkerchief into his pocket and grips my hand again. "But I can't tell from where."

Neither can I. Or rather, I can't until I glance toward the entrance of the development. The Camelot Lots sign has been obliterated. The gate no longer exists. Nothing exists except a dark gray mass.

"There," I say, and point, my voice thin and reedy. I turn toward the fence that borders the cemetery, but that's gone, too, along with the headstones and oaks. The void creeps closer, gaining speed, and the only thing that remains is the structure behind us.

Henry nods toward the showcase home. "It's our only option."

"If we can't get in?"

"Cover me." He unslings his umbrella and hands it to me. "I'll pick the lock."

We bolt, that gray mass to our backs, so thick and so solid, it's like a tidal wave. I can't even tell if these are Screamers or something else entirely. All I know is, this thing will consume us the first chance it gets.

Henry crouches at the front door, pulling out lock picks—of course he brought the lock picks—and works the lock. I stand, my back to him, reassured by his warmth against my legs. With a flick, I unfurl both umbrellas. They open with a pop that establishes a connection immediately, clearing a space around the door.

I peer through the gap between my umbrella and Henry's. I can't see across the street or even to the end of the front walk. Our world has shrunk to the span of two umbrellas, a wooden porch, and a tattered welcome mat beneath our feet. Everything else is painted in gray ash.

The fabric of our umbrellas shakes as if enduring gale-force winds. I clutch the handles, palms sweat-slicked and unsure. Worry batters my mind in time to the wind—rips, tears, the material stripped away, leaving nothing but naked spokes. I can't turn to gauge Henry's progress. I can't hold on much longer. I can't—

I tumble backward. Henry pulls me the rest of the way into the house and slams the door. He throws the deadbolt, for all the good that will do.

But maybe it helps. The space around us is quiet, if unsettling, the way abandoned spaces often are. And certainly, this house has never been lived in, has never truly been someone's home. I collapse both umbrellas and offer him his. In turn, he offers his hand and helps me stand.

He's still on high alert, peering into the rooms both to our left and right and then up a grand, sweeping staircase. "We shouldn't assume we're safe."

No, we shouldn't. He hits a light switch on the wall, but nothing happens. From his pack, he pulls out a flashlight.

Before he can turn it on, I say, "Wait a minute."

There's enough ambient light to navigate around the larger pieces of furniture. In the front room, curtains blanket a large picture window. My fingers find the center, and I pull back one side so we can peer through the glass. It's like a blizzard of ash outside, the world cast in tones of gray and sepia.

Henry comes to stand behind me, a steady hand on my shoulder, as if he's afraid I'll slip away through the window and into the nothing beyond.

"It's like the sandstorm," he says. "In the Sahara."

I plant a cautious hand against the glass. Henry's grip tightens.

"Is there anything out there?" I squint, but I can't see a thing. No evidence of the gate, a road, or even the porch where we stood.

"I don't know," Henry says.

"It's like..." I pause, trying to find the words to describe not so much what I'm seeing but what I'm feeling. "It's like there's an absence of everything, like nothing exists." Not even us, I want to add, but find that I can't.

"Perhaps it's merely a storm, and we simply need to ride it out."

I let the curtain fall, and the relief that washes over me comes out with a sigh.

"We can check periodically," he says, "to see if the storm is subsiding, but in the meantime, I think we should conduct a search, see how secure this space is."

So we do, from basement to attic, our flashlights carving a path in front of us. The pantry holds nothing but empty boxes meant to resemble a stocked larder. The comforter on the king-size bed in the master suite hides a bare mattress. And while you could do laps in the Jacuzzi tub, to quote Mortimer, it's clear no one has ever taken a bath in it. The closets hold nothing, not even skeletons. The basement is too dry and clean for ghouls.

But that's where we pause to inspect that egress window and the fissure that runs beneath the foundation. Both of us run our hands along the walls and floor. A light coating of dust sticks to my skin, but that's all I feel.

"Are we inside the fissure?" I'm on my hands and knees, working my fingers into the seam between floor and wall, the egress window a menacing rectangle above me.

"I dearly hope not," he says, and there is nothing reassuring in his tone.

We return to the front room, what the brochure for Camelot Lots would call the great room. From here, we can see the kitchen, the dining area, and both the front and back doors, along with the sweeping staircase to the second floor.

Henry's still scanning, still vigilant. "I don't think I've ever been in a place so completely without any character."

"It's a showcase home," I tell him. "It's not supposed to have character. It's like a blank canvas."

He nods, but even in the dark, I can tell he's unconvinced.

The curtain is still drawn across the large bay window, but the skylight remains unadorned. I stare up at it, pinpricks of cold puckering the skin on my arms. The open concept and large windows were meant to be a selling point, but the room feels cold and cavernous.

"We can set up base somewhere else," Henry says, as if he feels it too.

"I think here is best. Everything flows into this space." Oh, honestly, I sound like I've stumbled out of a home improvement show. "Which means if something comes our way, we'll see or hear it."

Henry gives me a nod of approval and yanks a sheet from a sectional. "Then let's sit and rest." As if to demonstrate, he eases the pack from his shoulders and then, once seated, places his feet on the coffee table. "We can work out our next steps, figure out how to make a break for it when this storm ends."

"If it doesn't?"

He sinks farther into the couch and pats the cushion next to his. "Then we think of something else."

The couch seems a great distance away, a yawning gap of a space that starts at the toes of my pink sneakers and stretches to the coffee table, where he's placed his umbrella and field pack. I slip my own field pack from my shoulders while my umbrella tugs me forward, urging me to deposit her next to her companion. Like we don't have bigger problems.

Shameless thing.

"Pansy, sit. You're making me nervous."

I glance up at the skylight before parting the curtains ever so slightly and gazing at the grayness outside.

"*I'm* making you nervous?"

He manages to laugh, and it's this that has me on the couch cushion next to him. From his pack, he pulls a small lantern and flicks it on. Light blazes before he adjusts the intensity to the lowest setting.

In the dim light, his expression is careworn, full of regret and apology. "I'm beginning to think this was one of those rules we shouldn't have broken."

I take his hand and give it a squeeze, but I don't have it in me to disagree.

CHAPTER 60
HENRY

Henry struggled against the seduction. Part of him found the experience curious, how easy it was to slip into the fantasy. Clearly, it was nothing more than that.

And yet, here he was, assessing this space as if he could set up housekeeping. True, he'd prefer something with more history and certainly more character. Even so? The kitchen was excellent, nearly perfect. Oh, the meals he could cook here. The barest hint of an aroma reached him. What was it? Something savory, perhaps with sage, something deeply comforting.

He jerked himself forward on the couch, planted his hands on the coffee table, and sucked in deep breaths. His heart thumped a warning, but nothing in the surroundings stirred. Only he and Pansy were here, and she was currently sleeping beside him. Earlier, he'd tugged additional sheets from the furniture, shook out the dust, and tucked her in as best he could.

Her sleep was deep, and he wondered, not for the first time, if he should wake her. Or was it more dangerous to be alert and susceptible to the seduction? The daydreams and fantasies only clogged his mind, making it harder to plan an escape.

His heart clutched at that thought and thrummed another warning. The house didn't want them to leave. If he were honest with himself, Henry was fairly certain something deep inside him didn't want to leave either. These two things were conspiring, or so he imagined.

He pushed to stand, shaking his head. Another circuit, another inventory to keep his mind from wandering. Henry checked both burner phones. Still no signal, no way to alert anyone to where they were. His umbrella merely vibrated with regret when it couldn't send a pulse, never mind an SOS.

"At least you're still with me," Henry murmured.

On the coffee table, Pansy's umbrella fluttered her ruffles as if to reassure him that she, too, was still here.

"And I appreciate your company as well."

He powered down Pansy's phone to conserve the battery and then picked up his own.

"Circuit three of the showcase home in Camelot Lots. According to my watch, it's 5:30 a.m., but I don't trust that it's accurate." He couldn't say why, exactly. Perhaps it was the quality of light, relentless in its sameness. No hint of sunrise or the sky changing color. Assuming, of course, there was a sky somewhere beyond those skylights.

He filmed as best he could, lighting the space with a flashlight. Tucked on the other side of that sweeping staircase was a room meant as a study or den, snug with a stone fireplace and built-in bookcases.

It wasn't a true replica of his father's study in Seattle, but certainly, it could be shaped into something just as satisfying. Henry stepped into the room, where a whiff of wood smoke suggested a recent fire in the hearth. Comfortable wingback chairs flanked the fireside, ready for an evening of excellent scotch and absorbing reading. The shelves were filled with a rather extensive, and impressive, book collection. Perhaps he'd relight the fire, pull a volume from the shelf, and...

Henry froze, his fingers gripping the phone until they ached. Slowly, very slowly, he panned the room, filming every last corner. Then he stopped the recording and scrolled back to the first video he'd made.

Jesus. He slumped against the doorframe. Hours ago, this room had been bare. The bookshelves held nothing but dust, and there were no furnishings save for a desk and chair at the far end. No wingback chairs. No thick Persian carpet on the floor. No tufted sofa where, he was convinced, Pansy napped on a regular basis.

The seduction wasn't all in his mind, then. The house was changing around him. Changing for him? Well, he *had* accused it of having zero personality. Perhaps it had taken offense. Perhaps it was out to prove something.

Perhaps he shouldn't think of it as sentient.

Henry started the recording again, aiming the flashlight as best he could. When Pansy woke, he'd get her opinion. But to do that, he needed evidence. He didn't trust his eyes, or his mind, enough to discern what was real and what wasn't. He navigated the room with an ever-present fear that the camera was picking up nothing but shapeless lumps and cardboard props, a Potemkin village of a house.

"If only I had more light."

In the corner, on the desk, a lamp flickered on.

Oh, no. No, no, no. Henry shook his head. This couldn't be happening. He slapped the switch on the wall, and the overheads blared on. He winced and turned them off again. Without recourse, he continued the circuit of the house, recording everything, light switches responding to his touch.

Upstairs, the master bedroom had changed drastically into something less suggestive and far cozier, the comforter the first victim. A dismissive: "Satin? Really?" had done it. Henry remained rooted at the threshold, watching the new spread change before his eyes. Goose down? Absolutely. Yes, that was more like it.

The lamp on the nightstand produced enough glow that he could read aloud to Pansy before bed. Unquestionably, Henry *did* read to her. See? Among the books on the nightstand was a thick tome with a fabric bookmark, complete with a tassel.

"Now, that's an appropriate use for satin."

The moment the words had left his mouth, Henry stumbled backward into a chair—one that hadn't been there moments before—and sat down hard. His chest was tight, his breath shallow. He had never read to Pansy in the evenings because they weren't married, and *that* certainly wasn't their marital bed.

Don't be daft, man. Of course you're married. You fell hard during her field agent examination, about the time she stole your umbrella. One of those irrevocable moments that changes everything. Naturally, you were a gentleman, taking an assignment in Minneapolis and striking up a true friendship. Nothing inappropriate about that. You wouldn't be the first field agent to...

"Stop!"

The nattering in his head subsided even as the room around him continued to change, auditioning items for his approval. An elaborate dressing table appeared, glimmering with silver brush and mirror set, lined with perfume bottles, and trimmed with a ruffled skirt.

Henry gave it a dismissive glance and muttered, "I doubt Pansy's the vanity type."

In its place, a stand appeared with an old-fashioned shaving kit, complete with a stainless steel bowl and badger hair shave brush.

"Well, yes. We know who the vain one is in this relationship."

There is no relationship, Henry. You're trapped in the housing development. Focus.

He stopped filming and tucked his phone away. Pansy would see the evidence herself once she woke up. She *would* wake up, right? Some tea, perhaps. He had bottled water and tea bags tucked in his field pack. Since the electricity was on, he could boil some water.

Tea. Yes. It would do them both good. Wake Pansy and clear all the cobwebs from his head. Tea was just the thing.

From the floor below came the whistle of a kettle, more cheerful than jarring. Henry rushed down the steps. True, he planned on waking Pansy, but not like this. A tray full of snacks and some perfectly steeped brew. Now, *that* was the proper way to rouse your wife.

The kitchen greeted his arrival, full of gleaming copper pots and pans along with bunches of herbs hanging from racks, each tied with a colorful ribbon. He eased the kettle from the burner and started in on the food. Before heading into the living area, Henry paused and glanced around, his chest swelling with pleasure.

Yes, this truly was the most perfect kitchen.

CHAPTER 61
PANSY

The aroma of tea creeps into my consciousness. The scent is light, full of jasmine, the perfect tea for the afternoon. I can't quite make sense of it, though, or of my surroundings. The cushions beneath my head are unfamiliar, and the blanket is lovely and warm, but nothing I've ever owned.

A subdued clattering has me bolting upright, eyes flying open. I glance around without really seeing anything, memories flooding my mind. Yes, the housing development and the showcase home. We're trapped. We need to find a way out. Somehow, instead of helping Henry, I fell asleep.

"I didn't mean to startle you," he says, "but I'm glad you're awake."

The look in his eyes is so tender that it has me peering over my shoulder for the object of his affection. Nothing except thick drapes. Nothing to explain the smile that pops those dimples, the deepening crinkles around his eyes, or the gentle kiss he bestows on my forehead.

I am breathless.

"Still sleepy?"

No, not in the least, but I manage the tiniest of nods. I am very much awake and very much confused. Henry folds a cup of tea into my hands. The bright scent of jasmine does little to clear my head, but the warmth against my fingers is reassuring. Until it isn't.

With care, I set the teacup on the coffee table. "The electricity's on?"

He chuckles at this. "That must have been some dream you had."

Yes, I *was* asleep, but this is starting to feel more like a dream. Something about the showcase home is different. Worse, something about Henry is different and vastly so.

"We're in the housing development," I say slowly, like I'm trying out each word. "We're trapped in the showcase home. Something chased us here. The Screamers, maybe?"

I take in our surroundings, which are far cozier than I recall. True, it was dark. But I remember the showcase home, have peeked through its windows dozens of times. It never had anything more than bare-bones furnishings and uninspiring, if high-end, decor.

Now it's something else entirely.

"Don't you remember?" My voice is thin and pleading, as if I already know the answer.

For a moment, concern clouds Henry's expression. "More of a nightmare, then. Or perhaps the Sight." He nods, mostly to himself, as if he's worked out this problem and can set things right. "Well, there's one way to take care of that." He heads for the pantry in the kitchen and returns with a small bottle, like so many that line my own pantry at home. "I'll let you add the dose." He places it next to my teacup.

I examine the vial. That's my handwriting, although the numbers swirl when I try to focus on the date. I uncap the bottle and sniff. The combination of bracing herbs would be just the thing to counteract the Sight. Assuming, of course, it had been giving me trouble.

The Sight seldom interrupts my sleep, and my dreams are almost never prophetic. But I'm beginning to think that *this* is the Sight inducing some sort of delusion. That's when it hits me.

A coma.

Fear thrums low in my belly, icy and sharp. The sensation inches upward, freezing my lungs until I can barely pull in a breath. Would I recognize a Sight-induced coma? I don't know. I'm always an observer, never a participant, watching the future or past unfold, but I always know it's not my reality.

This feels like reality.

"The tea," Henry urges. "You're looking a little pale. We can cancel dinner—"

I shake my head, because something inside me knows this dinner means the world to Henry, and I can't deny him that. Nonsensical, but I can't contradict him, can't insist there's no actual dinner to cancel. I pick up the teacup, and a glimmer on my left ring finger catches the light.

A wedding band, an elegant, low-key design that only hints at the expense behind it. And on Henry's hand? The ring's mate.

Never go into the housing development after dark.

But how was I to know? How on earth could I predict this situation? I rage silently at my mother, the Screamers, the Sight. But the burst of anger is meant for me. Henry was slipping into this fantasy even before we escaped into the showcase home. I knew he was. And yet I still fell asleep when I should've been on my guard and kept him safe.

"Are you sure?" he prompts, that concern flooding back into his expression.

"I'm sure," I say, and pretend to drink the tea. I really don't know if I should drink or eat anything. Despite my lack of acting skills, Henry seems to think I am swallowing his tea. For now, that's good enough.

"In that case, I'm going to head back to the kitchen."

He leaves me with another smile that shatters my heart.

With Henry in the kitchen, I do a quick recon of the first floor. On the mantlepiece, framed photographs take up every available space. Again, the images swirl, but I catch hints of me in a wedding dress, Henry in a tuxedo—devastating, of course—and a honeymoon somewhere with a rugged coastline and colorful villages clinging to cliffs. If I try to focus, the mirage fades, replaced by that same grayness surrounding the house.

Near the door, I find a stand with our umbrellas. They both quiver with anxiety, mine fluttering her ruffles in distress.

"Can you tell me what's going on?"

They agitate so hard that the stand clatters against the hardwood floor.

"Sounds like a party out there," Henry calls from the kitchen.

"They're just excited." I place a finger against my lips, not that it does much good. They calm the rattling, but the messages they send me, or try to send me, are a jumbled mess.

I turn to investigate the rest of the house, but a sudden thought strikes me, and I lean down. "Do you know where our field packs are?" I pat my pockets, but the burner phone isn't there. My field pack would have water and emergency tinctures. If I could get Henry to drink one, it might clear his head.

My umbrella points her strap in one direction, Henry's in the other. I sigh. They're completely unhelpful, and they know it. But they're together, at least. It's the one clear message that does reach my mind.

I've completed a full tour of the house when I realize our packs must be in the one spot I haven't searched: The kitchen. Where Henry is.

On purpose?

He knows the moment I slip across the threshold. He beams at me, the kitchen around him gleams at me, and the aroma steamrollers me. The double ovens are working overtime (of course his kitchen has double ovens). The counters are filled with ingredients, from fresh greens to breadcrumbs. Pies are cooling on wire racks, the scent of pumpkin, pecan, and mincemeat floating in the air. Sage, rosemary, spices. This is no ordinary dinner he's cooking.

Henry commands the center of the kitchen, so proud, so happy. He doesn't even appear startled when the back door begins to quake.

A pounding comes next, loud and insistent.

"Get that, will you?" he asks casually, kindly. "I'm up to my elbows in turkey grease."

The pounding continues. I cross to the door if only to make the noise stop. I've barely touched the knob when the door itself flies open. It slams against the wall and bounces once, twice. The emptiness beyond is vast and gray and hungry. I work to shove the door closed. But not before a figure comes tumbling through and spills into the kitchen.

And there, spread-eagled on the terracotta tile, panting for all he's worth, is my father, Max Monroe.

CHAPTER 62
OPHELIA

King's End, Minnesota
Saturday, July 15

At sunrise, Ophelia crashes through that invisible barrier. Or rather, at sunrise, it evaporates like mist, and gravity does the rest. Only her dignity is bruised, not that anyone has witnessed her faceplant. She rushes around the development, searching for footprints, although Henry would be careful about not leaving the slightest trace.

The acreage is empty of everything but the abandoned remains, the creaking frames of houses, and the sad-looking showcase home. Even so, she investigates. They were going to plant devices and reinforce the fissure as much as possible. Had they, and then left? Is this something the Sight simply hasn't shown her? Or refuses to? Leave it to the Sight to be that capricious.

Ophelia runs her hands along where she thinks the fissure should be, but she's not solid enough in this reality to determine if Henry managed to reinforce it. She peeks through windows, but curtains block her view, providing only glimpses of shrouded furniture.

Then? A hint of something pink.

Her heart clenches in her chest, a solid fist that sends the monitors into a frenzy back in Seattle. They'll give her something if she doesn't calm down, and the intoxication will pull her back into the hospital bed. She'll lose this thread. And she absolutely can't do that.

Ophelia presses her palms against her chest, pulls in modulated breaths, and even shuts her eyes against the pink of that umbrella. But the image pulls her not back to Seattle, but into the living room of the showcase home.

That's when she sees it. Two field packs, two burner phones, and two umbrellas. She leans close but senses nothing from them. They are dormant. Not transmitting. Not collecting any information. You might mistake them for the store-bought variety. Except. Something lingers in the air that feels intentional. They're playing possum. Which means?

She searches the house but finds no other traces of Pansy or Henry. Did they decide to sever any ties that might connect them to the Enclave? She can't lift the field packs, never mind search them. But it's entirely possible that they stuffed their pockets with cash and slipped away while she was busy pounding on that invisible barrier.

Are they safe? If they're not here, then yes. Anywhere is better than King's End. Ophelia pushes the wave of grief down past her heart, locking it into her belly. Later. She'll mourn later and then curse herself for not offering Henry a silent goodbye.

But if Henry and Pansy are truly gone, then why is *she* still here? Oh, that's the question, isn't it? Her thoughts drift toward the charming old farmhouse Pansy lives in and the two other players with agendas all their own. Then, Ophelia's there, in the foyer, silent and stealthy as a thief.

Footfalls sound above her head. Water gurgles through pipes. Some enterprising soul has brewed coffee, although Ophelia doubts the current occupants would extend that courtesy to the other. She flutters into the kitchen to find Mortimer, a full pot of fresh coffee, and three cups lined up.

The morning is so quiet in this part of King's End that the whisper of tires against asphalt reaches her, followed by a car door shutting and the beep of the lock. Ophelia can't move, although she dearly wishes she could.

Is this why the Sight hasn't released her? Why she isn't back in Seattle? Three cups, waiting patiently on the kitchen counter. Who else but Botten would be heading up the walkway, stepping across the porch, knocking on the door?

But that rap is too soft, too courteous, and Mortimer's smile is far too broad, nothing but anticipation and joy. He barges straight through her on his way to the door. He is so substantial, so forceful that Ophelia somersaults in his wake.

There, on the porch, is Jack Ling. Mr. Tall, Dark, and Nerdy, as Ophelia always calls him, and always to his laughter. The two men stand there, wavering, neither breathing. Their on-again, off-again relationship is one of the Enclave's worst-kept secrets.

"Hey, buddy." Mort's voice is tender, almost tentative. After the briefest hesitation, he pulls Jack into a hug. And after the briefest hesitation, Jack returns it.

"Sorry about the red-eye," Mort adds.

Jack pushes his glasses up and rubs the bridge of his nose and then rubs his eyes, which are dark and soulful and, yes, shot through with tired pink veins. "You got coffee?"

"I got you covered. Coffee for days."

Jack places his umbrella into the stand, easing it next to Mortimer's. Jack's umbrella is slate gray with a hint of silver threaded through the canopy. You have to peer closely to discern the sparkle, much like with Jack himself. They head for the kitchen, and Ophelia follows, curious about what Jack might sense. He has barely taken a sip from his mug when a frown clouds his brow. He surveys the ceiling.

"Pansy?" he asks.

"Sound asleep."

Jack's frown only deepens. Ophelia swears she hears his unasked question. *Are you sure?*

Mort must hear it, too, because he adds, "It's been a rough couple of days. She was exhausted and opted for a restorative."

No, you drugged her, or at least tried to.

"Rose's recipe, so she'll probably sleep until noon."

Jack nods, but Ophelia can taste the waves of doubt flowing off him. Jack Ling has always been perceptive, possessing a sensitivity bordering on the Sight, although without the annoying, and devastating, side effects. During her sabbatical, he often assisted Leah. While he couldn't channel what Ophelia saw, his gentle touch often eased her headaches after a session. After the coma struck, he'd spell Henry during those first horrible days when her brother tried in vain to bring her back.

Jack doesn't always trust his intuition. Like Henry, he needs data to crunch, to back up what he senses. This makes him an excellent analyst. But right now, he's warring with himself because he can't reconcile what Mort is telling him with what he perceives.

The clip of heels strikes the stairs. They pause, and the creak of the office door follows. Ophelia's heart rate kicks up. Will her presumptive sister-in-law even notice? The longer the deception, the better for Pansy and Henry. The door closes with the softest of clicks, and Ophelia lets herself melt into a kitchen chair. The heels take up the march again, down the hall, growing ever closer.

"Ah, Gwennie," Mort says as she clears the doorway. "So good of you to grace us with your presence."

All he gets is a frosty raised eyebrow in return. No one does the icy arch like Gwyneth, and anyone other than Mortimer Connolly would be sputtering an apology.

She turns to Jack. "It's good to see you, Agent Ling. How was your flight?"

"Not bad for a red-eye."

It's Jack, rather than Mort, who pours Gwyneth a cup of coffee, then lifts the pitcher of cream in question.

"Yes," she says. "You remembered." He hands her the cup, the gesture coaxing a genuine smile from her.

Jack always remembers those little things. How you take your coffee, your favorite color, and even where you left your keys. He scans the ceiling again and then peers down the hallway.

"How's Agent Darnelle?"

"Sleeping. I didn't want to disturb him. I'll check his vitals in a bit."

A hint of indecision washes across his expression, but Jack speaks, his voice calm rather than anxious. "Maybe you should check now."

Gwyneth's eyes widen in alarm, and Ophelia leans forward in her chair. This is either going to be very, very entertaining or disastrous. She's not sure which.

"Right. I'll do that." Gwyneth sets down her coffee cup, takes up her silver briefcase from the sideboard, and heads for the office.

Three ... two ... one...

Gwyneth's scream shatters the morning.

"Shit." Mort tosses his empty cup into the sink. The mug clatters against the stainless steel but only suffers a small chip. He races down the hall with Jack on his heels. Ophelia follows, spinning and dancing along the hardwood.

In the office, Gwyneth clutches a fleece throw. Pillows and blankets line the sofa in a human-like form, disturbingly so. Henry is very good at this sort of thing, also disturbingly so. Gwyneth looks to Mortimer, and a new kind of fear lights her expression, but not that of losing a loved one. No, this is a terror born from failing a tyrant. And if Reginald Botten is anything, he is certainly that.

"Pansy?" Jack doesn't wait for an answer. He takes the stairs two at a time and crashes against her bedroom door in a shoulder-splintering slam.

She's left it locked.

Oh, she is so very clever.

Jack pounds his fists against the wood, shouting her name, pleading, although he must sense it's a lost cause, that she isn't in the house, never mind her bedroom.

"Sweet pea, please. If you're in there, open up. Please, Pansy. Please."

It's enough to break your heart. Jack continues to pound until Mort shoves him out of the way, pulls out a set of lock picks, and gets to work. Yes, lock picking is one of those skills they teach at the Academy, although Ophelia never found much use for it. But since the lock on Pansy's door is more than one of those push-button models, it takes Mort several tries to thwart it.

When the door opens, Jack launches himself over Mortimer and yanks back the comforter. Nothing but pillows greets them.

Mort exercises his extensive four-letter-word vocabulary. He pulls out his phone and brings up an app.

"What are you doing?" Jack asks.

"Trying to get a read on her. She's still in the area, which means—"

Jack points to the nightstand and Pansy's Enclave-issued phone resting on the charger.

More delicious four-letter-words. Really, Mort's a genius, at least when it comes to swearing. His observation skills, however, could use a little work.

The next half an hour is both very, very entertaining and disastrous.

Jack heads outside, umbrella and laptop in hand. He scans the area—again, and again, and again—a futile exercise that neither Mort nor Gwyneth can get him to stop.

"Try again, buddy," he whispers to his umbrella. "She can't be too far."

Logic dictates that she can't be. After all, Henry's rental is still in the driveway, and everyone knows Pansy Little never drives anywhere. Her bike is in the garage, next to that bright-red vintage convertible hiding beneath a tarp. Jack even contacts the one and only ride-share driver in King's End, waking them in the process.

Waves of hurt and confusion roll off Jack's umbrella, so thick that Ophelia is forced to swallow them down. They clog her throat, get stuck next to her ribcage. Pansy is Jack's best friend, and by extension, his umbrella has bonded with hers. With Pansy's umbrella dormant in the housing development, the connection is broken.

And that feels like death.

In the office, Mort and Gwyneth exchange barbs filled with blame.

"You should've checked," he says, jaw clenched, molars grinding.

Gwyneth's spine stiffens. She has gone full-on ice queen and will brook no accusations from mere peasants. "Well, clearly, she didn't drink the tea, so maybe *you* should've checked."

But beneath the recriminations is the realization that they're both in this together. Because with Henry and Pansy gone, they're both in some very deep shit.

That's when Mort's phone rings. He pulls it from his pocket and stares at the screen, a pallor chasing the angry pink from his cheeks. His gaze meets Gwyneth's, and he looks like a man condemned.

"It's Botten," is all he says.

CHAPTER 63
PANSY

Even with the door closed, the space beyond feels so vast, so empty, that I step away, skirting the man on the floor. He's still sucking in deep breaths, as if he's just completed a marathon. His gaze meets mine, and his eyes hold a spark that's almost uncanny.

"Give your old man a hand up?" he asks.

Without thinking, I take a few more steps back, bumping into a long dining table that has made a sudden appearance, set with bone china, crystal goblets, and enough silverware to make me wonder how many courses Henry is planning to serve.

"Didn't think so," Max says. "Can't blame you. I wouldn't help me, either."

That self-recrimination hits low in my belly. I want to apologize or at least lean forward to help. All I can do is grip a dining chair.

Henry wipes his hands on a tea towel, dispatching the turkey grease. His stride is easy and unconcerned, as if visitors routinely tumble in through the kitchen door. He's the one to offer a hand.

With Henry's help, Max clambers to his feet. Then the two men do that forearm-grasping handshake thing. And yes, I'm having a hard time thinking of this man as my father, so for now, he's Max.

"Mr. Monroe, so good of you to make it." Henry's voice holds a hint of trepidation, as if he doesn't have a full read on this man who claims to be my father.

"I wouldn't miss this for anything. Appreciate the invite." He gives Henry's back a solid slap. "And we've talked about this, haven't we? Call me Max."

A hint of pink touches those razor-sharp cheekbones. "Yes, of course. Max." But Henry, as always, rallies. "I just heard from my father. He's picking up his rental at the airport. He should be here in an hour or so, in time to make his world-famous gravy."

"Looking forward to it. Besides, I believe he owes me a rematch."

I'm standing right there, so I see when the house shifts around us. An alcove off the dining area pops up, a cozy space complete with two comfortable chairs, a chessboard of gleaming wood, and a table set with a decanter and two tumblers.

Henry gives Max a conspiratorial grin. "And I believe he's looking forward to *that*. But if you'll excuse me." He points toward the kitchen.

"Go on, go on. Shout if you need help."

Henry returns to his oasis of the perfect kitchen. It, too, morphs around him, adjusting to his every whim. My mind whirls, trying to make sense of their nonsensical exchange. I'm still clutching that dining chair as if it's the only thing holding me upright. Max heads toward the alcove. Once there, he pours a generous amount of amber liquid into a glass and sips.

"Ah." He swirls the scotch, or cognac, or whatever it is. The sharp scent of alcohol mixes with the sage and the aroma of roasting turkey. "This is some high-quality fantasy your boy has going on here." He surveys the space, from the stone hearth in the living area to the soapstone countertops and radiant copper pans in the kitchen. "Such attention to detail. Trust me, most people aren't this meticulous."

"He's not my boy," is the only response I can think of. Because right now? I don't know if I can trust Max Monroe.

"Sure about that, are you?" He gives the ring on my left hand a pointed look.

"He ... we ... I've only known him a week. I don't see how—" I break off, unable to form the next words in my mind, never mind my mouth.

"And I don't see why not. I knew the moment your mother jabbed me in the gut with her umbrella and demanded to know how I breached dimensions."

"She knew you were a traveler?"

"Well, you come through naked, so I was either that or some sort of vagrant. Either way, she was prepared to deal with the situation. That's your mother for you."

My mind replays the events of that day my mother vanished. "But you had clothes." Absolutely, I would've remembered a naked man, and certainly this particular man. "When I saw you with her."

"Because your mother left me some."

I sag against the dining chair and then sit down hard.

"I'm glad about that, too, believe me." Max gives me a sardonic grin. "Don't need to be running around King's End buck naked."

I can feel my brow scrunch, the thoughts pinging around in my head. "But when did she—?"

"The summer before you returned from the Academy, when she still had the strength."

"But—"

"Sealed them up in one of those vacuum-packed bags, left me a knife and a key to the front door. I'm competent enough to handle both."

This can't be true—the clothes part, not the knife. From what I've gleaned, Max Monroe can most likely wield a knife. It's the glint in his eyes. He's not someone you want to meet in a dark alley or an abandoned silo. But then I remember those discarded plastic bags, the Swiss Army knife left behind.

"What if I'd changed the locks?"

"I would've blown the door off its hinges. Trust me, when it comes to your mother, I'm highly motivated."

"There's no place to hide anything in the silo." I think of it, the space stark, more disturbing in some ways than the housing development. "I would've noticed something."

"Would you?"

Would I? Of course I would. How could I help it? Except.

Never go to the silo alone.

And I hadn't. When I returned after graduation, I patrolled King's End by myself. The few times my mother was able, we merely repaired fissures in the housing development and anointed the fence with her springtime concoction of herbs and blood. The closest I ever came to the silo was viewing it from the road, well back from the property line, well within my mother's guidelines.

"There you have it, my rule-abiding progeny."

I glare at Max Monroe.

He raises his hands, expression softening in apology. "I'm sorry, sweetheart. Your mother's mentioned I've gone feral these past couple of decades. I don't mean to hurt you, but there's so much at stake." His gaze drifts toward the kitchen, where Henry is absorbed and happy. "And then there's that, and that could get sticky."

Max takes another sip. "Really, this is excellent." He pulls out a dining chair across from mine and settles in like he's enjoying an apéritif. "Can't fault your boy for his taste for the finer things."

"Should you be drinking that?" My attention is pulled toward Henry as he samples something simmering on the stove and then slips the spoon into the dishwasher. "Should he be eating? I mean, does that—?"

"Sweetheart, you're between dimensions, not in the underworld. It's not like Hades is blocking the way out. However, if you want to leave, you'll need to time it for sunset in King's End, and you'll need Darnelle's full cooperation. He can't be in his fantasy land when you make the attempt."

I spare the windows, shrouded in their curtains, a glance. How we're supposed to tell when it's sunset and how we're supposed to leave are things I do not ask. Instead, my mind keys in on something Max said a moment before.

"My mother mentioned you've gone feral...? Does that mean she's?" I want to say *here*, but I don't think *here* actually exists.

Max's eyes grow tender, the hard line of his mouth softening. For a moment, a memory flares. I've seen this face, those eyes, that smile, all focused on me.

"We have our own version of this." He waves a hand, indicating the house. "Right now, we're reliving the weekend Adele offered to babysit so we could have some time to ourselves." His laugh is low and amused. "We spent half the time trying to sneak next door to visit you and the other half otherwise occupied. So that's where we are. On the cusp of sneaking out or, of course, in bed."

I really don't need the details. Even so, I have to ask. "Can I see her?"

"Oh, sweetheart, no. I wish you could, and there's nothing she'd love more. But she's too far into this space, the fantasy. In the reality we've created between the two of us, you're never any older than four. To see you now, it would break her." Max shakes his head, both sorrow and anger in the gesture. "And she's been broken enough."

My eyes sting, my heart squeezes, and while I don't know what to think of the man across from me, we do agree on this.

"But that leads us to our current problem. If we're going to figure out the next steps, we need to extricate your boy from this dream he's curated without breaking him in the process."

"Henry might break?" Panic flares, fluttering low in my belly.

Max does another survey of the surroundings. "He's been working overtime on this. He is fully invested in this fantasy, and mind you, it's a deeply personal one." Max gives me a significant look. "His *father* is coming for Thanksgiving dinner."

I glance toward the kitchen, and the wave of happiness that rolls off Henry is palpable. To remind him of his father's death? I don't want to see that shattered expression from the cemetery return.

"Yes," Max says, and I'm not sure whether he's reading my thoughts or my expression, but he seems to understand. "Harry Darnelle is your boy's Achilles' heel. For good reason, I suppose."

He pauses, gaze drawn to the kitchen and Henry's dinner preparations. "Any idea how many holidays Harry was able to spend with his son?" Max doesn't wait for my answer. He simply makes a zero with his fingers and thumb. "He always deferred to Miranda on those things, although god knows they never agreed on anything else. So now it's Thanksgiving, and Henry plans on presenting his father with the perfect dinner. His perfect new bride." Max nods at me. "His perfect new home. Want to bet there's a suite just for Harry?"

No, I don't, because the house shifts yet again, assembling a guest suite on the upper floor. It's a stately room full of mahogany furniture and an elegant fireplace. The images fill my head as if I've seen this room, polished the furniture earlier that morning, laid wood for a fire in the hearth, anxious that Harry Darnelle will be comfortable while knowing he'd be content to sleep on the couch.

"He's even found a role for me." Max raises his palms toward the ceiling. "The curmudgeon father-in-law who doesn't quite approve of the union because our boy always needs a challenge, doesn't he? *Mr. Monroe*." Max rolls his eyes. "Indeed."

Henry chooses that moment to bring me a fresh cup of tea, perfectly brewed, of course. That light jasmine scent that woke me earlier bathes my face and loosens the knots in my shoulders.

"Feeling better?" The way Henry gazes at me makes my heart tender and fragile, like it might shatter. It's more than adoration; it's more than playacting. He sees all of me.

Even in this fantasy version, I'm very much me, who apparently couldn't bring herself to pull on a dress for Thanksgiving. I'm in a variation of what I wore on our trip to the farmers market: same cigarette pants, now paired with ballet flats and a boat-neck shirt with long sleeves. Same perky high ponytail with the same polka dot ribbon that I lost somewhere on the green.

Henry plants a gentle kiss on my forehead. "You look fetching," he says, reading my thoughts or perhaps the dismay on my face. Before returning to the kitchen, he gives Max a stiff nod.

Max manages to keep a straight face until Henry's attention is focused on the double ovens. Then he bursts out laughing.

"I do wish we could play out this little fantasy," he says, catching his breath. "How do you think he wins me over?" He raises the glass and gives the alcohol another swirl. "Perhaps with plenty of this?"

I ignore the questions and the undercurrent of malice. "What happens when his father doesn't show up?"

"What happens when your mother doesn't actually sneak over to Adele's? The scene resets and the scenario plays itself out again."

"Over and over? One endless loop?"

"Eventually, she, and he, will get bored and conjure up something new." He gives me a side-eye. "To be honest, I wasn't sure *what* I'd find when I came barging in, but I highly approve of this G-rated fantasy." Max places a hand on his chest. "Does a father's heart good."

Over in the kitchen, Henry glances up as if he knows what we're talking about. He gives me a wink, one that's anything but rated-G, and my cheeks flame in response.

"Well, it was nice while it lasted," Max adds, mostly to himself.

"Pansy," Henry calls. "Do you want to show your father the videos we made of the renovations? They're on my phone." He nods to the kitchen's built-in desk and the phones that sit on their chargers. Not Enclave-issued phones, and certainly not our burner phones.

I give him a numb nod. My feet are moving me across the room before I realize what I'm doing. Max said things could get sticky, and it feels that way. I'm being pulled forward, caught in a riptide. Henry wants me to show my father the videos, so that's exactly what I'm going to do.

My fingers know Henry's passcode because, of course, he's trusted me with it. Max comes to stand next to me, and we scroll through the videos. They are not of some dream renovation.

No, these are videos of the showcase home, ones Henry must have filmed while I slept. A thin wire of tension mars Henry's normally calm and measured narration as the space transforms around us. He knows something's wrong, knows he's losing his grasp on reality, but is powerless to stop it.

I look to Max, perplexed. "What does this mean?"

"It means our boy is still in there." He places a gentle, if tentative, hand on my shoulder. I don't flinch. "And it means that you can bring him back."

CHAPTER 64
OPHELIA

King's End, Minnesota
Saturday, July 15

Mortimer commits the cardinal sin of letting Botten's call roll to voicemail. More four-letter words, but these are desperate rather than delicious. He stares at the phone, cradling it cautiously in his palm like a man who has just realized he's clutching a live hand grenade.

"What the hell are we going to tell him?" he says.

"I don't know. Sounds like a problem for the response team lead." Gwyneth presses a finger against her lips and tilts her head in mock thought. "Oh, wait. That's you."

"Always a team player, aren't we, Gwennie." He nods toward the windows and the front yard beyond. "Can you at least help with *that* before the neighbors wake up?"

Ophelia peers through the sheer curtains. Yes, Jack is continuing his increasingly frantic search, going as far as to wander down the center of the street, umbrella outstretched like it's a Geiger counter.

A wash of pity melts the ice from her presumptive sister-in-law's expression. She doesn't bother with a nod. Instead, she heads out the door and down the street, the clip-clop, clip-clop of her heels loud in the early morning.

Maybe it's her medical training, but Gwyneth murmurs words that have Jack reeling in his umbrella, turning around, heading back for the house. Ophelia is too far away to hear either of them, but the closer they come, the more pure outrage rolls off Jack.

He charges into the house, Gwyneth trailing him, the kitten heels no match for his sneakers and the long stride of a former track star. He barrels into Mort, eyes burning behind those horn-rimmed glasses.

"What. The. Hell. Is. Going. On." His voice is deadly low, and each word is punctuated with a poke to the chest.

Mort deflects the last with the palm of his hand. He's already tucked his phone away, although Ophelia imagines it's burning a hole in his pocket. Ignoring a call from Professor Reginald Botten is another of those career-limiting moves.

"If you calm yourself, I'll explain."

Oh, it's always a bad idea to condescend to the angry, especially the righteously angry, the way Jack is at this moment.

"She's nowhere." Jack jerks an arm toward the front door and the street beyond. "He's nowhere. Give me one reason why I shouldn't call headquarters and request a competent response team."

Gwyneth wrinkles her nose in distaste as if she's not part of the problem but wisely keeps her mouth shut. Mort rubs his face, feigning amusement, but Ophelia can tell the blow landed.

"Here's the short version." Mort says these words as if he's spitting nails. "Botten believes King's End sits on top of a juncture, one that contains an actual gateway, one that Rose Little and Harry Darnelle damaged in an attempt to harness its power."

The anger deflates from Jack's chest, but he appears bemused and completely unconvinced by this proclamation.

"Now we're here to clean up the mess, and we need both Pansy and Henry to do so." Mort pauses, as if he's deciding how much to reveal. "It's a blood thing."

Of course it is. If there's anything the Enclave loves more than power, it's spilling blood.

"Are we talking about the arcane?" Jack asks.

"We are. They performed a ritual here, and when it went awry, managed some sort of makeshift hold, one that's threatening to disintegrate. You know as well as I do that things have never been quite right in King's End. This is why. Botten believes he's uncovered the correct text, but he needs direct descendants to reverse the incantation and heal the land."

Jack's brow furrows in thought. Of all the analysts Mort could have—and maybe should have—requested, Jack is absolutely the wrong one.

"Why not bring all this to light back—"

"Thirty years ago, or thereabouts."

The best sorts of lies are the ones that run parallel to the truth. For the first time, Ophelia unravels what Botten desires. She doesn't need the Sight for this, although it's offering her tiny peeks into the past. Yes, Rose Little crafted a stopgap measure, and when the construction company broke ground, they tore through the threads that held everything together. In the process, they tore through Rose.

But she did it to block the man whose quietly furious voicemail is now sitting on Mortimer's phone.

She did it to save the world. After making a terrible mistake, yes. But Rose's intentions? Ophelia can taste those still lingering in the air. Those were pure, as were the ones of the man who was like a second father to her.

"Enclave politics," Mort adds. "Darnelle senior had the High Council all tied up. Nothing could move until..." He trails off and shrugs one shoulder.

Yes, nothing can happen until people start vanishing and dying. Typical Enclave.

"So, what you're telling me," Jack says, his voice incredulous, "is that Rose Little and Harry Darnelle were both megalomaniacs who wanted to rule the world."

When you put it like that? Even Gwyneth blinks at this.

Jack is shaking his head as if he wants to shake out all the nonsense Mort's been feeding him. "That doesn't fit with the Rose Little I know ... knew."

"The Rose Little you knew was a broken woman. She should have paid for this, along with Harry Darnelle. But since they're not here, it falls to Pansy and Henry. Trust me, we're taking every precaution to protect them."

Please. I know better.

Jack makes a show of peering under chairs and behind the couch in the office. "Funny how they're not here, either."

Mort rubs his eyes and swears, and now it's just tedious. "Look, I'll be honest."

Oh, I doubt that. Ophelia snorts a laugh.

Jack startles, glances over his shoulder to where Ophelia is hovering. She catches the barest twist of his lips, the light in his eyes that's there and gone.

"Before we can deploy the task force," Mort continues, "we need to confirm the exact location of the epicenter. If anyone can pinpoint it, and quickly, it's you."

"Wait a minute. You're telling me you don't know where it is? That King's End is sitting on top of a juncture, and at any minute, someone could stumble across the epicenter and vanish?"

"Jesus, no. We know, more or less, that it's in the housing development, but again, after they broke ground, it may have rerouted itself. We can't deploy if we don't know exactly where it is. That's SOP."

Yes, it would be a shame if the ground opened up and swallowed an entire task force. Career-limiting move, indeed.

"So what you're saying," Jack adds, "is that Pansy's been patrolling all these years and could have vanished."

"That's on Rose and Darnelle senior, not the Enclave."

Yes, of course, the Enclave is always blameless in these situations.

Both Jack and Mort fall silent. In the quiet, morning filters through the screen door: someone starting up a lawnmower, the wet slap of a sprinkler, the catchy refrain of a pop song from a car radio. King's End going about its day, blissfully ignorant.

"Can you do this for me?" Mort stares at Jack, eyes alight with more than this request. *Do you believe me? Are you still mine? Can't we just get through this?*

Jack presses his lips together in thought. He looks like a man whose life's been cleaved in half, a before and after from here on out. After a long moment, he picks up his umbrella. Without a word, he heads for the door.

"Will you?" Mort calls after him.

Jack pauses at the threshold but doesn't turn around. "I'm going to go look for Pansy, assuming the housing development hasn't swallowed her up, that is. If I happen across your epicenter, maybe I'll report it. Or maybe I'll just keep on walking."

That's when Mort's phone rings. He knows better than to not pick up. So, instead of chasing after Jack, and his heart, Mort answers before the second ring.

Sonorous, terse words leak from around Mort's ear. He cringes, moves to the door, and peers through the screen, but Jack is already a shadowy figure on the gravel road that leads to the housing development.

"Everything's fine," Mort says when there's a pause in the recriminations.

To hear him, you might believe everything *is* fine. Even after watching his world crumble around him, Ophelia marvels at the confidence in his voice. He could fool her.

He might even fool Botten.

"We were outfitting Agent Ling, and he just left to conduct a survey."

Ah, yes, the best lies do run parallel, don't they?

Mort heads for the kitchen, phone to his ear. It's a short call, and he deletes the earlier voicemail without listening to it. He fishes his mug from the sink, runs a finger over the chip in its rim, and pours himself a fresh cup.

The kitchen window captures Mort's attention, but Ophelia doubts he's contemplating the view.

"He'll be back." The words are little more than a whispered prayer.

And if the best lies run parallel, then Ophelia suspects the worst lies are the ones we tell ourselves.

CHAPTER 65
HENRY

This truly was the most perfect kitchen. And that was the problem. Every kitchen had its quirks, every house its creaks and groans, every window a less than stellar view.

Every cook, every field agent, every man, his foibles.

When had he known it was all a dream? Before Pansy approached, certainly. Her eyes were full of regret, her fingers on his sleeve light and healing, the measured touch she used to mend fissures. Before she played the videos. Although those chipped away at the seduction and sent fault lines through the fantasy.

In the end, though, it wasn't a shattering. His heart didn't break. No, it was more of a shriveling, a contraction until the dream faded, and nothing was left but a few props and vast empty rooms.

And, of course, the sensation of someone taking a spoon and hollowing out his chest.

But then Pansy smiled at him, her expression nothing but relief, her hair mussed from sleep and perhaps worry. She urged him to sit on the couch and then pressed a thermos of tea into his hands, warmed from the canned heat he kept in his field pack.

"Drink. It will help."

The steam bathed his face and cleared his sinuses. "You added something?"

"Yes."

He sucked it down, greedy for his mind to return even as the liquid scorched his throat, the tincture soured his tongue, and the last fragments of fantasy fractured for good. He'd had everything he'd ever wanted, but nothing about that made sense. Better to face this reality than lose himself in what was nothing more than a castle in the air, held together with delusion and desire.

He exhaled, his breath rough, as the events of the last several hours clicked into place. Pansy poured more tea without his even asking, and he noticed she also had a thermos of her own.

"The construction company," she said. "Left behind, I guess." Maybe it was his expression, but she added, "Don't worry. I washed them out."

Would it matter if she hadn't? "Pansy, I want to apolo—"

"No time for that," a voice said.

Henry glanced up and into the sharp and assessing gaze of Max Monroe.

Damn. He'd hoped that had been part of the illusion as well. The disapproving father-in-law because why not? It made things interesting.

"Yeah, I know," Max said. "I'd rather not be here, either."

"Can you at least shed some actual light on this situation?" Henry swallowed more tea and cringed, but clarity, and cynicism, shot through him. "Or do you plan on talking in riddles and assuming I'm smart enough to figure it all out?"

Max laughed, but it wasn't a happy sound. "Your boy's got some teeth," he said to Pansy, whose gathering frown did not bode well for either Henry or Max. She looked ready to storm from the house.

Not that there was anywhere to go. Above them, the skylight was shrouded in that persistent gray. Nothing about their situation had changed except for the fact that they were in real danger of living out an eternal delusion.

Then something lit Pansy's eyes, clearing the clouds from her expression. She leaned toward Max, almost conciliatory. "*Can* you talk about it?"

Oh, of course. Henry should've thought of that. If he hadn't been so irrationally angry at Max Monroe, he might have.

"I can talk about some of it. I'll tell you what I know and help as best I can." Max spared Henry a glance. "Even you, Darnelle."

Henry let the gibe wash over him. But Pansy made a noise that sounded like an actual growl. She sat back, arms crossed over her chest, that frown blooming once again.

And though she be but little, she is fierce.

"Start talking, Monroe," Henry said, "or I'll start dreaming up a whole new scenario, one that doesn't include you."

"Promises, promises," Max muttered, but he pulled a dining chair toward the coffee table and sat. He cleared his throat dramatically and began in the way all fairy tales begin.

"Once upon a time, three Enclave field agents believed they could change the world. Or rather, two believed. One simply wanted to rule it. I'll let you figure out which one." Max turned to Pansy. "Your mother had, still has, I suppose, an extraordinary talent. For lack of a better way to describe it, she could bend Screamers, calm them, and then redirect them."

"It's why King's End is so delightful," Henry said. Even now, even with Rose gone, the vestiges of her work remained. "Extraordinary."

"It was, and is, and persists, despite the fact that King's End is sitting on top of a juncture. Rose only realized this ability after the Enclave forced her into a sabbatical after her time in the desert."

"Yes, that sounds familiar," Henry said.

"She spent several months watching the town transform around her. Then she located the juncture and realized it was feeding her ability. But without the prolonged break? Who knows? King's End would've continued to crumble, and Rose most likely would have taken a desk job once the field became too much."

"It's easier to burn through your field agents rather than let them develop," Henry observed.

"Had the Enclave known?" Max raised his hands, palms toward the ceiling. "They would've left her a husk, and gladly so. She decided to retire from fieldwork and settle in King's End." Max shook his head. The chuckle that accompanied it was warm. "According to Enclave rumor, Rose Little had lost her nerve after her time in the desert." He turned to Pansy. "Your mother never minded the gossip, not about herself, anyway."

"I'm assuming she brought in my father and Reginald Botten at some point?"

"See? I knew you were clever."

Henry made a colossal effort not to roll his eyes. They needed Max. Despite his obvious love for Rose and affection for Pansy, a river of spite ran through the man. Possible jealousy of Henry's father? A deep-seated resentment for years lost? Whatever it was, Max Monroe wore it with pride, like armor. Perhaps it hurt less that way.

"The plan was broken from the start."

Pansy's words startled them both. Her voice was dreamy, tinged with that precursor to the Sight. Max expression lost some of its spite, and he turned a tender gaze toward his daughter. Henry dug through his pockets and then passed her a handkerchief. The dots of red that stained the linen looked stark in the gray around them.

"You're right, sweetheart. Two agendas, one disastrous outcome. I can't give you the specifics. Your mother couldn't tell me, and there's only so much we can monitor from our side. In fact, it took me months to figure out who, exactly, had betrayed your mother. But she had planned a ritual to heal, to extend what was happening in King's End to the state, the country, the world, even. She had big plans, your mother. Unfortunately, Botten had big plans as well."

"Your side? Monitoring?" The notion of it pinged in Henry's mind. Of course the Enclave knew other dimensions existed. After all, their ancestors had originated somewhere other than this earth.

But did these dimensions have such advanced technology that they could observe others?

"I'll get to that, trust me."

Trust Max Monroe? No. Absolutely not. Henry felt certain that Max would avoid elaborating if not pushed, but he pursed his lips and nodded.

"Your mother planned to heal. Botten planned to subvert her ritual, reverse it, and use that power to open the gateway. From there, I imagine he thought he could use the force of that, the resources of an open gateway, to consolidate his own power."

"Who does that?" Pansy's scowl deepened. "I don't understand who..." She paused as if unable to articulate the necessary hunger, the soul-twisting desire for such a thing.

"Who has that sort of ambition?" Henry sighed. "I don't understand it, either."

You're a liar, Henry Darnelle. You understand it perfectly. Didn't his father always caution against unbridled anything, be it lust, greed, or ambition? And yet, didn't the Enclave encourage that sort of thing, to a point?

"A gateway always demands a sacrifice," Henry added. "I'm guessing that was the role Botten had planned for my father."

Max gave him a grin that was, in a word, feral. "Like I said. Clever. I don't know what Rose did. I'm guessing here, too. She could never say what happened, and she can't, even now. But she did manage a countermove. Instead of a killing blow, your father was literally struck dumb." Max nodded at Henry before turning to Pansy. "I imagine Botten launched a counter curse, since no one in King's End can speak of that day or tell you anything about Reginald Botten."

"'I can't say his name.' That's what Adele kept insisting," Pansy said. "The two of us thought it sounded like a curse, the kind from a fairy tale. And now you're saying there are such things?"

Max inclined his head toward Henry.

Henry steeled himself, swallowed back the revulsion. Curses ate away at something deep inside him. Their aftertaste was bitter and sharp, like nettles against his tongue. When possible, he avoided them altogether. "In the normal course of things, the Enclave uses curses to help calm the local population, help them forget. Failing that, render them unable to speak about certain events."

"I've never heard of such a thing," she said.

"It's classified. It's also something only a principal field agent can perform. In fact, it's a requirement for the rank. Not every agent can deploy a curse." Henry paused for a moment, considering that, wondering briefly if Pansy had inherited the skill from Rose Little. "And curses always involve blood."

Pansy turned toward him, eyes astonished. "Then you...?"

Henry pursed his lips and nodded. Yes. He had.

"*Oh*." Pansy was silent for a moment. "Remember how Adele tried with the photographs? It was almost like it was painful."

No doubt it was.

"Ah, yes. The photographs." Max rubbed his hands together. "They don't seem like much, but that circumstantial evidence would've been enough to launch an investigation, along with ruining several marriages and careers. That's how they've kept Botten in check all these years."

Pansy frowned. "Then, why didn't they?" She turned toward Henry, imploring, beseeching. "Why not give someone on the High Council the photographs and be done with it? Wouldn't it be enough? Wouldn't that have been the right thing to do?"

"Oh, sweetheart, the Enclave doesn't work like that." Max was shaking his head, and then his eyes met Henry's. Oh, yes, the two of them not only understood each other, but the Enclave as well.

"It was a scorched earth tactic," Henry said. "I suppose the Enclave would have gotten around to investigating King's End and come to the conclusion that Botten had done something irrevocable. In the meantime, it would've been chaos. The lives of multiple agents, many of them good people, on the whole, would've been ruined. It would've disrupted everything. Think of what happens to the world if no one's around to tame those level five hot spots." He pitched his voice softer. "Or what King's End might be like without you, or your mother, always on guard."

Pansy didn't look entirely convinced, but she nodded.

"Yes. That's it exactly." Max swung toward Henry and, for the first time, the man's expression was devoid of malice. "Your father was clever, too. He did everything he could to help Rose, and I believe he paid for it with an early death."

Words failed Henry, but he swallowed hard, kept his gaze locked on Max, and managed a nod.

"Your mother was able to close the gateway, but it was always a makeshift solution because—"

"The ritual isn't complete," Henry finished, "and the gateway is still expecting a sacrifice." The enormity of that blew through him. He felt paper-thin and helpless. When Max didn't utter a single sarcastic comment, Henry knew he was right and that the world was balanced on the edge of an abyss.

"I'm afraid so, and Botten needs both of you to complete it."

"So, is this our solution?" Henry gestured to the house around them. "Eternal exile?"

"Don't look so glum, Darnelle. You get used to it after a decade or two. Besides, I believe you have some unfinished business with my daughter. That should keep you occupied for a while."

"Stop being an ass." Pansy leaned forward and planted her hands on the coffee table, the full force of her glare aimed at her father. "Just tell us what we need to do."

The barely contained contempt drained from Max's expression. "Sorry, sweetheart. Your mother would be giving me holy hell for this. So, let's not tell her." He paused then, gaze contemplating the two of them as if he were auditioning and rejecting various solutions.

"You said something about sunset?" Pansy prompted.

"Yes, it's possible to slip through at both sunrise and sunset."

"It was sunrise when you—"

"When I came for your mother? Yes. And the silo is my ingress and egress point. Yours, however, is the housing development, as you've likely surmised. The question isn't can you return, but rather, should you? Tell me more about what's happening in King's End."

Henry told Max what he could of the data he'd collected, the imminent arrival of the task force, and that the right analyst, most likely Jack Ling, could pinpoint the epicenter in a matter of hours.

"They were waiting on us," he said. "Or, rather, for me to be strong enough to take part in the ritual. But they might deploy an advance party or even the task force itself if they're able to accurately locate the epicenter."

"Which means you could tumble right into Botten's grasp." Max pursed his lips. "That's not ideal. You'll only have a few minutes to clear the housing development before the next cycle begins."

Henry considered that, considered how easy it would be to deploy agents around the perimeter and block the routes from the housing development. "Risky," was all he said.

"Then, as much as I hate to suggest it, remaining here may be the best option." Max surveyed the space, his gaze assessing and critical. "Yes, with safeguards in place, it could work."

"Safeguards?" Henry asked, but Max continued as if he hadn't heard the question.

"We have to make sure your reality is secure. What did you bring with you?"

"Umbrellas," Henry said. "Go bags."

"Right. Those will be in the showcase home."

Pansy pointed to the umbrellas on the coffee table. "We're in the showcase home, and..."

The umbrellas flickered, momentarily transparent, before solidifying once again. Henry felt his heart clench.

"And it's your belief that keeps the image of them here."

"We're drinking tea." She peered into her thermos and took a tentative sip. "It's real."

"And Darnelle was cooking a real turkey. Don't think too hard about it, sweetheart. It's easier that way. The good news is, they'll assume you've fallen into a fissure."

Henry raised an eyebrow. "*That's* the good news?"

"It is. Granted, that's one half of the ritual. But agents fall into fissures all the time. You need an incantation to activate a gateway, and an incantation always requires blood," Max went on, almost as if he were enjoying himself. "Botten could stand at the epicenter for hours, reciting the incantation, but without fresh blood, it won't work. So, assuming neither of you has donated to the Enclave recently..."

Max trailed off. Perhaps it was their expressions. Henry was certain his must be as horrified as Pansy's.

"Don't tell me. Shit." Max stared at the ceiling, rubbed his hands over his face. "I know the Enclave loves their blood, but how long ago are we talking here? Routine check-up? A couple of months?"

Henry swallowed back bile and forced out the answer. "Yesterday."

"Well, children." Max clapped his hands together, and his laugh rang hollow in that gray, empty room. "Things just got sticky."

CHAPTER 66
OPHELIA

King's End, Minnesota
Saturday, July 15

Ophelia trails Jack around King's End. She's his invisible shadow as he ducks into alleys and peers into shops. She's curious about what he's doing and why. Jack is Pansy's best friend, more so than even Mortimer. She wonders what he knows about both her and King's End that no one else in the Enclave does.

Under different circumstances, she'd be curious about *how* Jack Ling goes about his work, the rapport with his umbrella—which is startling, but perhaps not surprising. After all, Jack thrives on a blend of data and intuition.

It's a sunny, sultry Saturday, and King's End is readying itself for an influx of visitors. Jack is so single-minded that he seems not to notice that an unusual number of day tourists carry their own umbrellas on this July day that promises to be both clear and hot.

Or perhaps he does. His eyes narrow. Abruptly, he swings around and heads back toward the residential part of town. He marches past Pansy's house without a glance. Mortimer doesn't come rushing through the front door, although Ophelia half expects him to. Jack continues his single-minded trek all the way to the housing development and through the gate.

There, he does pause, and raises his chin. His umbrella shudders. Within moments, they discover one of the devices Henry planted. Jack turns it in his palm before switching it off. Then he crouches as if he can track Pansy and Henry by the scuffed footprints they've left behind in their rush to safety. Perhaps Jack can, because he heads straight for the showcase home.

It's locked, of course, because Henry always locks the door behind him.

"Well, hell," Jack mutters, and lets out a sigh. Yes, he's an analyst, not a field agent, and his lock-picking skills are rudimentary at best. However, his motivation makes up for this lack of skill. He unfurls his umbrella to guard his back and gets to work. Ten minutes and a bloody thumb later, Jack stands in the foyer of the showcase home.

The house is so still, so deserted, that Ophelia feels herself congeal. She can barely push her way inside. Jack is a statue, his steps halting the moment he crosses the threshold. It's so quiet that when a single drop of blood slips from his thumb, they both hear it land on the tile.

Then the floor swallows it up.

"*Jesus.*"

Jack is on the verge of spinning around and leaving, not that Ophelia blames him. If she could, she'd give him a good shove out the door. This space is preternatural. Granted, so is she, in a way. But this space also wants something, craves it with a deep and abiding hunger, the sort that takes out its frustration by ripping holes in the surrounding fence.

Jack's gaze lands on the coffee table. He squints, then rushes forward, his hands pawing the burner phones, the field packs, and the umbrellas. He dumps everything onto the floor, sorts through all the items as if that will give him the clues he needs.

He rummages and rummages, so obsessed that Ophelia worries

he'll never stop. She can sense the shock that tightens his chest, the despair that clogs his throat, the full-body anguish that washes through him.

There, on the floor, are things that should be in Henry's pockets, assuming he and Pansy left everything else behind. A roll of twenty-dollar bills, another of fifties. A pocket knife. Pansy's emergency tinctures. The cash, though, is the most disturbing. Henry, she knows, would never leave without that.

Which means what? Ophelia doesn't know. Or rather, she's too scared to contemplate the possible answers.

Jack's umbrella is a blur of gray and silver sorrow. It flings itself forward onto the table, its strap covering Pansy's umbrella as if in an embrace. But Pansy's umbrella is silent; Henry's is silent.

Jack is on his knees, face in his hands. His body shakes, but not with sobs. Truly, he'd find solace in that. No, this is a man beyond devastation. This is a man who is channeling that righteous anger.

He raises his head, and the flint in his gaze has Ophelia skittering backward. Haphazardly, he shoves items back into the field packs, scoops up both umbrellas and bursts out the door, leaving it wide open.

He is far ahead of her, already past the entrance when she manages to leave the showcase home. Jack is heading straight for Pansy's, straight to confront Mortimer.

No, the Sight doesn't deign to show her *that* outcome, but Ophelia does know this:

It's the absolutely worst thing he could do.

CHAPTER 67
PANSY

I wait for my father, for Max, to elaborate on how things are "sticky." The house around us is gray and empty, so at odds with how it was in Henry's fantasy. My heart thumps with longing, because it wasn't simply his dream.

It was also mine.

Conflicting emotions war in Max's expression. Reluctance, yes. Regret? Possibly. He rubs his face, pushes hair back from his forehead, and exhales like a man who believes he's ruined everything.

"Botten knows the incantation," Max says. "He no doubt has enough fresh blood from both of you, and—"

"We're already in the fissure," Henry finishes.

"Exactly. You've done the hard part. No shoving or sacrifice required. He'll attempt to complete the ritual. At least, the Botten of thirty years ago would." Max turns to Henry in question.

Henry's mouth is a hard line, his jaw tight. "Wait a minute." He reaches forward before remembering are phones are useless. Instead, he shuts his eyes, deep in thought. I hold my breath, and not even Max interrupts him.

"Florence," Henry says at last.

"Italy?" I ask. I have no idea what this has to do with anything, never mind our current situation.

His lips twitch. "If only. No. Florence, Wisconsin."

"Wait." Now, tendrils of memory—and possibly the Sight—start weaving a pattern. "That was my capstone exercise at the Academy."

"Which was based on a very real mission where your Aunt Marigold vanished along with another agent, Gordon Darnelle."

My Aunt Marigold? I contemplate that, or try to. Then, all I can do is say, "He was—?"

"A second cousin."

"Of course. This isn't the first time Botten's brought you together, is it?" Max asks, although it doesn't sound like he needs an answer.

"No," Henry says anyway. "He tagged me to evaluate Pansy's class at the Academy, and then sent me to King's End to conduct her field agent evaluation."

"Classic." Max is nodding, mostly to himself. "Yes, Florence was the trial run, which means he thinks he knows the outcome."

"What was the outcome of that?" I ask. "I mean, for Botten?"

"About a year or so later," Henry says, "Botten secured his seat on the High Council. Mind you, that should have been impossible. He never married, which suggests he never honored his betrothal. That's a requirement for the High Council." He sits back and stares into the middle distance. "Appointment to the High Council is supposed to be unanimous, but there was one continuous dissenting vote. Arthur Connolly devised some sort of special dispensation, and the vote went through." Henry stares at the phones as if he's itching to fact-check. "I'm fairly certain there was a caveat. Botten could be seated, but he could never hold the chair position himself."

"And that dissenting vote?" Max asks, although his tone suggests he already knows.

"My father." Henry shakes his head, the sorrow in his eyes so close to the surface. "Of course, before then, Botten had taken over the Academy and started the ranking system, Botten's Best List."

"Amassing his own little army," Max adds.

"But that alone wasn't enough," Henry says, voice contemplative. "The High Council, though?"

"Ah." Max nods. "That comes with privileges, doesn't it?"

I remember my mother's sorrow at losing her sister and then her strange panic. Phone calls late at night, when she thought I was asleep, whispered words about keeping me home, not sending me to the Academy. Who was on the other side of that conversation, and what they said? I don't know. But I suspect it was the father of the man sitting next to me.

"Weren't you on Botten's Best List?" I say to Henry.

His lips twist in disgust. "Yes. Subterfuge, I suppose. I was never truly part of his inner circle."

Not like Mortimer, I think. "It would've looked really strange if he'd left you off."

Even as a cadet, Henry Darnelle was legendary. Leaving him off Botten's Best List would be like barring the valedictorian from the National Honor Society.

I turn to my father. "What does this mean? Can he really—?"

"Take over the world? No, it's worse. He most likely believes he can. Even if he were willing to share the power that opening the gateway will unleash, there are nowhere near enough agents in the world, never mind in a task force, to absorb the surge."

"He'll die," Henry says. "Everyone in the task force will die, and if I'm not mistaken, King's End will cease to exist as well."

"I see you've been doing your homework, Darnelle. Yes, all things being equal, that's exactly what would happen. Unfortunately, children, things aren't equal."

The gazes of both men land on me. My cheeks burn. I feel deeply and irrationally self-conscious, like I've done something terrible but can't say what, exactly, that terrible thing is.

"Oh," Henry says, and the word comes out with an exhale. "Your father is a traveler."

"And that means?" I ask.

"I don't know." He tilts his head toward Max. "But I imagine he does."

The quiet in the house turns oppressive and flavors the air with a mustiness that's thick against my tongue. For a moment, I'm not sure Max will elaborate. He takes a few breaths, clears his throat, and even then, I'm not certain he'll speak until he does.

"You, sweetheart, are a gateway walker."

I don't know what this means, but Henry leans forward, comprehension lighting his expression. His mouth makes an O of understanding as Max continues.

"Under the right circumstances, you can pass from your dimension to mine and back again. You're a paradox and should not exist. That you do is on me and your mother, I suppose. We brought you into existence. And when it was clear, when we knew what you were, I was supposed to..."

Max trails off, the anguish in his eyes like nothing I've ever seen. "And I couldn't, couldn't. So I chose eternal exile over the mortal sin of ending my own daughter's life."

I don't need the Sight to know these words are true.

He leans forward, head bowed, a palm planted on the coffee table as if he can't bear to look at me, can't bear the weight of the guilt he carries. I want to cross to this man, my father, and hug him. But I think if I did so, he might shatter. After a moment, I inch my hand forward and cover his.

The skin is rough, crisscrossed with scars. I slip to my knees so I can peer up at him. "I'm glad you didn't," I say, hoping my voice conveys my gratitude, my renewed love for a man I nearly forgot after all these years. "For both of us."

Max manages a laugh, the sound tinged with sorrow.

"Oh, of course," Henry murmurs, seemingly to himself. "Betrothals."

Max laughs again, this time sharper, with the cunning I've come to expect. "Adding up for you now, Darnelle?"

Henry appraises my father as if he's come to both expect and accept all the rough edges. "Indeed."

I, on the other hand, am completely lost. Betrothals? "I don't understand," I begin, but trail off because suddenly, I think I do understand.

"All these decades, all these *centuries*," Henry says, "the Enclave has been trying to manipulate genetics—"

"Eugenics, if you want to be precise," Max adds.

"In order to create someone like you," Henry says to me. "Someone who can travel through a gateway and then return."

"And it's a fool's sort of enterprise. The Enclave would be better off if they simply let agents procreate within the communities they protect. They're more likely to stumble across the trait that way."

"Did you know it would happen?" I ask.

Max shakes his head. "We knew it was a possibility, but even then, it's not a certainty. We only realized when your Sight began to manifest, and you started talking about fairy lights in the woods by the covered bridge."

My gaze meets Henry's. I catch a hint of how panicked he was back at the covered bridge, how I must have scared him.

"The fairy lights. I know it doesn't make sense, but I thought they would lead me home."

"In a sense, they would. They'd lead you straight through to my dimension. And that's the last place you should be."

"Why?"

"Because we're not kind when it comes to travelers. When one falls through and is discovered, and trust me, they're always discovered, we isolate them. An asylum, I suppose, is the best way to describe it. Although, to be fair, they do get to live out their natural life."

"And gateway walkers?" My heart pounds as if it knows the answer already.

Something crackles in the air, something full of static and blood.

"They're euthanized."

"And you were supposed to—"

Max stares at the ceiling as if it's too painful to look at me. "I was supposed to return with you to my dimension, where you would've been humanely…" He shakes his head so hard, it must hurt. "No, there's no humanity in that, even if they claim it's like going to sleep, that it's painless."

I consider that, consider what it is my father did and didn't do. What he sacrificed to keep me alive.

"We have other problems, don't we?" Henry says, his voice unbearably gentle. It's a lifeline, a peace offering, because the man holding himself rigid in the hardback chair across from us needs both.

"You do. It would be one thing for King's End to implode. A lot of cleanup for the Enclave, but nothing that hasn't happened before. But with Pansy as the sacrifice? That changes things."

"Because she'll pull power from your dimension as well."

"She will. And that will start a chain reaction that no one can stop. Apocalypse, Armageddon. It won't be like that. After one burst of agony, your world will simply cease to exist."

Henry slumps back on the couch and pushes his hands through his hair, his gaze now on the ceiling. "Yes, I see what you mean. Things really are sticky."

CHAPTER 68
OPHELIA

King's End, Minnesota
Saturday, July 15

Jack charges through the front door of Pansy's house. The rage that rolls off him is so strong, Ophelia must keep her distance or be consumed by it. The emotion is too sharp, too blisteringly hot. Although she's ephemeral, the sensation sizzles against her skin.

The screen door clatters behind him, loud enough that Mortimer and Gwyneth come rushing from the kitchen.

"What is it?" Mort says. "Did you find—?"

With all his strength, Jack flings the field packs so they strike Mort right in the gut.

"What the hell—?" The force of the blow cuts off the rest of Mort's words.

"They're gone!" Jack shakes the umbrellas at both Mort and Gwyneth. "I found all this at the housing development. They fell into that fissure you were so damned cavalier about."

Mort raises his hands like he's trying to gentle a wild animal. "Slow down and tell us what happened."

Jack doesn't bother with Mort. He turns his attention toward Gwyneth. "Tell me you drew blood samples. Please, tell me you did."

Gwyneth's eyes are wide with shock. Ophelia's never seen Gwyneth this silent, this scared. After a moment, she manages a numb nod.

"Then we can get them back. There's a way—"

"It's bullshit," Mort says. "Stories, nothing substantial."

Jack spins, and Ophelia cringes, catching the full force of his glare. "And you know this how?"

"I think I have the clearance to know these things, buddy. Maybe stick to your lane."

"You know what lane I've been in for the last year, *buddy*? I've been analyzing every last shred of data Henry Darnelle sends to the Enclave. Trust me, my clearance is higher than yours." He dismisses Mort with a wave of his hand.

"We can bring them back." Jack turns the full force of his persuasion on Gwyneth. "I know how."

"In theory," Mort observes. "In reality, you don't know shit. No one does. It's never worked."

"You're wrong. It has worked. The Enclave doesn't advertise it. Three months ago, someone *did* return. My uncle George told me, and he wouldn't lie about something like that."

This is news to Ophelia. It's so hard to keep track of time in this loop. But she counts on her fingers. No, three months ago, she was already comatose, cut off from all the gossip, which, all things considered, is the most reliable source of news in the Enclave.

"Do you know who this someone is?" Mort challenges.

"I don't. My uncle didn't say. He was on the debriefing team, though, and needed an outlet."

This, Ophelia understands. Like his nephew, George Ling has a sense for connections. Never mind emotional dysregulation; for someone like him or Jack, the buildup can overwhelm. Of course, in her case, it can send you straight into a coma.

"Right. So what you have are rumors and nothing else."

Jack ignores Mort and turns to Gwyneth, pleading in his eyes, his voice. "We need to move now, tonight, at sunset. I know what to do, but I need their blood to do it."

"Botten won't like—" Mort begins.

"I don't give a rat's ass about Botten, especially after what happened with Ophelia."

Her name brings Ophelia up short. She hadn't realized others in the Enclave might suspect foul play with her coma, other than her mother, but judging by the expression on Jack's face, he certainly does.

"Hasn't Henry sacrificed enough?" Jack returns that beseeching gaze to Gwyneth, his eyes dark and soulful and absolutely sincere. "Don't you want him back?"

The nod is barely there, but it is a nod. Gwyneth is still and silent, but something plays behind her eyes. Her thoughts are churning with calculation.

"The task force is set to roll in," Mort says in warning.

"They won't. I saw the advance party downtown. It's too busy. They'll have to wait until dark, and I'm sure they're telling Botten that right now."

Yes, the equipment—communications vans, the porta-potties, the tents—needed for even a small, elite task force might alarm the locals, catch the attention of the police and the town council. The Enclave never wants attention. Especially if this is an unauthorized task force, and Ophelia suspects it must be.

"They will deploy." Mort's words sound like a threat.

And if Jack is there in the housing development, spilling the blood that Botten had the response team so carefully collect? To quote Mortimer: heads will roll. Ophelia knows that much.

"Delay them until after sunset."

"Find me the epicenter, and I will."

The two men stare at each other, expressions unyielding. Jack won't give an inch, but then Mortimer doesn't plan to, either. There's a reason he's nipping at Henry's heels. No, he won't make principal field agent before twenty-five, but it won't be long after.

Assuming they don't end the world before then.

"All right." Jack continues to glare at Mortimer, but something has shifted in his expression. He wants Pansy back too much. Without another word, he turns from both Mort and Gwyneth and leaves the house.

Outside, he turns right toward where the sidewalk ends. Ophelia doesn't follow. Instead, she hovers by the doorway. She's still there when Mort's shadow eclipses her. His presence is unaccountably and undeniably cold.

"Fairy tales, buddy," he says, voice full of pity. "Nothing but fairy tales."

CHAPTER 69
HENRY

"You understand that it needs to be you."

Max Monroe's hand was heavy on Henry's shoulder. The man's voice was low, the words meant for Henry alone. And yes, Henry understood a great deal, including why, if it came to it, he would need to be the sacrifice.

"I do, and I will," Henry said. "But I'd appreciate—"

"Oh, here it comes," Max muttered.

"Information on why you ended up in King's End to begin with."

"Not *how*, Darnelle? Don't you want to travel dimensions and amass advanced tech, untold power, and—?"

"I'd prefer to stay in my own dimension, and I suspect it's better for everyone if no one travels and amasses untold power and technology."

What Henry wanted was here, in the showcase home, or rather, the showcase home of his own mind's devising. His father not only alive, but alive and well enough to whip up gravy and beat Max Monroe at chess (*of course* his father would win). Pansy as his wife? That had been impulsive, yes. Undeniably wonderful? Without a doubt.

Max stared at him now, those dark eyes uncanny. Pansy had her mother's classic bone structure. But the thick chestnut hair and the deep brown eyes that seemed unfathomable? Those were Max's.

"You're not what I expected, Darnelle." Max crooked a finger at Pansy and moved toward the kitchen door.

A bit of distrust replaced the warmth in her eyes. She pushed a palm beneath her nose, but if there was any blood, it was a minuscule amount. They gathered at the kitchen doorway, the gray through the windows as unrelenting as ever, static that seemed to have substance. Henry could feel it press against the door. This close, its staleness lingered on his tongue. No wonder he'd concocted an elaborate feast. Anything to banish this void.

"Back in my dimension, I was the equivalent of a field agent," Max said. "More or less. We monitor your world, along with others, for events that can tear fissures in our own. When required, we'll travel to assess the situation. That's what I was doing in King's End, essentially a scouting mission."

A faraway look crossed Max's face. "Your mother is so skilled that, at first, we thought the Enclave had moved in to contain the rupture. But then, progress slowed, and the powers-that-be grew concerned, so I was sent over to see what was taking your lot so long."

"And then you stayed?" Pansy said, although it really wasn't a question. "You fell—"

"In love? You might say love felled me. I couldn't leave your mother, not that I ever officially tendered my resignation. It's common enough, and certainly, my side wrote me off. There's plenty more where I come from. We're like cannon fodder."

Pansy tilted her head. "You must have a real name, then."

"Oh, I do, sweetheart. It's the one your mother found for me. I was more than happy to give up the old. But then, there was you. And the future. And only one thing I could do to save you and your mother."

Max raised his arms and turned a slow circle. "I set up shop here and waited. I secured your mother, so her stopgap measure remains —and that's no small thing."

"The list she left for me. She knew you would come for her."

"She did."

"And she couldn't tell me?"

"She left you a list. I'm not sure what more you expected."

Pansy's gaze narrowed, but she nodded. "I suppose there was a lot she couldn't say."

"We both knew this was the only chance to save your world, and you along with it." Max turned that sharp gaze toward Henry. "Good enough for you, Darnelle?"

Not really, but Henry doubted Max would give up more than he already had, but he decided to try. "Our ancestors, then? From your dimension?"

"Yes, which is why your lot gives us the most trouble. There are plenty who'd be glad to let you end yourselves and call it done." Max rubbed his hands together. "And speaking of your dimension, it's time for you to return."

Pansy glanced toward Max, the window, and back again. "And we do that how?"

"It's simple, really. The same way you got here. Just go around to the front and walk through the door."

"That's—" Henry began.

"Too easy? No, I said it was simple. It's not going to be easy."

Max flung open the door, and the static on the other side roared. It was like a beast, like the Screamers, Henry realized. Thick and viscous, and yes, sticky was the perfect word for it.

"Off you go, then."

No. Full stop. Absolutely not. Not without a guarantee. Not without some assurance that their dimension was accessible. Not without—

Max raised a foot and, with a gentle nudge, sent Pansy flying out the door. She vanished instantly, that greedy static swallowing her up.

"You son of a—"

"Better hurry, Darnelle. You only have seconds to catch her. Don't want to waste time beating me to a pulp. Besides, you have a world to save."

Without thought, without care, Henry leapt.

Although he knew it was impossible, that he couldn't see the space behind him, Henry had a distinct impression of Max Monroe sinking to his knees, palms pressed against his eyes, body quaking with unrepressed and unrepentant sobs.

CHAPTER 70
OPHELIA

King's End, Minnesota
Saturday, July 15

Ophelia shadows Mortimer. She knows where the epicenter is, has seen it many times in the loop. She hardly needs a preview of that now. Mort, on the other hand? Senior Field Agent Mortimer Connolly is up to no good.

Under different circumstances, she'd applaud that. Gwyneth has retreated to her room, leaving him unsupervised. No one should ever leave a Connolly unsupervised. Ophelia should know; she's one herself. He's dumped both Henry's and Pansy's umbrellas into the stand. They languish there, still inert. However, if one were to peer closely, one might detect that the straps are undone. And those two straps?

Somehow entwined.

Mort, however, does not peer closely or even give the umbrellas a second glance. Instead, he upends the field packs, items scattering across the floor. Unlike Jack, he doesn't paw the contents. He examines each item with care, weighing its purpose in the palm of his hand.

To be clear, Mortimer knows a go bag when he sees one.

It's those rolls of bills that give Henry away. The rest of the items, you could easily explain: Pansy's emergency tinctures, the wire cutters she tucked into her pack. Even the change of underthings, extra pairs of socks, sunscreen, and those thin emergency blankets. All handy when dealing with unpredictable Screamers.

But a couple of thousand in cash? So like Henry, what with his second laptop and burner phones. It's almost as if he's lived by Rose Little's rule five for all these years.

These items tell a different story, one Mort is reading now, and it casts doubt on everything else in the field packs. Why would Henry and Pansy attempt an escape? Unless they know something, unless they suspect that something—that threat—is here, in this house.

Mort stands and dusts off his hands but merely kicks the items to the side of the hallway. With purposeful strides, he charges through Ophelia with a force that tumbles her. When she's right-side-up again, he halts and studies the space where she hovers.

A chill of foreboding blows through her. Mort raises an eyebrow as if he's confirmed something. He's never manifested any hints of the Sight, true. But he is a Connolly; there is that connection, however tenuous. Does he simply know that someone's here, or does he know that she, Ophelia Connolly, is the one spying on him?

"This is none of your business." Mort aims these words right at her face.

"What's none of my business?"

The voice startles them both. Gwyneth stands at the foot of the stairs, nonchalantly easing the envy-inducing kitten heels back on her feet. Granted, her presumptive sister-in-law is no field agent.

She's not incompetent, either.

Mort gives his head a shake and offers up a self-deprecating laugh. "Got one of those sensations, someone peering over my shoulder. Probably nothing."

"Probably," Gwyneth says, tone arch. "But I presume whatever it is you're doing *is* my business."

Mort folds his arms over his chest. "Want to shed some light on why your betrothed would attempt an actual escape? Did you let something slip?"

"I did no such thing. As far as I could tell, Henry was so injured, we should've evacuated him to Seattle. But, no. We certainly couldn't do *that*."

"Not my call. That's on Botten. And he's not going to be happy about this." Mort kicks the detritus from the field packs. A couple of the twenties flutter and then float across the hardwood floor.

"Then maybe clean it up."

These two. They bicker like an old married couple, with all the animosity and none of the affection. Ophelia wants to referee. Almost.

"I mean," Gwyneth adds, and her voice is softer, approaching conciliatory. "Do we have to tell him that part?"

"How do we explain it?"

"Maybe we don't have to."

"We definitely need to report this. It's totally against Enclave protocol. Clearly, they were planning to go off grid."

"All right," Gwyneth says, and again, her voice is arch. "As response team lead, do you want to tell Botten? Perhaps even inform the High Council?"

Mort's silence speaks volumes. No, that's a one-way ticket back to Seattle.

"If Jack is right—" Gwyneth continues.

"Jack isn't right."

"If Jack is right," she says, as if Mort hasn't interrupted her, "we don't have to tell Botten anything. And if he's wrong?"

"We're screwed."

"No. Then we mourn and continue the mission, like we always do."

"We do that how?"

"I've been doing a little research into other incidents like this one. Florence, Wisconsin. Heard of it?"

"Yeah." Mort heaves a breath. "My capstone at the Academy. Thought it was shitty of them to pick that particular mission, what with Pansy and all. She never knew, and I never told her."

"Then you know. And you also know that the only explanation anyone could surmise was that the two agents in question were under a thrall. According to the after-action review, Botten himself was there. Tried to stop them but was unable to. There's a reason we pull our agents from the field. After the Sahara, this may have been too much for Henry."

Mort nods, lips twisting in derision as if this flaw, this addiction, will never touch him.

Recently, before the coma, that worry had been nattering at Ophelia. That Henry was close, that he'd give himself over to the Screamers, to the thrall. Now, even she begins to doubt. Is that what happened? Could Henry simply not help himself?

"He was in pretty rough shape," Mort says.

Building a case? Formulating an excuse? Neither will go down well with Botten; this, Ophelia knows.

"It's not ideal," Gwyneth concedes, "but we do have their blood. And Botten has the text. We can heal whatever needs to be healed, like Florence. They eventually repaired the fissure there to the point that it was no longer a hot spot. Saved the Enclave quite a bit of money over the years."

Death, destruction. What do those things matter as long as the Enclave can save a few dollars?

"We do have their blood," Mort says. "Right? Unless you let Jack have it."

Ah, and there's the rub.

"We'll make do."

The smile that unfurls across Gwyneth's face is both cunning and captivating, the calculating look of someone who knows the direct route to her spot on the High Council. Ophelia considers those kitten heels, oh-so-casually slipped back on.

Now, she wonders what her presumptive sister-in-law was doing upstairs. Ophelia assumed Gwyneth simply wanted to escape Mortimer, if only for a few minutes. Really, who could blame her? But another thought crosses Ophelia's mind.

No one should leave a Worthington-Wells unsupervised, either.

CHAPTER 71
JACK

King's End, Minnesota
Saturday, July 15

Jack doubles back for the blood, using a route that takes him over hedges and through vegetable gardens. Gwyneth Worthington-Wells has a reputation, a well-earned one, and he doesn't trust her to follow through with her promise.

He doesn't trust Mortimer, either.

From the moment Jack stepped through the door, he sensed something wrong, sensed it and ignored it. Now, look where that's left him. Stealing the blood of his best friend and the Enclave's premier field agent.

This has *wrong* written all over it.

So does slipping in the back door of Pansy's house. The stark absence of Rose pinches his chest, coats his tongue with sour bile. She is truly gone. The kitchen around him mourns, the blues darker, the cream-colored accents cast in shadows. He eases open the refrigerator and finds two vials of blood next to the orange juice.

Which also has *wrong* written all over it.

Voices come from the front of the house, Mort and Gwyneth squabbling. Jack tilts his head, an ear toward the hallway. Someone else is here, not physically, but a presence, ghostlike in its manifestation. Fortunately, the Sight is rare. Otherwise, Jack might never do anything slightly embarrassing. Getting caught in the bedroom? Or worse, the bathroom? No, thank you.

Fortunately, he can also tell when something, or someone, is hovering. Or he thinks he can. Like now. Someone other than himself is spying on Mortimer and Gwyneth. Images surface in his mind. The last time he saw Ophelia Connolly before she succumbed to the coma. Those bright eyes with their sparkle, the laughing way she always greeted him: Mr. Tall, Dark, and Nerdy. He never minded that, although anyone else would have earned a scowl. But then, nearly everyone indulged Ophelia Connolly. She was—is—so easy to indulge.

Could it be? Has the Sight brought her here, to King's End? Jack doesn't know and doesn't have time to investigate. He pulls a knife from a butcher block and then slips out the door, shoves his way through thorny roses and compact lilac bushes. He sprints to the housing development, his umbrella strapped to his back, canopy fluttering, urging him to run faster.

After he finds and switches off the transponders, locating the epicenter is child's play. Even Mort could find it. The location explains why he discovered the packs in the showcase home; the house sits right on top of the epicenter.

An eerie silence blankets the housing development. He flinches, casts glances over his shoulder. Despite the fissure that weeps like a wound, no Screamers invade the space. He wonders at that, considers what they know that he doesn't.

That sensation is so unnerving that he almost turns to leave. Instead, Jack finds a spot in one of the framed-in houses across the road. The structure gives him a full view of the showcase home's front door and the entrance to the housing development. But the rudimentary ceiling and walls shield him from the sun and anyone else who might stumble into this space.

Jack scrapes five years of gathered dirt and leaves from the floor and then sits. He leans back against the rough wood, the earthy odor of dry rot heavy in the summer air. He hopes no one—be it Mortimer or the advance party—will think to investigate the housing development before sunset.

He considers the vials of blood in his hand and hopes like hell he knows what he's doing.

CHAPTER 72
PANSY

I can't believe my own father just kicked me out of the showcase home like I'm some sort of fledgling bird. My arms pinwheel. It's almost like I can grab handfuls of the gray static that buzzes around me. I glance behind for Henry, but all that does is spin me in several rotations, to the point where a wave of nausea crashes through me.

I strain to invoke the Sight. It's the only tool, weapon, I have against this. I get nowhere. No hint of the future, no telltale dampness beneath my nose. Nothing. Scenarios run through my mind, but they're fueled by my imagination. I can't see anything—with my eyes or my mind—no matter how hard I try.

I keep trying, keep pinwheeling my arms until something catches me in the stomach with enough force that I nearly do vomit. My legs strike something as well, and a sharp sting blooms across my kneecaps. But I feel wood beneath my palms, the long top rail of the porch against my midsection, the supports against my knees.

I wedge a foot between the balusters, hold on with one hand, and reach my other into the void. This, I realize, is not an ideal way to find Henry, but it's my only option at the moment.

Fingertips, undeniably warm and real, brush against mine. I call out, but the static swallows my shouts. A moment later, a thump shakes the structure, solid and sure. A moment after that? Henry's hand curls around mine.

We cling to each other and the porch. Together, we inch our way in what I hope is the right direction, toward the front door. Henry tugs me closer. Warmth radiates off him. I get the impression he's speaking, but I can't hear his words. Static roars in my ears, fills my mouth, my nose. If we can't find the front door, is this our fate? An eternity of constant searching, together but cut off from each other?

The thought of Henry's dream home fills me with regret. I would've gladly given myself over to that fantasy. Perfectly brewed cups of tea? Cozy evenings without end? If only. *If only.*

Another thump makes me think Henry's knee has encountered something. His grip tightens on my hand. But it's the vibrations through the wood that give me an idea.

Granted, it's been a while since I've used this method of communicating, not since the Academy, to be truthful. But I learned it before then, thanks to my mother. No doubt Principal Field Agent Henry Darnelle knows his Morse code. I start tapping, hoping for muscle memory to kick in, hoping I'm not tapping out nonsense. When he squeezes my fingers, I know I'm getting it right.

This way, he taps. *Main column. I think.*

I hear the question in those last two words. I tap back: *Sight not working.*

We inch forward. Then Henry taps: *Watch out.*

My foot strikes a stair. In my mind's eye, I try to conjure the showcase home. I've passed by it so many times on my patrols, ignoring its cookie-cutter architecture. Now I wish I'd paid more attention.

But I'm fairly certain there's nothing between the stairs and the front door except a moldering doormat. Nothing to hold on to, to guide us. If we let go of the column, we're on our own. This static is greedy. It's sticky, to quote my father. We may never make it.

Leap, Henry taps, *on three.*

One ... two ... three.

I push off the stairs and fly forward. Henry clutches my hand. If we're lost, at least we'll be lost together. My shoulder slams into something solid and bruising, and then my cheekbone strikes wood so hard that I nearly let go of Henry.

I grope and find the cool metal of the door handle. Henry crashes next to me, his force shaking the structure. I take his hand to guide it toward the handle. If it's locked? Henry doesn't have his lock picks. Even if he did, we still can't see a thing. Could we break the glass? Crash through a window?

No, wait. According to my father, it's *simple.* Just walk through the front door. So I grab the handle and push. We tumble inside into an expanse that's devoid of the static but just as empty. I feel myself falling, like in those moments before sleep, down, down, down. Along the way, my hand slips from Henry's. A cry starts in my throat but emerges as a whimper, muted and heavy with fatigue.

Something catches me, something unaccountably soft. I'm not expecting soft, not after everything. Something else anchors me in place, not cruelly, but in a way that's familiar, secure, and genuine.

But it's the fatigue that wins in the end. I give myself over to it and close my eyes.

My sleep is dreamless.

CHAPTER 73
HENRY

King's End, Minnesota
Saturday, July 15

She was so damn clever. Morse code? Why the hell hadn't he thought of that? But his head had been filled with everything else—how to end up as the sacrifice, if it came to that, and how to ensure Pansy wasn't—that the practicalities of making it back weren't in the forefront of his mind.

Henry felt the gravity of their reality close around him like a cocoon. Everything was heavier here, but more solid, more substantial. In retrospect, the fantasy house was like strands of gossamer, sweet like cotton candy and undeniably lovely but ultimately counterfeit. A life built on daydreams couldn't truly be real. That was evident in Max Monroe's sorrow.

A breeze washed over him, puckering his skin. The heat of the day had diminished, which meant it must be close to sunset.

Henry's eyes flew open, that one thought propelling him upright. They had minutes, at best, to escape the housing development. He scrambled to his feet, using the coffee table as leverage.

The empty coffee table.

Henry pawed the surface as if that could make their umbrellas, the field packs, and the burner phones reappear. For a moment, his vision tunneled. Maybe Pansy had woken first. Maybe she had moved them somewhere safe. But no, she was there, on the couch, nestled in the dust sheets he'd tucked around her in what felt like a lifetime ago.

As if she felt his stare, she peered from her cocoon, face shrouded. She let out a single squeak and burrowed beneath the sheets.

What the hell?

"My father said that travelers come through naked." Her voice emerged from the depths of the couch, the words muffled. "I didn't realize that would apply to us."

That was when Henry glanced down.

Oh.

In the dining alcove, Henry tugged a dust sheet from a chair and secured an improvised toga. In the kitchen, he unearthed an old flannel shirt and blessed the extra large, extra tall worker for leaving it behind.

"Here." He tucked the shirt next to Pansy. "I'm decent, so whenever you're ready, we need to find our umbrellas and…"

The evening breeze puckered his skin once again, followed by ominous chills and a dread he hadn't felt even in the Sahara. The front door, the source of that breeze, was open. Footprints marred the dusty floor. The pattern looked almost like a scuffle, although there was only one set of footprints beyond their own.

"Someone's been here." He crouched and examined the tread of a pair of sneakers, but there was no way of knowing who had been here, or when.

"And they took our stuff?" Pansy padded over to him on nearly silent feet. "Our umbrellas?"

"So it would seem." He stood then, glanced her way, and forgot all about their missing items. "Pansy. What happened?"

He raised his hand to caress her cheek but thought better of it. A bruise bloomed bright across her cheekbone, the red livid, the purple coming in angry. She brought her fingertips to the wound and then winced.

"The door. I slammed into it."

Henry whirled. He had an instant ice pack ... in his go bag. He cast his gaze toward the ceiling and swore.

"I think we need to leave," Pansy whispered.

The air around them was congealing. A hint of seductive lavender filtered through the air. The grimy hardwood beneath his feet felt slicker, recently polished. Yes, if they didn't, they'd end up right back where they started, and returning at sunrise was not an option, assuming they could make this journey a second time.

"I'll check the way out." He moved toward the front windows, peering cautiously from behind the drapes. The way appeared clear. No task force, at least not yet. That didn't rule out a sentry tucked away in the shadows. "Can you see if our umbrellas are still here?"

"They're not." She said it with such certainty that worry pinged in the back of Henry's mind. "At least, mine isn't."

"The Sight?" he asked. She had that look, a disconcerting dreaminess in her eyes, but a hint of a smile curved her lips.

"I don't need the Sight for that. She isn't here. I can tell."

His wasn't either, although it could certainly drop into stealth mode when the mood struck. But this wasn't one of those times. No, neither of their umbrellas was capricious like that. But without them? Here they were. No money, no clothes, no way to even walk down the street without calling attention to themselves.

Henry surveyed the great room. Both the windows and the front door were too exposed. The egress window in the basement was too risky. So was the kitchen door, for that matter, but that way provided more cover. "We should head out the back. After that, I'm not sure—"

"Guy and Milo. They'll help, and so will Adele. If we're not in the fissure, then we just need to be gone, right?"

"Botten still has our blood."

"But he doesn't have *us*."

The tiniest bit of hope kindled in his chest. "He doesn't have the sacrifice." All the blood samples in the world wouldn't change that. The gateway would still be hungry, true. But that was all it would be.

"Not even Mort will think to check Guy's place for a while, I'm certain. By then, we can be somewhere else. It's not like the Enclave is going to alert the police and put out an APB on us."

Wouldn't they, though? Henry could think of several scenarios where they might. The most likely ruse would be an abduction, with him as the culprit and Pansy as his victim. Yes, the Enclave could get local law enforcement to play along with that. And if the image of Pansy's bruise ended up on closed-circuit television? Most definitely.

"Is there a back way out of the development?"

"Not unless we cut a hole in the fence, or maybe climb it." She wiggled her bare toes and frowned. "But if we can make it out of the gate, we can take the long way around, past the silo and the fields. It's rough going." She stared down at her bare feet again and sighed. "But it might be our best option."

Someone knew they'd been here. That same someone might have eyes on the gate and the main road. Mortimer Connolly would, as would any member of the advance party. What Max had observed was true. Botten really had amassed his own little army, and now he and Pansy were up against it. Henry didn't like those odds. But with the air shifting around them, hints of that fantasy teasing the back of his mind, they didn't have a choice.

They paused briefly in the kitchen, but no one had left behind boots or shoes or even a pair of socks. Certainly nothing as useful as wire cutters. Before opening the door, Henry scanned the area. As far as he could tell, no one was in place, but that meant little.

Before they stepped outside, Henry did cup Pansy's face, brought her gaze to his, and let his thumb travel her uninjured cheekbone.

"If we're caught, I want you to run like hell."

"But—"

"I'll do what I can to fight, to create a distraction, but you need to do everything you can to escape."

"But he'll still have you, and he still has my blood."

"I know, but it's the difference between sacrificing King's End and sacrificing the entire world."

"And sacrificing you." Her voice was so quiet that Henry wasn't certain he'd heard her correctly.

"Promise me, Pansy. Promise me this one thing."

Her eyes, again, uncanny and dreamlike. If the Sight was this close, they really needed to find shelter. For a foolish moment, Henry didn't care. He wanted to remain here, let the kitchen reform around them, bar the door from Max Monroe, and step into the fantasy again. Step in and never return.

Step in and end the world.

"All right." Her soft words broke the spell thickening around them. "I promise."

The determination in her eyes spoke volumes. Briefly, he wondered if she saw something, if the Sight—for once—was helping rather than hindering.

She took his hand, and together, they left the showcase home behind.

CHAPTER 74
JACK

King's End, Minnesota
Saturday, July 15

Jack ignores Mortimer's calls and increasingly terse text messages. He ignores the reminder that Mort is his response team lead, and as such, Jack needs to check in with him. With this last, Jack rolls his eyes.

"Pulling rank, buddy?"

But tendrils of anxiety infiltrate the back of his mind. He doesn't want anyone searching for him—or Pansy and Henry—before sunset. So he fires off a terse message of his own.

Almost there. Need silence.

It does the trick. The quiet is blissful, if uncanny. He'll need to time things perfectly and keep an eye on the sun's trajectory. But he already knows the location, around the back of the showcase home, near that egress window. That space, too, is quiet and uncanny.

Then that anxiety rears up, more of a roar, almost tangible, as if it could shake him by the scruff of the neck. It's a full-fledged warning cry. Forget about the blood, the incantation, it urges. His bags are still in the rental, and what he should do is get behind the wheel and start driving. North first, jump on I-94 and then I-90 straight back to Seattle. The route plays out in his head, including stops for fuel and caffeine.

Jack shakes the suggestions from his mind. These visions occur from time to time, generally when he's under stress. At the Academy, he entertained several scenarios that involved sneaking off Joint Base Lewis-McChord and making a run for Puget Sound. What he, along with Pansy and Mort, would do there was anyone's guess. Then Pansy's nose would start to bleed, and he'd abandoned the idea.

Pansy. That's why he can't run away. The reminder on his phone pings, but he's already stepping from the framed-in structure and toward the showcase home. The sky is in that liminal space between the golden hour glow and twilight. The air, too, is sweeter, more seductive, and, for the housing development, almost pleasant.

He kneels, soaks the small patch of earth in front of him with blood, and watches as the soil sucks it down, greedy, greedy, greedy. With that pilfered kitchen knife, he slices his own palm, the sting angry and outraged. From all his research, from all his talks with his mentor—his uncle George—Jack knows that this is the crucial step the Enclave so often dismisses.

You have to want it badly enough to sacrifice your own blood as well; the more immediate, the more violent, the better.

And there's nothing Jack wants more than for Pansy to be safely returned.

Their combined blood bubbles and churns. The wind whips up, ruffling his hair and his umbrella's canopy. Static fills his mouth. Will this work? It must work. He chants the incantation again, louder, with authority he doesn't feel.

He chants and he chants, bleeds and bleeds. A creaking catches his attention. The sound of hinges not often used, followed by the clatter of a screen door.

And there, on the back porch of the showcase home, is Pansy.

CHAPTER 75
PANSY

"Pansy!"

Someone calls my name, someone who sounds like Jack, his voice filled with anguish and relief. I've made it down the porch steps, the ground rough beneath my bare feet, when a blur comes tearing for me.

I flinch before realizing it *is* Jack, sprinting across the desiccated lawn. He captures me in his embrace, pinning my arms to my sides, his exhales rough and ragged against my ear.

"It worked. It really worked. You're here, you're really here. I can't believe it worked, but it did."

Then Henry is at my side, prying me from Jack's arms without much success.

"Agent Ling, please. I need you to listen. This is crucial. Pansy's life may be in—"

But Jack *isn't* listening. He cups my face, one palm tacky against my skin. I wince, the pressure against my injured cheekbone prompting a spike of pain. Only then does Jack ease up.

"Pansy, what happened?"

"No time," Henry says. "We need to leave the housing development before dark."

"Shit, you're right." Jack takes my hand and starts pulling me toward the entrance. His slate and silver umbrella flutters a chaotic greeting.

Henry catches up to us, yanking on his makeshift toga and securing my hand in his.

"I think the way is clear," he whispers. "I don't see anyone else, no evidence of an advance party." His words are cautious and quiet, and I barely hear him over Jack's frantic narration.

"When we discovered you were gone ... I found your packs and umbrellas ... Mort's being an asshole. I think he might be hiding something. Do you feel it?" With this last, he spares me a look, and I try to nod. But he's off again, relating the last several hours.

Henry joins the fray, adding his own narration, trying to convince Jack to let me go. His tone is coaxing, if urgent, full of the authority of a principal field agent.

But Jack is frazzled, utterly convinced of something, imploring both of us. His words blend with Henry's until my ears buzz. Loud. So loud. My vision clouds and then clears, but each time I see less and less, like my world is slowly but inexorably collapsing. Every few steps, I forget how to walk, or so it seems.

"Jack, listen to me," Henry says. "Pansy needs medical attention. She needs Rose's remedies." He glances at me, blanches, and then swears.

With a corner of his makeshift toga, he dabs beneath my nose. Haltingly, we inch forward and through the gate. Even then, Jack won't pause. I don't think he can. He's pulling us toward something, something that feels predestined. The notion punches through the buzzing in my ears and sends shivers across the exposed skin of my legs. The day is still warm, but I'm freezing.

When we reach the shade of the Camelot Lots sign, I freeze completely. I'm a block of ice, cold, unmoving. Someone will have to carry me. I'm hoping that someone is Henry and that he'll turn back around and head for the showcase home.

Because our blood. *Our blood.* Jack's frazzled words finally penetrate. He performed some sort of ritual and thinks it worked. Whether it did or not, I don't know.

What matters is, it didn't end the world.

What matters is, Botten won't have our blood.

This must be why the Sight has clamped down my entire body, why my nose won't stop bleeding.

"Pansy?" Jack tugs at my hand, but I'm stiff-legged, an ice sculpture.

I feel as if my feet have gained a hundred pounds each. My limbs refuse to cooperate, and I'm still so cold that the rush of blood across my upper lip burns.

"Henry," I whisper. "Jack used our blood."

He continues to dab, but understanding and astonishment light his gaze. Henry swings around, secures the toga, and steps between me and Jack, at last prying his grip from mine.

"Agent Ling, this is important. How many vials of blood did you use for the ritual?"

At first, Jack squares off, looks as if he's planning a left hook, then hesitates. Even in a toga, Henry can hold his own. But that glazed expression hasn't faded from Jack's eyes. With strange deliberation, he pulls two empty vials of blood from his pocket, and they clink in the palm of his hand.

Henry shuts his eyes, a look of pain crossing his face. Two vials, which means two must remain, somewhere, still untouched. That last bit of hope slips away from me. That full-blown fantasy of returning to the showcase home evaporates. It would've worked. The Sight insists that it would have, and marvelously so. Even as it insists this, I have to wonder.

Why won't it let me move?

That's when I notice the rumble beneath my feet and the dust cloud rising in the wake of an SUV, one that's headed straight for us.

Mort springs from the passenger door before the vehicle comes to a complete stop. He charges across the gravel, feet kicking up rocks. Head down, he rams his shoulder straight into Henry.

The two men crash to the ground, all elbows and fists and knees.

"You son of a bitch," Mort grinds out, jaw clenched, hand tightening the sheet wrapped around Henry's neck. "I'm ending your career over this. By the time Botten's through with you—"

My throat aches from shouting, but at least my feet are lighter. I'm at Mort's side, yanking on his shirt. His skin is ruddy, an unhealthy, aggressive pink. He spares me a glance and then goes absolutely, dangerously still.

"What did you do to her?" This is directed at Henry with cold, deliberate venom.

"He didn't do any—"

"What. Did. You. Do. To. Her." He twists the sheet even tighter. "Forget your career. I'm ending you."

Henry himself has gone absolutely and alarmingly still. I don't think he can breathe. No, I'm certain he can't. I don't have the strength to pull Mort off him, not when he's in a rage. Neither does Jack. He's there, on Mort's other side, working to tug the sheet from Mort's grip. I suspect he's making it worse.

The blast from a car horn cuts through the air, long, loud, and unrelenting. The sound banishes the buzzing in my ears. We all freeze now, a strange tableau: Mort priming to land a killing blow, me reaching for his fist, Jack still trying to pry the sheet from Mort's other hand, Henry unnaturally pale and immobile.

At last, the noise cuts off. The driver's side door swings open. A delicate pair of kitten heels makes an appearance. Gwyneth steps from the SUV and picks her way across the gravel.

She comes to stand over us, expression mild, as if we're merely four children tumbling on the grass.

"Botten just called," she says to Mortimer. "He wants an update."

CHAPTER 76
HENRY

Henry felt certain Mortimer Connolly's fist would have met gravel rather than his nose.

Well, nearly certain.

"You should probably check in," Henry said now, voice ragged through his bruised throat. "You know how Botten dislikes delays. Hate to see you lose *your* career over this."

At his words, Gwyneth hissed. Yes, he was goading Mort. To be fair, the man absolutely deserved it. Besides, Henry was done with everything. His path was clear, and he was going to wring as much enjoyment from that dismal prospect as possible.

Then he made the mistake of glancing toward Pansy. The blood gave her that fierce appearance he'd first seen on the green, but her eyes were so tender when they met his own. His heart couldn't take much more of this. Even now, he fought the urge to grab her hand and rush back into the housing development.

The fantasy was in the air, thick and sweet. It beckoned. Through the gate, the houses glimmered. Street lamps flickered in and out of existence. The showcase home was presenting ever more appealing façades. Now that it knew him, it was quite the temptress.

And then, from the open car doors, came the sound of a ringtone.

Gwyneth raised an eyebrow at Mort. He let a second ring pass before lumbering to his feet and jogging toward the SUV.

To Henry's surprise, Gwyneth leaned down and helped not him but Pansy to her feet.

"Are you all right, Agent Little?" Gwyneth tilted Pansy's chin for a better view of her bruise. "A blow like that could certainly cause a bloody nose. I'd like to check for a concussion as well."

Henry cleared his throat.

"Please." She eyed him, her expression full of disdain. "You were faking."

Well, not entirely. The wound on his chest had renewed itself, a dull ache that coiled around his heart. Mort had landed a couple of blows along his ribs and had grazed a cheekbone with a watch, a wound that alternately stung and throbbed. Brawling in a toga? While trying to maintain some dignity? Nearly impossible.

Henry clambered to his feet, or tried to, the damn sheet impeding his progress. He adjusted it as securely as possible, readying himself in case Mort came back for round two. Since the man was heading in their direction, phone clutched in his fist, that was entirely probable.

Instead, Mort merely passed the phone to Gwyneth with the sort of payback smile reserved for a pesky sibling. Gwyneth listened for a moment and then responded with that cold, calculating Worthington-Wells reserve.

"No, I don't think so. While Agent Darnelle has recovered—" She cast a gimlet eye his way. "Agent Little has taken a tumble. I'd like to delay to ensure she doesn't have a concussion. By morning?" An icy pause. "Perhaps." With the air of an empress, she offered the phone to Mortimer, hand outstretched, unconcerned whether he took it or not.

"Yes," Mort said into the phone. "Agent Ling has located the epicenter."

Jack startled at the sound of his name, but he gave the smallest of nods. Henry kept his face impassive, as if the epicenter were the least of his concerns.

"No," Mort said after a long pause. "Not in the housing development proper. The terrain there is unpredictable. The field to the west is the best place for the task force."

And so it begins. Again, Henry remained expressionless, bordering on clueless, as if he had no idea what the task force was actually for or what Botten had planned. Only when Mortimer had tucked the phone in his back pocket did anyone speak. That someone was Gwyneth, her voice gentle, the words meant for Pansy.

"Eight hours."

In her tone, he heard the message: *I can give you eight hours, but no more.*

What did Gwyneth know? What had she figured out? Certainly not all of it. Henry shook off the thoughts, doubtful they'd get a chance to confer. But she understood Pansy was the key and was acting accordingly. Over the years, he'd felt any number of things about Gwyneth: admiration and annoyance, indifference and brotherly affection. This wave of sudden gratitude brought him up short.

"We should probably head back," she added. "I'd like to get some ice on that bruise before her eye swells shut."

But none of them moved. The sun flirted with the horizon, painting the sky magenta and orange, startling colors from a child's box of crayons. Were they still too close to the housing development? Had he and Pansy triggered something irrevocable? Had Jack, when he spilled their—and his—blood?

No, it was Pansy herself. Henry knew that look. It had been brewing ever since they'd returned to their reality. And now? There was no stopping it.

Henry broke the spell, broke free of the strange, cloying inertia that crept from the development. He crossed to Pansy and—for the second time in less than a week—slipped an arm around her waist to break her fall.

CHAPTER 77
PANSY

King's End, Minnesota
Monday, May 25 (thirty-one years ago)

I'm standing in the housing development. Or rather, where it will be. Now, it's a meadow full of waving grasses, wildflowers, and gently rolling hills. Wild roses climb the fence that borders the cemetery, a robust pink reminiscent of strength rather than shyness.

My only thought is: What a shame. It was perfect like this.

A voice startles me, low and sonorous, a voice I recognize, one I came to dread during my summers at the Academy and one that dismissed me so casually to Henry not so long ago. But these words aren't clipped. Instead, they hold a wealth of latent promise and suggestion.

"Look what I found. A wild rose for our wild Rose."

There, in an outstretched hand, is the largest bloom from the fence. The man holding that bloom?

Reginald Botten.

Except the man standing there is barely older than I am. His build is powerful, but he lacks the gravitas of gray temples and frown lines along his brow. He could, at this moment, be anyone, go anywhere, and make different choices. Instead, he has his gaze trained on the woman before him.

My mother.

I've seen photographs, of course; most recently, the ones Henry brought to King's End. They never captured just how startling her beauty was, or is. How full of life and energy and power she was. She must have intimidated the hell out of everyone in the Enclave. Except maybe for the man at her side, whose hand clasps her waist in a way that speaks of intimacy, the gesture adoring without being possessive.

Harry Darnelle.

Harry is a slightly shorter, more barrel-chested version of his son. But there's so much of Henry in his expression that my heart lurches. If I squint, he could be Henry, right down to the dimples. He is studying not the rose in Botten's outstretched hand but the expression on my mother's face.

Perhaps this is why he misses the deception. Because it's there, lingering behind the offer of the rose. It's there when they move to what must be the epicenter, a cleared space of grass in the center of the meadow. It's there when they each pull out a knife.

The blades glint in the sunrise.

"Soon, if we're to do it," someone says, although who, I can't tell. The Sight is being particular about what I can see, what I can hear.

Mouths move, but if they're chanting an incantation, I can't discern the words. My mother tips her head toward the sky, eyes closed, but whether she's praying or merely composing herself, I can't tell.

The gravestones are obscured beyond the rose-covered fence. Behind me, I catch the flash of a red convertible but can't see the gravel road it traveled. I open and close my hands, take a tentative step or two. I'm no longer frozen.

I am, however, transfixed.

When my father said Botten delivered a killing blow, I thought he meant figuratively. Some sort of fairytale curse that would incapacitate Harry Darnelle to the point of death.

Botten uses his knife. The arc of the blade sweeps through the sky at the moment the sun touches the horizon. The silver flashes. The point pierces skin.

I scream.

The eruption of blood paints the grass, the ground, and the wildflowers in a red so bright it's obscene. It gushes in a horrible torrent. Harry drops his own knife and clutches his throat. Blood seeps through the seams of his fingers.

Without thinking, I rush forward. I forget that I'm not here and can't participate. Or rather, I ignore all that. Because the only thing on my mind is that I will not let Henry's father die. I hold my hands above his, that same gentle move I used with Mort's umbrella at this same man's funeral. For *that* to happen, this must. For *Henry* to live, his father must. There's no other way. Harry Darnelle lives, and I'm going to make certain he does.

The meadow is silent the way the housing development always has been. No birdsong. No buzzing of insects. The wind whispers, and it's a cruel sound indeed. Blood is hot against my palms, but my skin burns with something more. This wound is both physical and psychic. That field agents can do this to each other? That they'd want to? I can't fathom that.

Then someone gasps.

I glance from my task to see both my mother and Reginald Botten staring at not me, but Harry. Or rather, the blood that isn't flowing from his wounded neck. Even when he removes his hands, the blood bubbles but doesn't flow, as if his body refuses to bleed out.

"How is that possible?" Botten begins. But he knows, he must know, because he glances around, guilt and guile in his expression.

Before he can speak again, my mother lunges for him, knife still clenched in her hand. She will kill him without regret or remorse. It's there in her posture, in the way the knife finds its mark and tears a long, jagged gash down Botten's arm.

Harry cries out, but no actual sound emerges. He brings his hands to his throat again, and they pass through my own. Then he turns his head, and my own gaze is drawn from where my mother is holding her own against Botten.

Harry's eyes are as dark as Henry's and flecked with that same gold. But there's nothing unfathomable in this man's gaze. He doesn't have to speak. I already know what he'll say. He does, anyway. Or at least, he tries.

"Thank you."

These silent words crush me.

Across the meadow, my mother lets Botten go. But as a parting gift, she throws her knife. It spins, blade over hilt, before finding its mark in the back of Botten's thigh. It's a glancing blow, tearing his jeans, but not much more. Still, he stumbles.

With grace that belies his injuries, he takes the knife. He spins the handle between his palms, another incantation on his lips, one that makes them twist cruelly. Before he whips the knife at my mother, Botten slices open his palm and coats the blade with blood.

But in his haste, his aim goes wide. Then he runs, and the meadow swallows him up.

"Harry!" My mother races across the meadow but stops short when she reaches the clearing.

A fissure has opened up, that familiar gaping maw. It undulates as if it's smacking its lips in anticipation of its sacrifice. My mother retrieves her knife and then returns to the edge of the fissure. She waits until my gaze is locked on her. How she knows, I can't say. Except she does.

"Watch me," she says.

And then she slices open her palm.

Her blood soaks into the earth. Her blood heals the earth, or rather, it's like a gauze placed upon a wound. A crosshatch pattern that runs back and forth, back and forth, lines intersecting and then joining with the fence that borders the cemetery.

She nods to Harry, who picks up his own knife and, despite major blood loss, does the same.

It is, as my father said, a stopgap measure. The pattern is clear; the random spots that she painted in the spring are no longer random but crucial connections that hold everything in place. I understand now why, if the fence goes, we all do.

I wonder, too, how many times Harry Darnelle visited King's End in secret, for his blood binds this wound as much as my mother's does. I wonder, when the construction company broke ground, whether it broke part of him as well.

At last, the fissure shrinks and then vanishes altogether. It lingers, though, just beneath the surface, a festering wound that will plague my patrols in years to come.

I'm still crouched next to Harry, still holding my hands whisper-close against his neck, when my mother steps beside me.

"You can let go now." Her voice is unbearably gentle, as if she understands that I, too, have experienced this trauma.

I ease my hands away. In a flash, I tumble through the years to come. I see what it is Harry Darnelle has done, how he stood sentry for three decades, protecting the world from the man who attempted to slit his throat. The strength, the integrity, the patience to do such a thing. The weight of the burden, the steel of his resolve. It's easy to draw blood, easy to kill. How much harder is it to keep the vigil, to never waver, especially when there's no reward at the end?

No wonder Henry is such a good man. His father most definitely was.

Before the blood can rush down Harry's throat, my mother pulls off her T-shirt and catches it. They hobble away from me, a slow trek through tall grass that parts and then closes behind them. I try to follow, but a wave of sleep nudges me backward, a gentle push against my shoulder.

I fall through that endless expanse. I feel nothing except for the sticky sensation of Harry Darnelle's blood on the palms of my hands.

CHAPTER 78
OPHELIA

King's End, Minnesota
Saturday, July 15

Pansy's front parlor is crowded with people and a herd of unspoken elephants. Really, it's a wonder there's any room left at all. At least everyone is now fully dressed. Henry in field gear, because he knows what comes next. Pansy in something that looks incredibly soft because she's still unconscious.

Gwyneth managed that task herself, a fact that surprises Ophelia. True, Gwyneth ordered Jack to retrieve those soft sweats and ordered everyone from the front room. Ophelia found herself complying, as if seeing Pansy so vulnerable was too much, even for her, who has seen how all this ends.

They gather in the hallway. No one speaks, although the air is filled with recriminations and rancor. Ophelia notes, alarmingly, that neither Henry's nor Pansy's umbrella is currently in the stand next to the door. She wants to go search for both but doesn't dare.

Gwyneth emerges, a corner of that blood-soaked flannel shirt pinched between index finger and thumb. Her gaze takes in the three men hovering outside the door. For a moment, it appears to stray toward Ophelia as well.

"Burn this," Gwyneth commands.

When no one comes forward to do so, she lets the shirt drop to the floor.

Of course, her presumptive sister-in-law realizes this is no fainting spell. She is like the strategist who anticipates the cold war while the hot one still rages. She's several steps ahead of everyone else, on a path that clearly involves Pansy.

Except Gwennie should really pay attention to the here and now. Because the allies won't be storming the beach at Normandy, and the here and now will come to an abrupt and rather unpleasant end.

They all flow into the front room, crowding each other. An elbow jab here, a hip check there. Pansy is on the floor, a pillow beneath her head, a blanket tucked around her. The sun has set, and lamplight bathes the room in a gentle glow. Yet the bruise on Pansy's cheekbone blooms unnaturally bright, and Jack sucks air through his teeth.

"I'm going to assume all three of you know what to do," Gwyneth says. "I suggest one of you do it."

Henry steps forward, but Mortimer shoots out an arm and shoves him against the fireplace. Framed photographs rattle on the mantelpiece. One teeters and then falls, glass cracking against the stone hearth.

"Not. You."

"I have her consent," Henry replies calmly, as if Mort isn't pinning his shoulder to the chimney.

"You don't have mine."

Ah, yes, Mortimer. So fond of pulling rank.

Mort swings his head around, gaze bulleting toward Jack. "See what you can do."

Jack rushes forward, his movements smooth, tender, but tense.

He eases Pansy's head to his thigh, adjusts her position, and whispers encouraging words.

"I know you're in there, sweet pea." His voice is almost teasing, as if this is a game between the two of them. He pulls in a breath and then lets his fingers come to rest on Pansy's temples.

A guttural cry emerges from Jack's throat. He jerks his hands back as if they've been burned.

"What's wrong, buddy?" Mort lets up on Henry, who immediately slips from Mort's hold and moves to Pansy's other side, well out of reach.

Jack is shaking his head. "I don't know. I don't know. It feels wrong."

"Try again."

Jack nods, licks his lips, and then sets his mouth in grim determination. But the moment his fingertips light on Pansy's forehead, his expression twists in pain, in despair. He looks like a man who has no choice but to press his palms against a stove's hot burner.

With a gasp, he pulls his hands back, head shaking again, shoulders hunched and trembling. "I can't do it. I just can't do it." He looks not at Mortimer but straight at Henry. "There's nothing there, like with Ophelia."

The proclamation tumbles Ophelia, sending her reeling backward toward the hearth, where, she imagines, the chimney might draw her upward, out into the air, the sky, to somewhere far away.

"No," Mort says, his voice distant. "She can't be. She must still be—"

"Here?" Jack is still shaking his head, and Ophelia doubts he'll ever stop. "Sorry, *buddy*. But she's not."

Oh, and the blame is squarely on Mortimer.

"Let me," Henry says.

Those two words reel Ophelia back down the chimney, whooshing her into the room, where she comes to rest on the sofa behind Henry. He is so solid, so sure. No one can deny him.

"Absolutely not."

Except Mortimer. He raises a foot as if he could step across Pansy and pin Henry to the window frame this time.

"Don't be stupid," both Jack and Gwyneth say at the same time.

For a moment, their gazes meet, an odd alliance, this. Jack inclines his head, deferring to Gwyneth.

"If you'd like to explain to Botten why she's unconscious, by all means, do so. If you'd like to explain how you know that *and* for how long you've known that?" Gwyneth raises her hands. "Again, by all means, knock yourself out. I'll be happy to watch."

No doubt Gwyneth would, complete with a front-row seat and VIP access.

But another odd alliance is brewing here in Pansy's front room. No one has to say it. No blood oaths. No promises. Just the simple fact that no one here will ever speak of Pansy's Sight. Ophelia's heart pounds. In a distant part of her mind, she hears the beep, beep, beep of the monitor.

She slips from the sofa and slides next to Pansy. She leans down and whispers, "Can you believe this?"

It's another one of those pyrrhic victories. True, Gwyneth has any number of ulterior motives. But both Jack's and Mort's affection run deep. Not even Botten can touch that. As for Henry?

He moves with subtle grace, easing into Jack's spot on the floor so seamlessly, you'd never suspect he was recently brawling and holding his own, despite the toga.

Well, mostly.

His fingers come to rest on Pansy's forehead, his expression tender and then anguished. But Henry stays the course. Ophelia knows he can remain like this for hours, for days. She always believed that the only reason he couldn't bring her back was that he arrived too late. He was, after all, in the Philippines.

But what if he was never meant to bring her back? What if that was a practice run? What if, all this time, the Sight has been trying to propel her into action? Instead of hovering, wringing her translucent hands, and offering suggestions, maybe Ophelia *can* actually help.

She settles next to Pansy, her hands joining Henry's. A connection fizzles through her, not with Henry, not with Pansy, but with both of them.

Back in Seattle, someone is panicking. Monitors beep and whir. Something cool enters her veins, but Ophelia hangs on for as long as possible.

CHAPTER 79
HENRY

King's End, Minnesota
Saturday, July 15

Only when Ophelia slipped away did Henry realize she'd truly been there, that it wasn't his imagination. She left behind a path for him to travel through the grip the Sight had on Pansy's mind.

If only he'd known how, all those months ago, perhaps Ophelia would be free of the Sight's hold as well. Then something breezed through his thoughts, banishing the recriminations, smoothing over the rough edges of guilt.

It wasn't your fault.

For the first time since Ophelia had succumbed to the coma did Henry believe it. When Pansy opened her eyes, the larger why came into focus, not that he could articulate it, not in words, at least.

Pansy gazed up at him. For a moment, it was just the two of them, like that first time he'd brought her back. The wonder in her expression. The well of joy in his chest. That sweet, tentative truce. What he wouldn't give to travel back a week.

If only.

Now, he raised a finger to his lips and caught Pansy's nod of assent.

Outside, a large vehicle rumbled down the normally quiet street. That, he surmised, was the communications van. He wondered how extensive the setup would be. Eight hours wasn't a lot of time for a large task force to deploy. A streamlined one, filled with some of the best, and hungriest, agents in the Enclave?

More than doable.

"Pansy?" Jack's voice shook, her name a whispered prayer. He knew better than to lean forward, to crowd her.

She turned toward him, a tired smile lighting her face. "I'm here."

Her gaze flickered, first to Mortimer and then Gwyneth and then back to Henry.

"Are you able to sit?" he asked.

"I think so." Already, she was moving, easing up to her elbows, although once upright, she leaned heavily against his chest.

The feel of her there, in his arms, was as familiar as if in some other lifetime, they'd sat like this often. Her head came to rest in the crook of his shoulder, and she sank against him, solid and warm in his embrace. Certainly, everyone in this room sensed this strange intimacy. Jack glanced away, and Mortimer scowled.

As for Gwyneth? The inscrutable scientist was gathering data. To what end, Henry could only guess. Although Gwyneth, their betrothal, and even the Enclave wouldn't be a problem for very much longer, at least, not one of his problems.

It was Gwyneth who broke the spell. She crouched in front of Pansy, her expression full of clinical concern.

"How are you feeling, Agent Little?"

"Better. Grounded. I'll be okay."

Gwyneth's gaze flickered to his before returning to Pansy. "I don't mean to rush you, but I've booked a room at the bed and breakfast. Agent Darnelle and I should probably head out."

So, they were going to maintain the polite façade, then, no one in this room willing to broach Botten's hidden agenda. Henry supposed he could, but what little advantage he had was in appearing ignorant.

He shifted his position, knelt to help Pansy stand, and instead, found her in his embrace. She brought her hand to his heart and let it rest there. The heat from her palm penetrated through his shirt, his skin, down deeper through muscle, until it finally touched the bruise left from his betrothal ring. Warmth spread through his chest, soothing the ache, mending the fractures in his heart. Then she stood on tiptoes, brought her lips to his ear, and whispered words meant only for him.

"Your father was a good man."

THEY DIDN'T BOTHER with the luggage. That was the most obvious tell. They left his SUV and took Gwyneth's high-end sedan, one with leather seats, the sort only she would have the audacity to expense. When she slipped behind the wheel? That, too, was a tell.

But then they turned left out of Pansy's driveway, not right, not toward the housing development. That was promising, although Henry remained silent, on alert. He scanned the area with a Z-pattern and checked the side mirror, looking for hints that Botten had the neighborhood covered. The Enclave was often far too careless with small towns, as if video surveillance only existed in cities, as if no one here might keep an eye on their neighbors.

But any number of home security cameras were recording their slow trek up the street. No doubt those same cameras had caught the communications van heading in the other direction.

Gwyneth slowed the car, pausing at the first stop sign. Another vehicle shot into the intersection, blocking the way forward. Yes, Henry could unlock the door and make a break for it. He could split the task force's efforts, lead a portion of them on a chase, into the cemetery, perhaps. He suspected he could even hide in the arms of that willow tree; there was something preternatural about it.

Except that would solve nothing. Botten had his blood. With Mortimer on guard, Botten had Pansy as well. Max Monroe's words surfaced in his mind.

You understand that it needs to be you.

Only now did Henry discern the compassion in the other man's voice.

They sat there, high beams from a second vehicle joining the first and flooding their car, painting them both in a garish light.

"It's not going to end like you think it will," Henry said, venturing to say the quiet part out loud.

"You don't know what I think." Gwyneth stared straight ahead, chin jutting toward the windshield, knuckles pale on the steering wheel.

True enough. Perhaps he never had. Perhaps that had been the problem all along, at least between the two of them.

"I never meant to hurt you," he added.

"What makes you think you have?"

He exhaled, half sigh, half sorrowful laugh. "How about this. In the next several hours, I don't mean to hurt you, but I suspect it could be part of the collateral damage. In fact, I suggest you hand me over." He nodded toward the cars in the intersection. "Then drive straight to the airport and take the first flight back to Seattle."

Only then did Gwyneth shift in her seat, head turning slightly. "What are you saying, Henry?"

"I believe I already told you. It's not going to end like you think it will."

When Botten stepped from that second vehicle, Henry knew he was right.

CHAPTER 80
PANSY

King's End, Minnesota
Saturday, July 15

I make my own tea. This, I insist upon. Jack hovers, but I don't let him close enough to help. I pull vials with unbroken seals from the pantry, run the water myself, and watch while steam coils in the air.

With this last, I hope that adage is true that a watched pot never boils. Perhaps we, the world, everything can remain like this, perpetually waiting for my tea to brew.

Of course the water boils. I suspect that at the end of the world, time moves very quickly indeed.

The tea steeps, and Jack makes me some toast. I doubt you can poison toast, so I trust him with this. I train my gaze on Mortimer, who's standing with arms crossed over his chest, a petulant frown on his face. I have so many questions, but the one that springs from my mouth surprises even me.

"Why don't you like Henry?"

Mort gives a dismissive snort, as if the answer is far too obvious.

"You didn't grow up in the Enclave, in Seattle." His expression turns sour. "You didn't grow up with Darnelle."

What that has to do with it, I'm not sure, but Mort isn't finished.

"Oh, he loves his rules and his protocols, but he doesn't believe they apply to him."

I'm pretty sure Mort just described himself. Jack's gaze touches mine, and I catch the barest hint of an eyeroll.

"Jesus, you should've heard my old man over the years," Mort continues, warming to the subject. "It was constant. I mean *constant*. 'Why can't you be more like the Darnelle boy?'"

Oh. A sudden sharp pain stabs my heart, despite everything Mort has done, has kept from me. Living with something like that? I can't imagine it. Yes, my mother always encouraged me to appear unremarkable.

She never made me feel that way.

"The man is an insufferable prick," he adds, as if this is the last word on the subject.

And I don't know if Mort means his father, Henry, or both.

I try to carry the tea things upstairs myself, but Jack insists on helping. His eyes are so sad that I relent. We're in my room when he speaks, and his voice is a match for his eyes.

"Pansy, what's going on?"

I don't know what to tell him.

"Mort's lying," he adds. "I know he is."

"I know he is, too." And it hurts my heart all over again.

"And Gwyneth?" Jack shakes his head. "I don't understand anything about Gwyneth."

I'm certain no one does.

Jack lets out a long breath, as if he's afraid to touch this next subject. "What's Botten after?"

I suppose this question makes sense, that Jack's ability would lead him to the culprit in all this.

"Because I know it's something, but I can't tell what. Only that it tastes wrong. It tastes like revenge. Mort said something about a gateway, something Botten told him. But it isn't the truth." Jack pushes his hands through his hair and then stares toward the ceiling, as if he can find all the answers there. "I doubt Mort knows the truth."

Jack's right, of course, even if I can't articulate why, as if Botten's curse extends to me as well. Then the memory of his voice makes my heart skitter.

A wild rose for our wild Rose.

That offer, palm outstretched, the seductive lilt of an invitation. Had he expected my mother to accept that offer, to betray Harry Darnelle? Botten was presenting her with the world, crowning her his queen.

And she refused.

Dread fills my stomach, and I sniff, just a bit, but it's enough to alarm Jack.

"Oh, god, Pansy, sit, sit." He urges me toward the bed, and I relent again because it's easier this way.

"It's okay," I tell him. "Just an aftershock."

After a good ten minutes of fussing, I convince him that all I want is sleep. He's at the door when I call out to him.

"Maybe you should head back to Seattle. Fly standby if you have to."

"You mean tonight?"

I nod. He hasn't asked me what I saw when I was unconscious, and he won't. But a sudden steel invades his gaze. He raises his chin as if he can taste fleeting visions of things to come.

"I will if you will."

"I can't."

"Then I can't, either."

The sadness in his eyes pierces me. Then, with resolve, my best friend turns and shuts the door behind him.

THE TEA in my cup is the perfect temperature for drinking, but I resist the urge to gulp it down. I brewed one of my mother's most potent recipes, and I don't need it coming right back up. Tiny sips, the herbs tangy against my tongue.

The potion works. It will keep me sharp, keep me focused, keep me awake for the next six hours. After that? Well, after that, it might not matter anymore.

With the bedroom door locked—I don't need Mort bursting in at an inopportune moment—I head for the closet. I plan to pull out the memory box, but the disarray stops me short. Sweaters and shoes shoved to one side, lids on the file boxes askew. Someone has conducted a very hasty and somewhat casual search of my closet, the file boxes in particular.

Someone who clearly doesn't care if I notice or not.

I crouch and inch closer, inspecting the ransacked files, observing the spilled photographs, and plucking the single strand of blond hair caught on the cardboard corner of one box. A strand of hair that is, mind you, far too long to be Mortimer's.

What, if any, photographs are missing, I can't tell. Some, certainly. But I don't have time to sort through the mess. What I want is the memory box, which is still tucked in its corner, flush against the back wall.

It's only when I'm seated cross-legged on my bed, fingers clutching a lock pick, that I notice that someone has been here before me, too. Henry's efforts left the brass around the lock pristine. Now, several scratches mar the surface.

My lock-picking skills reside somewhere between Henry's excellent ones and those of the person who gouged the front of the memory box. Again, did they think I wouldn't notice?

I shut my eyes and pull in a breath. In the grand scheme of things, does it matter? Because I don't think they found what they were looking for, the same way Henry and I didn't. Because sometime between Henry leaving and my tea water boiling, the reason why memories are precious and I should keep them close came to me.

The lock springs open on my fifth try. With care, I remove the photo albums, wondering what Gwyneth Worthington-Wells made of my prom and if it captivated her as much as it did Henry. Somehow, I doubt it.

I run my fingers around the inside edges of the box, pushing gently against the base. One corner gives ever so slightly before it pops open to reveal a false bottom.

There, in my mother's hand, is a letter addressed to me.

CHAPTER 81
OPHELIA

King's End, Minnesota
Saturday, July 15

This part never changes. Although to be fair, this particular event has never happened at an intersection in King's End. Ophelia wonders about that, about this public display of aggression. But Botten stands there, leaning against the passenger side of an SUV while three Enclave agents take turns roughing up Henry.

Henry has made his fair share of enemies on his way up the Enclave career ladder. Certainly, Botten wasn't short on volunteers for this particular task. No doubt there was a waitlist.

After the first blow, Gwyneth half emerges from her car, fingers curled around the door as if she needs the physical support. When Botten points a finger at her, the command clear, she defies him. But when Henry meets her gaze and gives his head a tiny shake, she complies and tucks herself back inside.

A moment later, one of the agents splits open Henry's cheekbone with a left hook. Granted, that agent also suffers a fractured hand. Henry is stoic while the other man howls in pain.

Serves you right.

Ophelia hovers next to the man, whispering sharp words in his ear. He blinks in confusion. The pain, she thinks, opens a passageway. He can't quite hear her or comprehend what she says. Still, she's an unnerving presence in this unfair fight. He remains crouched, hand tucked against his chest as if he's tapped out of this particular bout.

The remaining two are brutes, the sort who enjoy the more violent duties of an agent's job, the sort you point at a problem and hope for the best.

Right now, Henry is that problem.

"Not too rough, boys," Botten says, gaze on his cuticles, supreme unconcern in his voice. "I do need him conscious."

The benign-sounding words send shivers of ice through Ophelia. This, too, hasn't changed. Worry churns inside her. Have all her efforts been fruitless? Do all paths eventually come to a single point? This, right here, Henry beaten down, physically and then emotionally.

"You're going to need more than that," Henry says, oddly calm, as if all Botten needs is an extra helping of mashed potatoes.

Botten condescends to look at Henry. "Do you imagine I haven't considered that?"

Henry wipes away blood with the back of his hand. "I imagine you have."

The two brutes move forward and grab Henry by the arms, but otherwise, they're frozen by this strange conversation. To be honest, so is Ophelia. Words are always exchanged between these two men, true. Henry's sometimes involve more blood and teeth. Botten's are predictable to the point that Ophelia wants to tune them out.

"So disappointing." Botten shakes his head in mock chagrin. "You could've gone far, my boy. Such a simple task I set before you. And yet, you always falter at those moral junctures. So like your father that way. We wouldn't be standing here now if not for him."

Botten knows, better than most, Henry's weak spot. That weak spot is Harrison Darnelle, and the uncertainty in Henry's mind about his father and what happened here in King's End thirty years ago. Had his father succumbed to the lure of a gateway, wanted power the way Botten did and still does?

In all the paths Ophelia has traveled, this blow always lands and lands hard.

But Henry stands there now as if Botten has spewed nonsense at him.

Ophelia swirls around Henry, battering those two brutes at his side. To no avail, but she takes great pleasure in trying.

Botten inclines his head. The agent on the right delivers a sucker punch to Henry's gut. The air whooshes from him, and Ophelia is blown backward. Henry gasps for breath, knees buckling beneath him. But then he stands and raises his chin.

Botten frowns, furrows deep on his brow, as if he can't quite discern why things aren't going according to his plan. Ophelia wonders if he can sense all those other paths and intuits that this one isn't quite right, isn't delicious enough.

"Your father was a weakling," Botten says, trying a different tack. "Always doing some woman's bidding. Rose. Miranda. It hardly seemed to matter as long as Harry Darnelle had a mommy to tell him what to do."

Henry tilts his head as if he's truly considering what Botten has said, as if the man's words are worth anything. Botten, seeing he's caught Henry's attention, continues.

"Your father was a sad, pathetic, craven man who gave up everything. For what? So he might live vicariously through you? Tell me, how did that work out?"

Ophelia boils with outrage on Henry's behalf. She wants to beat her fists against Botten, kick him in the shins repeatedly. She swoops around, gathers speed, and shoots straight through the man. But Botten has warmed to this subject—indeed, he's been planning this moment for ages—and her presence has no effect.

"He never met a decision he didn't want to delay. Gummed up

the entire Enclave with procedural nonsense. A man of action?" Botten scoffs, the sound dismissive. "How he got that reputation is beyond me. Then again, Rose was always at his side, picking up the slack."

Henry is stoic, so like his father that fear thrums through Ophelia's veins. She knows the photographs, the evidence of his father's other—possibly happier—life have planted seeds of doubt in Henry's mind. The before and after is *so* stark, she might wonder as well. Who was Harry Darnelle? Was he the man his son always believed him to be?

Panicked, she flits back to Henry and swoops around his head.

Don't listen to him. Don't listen to him. This isn't true. It can't be true.

"How he made principal field agent is anyone's guess. Do you know how he got that scar on his neck? Do you? Oh, it's not a pretty story. Then again, Rose was there. Did she tell you about it, about him, about his incompetence?"

Each time through the loop, the mention of his father's scar shatters something inside her brother, something fragile, already on the edge of splintering. Why that and not all the other garbage Botten's been spewing, she's not sure. But it always works. The fear in her veins turns to sludge. Watching her brother break this one last time may break her.

Something wars in Henry's expression. His gaze has never left Botten's face, but now he glances away as if he's hiding something, something that looks like a smile.

"My father," Henry says, his voice full of conviction, "was a good man."

Ophelia doesn't see Botten signal for another blow, but this punch sends Henry to the ground. This time, he doesn't get back up. The agents approach, one aiming a field boot at Henry's stomach, the other at his head. Ophelia's heart thrums, and the monitors back in Seattle scream. She knows what this blow does to Henry, or, more accurately, to his mind. This is the killing blow. This blow steals his clever, astute, and marvelous mind.

Ophelia can't bear to watch.

"Enough!" Gwyneth has rounded the front of the sedan, cell phone clutched in her hand, finger poised to dial.

Everyone stills at the sound of her voice, one full of outrage and the absolute certainty that no one defies a Worthington-Wells.

"Stop right now, or I'm calling 911." Gwyneth shoots Botten a glare, and then her gaze travels this very public intersection. "Assuming, of course, that someone hasn't already." That icy eyebrow and chilling smile come next. "Enjoy explaining this to a small-town police chief."

Ophelia flutters, not daring to hope. Yes, it's true that Gwyneth, on occasion, has tried to intervene. Often, she's too late, stepping in only after the blow that leaves Henry with a traumatic brain injury, his mind muddled, unable to think, slow to react.

Botten scrutinizes the area as if, only now, he's realized that, in his arrogance, he's let things slip. Then he assesses Gwyneth and the threat she poses. Will she make that call?

Oh, undoubtedly.

A crafty grin splits his face. Botten holds up his hands in a gesture that says, *Yes, boys, it's been fun, but let's wrap this up.*

They drag Henry into that second car, his feet scraping against the asphalt. Deliberately, they knock his skull against the doorframe before shoving him into the backseat. He's sandwiched between those two brutish agents, and there is no escape, not that he appears conscious enough to try. Botten heads for the sedan, the agent with the fractured hand hobbling after him.

The cars swing around, speed past Gwyneth, and head down the street toward the housing development.

Gwyneth remains at the stop sign. Her gaze travels in the opposite direction. She peers at the road that leads to the center of town and the exit onto the interstate. She could be at the airport in an hour, Ophelia thinks, less if she floors it. And Gwyneth would most definitely floor it.

Instead, her presumptive sister-in-law leans across the driver's seat and digs out a second phone from that silver-sided briefcase. She pecks out a quick message—one Ophelia can't see, never mind read—and tucks the phone away once again, the picture of efficiency.

Then Gwyneth Worthington-Wells gets behind the wheel, executes a precise three-point turn, and drives after Henry.

CHAPTER 82
PANSY

"Pansy, Pansy. Are you awake?"

Why Jack is bothering to whisper, I'm not sure. He wants to wake me. Maybe I shouldn't be feigning sleep. My hand rests on the letter my mother wrote, tucked beneath my pillow. Her words play in my head over and over again. Her voice, so close, so strong, it's like having her here again. I want to remain in that space, warm, cozy, and unmoving.

But I must move; I must appear unremarkable. I've been practicing for this moment—and the ones to follow—all my life. Waking up groggy after an episode with the Sight is part of that.

"Pansy?" Jack still speaks in a whisper, his voice tender and worried. "Are you okay?"

"Hm?" I make a big show of rolling over. "Jack?" I lift onto one elbow. "What's wrong?"

"Mort's gone."

This I know. Mortimer never fails to hit every creaking floorboard on his way down the stairs. While he can manage stealth, he clearly didn't bother to an hour ago. In his wake is the aftertaste of betrayal.

"He left without saying anything, without even waking me up."

The anguish in Jack's voice makes my heart ache. While I understand why Mort involved Jack, I dearly wish he hadn't, that my best friend was tucked safely back in Seattle. Then again, depending on how all this ends, even that might not keep him safe.

"I don't like what's going on," Jack says. "We should leave. I know you said you couldn't, but things are different now."

I'm sitting up, nodding like I agree with him. He's crouching next to the bed, field gear on, umbrella strapped cross-body.

"I think Mort hid your umbrella, or maybe took her." He touches the handle of his own umbrella, and it shudders. "We've spent the last half an hour searching."

"You won't find her."

She is in stealth mode, that's all I can tell; it's the safest thing for her and me. No one will think to use her to find me. No one will think to deactivate her permanently, either.

"Let me get changed," I say.

"So, you'll go?"

The hope in Jack's voice nearly crushes me, but I nod. Since the only light in the room filters in from the hallway, I hope it's convincing. I palm my mother's letter, slip from bed, and ease into the closet, shutting the door behind me.

Back against the door, I ease the letter from its envelope. One last time. I can read her words, let them soak in and flow through my veins. I can read her words and know, absolutely, that rule seven on her last list is true.

Always know that you are loved.

My mother did everything in her power not only to tell me that but also to make certain I'd live as well.

CHAPTER 83
ROSE

King's End, Minnesota
Tuesday, May 29 (five years ago)

My Darling Girl,

Every summer, while you're still at the Academy, I write one letter I never mail to you. I tuck it into the false bottom of the memory box and vow not to look at it again. Invariably, the following summer, I do, only to watch it disintegrate into so much ash.

This is your last year and my last chance. Through the front window, I can see my destiny rumble down the road. That backhoe in particular looks ominous. I've done all I could to warn King's End. Sadly, it wasn't enough.

By now, I hope you understand why that is, and why I couldn't sit you down and explain what happened three decades ago between myself, Harry Darnelle, and that third agent. How your mother—unwittingly, it's true—helped unleash a curse on King's End and the world and then barely had the capacity to contain it.

The weight of that can't compare to this: I must ask my own daughter to risk her life to fix the mistake I made.

I will never forgive myself for that.

I imagine you have questions, any number of which I can't answer directly. I will do my best to point the way, to guide you through this journey fraught with ambition, avarice, and malice. For yes, I was ambitious, as was Harry. We were greedy for a different world, a better one. Perhaps we were arrogant as well, believing ourselves the ones who could bring that about.

As for that malice? I'd like to think neither of us brought that into the equation.

It's perhaps not the most pressing question, but I suspect it's one you have. Yes, I was deeply in love with Harry Darnelle. If Henry is anything like his father—and I imagine he is—oh, my dear girl, you may be in for it. Darnelle men have an undeniable charm.

As for your father? Ah, your father. Combative and prickly, fiercely loyal, and, in short, a born curmudgeon. And yet, there's no one I'd rather spend eternity with. Indeed, I'll have an eternity to convince him of that.

Given half a chance, your father would have upended the Enclave. Let's be real. He would've destroyed it and brought forces from his dimension to do so. That, however, wouldn't solve the issue in King's End. What was put into motion must be completed. With each passing year, the hunger for that completion grows. Fortunately, the instigator in all this—yes, I'm choosing my words carefully and not naming names—doesn't know what you are.

You are the key to everything.

Do you remember the willow tree and that ill-fated picnic with Daniel? That was a trial run. Strange as it seems, that was the Sight, preparing you, arming you for the events to come. I don't know if you've visited the willow since then. I wouldn't blame you for avoiding it. I have, however, returning there after you left for the Academy that summer.

The space around the willow tree was my first and most

successful experiment in King's End. Perhaps because the fissures in the cemetery are so small. Indeed, if those were the only fissures here, King's End would not be a permanent post. But do you remember how it felt there, secured in the willow's embrace? The calm, the peace? I was able to bend the Screamers there, redirect them back in on themselves, in a sense, creating a loop. In doing so, I created tranquility.

When the Sight attacked you there, it was showing you what's possible. The space around the willow is now even more tranquil. You did that. You healed those fissures even further. You can continue to heal them, all the ones I've bent and looped. Oh, my dear girl, what we could have done together, given half a chance.

However, there's a catch. There always is, isn't there, especially with the Sight. Do you remember how the blood flow stopped only when you let go of Daniel? Remember that feeling, because you must be willing to let go of everything, and I do mean everything, everything and everyone you cherish.

The other catch is this: You can't appear willing. Instead, you must appear clueless and, yes, unremarkable. The instigator in all this will expect many things from you: fear, hatred (you are your mother's daughter, after all), incomprehension. This person will not expect obedience, never mind willingness. Appearing clueless is your armor; appearing unremarkable is your shield.

As for your sword? You know what to do, because I showed you myself. It was you there that day, back when the housing development was still a meadow. Our silent witness that all three of us have been searching for ever since. Harry believes it might be Ophelia Connolly, as does the instigator in all this. Harry is doing everything in his power to protect her.

I know better, because I know who your father is. What you accomplished goes far beyond power fueled by a single dimension. The first time I coaxed you back to consciousness, I knew that I'd already met you. On that day, in the meadow, you not only saved Harry Darnelle and King's End. You may have saved the world.

I knew I would have to prepare you, train you, and, in the end, be willing to let you go. Your father knew what was to come as well. He loved you so fiercely that he gave up life in both dimensions on the minuscule chance you might survive all this.

The end won't be easy for me. This is also something your father saw, and it nearly broke him. I hope it won't break you.

Now, I must trust that the Sight will offer up the memory of the Mother's Day event at the community center, where our efforts left us sticky with decoupage, and you found the secret compartment so delightful. I must trust that the Sight will lead you to these words in time.

As with most everything else, I'm giving Adele the memory box for safekeeping. That way, I won't be tempted to open the secret compartment and check to see if this letter remains, even if that means never seeing the other items again.

But my days are short, and I'd rather spend them with you, in the here and now. Even if by the time you return home, I won't be fully myself. No, that backhoe won't physically slice through me, but I'll feel it as if it had. In a few weeks, King's End will feel it as well.

My darling Pansy-Girl, my sweetest of flowers, know that you brought light to my life and joy to my heart. If I must leave you with this unspeakable burden, also know that I leave you with every ounce of my love.

CHAPTER 84
PANSY

We're barely off my front porch when half a dozen Enclave agents surround us. Yes, we could've left by the back door, and maybe should have. Then again, three agents are currently there in the garden, trampling the lavender and rosemary. The results would most likely have been the same.

But the front door? That way, someone's doorbell camera—most likely Guy's—will pick up the commotion. The Sight insists this is a very good thing. For once, I agree.

Jack is howling, not caring if he wakes the neighborhood. Or perhaps that's his goal. I can't shush him. No one can. It takes a punch to the face for that.

I rush to his side and help him sit up. He rubs a hand across his jaw, wincing, spitting out a few blood-laden curses. The three agents from the backyard round the corner of the house. Jack looks to them and then the other six. His thoughts ring as clear as mine. Really?

Nine agents? Just for me? I blink a couple of times and feel the trickle of blood before the question pops into my mind.

What would clueless and scared Pansy Little do?

What *have* I done? For there are choices to make, and certainly other dimensions where I made those choices.

"Why do they want you?" Jack scoots closer, and we huddle together. "Mort said it was something your mom and Henry's father did, that they damaged a gateway. But that's not quite right, is it?"

"No, that's not quite right." My words come out stiff and formal. I suspect this is all I can, and should, say to Jack. Oh, how I wish he'd left, was already at the airport. I wonder if there's a version of these events when he does leave.

The night around us is silent and still. A few chirps from crickets. A single bark from a dog a few blocks away. Typical of July, the air is oppressive, and sweat sprouts along my spine. Light from the street lamps illuminates Jack's expression. And I know.

There is never a version of events where he leaves me.

None of the Enclave agents have done more than trap us in a circle. They aren't even speaking, which is strange. One agent presses a finger to an earpiece, tilts his head, but otherwise doesn't move. My gaze meets Jack's, and I see the thoughts churning. Yes, these agents are waiting for something, or, more likely, someone. They don't dare do much more than keep us surrounded while waiting for their next set of orders.

"I'll create a distraction," he says now, rubbing a hand over his mouth as if he's wiping away blood. "You get the hell out of here."

Jack bursts forward with speed and strength that belies his injury. I don't waste this effort. I do what scared Pansy Little would do.

I run.

A startled shout goes up. Footfalls pound behind me. I make a point of leading my pursuers straight past Guy and Milo's place, right through the line of sight of the doorbell camera. Then I use my knowledge of King's End to my advantage and cut through everyone's gardens and backyards.

Someone gets tangled in a tire swing. Someone else hurtles into a raised garden bed. I dash down an alleyway and shove a recycling bin into the space behind me. That crash is undeniably satisfying in a way it probably shouldn't be. Still, I savor that tiny triumph.

Up ahead, a dark ribbon of asphalt bisects the alley. If I make it there, I have options. Hide long enough, but not too long. Will Botten proceed without me? Without Henry? Assuming, of course, he doesn't already have Henry. I swipe a quick hand beneath my nose. The Sight offers nothing except the reminder that Botten has our blood and that Jack has already spilled some of it. And that I am, annoyingly, the key to everything.

But if what my mother showed me in the meadow is correct, *I* can't proceed without Botten. Whether I heal the wound or Botten ends the world doesn't matter; we both need the ritual, and we both need Henry. Oh, what a strange and sordid symbiotic relationship this is.

Before I can decide my next steps, a sedan pulls onto the road, blocking the alley and my way out. I skid, arms flailing. Two agents spring from the car and give chase. I dart into another yard, the thwack and whoosh of a sprinkler catching me off guard. My toes hit wet grass, and I slip before catching myself. My feet churn up mud, my thigh muscles scream, and I inhale a few drops of water. My lungs burn and wheeze.

I push through, losing one agent in a tangle of hose and then another who slides into a play structure. One agent remains, and he's gaining on me. I don't dare glance back, but I can feel his bulk. So few people are this large and this fast, but I try not to dwell on it. I try not to think at all. When I do, my heart sinks and my legs feel sluggish.

But it's no use. His arms clamp around my chest. He lifts me from the ground. I kick hard, striking his shin and earning an obscenity. It's then, of course, I know for certain. The man who captured me?

Mortimer.

He tries to calm me, Mortimer-style. One arm traps me against his chest, and the other holds my head. His urgent whisper is hot in my ear.

"Pansy-Girl, listen, before the others get here. Everything depends on your cooperation."

Yes, obviously. I fight on, squirming in his grasp. Oh, he is too damn strong. I'm about to bite down, with plenty of teeth, when his hand clamps over my mouth. He knows me too damn well. No wonder he was the one to catch me.

"I understand this is scary," Mort is saying, "and that Rose may have not told you the truth. I know it's hard to believe that she may have done something terribly wrong. We need your help to fix things. All we're doing here is setting things right."

He lifts his hand as if he's certain I won't bite.

I do, with words instead of teeth. "How do you set things right with secrets and lies?"

Mort falters, but only for a moment. Other agents approach now, a few limping, a few others with vengeance in their expressions. A couple are drenched. This, too, pleases me more than perhaps it should.

"Let me deal with her," Mort calls out.

They back off, but not so far that, if Mort lets go, I can make a break for it.

"Are you calm now?" he says to me, grip still tight around my chest.

"You could always make sure and drug me again."

"I'm serious, Pansy. This is no joke."

"That wasn't, either."

His sigh is so massive that it resonates through my ribcage and all the way down to my feet. His grip is as oppressive as the night, and I can't pull in a full breath.

"Listen to me," he says as if he's talking to a small child and not an overly bright one, either. "I'm going to let you go, you're going to cooperate, and I'm going to show you why."

"I'll run," I say with a lift of my chin.

"No, you won't." He pulls out his phone and speed-dials a number. "Put him on."

And there, on the screen of Mortimer's phone, is Henry.

I let myself go limp then, because that's what clueless Pansy Little would do. Because that fits the narrative. Isolated Pansy Little with a tremendous crush on out-of-her-league Henry Darnelle. There he is, her savior, bruised and broken, unaware of the agent recording him.

I can be her. In truth, I don't have to try too hard, not with how injured Henry is. The shock of that makes my heart pound painfully against my ribs. It's only now that my last hope for him blooms bright in my mind and withers: that Gwyneth had sped them straight to the airport.

I don't think there's a scenario where that ever happens, either.

For one intense, excruciating moment, the urge to tell Mort that Jack knows all about this betrayal rushes through me. But the screen of Mort's phone is awash with red. While that's something I suspect only I can see, the image stills the words in my mouth. I don't need to inflict that on Mort, no matter what he's done.

Because I also know this. There isn't a scenario that doesn't involve a great deal of damage, betrayal, and blood.

CHAPTER 85

OPHELIA

King's End, Minnesota
Sunday, July 16

Botten can't help himself. This, Ophelia knows. It's another of those pyrrhic victories that he succumbs to this urge to gloat. Without fail, he always makes his way across the task force's bivouac and enters the tent where they're holding Pansy.

Like the confrontation with Henry, this meeting always happens. Ophelia has seen enough photographs of Rose Little to know that, despite her coloring, Pansy resembles her mother. Here, in the shadow of the olive-drab canvas, the similarity is startling.

So much so that Botten hesitates, the tent flap still clutched in his hand as if he plans to leave rather than enter.

But enter, he does. He always enters the tent, pulls up a folding chair, and sits just out of spitting range of Pansy. After all, the man isn't a fool. However, there is a scenario where he miscalculates the distance.

That's one of Ophelia's favorites.

They always have Pansy secured to a chair, sometimes with zip ties, sometimes with rope. Once, they forgot about her hands, and she greeted Botten with a double middle-finger salute.

This is also one of Ophelia's favorites.

Botten regards Pansy in what is meant to be a judgmental, unnerving manner. He's channeling his Academy headmaster persona, bringing its full weight to bear. While the maneuver certainly works on thirteen-year-olds, it has little effect on the woman who sits across from him now.

Or rather, it shouldn't. Pansy's lip quivers ever so slightly. But she doesn't speak. She never does. Always, it's Botten who initiates the conversation, such as it is.

"I see my evaluation of your skill set was correct and that the talent Agent Darnelle spoke so highly of appears quite absent." His gaze roves in a lewd manner. "Perhaps it was a different sort of talent that had him so enthralled?"

Botten doesn't know Pansy as well as he does Henry. Truthfully, he all but ignored her existence at the Academy. So, this blow? Doesn't land.

Or, again, it *shouldn't*. Pansy looks like she's about to deny the accusation. Then she lowers her eyes to her bound hands.

"My mother said I should do everything I could to pass my exam."

What! Never in all these trips through the loop has Pansy said anything remotely close to this. Where's her strength, her defiance? If nothing else, Pansy always calls Botten on his bullshit. Ophelia is outrage itself. She swirls and swirls and swirls. Her outburst reverberates around the tent with so much force that the canvas shudders.

Botten's attention is pulled upward toward the rippling fabric, but Pansy's gaze never leaves her hands.

"Hm. Interesting," is all he says, but whether he's referring to Pansy's confession or the wayward canvas is hard to say.

Worry churns inside Ophelia. A faraway beep, beep, beep starts up. She tries to clamp down her rampaging anger, her ragged breathing, her bruised and battered heart. This is Pansy's last stand. Why isn't she making the most of it? She's as vulnerable and cowed as a first-year cadet during the intake interview.

The confusion that plays across Botten's features confirms that he, too, is perplexed, or perhaps dissatisfied with this encounter. Taunting Rose Little's daughter is right up there with watching those brutes tag-team Henry. Where is the fiery defiance her mother was so famous for? Why no swearing, no spitting, no double middle-fingers? This is clearly not what Botten expected. It's certainly not what Ophelia expected, either.

This is like poking roadkill with a stick, mildly interesting but hardly worth the time or effort.

Botten heaves a sigh and pushes against his thighs to stand. "You must have been a great disappointment to your mother."

Pansy merely drops her head lower, as if this accusation is too much to bear.

Botten pauses at the tent flap, as if he's waiting for Pansy to meet his gaze one last time. Her shoulders remained hunched, nearly to her ears. She's folded in on herself, defeat and despair swirling around her.

Ophelia wants to weep.

"Try to pull yourself together, my dear. Despite everything, you can still be useful to the Enclave." With that, Botten lets the tent flap close behind him. His voice is light as he calls out to someone across the bivouac, something about sunrise and preparations. His tone, his demeanor, and his entire being radiate triumph.

Now, Ophelia wants to scream. She wants to take Pansy by the shoulders and shake her hard. She wants...

Across the tent, Pansy squirms in her chair. She's muttering something, something that sounds like, "Stop, stop, stop. It's not time yet."

Ophelia swoops across the space, floats next to Pansy. A pattering hits the dirt floor, a light and persistent drip, drip, drip.

Blood.

Pansy is trying to stem the flow as best she can with her bound hands, leaning so the blood doesn't soak her shirt. She frowns and tosses her head as if to shake off the sticky sensation.

Ophelia knows it must itch. She's always hated the feel of blood beneath her nose.

Pansy lifts her head, and a splatter of blood flies through the air and strikes the space where Ophelia hovers. For one brief moment, she is ... not solid; she'll never be solid in this loop. But she catches the hint of her form: a disobedient curl here, a double-knotted boot-lace there. (Even in these visions, Ophelia dresses appropriately; she is currently in full field gear.)

"Ophelia?"

Ophelia nods, and for once, Pansy can see her.

"I'm sorry, I'm sorry. I'm so, so sorry."

You don't have anything to be sorry for.

It occurs to Ophelia that this is the first time that she's seen Pansy's nose bleed at this point. In the other scenarios, in all the terrible times through this loop, it's as if the Sight has deserted Pansy. The Sight is never that capricious, not when it comes to self-preservation.

"All this time," Pansy is saying, "Botten thought it was you, but it was me. And I'm so sorry—"

Shhhh.

Ophelia hushes Pansy with a strength that sends the canvas rippling again. It's a wonder no one in the bivouac notices.

It doesn't matter. He would've come after me anyway.

But it's like Pansy to think of that, to think of her.

"You've seen this how many times?" Pansy is still shaking her head, as if she understands what Ophelia has been through and finds it incomprehensible. "How many times?"

And Ophelia finds she's shaking her head, too, because she doesn't know, has lost count.

All of them. Except this one.

Pansy stares as if Ophelia has painted the words in the air and they linger there.

Except this one. Hope is a cruel, cruel thing, and it has seduced Ophelia far too many times for her to trust it now.

But she can't help herself.

He's going to kill you and Henry.

"Yes, I know."

He'll have a knife.

"I know that too."

He always goes for Henry first. Always.

Pansy shuts her eyes, but not before a single tear escapes and travels down her cheek. "I know."

Ophelia wonders just how much the Sight has shown Pansy. Before she can ask, Pansy exhales a breath, brings her bound hands to her face, and scrubs her knuckles against her cheek and beneath her nose. Then she looks directly at Ophelia.

"I know what I have to do."

With these words, Pansy smiles, but it's not triumphant, not arrogant. It's the battle-scarred smile of a woman who's about to push a piece across a chess board, a move that will result in checkmate.

If Botten had seen *this* expression on Pansy's face, he wouldn't have left the tent so cavalierly. He wouldn't be filling the bivouac with the sound of his whistling and dreams of things to come. He wouldn't, Ophelia realizes, have let down his guard.

Oh, yes. Hope is cruel, indeed.

CHAPTER 86
PANSY

King's End, Minnesota
Sunday, July 16

They come for me just before sunrise. I've tried to kick dirt over the splotches of blood, but there's nothing I can do about the stains on my shirt.

No one, notices, though. Mort isn't among the agents sent to haul me up and out of the tent. He would have certainly questioned both the blood and me. But no, Botten has sent near strangers, agents from Academy classes before and after mine. Which, considering what he's planning, makes sense. No allies, no friendly faces, no one to intervene. To them, this blood is merely collateral damage.

The trek to the housing development is rough. My hands are still bound. Apparently, protocol demands that we walk rather than ride in one of the many SUVs and sedans about the bivouac. But it gives me time to think and to sniff back the blood that seems to build. The dam is about to burst, and I must be careful.

Because I still don't know if this will work. The Sight never let me hear the words of the ritual, so Botten must speak those. I have mere seconds between that and the knife that will find Henry's jugular. This is something the Sight insists will happen if I don't act fast enough.

The image of that buckles me with terror. I stumble. The two agents gripping my arms jerk me upright so my feet skim the gravel road for several steps.

The oppressive night is slowly transforming into an equally oppressive and brilliantly red dawn. The sunrise stains the entire area, even the space beneath the Camelot Lots sign. Mosquitoes natter in my ears and light on my neck, attracted by the blood, no doubt. They probe the skin, and while this is the least of my problems, I give my head a shake just as we pass through the gate.

One, two, three drops of blood strike the ground.

The earth rumbles beneath us.

"What the f—" one agent begins.

"Keep moving," another one snaps.

We round the showcase home, and my gaze lands on the fissure there. The expanse is deep, an endless gray, but rimmed with teeth. I blink, and they vanish. No one else seems alarmed, so perhaps it's only my state of mind, or the Sight. But no, there, from the corner of my eye.

Teeth. A double row. So very ravenous.

I think of my mother's words: *With each passing year, the hunger for that completion grows.*

The gateway must be very hungry, then. Perhaps by feeding it our blood, Jack was essentially offering it an appetizer. The epicenter itself is beneath the showcase home. Short of total demolition or raising the house off its foundation, it's still inaccessible. But this current fissure is like a tentacle, grasping, reaching. It's more than enough to do the job, to seize the sacrifice and sate its hunger.

Botten and Henry are already standing at the fissure's edge. I'm being paraded forward like a reluctant bride in some perverse marriage ceremony. It strikes me then. That's what this is, an unholy sort of marriage. Of course, Botten sacrifices Henry—because Henry is every inch the man his father was. Botten needs to rid himself of this constant reminder that this better man exists.

Woven into that is another layer. Once upon a time, Botten wanted my mother, wanted her power along with that of the gateway. One is inexorably linked to the other. Did he ever love her? I don't think that matters.

My mother wasn't entirely wrong when she told me to give Botten what he expects. But I went one better. Maybe it was the Sight, or Jack's words about revenge. I gave Botten what he needed. Deep down, what he needed, *craved*, was proof that Rose Little lived a sad and pathetic life.

I presented him with that, gift-wrapped in the form of her sad, pathetic daughter.

This might be the only advantage I have. Botten remains within striking range of Henry. My heart skitters and I waver, legs wobbly once again. One of the agents jerks me by the elbow, and I stagger forward.

"Not too close," Botten instructs. "We don't want her tumbling in."

In the air hangs the unspoken: *Not yet.*

The agents position me opposite the two men. My mind scrambles, sorting out the choreography of how Botten plans to sacrifice us both. That, too, is part of his revenge.

Henry first, yes. That's obvious.

Across from me, Henry appears devastated but determined. Up close, his bruises are the same brilliant red as the sunrise. The sorrow in his eyes shoots through me. But that's all I see. No confusion. No befuddlement. No traumatic brain injury. The Sight has shown me that this isn't always the case. Something about Henry's condition feels like hope.

Let me. He mouths these words. Despite everything, the principal field agent is still in place. And yes, Henry would sacrifice himself to save me and the world. But that's not going to work. Even if it could? I'm not as heroic as all that. I can't sacrifice Henry.

The dam builds, and I sniff. We are very close now, but not close enough. Botten must speak the ritual. So I do the one thing no one should do when staring down her own death, never mind the end of the world.

I wink at Henry.

No, I certainly haven't mastered the sexier-than-it-has-a-right-to-be variety, but Henry's eyes widen. Then he schools his expression, churning out a schoolmaster frown.

Botten dismisses me with a shake of his head and pulls a sheet of paper from his trouser pocket. I don't think he needs this; he's no doubt memorized the words, but he makes a show of reviewing the text, running a finger down the page. He begins, his voice deep and sonorous, spreading out across the housing development.

Agents on the perimeter bow their heads as if in prayer. Some, I suspect, even have their eyes closed. A second row stands with their backs turned, umbrellas unfurled, although the Screamers are dormant, or perhaps only waiting. But the setup is deliberate, a way for Botten to ensure there are no witnesses. Or at least very few.

The last of Botten's words ring out across the space. His chest swells with satisfaction, and he lets the paper drift to the ground. It flutters like a dying leaf before being sucked into the fissure. The ground undulates, a rise and fall beneath our feet that feels like impatience.

Hungry, indeed.

Unencumbered, Botten reaches for the knife, the one unobtrusively attached to his belt. He unfastens the catch, the sound so loud in a morning without birdsong. Before he can extract the blade, I speak.

"Are you sure you're ready?" My words still his hand.

Botten glances toward me but doesn't respond.

Once I'm certain I've caught his attention, I give him my most beatific smile. "Don't you first need to pick a wild rose for your wild Rose?"

He grips the knife's handle, knuckles white and protruding. Slowly, he turns from Henry and toward me. "What did you say?"

I continue to smile as blood streams from my nose. It's not a gush, not yet, but the dam has fractured.

Comprehension lights Botten's eyes, followed by a wrath so vicious, I take a step back. His expression contorts, but he calculates the distance between us. No, he's not fool enough to jump the fissure, but he unsheathes the knife.

Then, as I hoped, Reginald Botten comes for me.

CHAPTER 87
HENRY

King's End, Minnesota
Sunday, July 16

Pansy's wink nearly did him in. Made his mind blank in confusion. Made his skull pound.

Made his heart soar.

What had she seen? Something crucial. Something devastating, perhaps. Something that triggered Botten and gave them a fighting chance. And that wash of obscene red? Somewhere, in the back of his mind, he'd expected that.

The key to everything. Henry wanted to damn everyone. Reginald Botten. Max Monroe. Rose Little. Even his father. Everyone who'd brought them to this moment and forced Pansy into this role.

Before he could act, a massive blur flew forward, an impressive combination of speed and bulk, someone with a cobalt blue umbrella strapped cross-body, the canopy reverberating with fury.

"No!" Henry shouted, but it was too late.

Mortimer Connolly barreled into Botten. The knife flew skyward, spun end over end, and landed wide of the fissure. With a roar that spoke of betrayal, of anguish, Mort used the full force of his strength and weight to send the older man plummeting into that gray and endless expanse.

An angry tremor rumbled beneath their feet. Shouts went up. A few agents simply bolted from the housing development. Another quake knocked Mort off balance and sent him stumbling toward the fissure.

He teetered at the edge. His arms flailed, boots skidded against loose dirt. Henry lunged forward and stretched out his bound hands. Mort looped an arm through his. For one breathless moment, they hung suspended, not quite defying gravity. Henry's back, his ribs, his gut all protested the move, but he yanked, and they went tumbling across the sparse grass.

Mort panted, face down, chest heaving, obscenities flowing despite lack of breath. Henry pushed to his knees, held up his bound hands. Someone—he wasn't sure who—sliced through the rope. He scrambled to his feet and started forward, certain he was too late.

In the moments since Botten had plunged from view, the fissure hadn't grown, but Henry didn't dare jump it. Pansy was on the other side, on hands and knees, blood drenching the earth in front of her.

Oh, no, no, no. The ground rumbled again, shaky and unstable. Henry did a quick survey, calculating, assessing. A groan emerged from the fissure, almost human-like. The start of the implosion, then? But no, the fissure itself was no larger. What, then? He dismissed the question and raced for Pansy.

By the time he reached her, she was already pale, those dark eyes impossibly huge. The soil was soggy with her blood. He knelt to gather her close, but she shook her head.

"Watch me," she said, her words little more than air.

She took Botton's knife and sliced her palm. Henry jerked forward, intent on grabbing it from her. But she flipped the blade around and handed him the hilt.

"You must be willing. That's the only way it will work." The pleading in her eyes nearly did him in once again. "You must be willing." With that, she planted her bloody palm against the earth.

He didn't hesitate. He didn't think. He gave himself over to the impulse to follow this woman wherever she might lead him.

Henry wiped the blade against his trousers.

Then, with the knife's edge pristine, he sliced through his own palm.

CHAPTER 88
PANSY

King's End, Minnesota
Sunday, July 16

"Pansy ... Pansy ... Pansy..."

From somewhere very far away, Henry's voice infiltrates my thoughts. Warm, lovely, coaxing, but beyond my reach.

"It's over. You can come back now."

Can I? He is so very far away, and all I can do is float. It's dark here, but not frightening.

"Pansy, please. Come back to me."

I want to tell him that I'll try, but I don't want to lie. I never want to lie to Henry.

"Come back."

The misery in his voice is almost too much. But I must let everything go, everything I cherish. And I must do so willingly.

So I say goodbye to King's End, to Adele, Guy, Milo, and Matilda. I say goodbye to my frivolous and fierce pink polka-dotted umbrella. She is somewhere nearby, shaking with sorrow. Mort and Jack—I let them go as well, like after every summer at the Academy, the sensation both sweet and bitter. I want to tell everyone that this is a journey I must make on my own, but I don't think anyone can hear me.

Last of all, I say goodbye to Henry. I want to reassure him that this isn't his fault; he did nothing wrong. I know he won't believe me. He's too stubborn, too honorable.

Instead, I let him slip away, bit by bit, until all that's left is the echo of his voice, those soft, coaxing words I must refuse.

Come back.

CHAPTER 89
OPHELIA

Seattle, Washington
Sunday, July 16

Ophelia opens her eyes. Gradually, at first, a soft blinking against a nightlight. Then, all at once, they fly open. The ceiling of her childhood bedroom looms above her, speckled with glow-in-the-dark constellations she painted after her first summer at the Academy. The ceiling she refused to repaint even after outgrowing things like artificial starlight and boy bands.

So, yes, Ophelia recognizes the view. She certainly doesn't understand it.

Her mouth is parched. She tries to roll over and finds she can't. Her muscles revolt, insisting that she hasn't done this sort of activity for a very long time and what's the sense in starting now.

An insistent beep, beep, beep sounds somewhere behind her. What an annoying sound. She grimaces and then notices how dry her skin feels.

Footfalls approach. A soothing voice follows.

"Hang in there, lovey, give me a minute, and I'll..."

The voice and footfalls come to an abrupt halt.

"Lovey?" It's a sweet voice, but now it's filled with near terror. There's a grappling, a small burst of static, and then a frantic, "Mrs. Connolly? Mrs. Connolly, are you awake? Please, come quickly."

Bare seconds later, a commotion comes from down the hallway. A presence crashes into the room, nearly smacks against the bed. Now her mother looms over her, hair mussed, dark circles beneath her eyes, an old tattered robe tossed over her shoulders. Ophelia can't remember a time when her mother has been so disheveled. It's as if she's coming apart at the seams.

"Ophelia?" Her mother's voice cracks with agony and hope.

She wants to tell her mother to never trust hope, that it's cruel. Except, of course, when it's not.

"If you can hear me, sweetie, blink twice."

She complies. Her mother weeps.

And for the first time in nearly a year, Ophelia Connolly smiles.

CHAPTER 90
MAX

Sometime during the first decade, Max Monroe lost the habit of sleep. He doesn't need to, not here in the in-between. So he's alert when the space shifts, expands, and then collapses again. Another visitor trapped in this realm—a realm of Max's own making, it's true.

For some, this space is a sanctuary. He tends to his caretaker duties and makes certain these visitors are content. For others? This space is a prison. When warranted, Max enables their escape.

But this newest guest? Unexpected, to say the least.

His bed is warm. The woman curled next to him is a miracle that Max still can't allow himself to completely believe. Rose has yet to lose the habit of sleep, so he pretends. And really, if you have an eternity before you, why not spend it in bed? Especially when your companion is the most desirable woman in any dimension.

But today? Today, Max Monroe has something else on his agenda.

"Rose, honey?"

"Hm?"

"I'm going to head out for a bit, pick up some bagels from The King's Larder."

"No, you're not." Her normally crisp voice is soft with sleep and amusement. "You're sneaking off to see Pansy."

Oh, if only that were the case. Max shuts his eyes, lets his mind travel a multitude of paths. He can see many things, many scenarios, many outcomes, it's true. But not everything is available to him. Right now, one of those things is the outcome of that confrontation in King's End.

Still. There is that newest visitor. And that's something.

"I think she's safe," he murmurs, hardly daring to believe it.

"She's with Adele. Of course she's safe."

Max sighs. Some days, he wishes he could immerse himself fully in this fantasy. But on days like today? He smiles, and he knows—without Rose awake to tell him—that it's a feral thing, indeed. He slips from his warm bed, his warm wife.

Max Monroe has a score to settle.

And all the time in all the worlds to do so.

CHAPTER 91
PANSY

King's End, Minnesota
Sunday, July 16

There are voices. But that's all there are. This doesn't alarm me, although maybe it should. Words float in and out, in and out, until, at last, they resolve.

"You kept a cool head in the aftermath. I'm impressed." Mort, I'm nearly certain, although he isn't speaking to me.

"You contributed."

Mort laughs, the sound tinged with sadness. "Ah, Gwennie, we'll make a team player of you yet. Still, I'm not sure when you had time to call for medical backup and a cleanup crew."

"Well, you know, women are better at multi-tasking. And I managed to unearth a bit of leverage along the way. It speeds things up when you can skip echelons."

"Why let a good crisis go to waste?"

"You could say that. Now, before we do this, are you absolutely certain you're the same blood type?"

"Should be in her records, shouldn't it?"

"There's a lot in her records that's erroneous. I don't trust them. I don't trust *him*. And after everything…"

A pause. The air around me is strange, silent, and sorrowful.

Mort coughs out a sigh, the sound full of regret. "Yeah. After everything. How about this." Now his voice perks up. "You might say I couldn't *be* more *positive* about our blood type."

And yes, Mort never lets an opportunity for a joke go to waste.

"Try to be serious."

"I did that once. Didn't take." Another pause, a hiss of breath. "Ow. Damn, you're vicious."

"Thank you."

"How's Darnelle?"

Henry? I want to sit up, find him, make sure he's okay. My body won't comply, like something or someone is holding me down. I concede that something may simply be gravity.

"Stubborn. Refusing treatment until I…"

"Well, what are you waiting for? Tap a vein."

Another pause, but this one is filled with a rush, a wash, a roaring that crashes through me, something hot and most definitely aggressive, something that feels a lot like Mortimer.

"What did you end up telling the High Council?" Mort again.

"That we had an unfortunate incident at a level five hot spot and that one of our most beloved members stumbled upon a portal and vanished."

He snorts. "He may have had a little help, but I suppose that's close to the truth."

"The best lies are."

"You might be overselling it with *most beloved*."

"Hm. Perhaps."

"Half the High Council will be popping champagne corks tonight."

"I might join them."

Oh, and there's that Enclave malice.

"You're not worried about the others, what they might say?" Mort asks.

"What can they say? I mean, without implicating themselves. We were all hand-picked, the best of Botten's Best." This pause is contemplative. "No, it will just be one of those things, like any other Enclave mishap."

"That will dog us the rest of our days."

"Like any other mishap." Gwyneth's voice is unusually precise. "With the after-action review tucked away in the files to gather dust. Just like *Florence*."

My ears prick up at that, but it's not like I'm participating in this conversation, such as it is.

"No one's blackmailing anyone, not over this," she continues. "At worst, we'll have to make awkward small talk at social functions."

"I suppose you're right." Mort gives a curt laugh. "I always wondered why my parents hated Enclave parties."

"Not *all* parties." This response, I'm certain, is too soft and too sly to reach Mort.

"She's coming to," he says.

Am I? I hope so, because I have questions, lots of them. Before I can pry open my eyes, something seductive flows through my veins, mingling with what must be Mort's blood. The sweetness of sleep is too tempting, the weight of it too sure. I forget my questions. I float, in and out, in and out, until I land in a dream.

In my dream, I hear the sounds of camp being struck, the clang of equipment, the rumble of vehicles. In my dream, someone squeezes my hand and places a gentle and reverent kiss on my forehead.

In my dream, someone tells me goodbye.

THERE ARE VOICES. But that's not all there are. Creaking boards, far below on the front porch. Warm sunshine against my eyelids. The yip of a small dog and the robust bark of a larger one.

A doorbell.

My bedroom is bright and cozy. That's startling. Even more so? I'm in bed, also perfectly cozy, wrapped in the cocoon of the comforter. The clock on the nightstand reads 3:05. The only clue something might be amiss—other than waking at three in the afternoon—is the pink medical wrap around the crook of my left elbow and the gauze it's holding in place.

The bell rings again.

I ease from bed, test the floor and my balance, but really, I'm feeling fine. A little groggy. My mouth tastes like cotton and quicksilver. Before the doorbell rings again, I head downstairs.

Belatedly, I think to check a mirror and duck into the powder room beneath the stairs. If I peer closely, the remains of a bruise are still evident. With careful fingers, I probe. The slightest ache, and then it evaporates. More like the memory of a bruise than an actual one.

I'm not sure how, but it's fortunate, because on my front porch is a crowd. Guy and Milo, Adele and Matilda, Prince and Tiny, these last two straining at their leashes and scrabbling against the wood slats. Everyone has a box, a bag, or a bottle of something.

Adele beams at me, crinkles deepening around her eyes. "We were worried you might be out on rounds."

Rounds? I suppose that's something I need to do. Maybe? But I'm not going anywhere at the moment.

"I don't understand," I say because I'm not sure what's brought some of my favorite people, and dogs, to my front porch.

They grin at each other, co-conspirators in my confusion. Then Guy lifts the lid on an enormous box to reveal a cake, one with chocolate frosting and decorated with pink polka dots.

"Happy birthday, Pansy-Girl," he says.

In the stand next to the door, my umbrella pops out of stealth mode and flutters in excitement.

"My birthday?"

"It's the sixteenth, isn't it?" Adele tilts her head in thought, although she most definitely knows the day I was born.

But is today the sixteenth? My mind scrambles, tumbling through all the events of this past week. Yes, it is. It's my birthday. And I'd completely forgotten.

"First sign of getting old," Guy teases, as if he's reading my thoughts.

"I don't mind that," I say, and invite them inside.

No, I don't mind at all.

☂

Later, it's just Guy and me in the kitchen. We're cleaning up, which he insists I don't need to do, that it's my birthday, and all I need to do is keep him company. We're talking about inconsequential things—the newly cracked asphalt on our street that needs to be reported to the town council, the teenagers who apparently tore through everybody's gardens last night, and the fact that his neighbor needs to buy a new hose.

I make sympathetic noises and attempt a blank expression. I'm not sure it's working, because Guy has a hang-dog look to match Tiny's when the latter is caught counter-cruising.

"Pansy-Girl, I want to make sure I didn't overstep my bounds." He's wiping one of my thrift store teacups like it's fine china, and it's already beyond dry. "My doorbell camera was pinging all night long, and I maybe checked this morning and saw that your friends had left." He shakes his head, anguish in his features. "I couldn't bear the thought of you spending your birthday alone, especially this birthday, and—"

"It's okay," I assure him. "They couldn't help it. They were called back to Seattle." With my thumb, I rub the thin scar that bisects my left palm, back and forth, back and forth. Healed, and yet it too has the aftertaste of pain. "Besides, I'd rather spend my birthday with all of you."

Carefully, he places the teacup in the cupboard, and there's nothing but doubt and guilt in the gesture. Then he turns to face me.

"It's true," I insist.

He opens his arms, and I accept a giant birthday bear hug from this giant bear of a man. "It's good of you to say that."

The kitchen is blue and white and brilliant in the afternoon sun. The scent of coffee lingers enticingly in the air, and that chocolate cake is ready for round two. Something about the house has shifted, and I ease into it, like easing into a comfortable pair of slippers.

And I think to myself: *It's good to be home.*

It's dusk when my doorbell rings again. I'm already in pajama bottoms and a cami top, curled on the couch where I've spent most of the evening, everything silent and serene. Tomorrow, I plan to confront the housing development. Today, though? I've done little more than some gentle yoga and checking notices from the Enclave. Other than a memorial post for Professor Reginald Botten, all is quiet.

But someone at my door? The thought makes my heart thump in anticipation and hope, although this isn't the Sight, and it won't be for a while. The Sight is a sluggish thing that's recovering somewhere deep in my mind.

I'm on my own for the next few weeks, a sensation that's both freeing and a bit frightening. So I straighten my ponytail in the powder room mirror and head for the door, toes tingling, stomach fluttering.

On the other side is Denisha from The King's Larder. I try not to sag in disappointment. I try to pretend that I wasn't expecting well, someone. In the stand next to the door, my umbrella sags as well. Her sigh is nearly audible.

"Special delivery," Denisha says, holding out a small box, her grin bright.

"For me?"

She laughs at this. "Yes, for you. He ordered it special, all the way from Seattle."

I take the box along with the card she hands me. I try to tip her, which she refuses with a quick, "Already taken care of, too. I like him. We all do."

She's on the sidewalk, swinging a leg over the seat of her moped, when she calls out, "He really is a keeper, Pansy."

Once she's gone, I shut the door and confront this mysterious package. I stare for several long moments as if I have x-ray vision.

At last, I tear a corner, and then can't stop myself. Inside is a jewelry box, oblong, a deep midnight blue.

The rich velvet of the box doesn't scream *expensive*. No, it's more of a whisper, one that insists—politely, mind you—*If you have to ask, you can't afford it*.

Then I open the box, slip my palm beneath the necklace, and dangle it in front of me. The silver flower is exquisite. I examine the pendant. The intricately carved details are so precise. It's a marvel that anyone could create such a thing. A flower, yes, but not just any flower. A pansy.

Of course.

A little pansy for Pansy Little.

The logistics of this make my mind spin. When did he find the time for such a perfect gift? How did he ship it here so quickly? That alone must have cost more than the necklace itself, which I suspect was a sizable amount.

I open the envelope, hoping for an explanation, for something more.

Tucked in the envelope is a card, the stock rich and creamy. No greeting. No signature. Just one simple line in elegant script:

And though she be but little, she is fierce.

The only other item is a pink and white polka-dotted ribbon, the one I most definitely lost on the green, considering the telltale grass stains.

I shake my head as if I can shake away the thickness building in my throat, soggy and full of salt. No, no, no. I know what that ribbon means and why he returned it to me. I can almost hear those exact and utterly correct words.

This is yours. I have no right to it. I have no right to you.

Yes, I know what the end of a relationship feels like. This time, I refuse.

For all the good it will do me.

Maybe it's the Sight, rousing itself to offer up a tidbit. Maybe it's merely a memory. I secure the pendant around my neck and then head upstairs.

My closet is still a jumble of files and spilled photographs. Tomorrow, I vow, I will clean. I will sort all these papers and place my mother's umbrella back into the stand. But now, I'm pawing through the mess. Of everything here, I'm certain Gwyneth Worthington-Wells found nothing interesting about this particular piece of paper.

I find it carelessly shoved to one side, along with my birth certificate. Yes, this will do nicely.

After all, Henry Darnelle isn't the only one who can quote Shakespeare.

CHAPTER 92

OPHELIA

Seattle, Washington
Monday, July 31

"What are you doing here?" Ophelia asks her brother.

Two weeks have passed since she broke free of her Sight-induced coma. Two weeks in which Henry has barely left her side except to dart home to shower and change clothes. She's tried to tell him it's unnecessary, that while the Sight hasn't exactly abandoned her, she's picked up a thing or two through that endless loop.

True, she lacks Pansy's knack for locking down the Sight completely, but watching her do so—over and over and over again— has rubbed off on Ophelia. Who says you can't learn by osmosis?

She's still confined to the hospital bed. She needs the handrails, the bed's ability to move up and down. A walker has replaced the IV stand and the other equipment that crowded the room. Her physical therapist assures her that in the next few weeks, she'll graduate to a big-girl bed. (Ophelia's words, not the therapist's; her therapist is far too kind for that.)

Henry plops down in the wingback chair he lugged to her

bedroom on his first day back. At his feet? Today, it's a plastic milk crate stuffed full of files and correspondence, a few thick packages spilling over the sides.

"I'm tackling the estate and trust paperwork these next few days," he says. Really, the man looks gleeful at the prospect, but then he sobers. "And I really should acknowledge all the condolences. It's not too late for that, is it?"

He's asking *her*, the irresponsible one? Ophelia wants to tell him that after his helping to save the world, all can be forgiven, even belated thank-you notes.

But he hasn't answered her actual question, and he won't. Henry's avoided the subject of King's End, of what happened there, of one of its residents in particular. And, certainly, Ophelia hasn't confessed all. She can't mortify Henry like that. She can't risk anyone overhearing those conversations, either. The Enclave's reach is still long and grasping. She needs to keep the strength of her Sight a secret. That goes for Pansy's, too.

"Estate work first, I think. I had Cam sort everything by category, and I'm sure the lawyers and accountants would appreciate—"

She points to a package wedged between bundles of bound mail. "Actually, you should open that one."

"I..." Henry glances down and pries the package from the others. "I should?" Then his gaze lights on the return address. He places a palm over it, as if that can negate everything. "No. She didn't."

"Didn't what?" Ophelia asks, feigning innocence.

He sighs. "I sent her a birthday gift."

You sent her a kiss-off and then ghosted her. Ophelia manages to bite back the words before they can leave her mouth. Honestly, despite his intelligence, her brother can be clueless sometimes.

Henry turns the package in his hand, inspecting it, a frown deepening on his brow. Clearly, this package isn't the right size or shape for a return.

"I can't imagine what—" he begins.

"Then open it."

He gives her a wan smile. "Yes, I suppose I could."

Still, he hesitates, his grip loose and uncertain on the brown paper wrapping. Then he rallies, because Henry always does. But precisely, with a letter opener to slice through the tape. Inside is a slender box, the sort that might hold stationery, a box adorned with a pink and white polka-dotted ribbon.

Ophelia stifles a laugh. The last time she saw *that*, Henry was surreptitiously slipping it into his suit coat pocket.

Her brother is not pleased. When he opens the box, his displeasure only deepens, a full-on schoolmaster scowl. He slaps the box shut and leans back in the chair, aiming a frustrated breath toward the ceiling.

Ophelia holds out a hand. "May I?"

For a moment, Henry doesn't respond. Then he shoves the box her way.

True, she doesn't know much about cars. If you asked her what an Alfa Romeo Spider looks like, she couldn't tell you. But undoubtedly, she's seen one before, if only through Pansy's eyes.

Now, it appears that Henry owns one.

Then she notices the card attached to the automobile title and the painstaking words inscribed there.

What's past is prologue.

Now, Ophelia does laugh.

Well, brother mine, it looks like she called your bluff and then raised you.

"Henry." Only when he glances toward her does Ophelia continue. "What are you doing here?"

"I'm—" He waves a hand at the milk crate.

"No, I mean *here*. In Seattle. In this house. You've already watched me learn how to walk once. You don't need to stick around for the encore."

Her father has hired an army of therapists: physical, occupational, even speech, and when she's ready, a physical trainer. Then there are debriefers and specialists from the Enclave. All of which are necessary but exceedingly boring.

Henry shakes his head. "After everything—"

"Especially after everything. You need to live your own life, not put it on hold for mine. Besides." She tilts her head and gives him a sly smile. "I hear they're opening a field office in Minneapolis, and they need a principal field agent to head it."

"How do you—?"

"Like I said." She waves a hand in the air. "I hear things."

"I can't."

"Tell me one good reason why not. Because I don't see why you shouldn't."

"Don't you? Because I can think of several reasons, the main one being that I'm still betrothed."

The anguish in Henry's voice startles her, each word scraped against gravel and broken glass. Hunched forward, he rests his head in his hands.

"I can't do that to her." These words sound like an oath. "I can't hurt her any more than I already have."

Emotions swirl in the air, thick and complicated. If Jack Ling were here, he could probably name them for her. But Ophelia catches the undercurrent, and their meaning washes through her. This thing between Henry and Pansy runs deeper than mere flirtation and the obvious feelings Ophelia witnessed.

No, Henry's in love. Deeply in love. The once-in-a-lifetime kind of love that says if you don't grab it, you'll live with nothing but regret. Along the way, she missed this. Blame the end of the world for that; everything came too fast, was too dire. She should've guessed. Henry never does things by half-measure.

But Ophelia has an ace up her own sleeve, one she plans to play on Pansy's behalf.

A recent, albeit awkward, visit from her once presumptive sister-in-law. Yes, Gwyneth Worthington-Wells came around, carefully collecting data to support a hypothesis. But Ophelia has adopted Rose Little's rule five. It's a good one. It's easy to bat away questions about what she saw during her Sight-induced coma. It's not like those with the Sight routinely wake up from such things. In fact, Ophelia is the first on record.

Besides, Gwyneth wouldn't like all of Ophelia's answers, and Ophelia may have hinted as much.

Even so, before Gwyneth left that afternoon, she extended a peace offering along with the air hug and kiss, the words an aside, as if they held no importance at all. "I've submitted my own petition for annulment."

Ophelia blinked, all big eyes and naiveté. "Can you convince Wendell to do the same?"

"We'll see," was all Gwyneth said, an implicit promise in her tone.

But all Ophelia heard was Rose Little's rule four:

If the Enclave makes an offer, remember they always require something in return.

She will need to think about that. But later. Now, she has a mission.

"All right, then," she says to Henry. "I see your point."

The words catch his attention. He does not expect her to agree, never mind so readily.

"In fact, we should start planning. These things take time. Wait! I know! We can make it a double wedding!" Ophelia claps her hands together as if the idea of Wendell waiting at the end of the long walk down the aisle is her life's dream. She even squeals, just a bit. "I want my colors to be sage green and glitter. Do you think Gwyneth will mind?"

"Glitter isn't an actual color."

"Of course it is."

Henry rubs his temples. "I know what you're doing, and it won't work."

"Then maybe this will. Gwyneth submitted her own petition for annulment."

"How do you know that?"

"I hear things." Her words come out light and musical.

He sags farther into the wingback chair, his posture slumped, defeated. And yet, almost absently, he runs that pink and white polka-dotted ribbon through his fingers. It's a caress so soft, so tender, so intentional, that a blush heats Ophelia's cheeks, and she has to glance away.

"Her parents will contest," he says. "And her mother—"

"Please. This is Gwyneth. She's already thought of a way around that."

"Gwyneth," Henry murmurs, then shakes his head and releases another sigh, the sound full of exasperation. "What the hell are you up to now?"

She wants him to go back to King's End.

This burst of Sight is so strong, so insistent, that Ophelia gasps. She sniffs, and her fingers come away with a hint of blood. Henry leans forward, a handkerchief in his hand and alarm in his eyes.

"Ophelia?"

She takes that unbearably soft handkerchief but brushes away his concern. "I'm okay." She considers what this means and what she should do about it. "I want to meet Pansy."

"She's certain to travel to Seattle for advanced training sooner or later."

"No. I want to go to King's End and meet her there. I need her. And, Henry? I think you need her."

Her brother doesn't answer. Instead, he picks up a stack of official-looking paperwork full of numbers and mind-numbing small print.

"You know what?" he says, thumbing through the stack of papers. "I'm going to work on your trust first."

Ophelia flops back, disappointment thick in her mouth. She's working up a good sulk when she notices her brother. Before turning his attention to the paperwork, he threads the ribbon through his fingers.

Then, in a gesture that's both deliberate and absent-minded, Henry slips it into his pocket.

CHAPTER 93
PANSY

King's End, Minnesota
Monday, August 14

The last thing you want to see after a prolonged patrol in the housing development is someone from the Enclave on your front porch.

Even if that someone is Principal Field Agent Henry Darnelle.

Once again, he's on the porch swing. Once again, he's in full regalia: a charcoal gray suit, a pop of white dress shirt at the collar and cuff. Yes, even that ridiculous hat has made a return. The swing creaks under his weight, the sound deliberate and patient.

My umbrella shudders in my grip. I clutch her tighter, expecting an all-out rebellion. But she snuggles close, as nervous and uncertain as I am. What is he doing here? The question is both mine and hers, and the Sight isn't offering up a single hint.

Typical. Just when you actually need it.

The last time I heard anything from Henry, it was in the form of his signature on my field agent examination report. Yes, after everything. He filed my report. On time, mind you. Not only did I earn a superior rating (the official Enclave term for *passing with flying colors*), but he recommended me for the accelerated track to senior field agent.

I'm not sure what to do about that. It means time in Seattle, away from King's End.

Henry still hasn't moved except to set the swing in motion, so I glance behind me, toward the housing development. Then I turn back to Henry.

There are things I long to tell him. How my renegotiations with the Screamers are going. How the housing development has changed. How I can see those fairy lights flicker whenever I pass close to the woods.

How I'm not sure I can leave King's End. Ever.

And, most of all, how much I've missed him.

I can't stand here forever, and I lack the will to push through my neighbor's lilac bushes. Plus? I don't feel like hiding anymore.

I glance down at my umbrella, my question little more than a whisper. "What do you think?"

She shudders again, this sensation mischievous. She flies from my grip. Although, really? I give her a bit of a boost. She soars forward, sticks the landing, and then tumbles end over end until she reaches my house. There, she plummets to the sidewalk, not so much a damsel-in-distress as a prima ballerina.

She is, however, still absolutely shameless.

Henry's umbrella topples down the front porch steps. How, I don't know. There's nothing in the Enclave's *Umbrella User Manual* that explains these two.

Then? They cavort to the point where I'm blushing on their behalf. Fortunately, they move the canoodling beneath the hydrangeas before it strays into PG-13 territory. How I'd explain *that* on Hey Neighbor, I have no idea.

Henry's studying the shaking hydrangeas with concern and a

touch of amusement. It's there in the twist of his lips. Then he looks at me, and I'm pinned in place, sneakers glued to the concrete.

"Shall we let them get reacquainted?" he says.

My throat is so thick, my heart so tender, I can only nod.

"How are you?" The inquiry is polite and so very much like him.

Again, I nod. The man has stolen all my words, the ability to speak. Hat in hand, he makes his way down the porch steps.

"The Enclave is opening a field office in Minneapolis. Have you heard?"

I feel my eyes widen and give my head a little shake.

"Well, they are, given the recent activity in the area." For a moment, his gaze strays from my face to take in the view toward the housing development. "They need a principal field agent to run it. You might say I've tossed my hat into the ring."

And then the man winks at me.

I don't know if it's his silly joke or that sexier-than-it-has-a-right-to-be wink, but the dam breaks, and I start to cry.

Everything stops. Our umbrellas halt their frolicking. The air around us stills. Henry looks stricken, and the hat lands on the sidewalk with a plop before rocking gently from side to side.

Then he rushes forward, linen handkerchief at the ready.

"Pansy, Pansy, I'm sorry. If you don't want me here—"

"No ... no, that's not..."

He begins to back away, and I grasp his lapels and lock him in place.

"I mean, yes. I want you here." This close, I can detect a newly acquired bump on his nose. Other than that, the rest of him appears healed and whole. Those dark eyes, as always, are a bit unfathomable. But the grief has faded along with all his bruises.

"I was waiting on the annulment." His voice is thick, latent regret lingering beneath the surface. "It's finally made it to the High Council's docket. I've been assured that during the next session—"

I shake my head, pouring my full self into the gesture. The

betrothal, the annulment. None of that matters, not to me. "I don't care about that."

"But I do." With his thumb, he chases away a final tear. "I needed to do this right, for you, for me, for both of us. Do you understand?"

Do I? Oh, yes. Absolutely. He is Henry Darnelle, and he can't do the most important things in life any other way.

He steps closer, bringing with him a trace of warm vanilla and sunshine. He cups my face, his fingers lingering where my own bruises have faded. A smile lights his face, and from beneath the collar of my shirt, he coaxes the pansy pendant free.

His gaze meets mine, and the gold flecks in his irises positively glow. "May I?"

His whisper is such a soft, inviting, seductive thing that my ability to speak and think vanish once again. But I manage a single, silent word.

Yes.

Then Henry kisses me, and it's correct and perfect and full of unspoken promises, a slow, lingering caress—as if we have the rest of our lives for these sorts of kisses. No doubt Hey Neighbor is exploding. At least three cell phones are aimed at us, but I don't care. Henry Darnelle has returned, and I want everyone in King's End to know.

He breaks the kiss by planting a gentle one on my forehead. His arms gather me closer as if he's afraid I might be spirited away. His heart pounds against my ear, a match for my own. Something strikes my cheek, and I glance up in time to catch a second tear with my fingertips.

"I thought I lost you." His words are quiet, almost calm, but beneath them, I taste terror inspired by the gray expanse, the knife, and all that blood. "I thought I lost you forever."

"You'll never lose me, Henry Darnelle."

I take his hand. Together, we gather our umbrellas and head up the porch steps. Together, we step inside and shut the door behind us.

Maybe I say it. Maybe he does. Or maybe we both do. But the words flavor the air with both hope and a contentment I feel all the way down to my toes.

At that moment, I know this without a doubt:

It's good to be home.

THE END

ACKNOWLEDGMENTS

I would like to express my heartfelt gratitude to *Pulp Literature* magazine. Yes, it was lovely to win first place in The First Page Cage contest. Better still was the deadline, which motivated me to complete *The Pansy Paradox* in the first place.

Hats off to Julie Fasciana for ~~volunteering as tribute~~ volunteering to beta-read both *The Pansy Paradox* and *The Capstone Conundrum*.

As always, thank you to Carol Davis for proofreading and corralling all my commas (any remaining typos are mine).

Thank you to my kids for always wanting to go to a bookstore with me, my sister for listening to me ramble about *The Pansy Paradox*, and to readers everywhere for being a crucial part of the writing process.

ABOUT THE AUTHOR

CHARITY TAHMASEB has slung corn on the cob for Green Giant and jumped out of airplanes (but not at the same time). She spent twelve years as a Girl Scout and six in the Army; that she wore a green uniform for both may not be a coincidence.

After twenty years as a technical writer, she now writes fiction full-time. Her short speculative fiction has appeared in *Flash Fiction Online, Pulp Literature, and Escape Pod.*

See what she's up to at https://writingwrongs.blog/

Also by Charity Tahmaseb

The Chronicles of King's End

Book 1: *The Pansy Paradox*

Book 1.5: *The Capstone Conundrum*

Coffee & Ghosts series

Available in ebook, print, and audio

Coffee and Ghosts, Season 1: Must Love Ghosts

Coffee and Ghosts, Season 2: The Ghost That Got Away

Coffee and Ghosts, Season 3: Nothing but the Ghosts

Coffee and Ghosts, Season 4: The Ghosts You Left Behind

Young Adult Fiction (with Darcy Vance)

The Geek Girl's Guide to Cheerleading

Dating on the Dork Side

Young Adult Fiction

The Fine Art of Keeping Quiet

The Fine Art of Holding Your Breath

Now and Later: Eight Young Adult Short Stories

Short Stories

Straying from the Path, Stories from the Sour Magic Series of Fairy Tales

Dragon Whispers: Six Tales of Dragon Adventure and Lore

Here's How We Survive: The (Love) Stories for 2020

9 781950 042227